# DARK FORCE UNIVERSE
## THE BATTLE FOR HYDRA V

# Maria Cowen

# TABLE OF CONTENTS

# CHAPTER ONE

Captain Rebel Morningstar shifted uneasily in his chair. It had been three hours since the Democratic Galactic Senate had come to session and they had not yet reached a decision. Two standard years ago, following the death of the Emperor Drakkor, the Senate had been convened to rule most of the planets of the Old Order. But the resistance movement was still alive on a few far flung systems not under the Senate's control. And this was to be the subject of today's session. To be specific, Hydra V, in the system X5LZ, was a planet asking for help... or, rather, her pro-Democrat contingent was.

Hydra V was dominated by a tyrant who would not bow to the new government because it would herald the end of his absolute power on this watery world. Hydra V was almost completely covered by ocean, with only a handful of islands and archipelagos rising above its surface. Not much was known about this planet, since its isolation rendered it useless to the Old Order.

Reb stifled a big yawn. Sitting in the senate antechamber wasn't exactly his scene, but Countess Liana Galaxia had asked him for help in her project to reunite the new Democracy, and he was incapable of refusing her anything. Liana was the first and only woman in the entire universe to captivate him so completely and sate his thirst for adventure. Reb and Liana had been lovers for two years now, and their happiness only seemed to increase with time. Surprisingly, they were a perfect match, despite differences of opinion and social background.

He glanced at her now, with a possessive tenderness, and she returned his smile. Sensing her tension, he knew she had been inwardly rehearsing her speech. Now it was her turn. She rose, and the room fell silent.

With her nubile body draped in a white gown and her golden hair braided around her head, Liana looked both beautiful and fragile. "Dear friends," she began in a clear, strong voice. "Since we won out over the forces of the Old Order we have striven to maintain peace in all member systems. Today, we have assembled here to determine whether or not we should intervene in Hydra V's civil rebellion. I believe their situation calls for intervention. And I believe we cannot ignore this cry for help we have received from their revolutionary forces. Hydra V may not have reached our high level of technology, but the Hydran people certainly don't lack the intelligence to develop and, moreover, they are endowed with a highly evolved sense of beauty and harmony."

Countess Liana pointed at the table before her to where a small statue stood. It was perhaps eleven inches high and carved from a dark, rich, beautifully colored piece of amber. It represented a beautiful, slender young woman and displayed the perfection of youth. Its long hair was laced with black onyx and two sapphires were masterfully set in the eye sockets. The total effect was extraordinarily beautiful. The sculpture seemed to radiate a gentle light from within. Liana reached out and, at her touch, the form recited a message in a silvery female voice.

"I am Princess Iris, daughter of the noble house of Odman. My father, King Handor, the leader of the opposition faction on Hydra V, has been kidnapped and is now held prisoner by Sadra, the tyrannical ruler of this planet. All attempts to recover custody of my father or to free our people from Sadra's tyranny have failed. Many of our people have died in protests and uprisings and we are desperately short of skilled warriors and weapons. We beseech the Senate to send help without delay."

Reb knew it had cost many people their lives to smuggle this message to the Senate. All of a sudden he wasn't bored anymore. He hoped the Senate would decide to send help to Hydra. He was getting soft, after his long furlough on Carrandon, and he needed some action. A fresh spurt of adrenalin flowed through his veins in anticipation.

Liana looked around the room, crossed her hands in front of her and continued. "I volunteer my services to conduct this expedition. And I request the services of Captain Reb Morningstar, who is present in this room, plus his co-pilot, Digerawicz the Prozoan, my brother, Commander Marcus Galaxia, who is currently serving on the Saldusa VII, and Buck Salladian, the Minister of Arts here on Carrandon. My wish is that you approve this intervention by displaying a majority of votes on the main screen. Thank you."

Liana sank gracefully into her seat, exhausted. An enormous screen suspended above the table was illuminated with a mixed pattern of red and blue lights. Blue was for yes and red was for no. Gradually the pattern shifted, colors separated so that the majority of the screen was a brilliant blaze of blue and a small portion was red, and permission was thus gained. Liana rose to depart, acknowledging congratulations and wishes of good luck as she left. The President of the Senate, an ancient humanoid creature native to the planet Carrandon, with enormous grey eyes and silvery, scaly skin, approached the Countess and intoned warmly, "Dear child, I wish you luck and trust that you will successfully complete your mission. May you and your team walk in the Light."

\*\*\*

The preparations for departure took three days, during which the *Golden Phoenix* was loaded with supplies and Digerawicz checked every circuit in the ship.

Countess Liana's assistant, the silver android unit, 4-2-N0 was now seated at the Countess' personal computer. A message had just been received from Saldusa VII advising that Marc would intercept them at a rendezvous point on their journey to Hydra V, and the android was having trouble concentrating on his screen. "I'm so excited, I just can't wait to see Master Marc and Tootee again!" he caroled.

"Fortuno, I must remind you that you have a great deal of work to do on the Ordano Project," said Countess Liana impatiently as she paced nervously through the Captain's quarters that she shared with Reb.

Fortuno turned back to his console in resignation. "I'll begin at once, Countess," he replied without enthusiasm.

Countess Liana paused in her pacing and looked down at the little statue of the Princess Iris from Hydra V.

She picked it up and held it thoughtfully. There was more to this statue than just a recorded message, she felt. She wished Marc were here now. She wasn't trained in the lore of the Light, as he was, but she could sense an unusual concentration of energy in the little figurine, and it seemed to pulsate in her hands as though there was a heart beating inside. "*My imagination must be playing tricks on me,*" she thought, "*But there is certainly something strange about this little sculpture, something...*"

"Darling," Reb burst into her thoughts. "We are taking off in just a few minutes. You can take your position. Oh, I almost forgot. Buck wanted to take a look at this." He pointed to the amber figurine.

\*\*\*

By evening their ship was traveling through hyperspace, far from Carrandon. Reb and Liana had retired to their cabin and all was quiet. Buck finished his second Hologame with Digger, beating him 20 to 5, then stretched out lazily on his contour couch. After two years as Minister of Arts to the new Democracy, he needed a vacation. Not that he didn't like his job... he loved it. But he wasn't used to being tied to one place for such a long time and he had a bad case of rock fever. Hydra was very much like his home planet: plenty of water, hot climate and lots of beautiful, unsophisticated native women. "*Yes, it would do very nicely*", he thought. He suddenly chuckled at himself. "*I'm getting romantic in my old age,*" he thought and then sighed longingly, "*I wonder how long it's been since I had a good, long swim?*" He smiled, and lifted the little statue, it glimmered on his outstretched palm. Someone seemed to be calling to him from far away, and he shook his head involuntarily to clear his ears. *"I'm so sleepy, I'm hallucinating"*, he thought, as he put the figure down and headed for his cabin.

*** 

*Star Wind* was a small V-wing fighter adapted for deep space travel, and it glided smoothly into the orbit of Saldusa VII. Marc leaned back in his control seat and relaxed his shoulders. He had arrived early for the rendezvous, in his eagerness to be reunited with his sister and friends, and it was now T-minus-30 to encounter. He set his chronometer alarm and leaned back, letting his mind wander.

For more than a year now, Marc Galaxia had been working as a coordinator on the construction of a new intergalactic spaceport at Saldusa VII. The Galactic Senate had offered him some attractive positions in government, but modesty prevented him from accepting them. Marc wasn't a humble architect from Argalon, any more, but he wasn't ready for the razzle-dazzle of politics, either! Thus, he had welcomed the message from Liana about her expedition. He had missed his friends and could certainly use a little action. He smiled at the thought of soon being with Liana, Reb and Buck. It would be exciting to be a part of their peace enforcement team once again.

An urgent bip'bip'bip sound interrupted his thoughts. Tootee was advising him that *Star Wind's* scanners had picked up the *Phoenix*. "Thank you, Tootee," Marc called to his friend, the rotund little droid which accompanied him everywhere.

Concentrating on his controls, Marc made a smooth landing, attaching his small V-wing to the *Phoenix's* hull. He was an excellent pilot, and completed the maneuver expertly.

Two minutes later he boarded the *Golden Phoenix*, and was almost suffocated by Digger, then kissed and hugged by his human friends. It was like coming home.

"Hi, Kid!" yelled Reb enthusiastically, "Seems like our combat skills are not going to rust away just yet. This expedition sounds like fun. My hands are just itchin' to use this baby," he caressed the blaster at his waist. "Digger, you too, right?" He clapped the Prozoan's shoulder with such force that Digger groaned and gave a good natured hoot.

"Oh, dear. I thought this was going to be a peaceful mission," Fortuno said nervously. "Besides, water is a dreadful stuff. Humidity isn't good for my joints." He fluttered about in dismay, continuing, "We must be sure to pack along enough liquid silicone lubricants when we disembark down there."

"Take it easy, Fortuno," interrupted Marc. "I don't particularly like water any more than you do." The planet Argalon, where he was raised, was a dry, hot, arid desert. On Argalon, water was as precious as gold. "We will just have to stick together," he winked at the droid. "At least Buck will be happy, he'll have a chance to show off his swimming skills. He's sure boasted about them enough, over the years." Marc grinned at Buck Salladian, who was lying comfortably on his recliner, smoking a cigar.

"I'd be honoured to demonstrate what the art of swimming is all about. I might even teach you guys a thing or two."

"You all talk as though you're taking a vacation on Hydra V," admonished Countess Liana. "What about the crisis concerning Princess Iris, not to mention her father, the king, whom we are supposed to free, and the Tyrant we must quell?" There was a note of reproach in her voice. "Shouldn't we sit down together and plan our approach?"

"She's right," Marc was quick to agree. "We should work out a plan of action."

\*\*\*

Later that night, Countess Liana and her brother, Count Marcus found a moment to talk in private. "Something's wrong, Sis," said Marc, "I can see it in your eyes. Is it this sculpture that's bothering you?"

Liana nodded, with an expression of grave concern.

"I can sense an enormous concentration of Light in this little statue. It's almost like a living presence. It's as if Princess Iris is here with us. But the vibration from the Light feels positive, so I believe Princess Iris will be our friend. She definitely represents no danger to us. But, the culture this comes from, worries me." He walked his fingers up the figurine thoughtfully. "This culture was capable of manipulation of the Light when they created this sculpture and this is something that could be very dangerous if it were turned against us."

"I wonder if all the inhabitants possess this gift, or if there are a minority of Light-sensitive beings on Hydra

V?" Countess Liana frowned at her brother. "I wish I had more knowledge and training with the Light. When we complete this mission, I want you to teach me."

"Gladly," he nodded. "But for now, please notice that the method by which this message has been recorded is completely unknown to us. The voice is very charming, though," he added.

"You just be careful, Marc," she wagged a finger. "You've been stationed in a womanless world for a long time now and I don't want you to fall in love with the first girl you meet. The natives are reputed to be very bewitching on Hydra V". There was a hint of envy in her voice.

"Don't worry, Sis, I can take care of myself," Count Marcus replied soothingly. "By the way, when are you and Reb going to do something to legalize your relationship and give us an heir to the royal bloodline?" he teased.

The Countess responded with an angry jab at his ribs but said nothing.

"Well," he concluded, "let me study this sculpture a little longer and see if I can come up with some more answers." He picked it up carefully and waved good night to his sister. But it was nearly morning on the ship's chronometer before Count Marcus finally put the statue away and lay down to rest.

# CHAPTER TWO

Before he even opened his eyes, Marc knew something was wrong. He jumped to his feet in one fluid motion and saw the red alert lights blinking in the corridor, in sync with the intermittent, high pitched trill of the warning bell. Outside his cabin Marc bumped into Buck, who was running and trying to button his jacket at the same time. On the bridge, Reb leapt into the pilot's seat and struggled to regain control of the ship. Digger was in the co-pilot's seat, doing his best to help.

"We're under attack!" called Countess Liana to Marc, leaning over her partner's shoulder to get a better look at the console screen.

"There appear to be three big battleships and approximately twenty V- and H-wings closing on us, fast. They would have to be from the Gandra System which is a neighbor of X5LZ, our destination. Systems like Gandra still cling to the old order." Reb Morningstar was talking rapidly to his friends. "We'd just emerged from hyperspace when the attack occurred. It's as if they were waiting for us." Then he added suspiciously, "I don't like this at all. It's as if they knew we were coming and were waiting for us."

"I'll ready my V-wing for battle," offered Marc, heading for the airlock. Unit 4X-2T hurried off after him.

"Oh my goodness, please be careful Master Marc," Fortuno called after his vanishing shadow. "Be careful, Tootee," he amended in a smaller voice. He was answered by a few impatient beeps.

The overhead cockpit screen was turned on to display the battlefield. It was obvious the enemy was attempting to surround their craft. Those bulky battleships, heavily armed and well-shielded, were flanking their position: one in front, one to the left, and one to the right of the *Phoenix*. The V- and H-wings were filling in the gaps and closing off routes to escape.

"We have to do something, fast!" Buck said nervously. "It's too late to try for a jump into hyperspace, I suppose?"

Before Reb could reply, a familiar Marc's voice was piped through the control unit. "Reb, can you hear me?"

"Receiving you loud and clear," Reb replied.

"Look! In back of you! There's still an opening in their flanks. Let's try for it, Buddy."

"You got it!" Reb rotated his ship one hundred and eighty degrees and said to Marc, "Let's go!"

\*\*\*

*Star Wind* had detached itself from the *Golden Phoenix* and made a turning maneuver which placed it above and ahead of the *Phoenix*. Then, accelerating to full thrust, the *Phoenix* jumped for the opening too, nearly throwing Countess Liana to the floor. Buck, who was not strapped down, flew off his contour chair and collided with the wall.

Collecting his body from the floor, Buck hauled himself back into position, moaning softly and rubbing his elbow.

Just then, nearby explosions rocked the ship violently. Fortunately, Liana, Buck and Fortuno had hastily buckled themselves in. Just then, three V-wings appeared right in front of them. Reb aimed and pressed a button, firing the laser. "Missed!" he swore under his breath. But the V-wings were still closing. Reb fired again and again. One V-wing exploded in a bright ball of fire.

"Gotcha!" hollered Reb.

"Wooooo!" Digger called out excitedly.

Marc, in his V-wing, engaged one of the H-wings in a crazy chase, with the three big battleships right at their backs. Two enemy V-wings were still buzzing about in front of the Phoenix irritatingly.

"It's getting hot, here, Digger. Why don't you take a seat in the artillery tower and Buck will replace you down here?" suggested Reb. The Prozoan barked in agreement.

The change was an improvement. Two minutes later, another V-wing was converted into a flash of light against' the black tapestry of space. A moment after that, a second burst testified to the fact that the third pest was gone.

Marc still couldn't get a fix on the H-wing he was chasing. Now another appeared out of nowhere, closing on his tail.

"Marc's in trouble," cried Liana. "Do something, Reb!"

"I know, I know." he complained. "Let's see what we can do to make it an even contest for Marc." He took aim at the H-wing on Marc's tail and the little ship spun out of their path in flames.

"I got him!" Reb called triumphantly. "Now Marc can take care of himself."

Suddenly, the *Golden Phoenix* shook violently. Then a crashing sound came from the back of the ship and all lights went out, leaving only the glow of the control panel which had switched to auxiliary power. Reb and Buck unbuckled and swiftly dispatched themselves to investigate the damage.

"It's a rear cargo compartment," said Reb to Buck as he activated the hydraulic safety doors to close off that area. We have a fire, but that will snuff soon enough without atmosphere to feed it." He nudged Buck and pointed in the direction of the cockpit, indicating that they should go back. "Obviously, we cannot escape them now that we have sustained these damages. We'll have to stand and fight. But I have a plan..."

By now, everyone knew about Reb's crackpot schemes. But they usually worked, so he was given the benefit of the doubt when he came up with a new one. Under Reb's direction, the *Golden Phoenix* made a one hundred and eighty degree turn to face the command ship full-on. Its enormous, hulking shape grew with each heartbeat until it filled their screen like a shadow of death.

\*\*\*

Marc was still trying desperately to get a fix on the H-wing when he picked up a new V-wing on his tail. A lucky shot took care of it, causing enough damage to cripple the craft and eliminate it from the fight. But the pilot of the H-wing was a good flyer, he just couldn't catch it. Marc wiped the sweat from his forehead and put his craft into a dive and reverse loop maneuver which would put him on top of the H-wing if it was successful.

"*I'll have to act fast; shoot him before he sees me,*" he thought.

Marc came out of his reverse roll and was on top of the H-wing. He took aim, and in an instant the little ship ceased to exist. "*Too bad you were on the wrong side*", he said silently to the other pilot, "*You were one helluva flyer*".

Sighing with relief, Marc looked around. He'd been so absorbed in his own problems, he hadn't realized he'd flown far offside of the battlefield. What's more, the enemy seemed not to have taken notice of his absence. He decided to capitalize on his good fortune. The *Phoenix* was headed straight for the enemy command ship and he guessed what Reb was up to. He also felt a strange flicker of disturbance in the Light, it was coming from the command vessel. There was something familiar... someone he knew was in that ship. Someone... Princess Iris! Marc had identified the vibration, he knew he was right, yet his brain refused to believe she was in that enemy ship. Unless she was a prisoner. For whatever reason, Princess Iris was definitely there. Her presence was like a ripple of purity in that ocean of latent evil. Marc punched the coordinates into his computer console and his little craft pivoted and flew straight toward the hulking battleship.

*\*\*\**

Blackness. Blessed blackness. She didn't want to think. It hurt to think. She didn't want to move. It hurt even more to move. But thoughts pushed their way into her aching skull, thoughts of death. Thoughts of torture. Her lips were dry and cracked, and she knew the warm stuff she was lying in was blood. But not her blood. She stirred and stretched out a hand. The pain was excruciating. She touched a little body on the floor next to her. The body was cold. *"My dear, faithful little Lony,"* she sobbed silently. *"There is nothing I can do for you, anymore. I can't even give you back to your Mother Sea, as our custom dictates."* She pulled back her arm. *"Oh, Lony, I am so sorry, so sorry."*

She tried to sit up. The back of her head was throbbing where she had received the first blow. She tried to open her eyes, but they neither wanted to open nor to focus. She tried again. All was dark and indistinct, at first, but then the gloom lifted and she was able to distinguish two small shapes on the floor next to the wall.

*"Estri and Herme. Are they still alive?"* she wondered with dismay. She projected her thoughts outward, in inquiry, the way she had been taught to do as a child. *"Yes, they're still alive. But they're unconscious, and probably wounded."* She brushed her long hair away from her face and touched her temples, trying to concentrate. She remembered, now. She had been captured four days ago, along with her escort of royal guards and her three servants, one of whom had been killed defending her. She tried to analyse the situation. Surrounded by the cruel, brutal enemy, there wasn't much hope for survival. But something told her not to give up. The message which she had sent to the Democratic Senate was her last hope --her only hope-- and that hope was not dead, yet. *"Even if I die, they will never learn the Secret of Hydra",* she grimaced painfully.

***

Reb Morningstar steered his ship straight toward the enemy's command vessel. Enemy missiles filled the space around them, doing little damage. Suddenly, Reb altered course and steered instead toward the battleship on the left. The *Phoenix* was now situated between the two enemy craft and caught in the crossfire of plasma missiles. Abruptly the *Phoenix* tilted just in time to avoid a hit by two arrow-shaped missiles which missed her by mere inches and exploded the battleship's power-plant instead.

"Good shot!" cried Reb enthusiastically, as he changed course in order to avoid a collision with the exploding enemy ship as it blew apart and jolted everyone aboard the *Phoenix*.

"One down, two to go," Reb said with relief. "Sometimes their self-destructive tendencies cause me to wonder!" He laughed and winked at Liana, who was struggling to recover her poise.

"Well done," said Buck. "Now we only have to eliminate two more of the monsters, and Marc is nowhere in sight."

"He's okay," murmured Liana. "I can sense he's unhurt."

"What course now, Captain?" asked Buck.

"Steer straight for the main ship again," barked Reb, already fully absorbed at his console.

\*\*\*

Marc was nearing the enemy command ship and luckily no one had yet noticed him. Using the distraction created by the explosion of one battleship, he moved closer to the vessel and landed softly on its stern, near the

16

emergency exit. Anchoring the *Star Wind*, he donned his space helmet, checked his suit and made ready to board the enemy ship.

"Tootee," he called softly, "I'll need your help now. See if you can open this thing for me."

The little robot beeped its readiness and they got underway. Hermetic coveralls and helmet protected Marc from the deadly void outside, but the little robot needed no protection, whirring silently along beside his master as Marc jetted himself over to the emergency exit of the big ship. It took them only a minute to arrive, and another minute while Tootee worked at the lock with his electronic probe, then the heavy door swung open and they were inside!

After decompression, Marc lowered himself cautiously into the dark passage below the airlock, and then helped Tootee to pass noiselessly into the corridor beyond. With the hatch door closed, they were in total darkness. Marc's hand groped for the laser sword in his belt, removed and activated it. A bluish glow now illuminated the narrow corridor. Together, Marc and Tootee moved forward. The corridor took a few bends before they found themselves in the cargo loading area at the rear of the ship. Moving silently and carefully, they passed through the area and found a hatch on the other side.

*"We must locate the cells where they are holding the prisoners"*, thought Marc. Passage after passage, they moved silently through the labyrinth of the ship, letting Marc's instinct guide them, just as Benja-Ko Menjoro had taught him to do. Now they were passing through a storage area. Several doors were open, displaying all kinds of equipment inside. Then Marc heard a noise

ahead of them and doused his laser sword, jumping into a dark storage locker on his left. Tootee whirred quietly beside him.

Two soldiers were approaching Marc's hiding place and the young Jaira quickly buried himself in a pile of space suits.

"I wish we would be furloughed soon. My son will be born sometime this week and I want to be back home for the event," said one soldier.

"Why all the fuss about one stinking ship, anyway?" asked the other. "We have Hydran hostages, and we have their leader." Then he added, "Oh, here's a new helmet. Just what I've been looking for! My old one is only good for recycling. Let's go, the Admiral can get pretty nasty to soldiers who go AWOL on board ship."

Their footsteps echoed fainter and fainter until silence prevailed again. Marc scrambled out from under the pile of suits and was walking in the direction the soldiers had taken when a thought stopped him in midstride. He returned to the room and re-emerged a few moments later dressed in a shiny black uniform and helmet, his face obscured by the smoked glass. Together, the imitation soldier and his robot companion moved soundlessly along the corridors toward the heart of the ship.

***

When the door of her dark cell burst open and two armed guards entered, Princess Iris' dark shape on the floor didn't move.

"You, there!" One of the guards approached the crumpled figure and gave it a kick. "Get up and come with us. The Admiral wants to see you." The figure was unmoving. The guard reached down and grabbed a fistful of long hair, dragging Princess Iris to her feet. "Hurry," he added, giving her a brutal shove.

The girl groaned, but followed the guard without protest. Outside the cell, in the lighted passage, the guards could see that she was in a wretched state. "The Admiral gave orders to prepare her, so we'll have to clean her up a bit." Bracing her between them, they led her to their bathing quarters where she was turned over to a pair of equally rough female attendants who gave her a scalding bath, followed by an icy plunge.

Torturous though it was, Princess Iris was surprised at how refreshed and competent the bath had made her feel. The attendants toweled her roughly and dropped a silken creamy robe over her head. Her mind was racing. By the Holy Mother Sea, she knew what was coming and her stomach was churning in nausea at the thought. *"I won't let them do this to me. I'd rather die and take my secret with me."* Again she smiled bitterly, as she had in the cell, with the thought. *"They don't know the extent of my training. I can stop my heart at will, and escape whenever I choose"*. She tried to look regal and not squirm, as she watched in the mirror while the female attendants worked to make her presentable for their Admiral.

Once the bruises were covered with cosmetics, Iris almost looked like her old self, except that she lacked her usual shimmering radiance. *"I must prepare myself for the final effort"*, she thought sadly, beginning a series of deep breaths. *"Inhale... exhale, slower... deeper"*, she was entering a light trance already. Her eyes clouded, her pulse slowed, her heartbeats became less and less noticeable. She was entering a deep trance state, making herself immune to whatever would happen to her.

"Well, that's the best we can do," said an attendant who was completing a critical inspection. "Let's deliver her to the guards."

"What a pity such a beautiful girl is going to be wasted like that," the other attendant replied, possibly remembering her own lost youth and beauty.

They lifted her to her feet, and called the guards who marched in and once again braced Princess Iris between them. Rather than offer resistance, she leaned on them, as if her strength was failing, and they led her thus towards her humiliating destiny.

\*\*\*

Countess Liana had to put her hand over her mouth to keep from panicking and shrieking out loud. The air on the bridge was thick with smoke from hits they had taken to the ship, and they were on a collision course with the enemy vessel. Then she noticed the *Phoenix* was losing speed and slowing down and she raised an inquiring eyebrow at Reb.

"We'll land on enemy territory in a few minutes," said Reb as he busied himself at the controls.

Reb knew the shielding system of the big vessel was activated, to protect it against missiles or meteor showers. And he also knew that anything slow moving could penetrate that shield easily. In minutes *Phoenix* had set down lightly on the surface of the battleship, thanks to its skilled captain.

"Fortuno, begin reconnaisance of our damage and

carry out repairs while we're gone," instructed Reb. "Digger, please supply everybody with weapons. Liana, Buck, get your light suits and helmets on. Fortuno will remain on the ship, ready it for take-off and await my orders." He snapped on his own helmet and spoke via the internal speakers. "Okay, everyone, we are ready to board the enemy ship. Our only chance for survival is to reach the main reactor, immobilize it, and gain control over the enemy." There was never a doubt in Reb's mind that to surprise the opponent was their best hope for survival, since the enemy would never expect to be under attack from such a small rebel force.

"Excuse me, Master Reb," interrupted the ever helpful Fortuno, "Your odds of survival are 578.2 to one, and under such circumstances I would not recommend that you board that vessel."

"Spare me your statistics, Fortuno," Reb cut him short. "We are proceeding with my plan."

Moments later, a heavy door swung shut behind them and they were floating in a freezing void. All around them, thousands of distant star systems shimmered indifferently at their plight. Countess Liana clung to Reb's gloved hand. Open spaces always made her dizzy. Only the magnetized soles of their boots prevented them from drifting away into an eternal nothingness.

Reb was leading the others, followed by Liana. Buck and Digger brought up the rear. They could all see that the V- and H-wings were returning to base, and knew that *Phoenix* was safe from harm. However, the *Phoenix's* crew had no time to lose. Reb signalled them to stop. He'd spotted a dark rectangle, a hatch door, in the solid wall of the ship. Reb and Digger set to work. It wasn't easy to gain access to a battleship of this type. Beads of sweat floated around inside Reb's helmet as they worked silently to release the catch. Abruptly, the big hatch door swung open. The little band of adventurers quickly slipped inside and sealed the hatch behind them.

Adjusting their weapons, they were ready for battle. Together they moved through the corridors toward the center of the ship. To their surprise, the passages were empty.

"Marc is somewhere inside this ship." Liana said. "I can feel him."

"He must have sneaked in before us," suggested Reb. The corridor they were walking through was poorly lit and very narrow. The area was obviously restricted to maintenance. They saw the water and air recycling plants, as well as food synthesizers, garment synthesizers and so forth.

Without warning, a blinding light was turned on them. "Drop your weapons. You are surrounded. Any attempt to resist is pointless," a metallic voice boomed out.

Reb froze in mid-step. Blinking his eyes, he tried to focus on the area in back of the light.

"If you do not drop your weapons instantly, you will be exterminated," said the disembodied voice.

Reb's thoughts were racing. He felt trapped, and angry. "*There **must** be a way out!*" he thought feverishly. He could see his opponents now, at the far end of the corridor. He looked back, the way they had come. That passage, too, was blocked by soldiers.

His foot stubbed against something. He looked down. There, underneath them, was a trap door opening into the ventilation system.

"Liana, Buck, get into the ventilation tunnel. Quick!" he commanded, leaning against the wall and opening fire on the soldiers ahead of him at the same time.

Digger assumed the same position, flattened against the corridor wall, he opened fire in the opposite direction.

"Digger, get inside!" hollered Reb impatiently. "I can't hold them off for long."

But Digger's big hairy body could not squeeze into the tunnel opening. Liana and Buck pulled and tugged, but was impossible. Reb was now sweating profusely, and the enemy was closing in on them. In another minute, it would be over.

# CHAPTER THREE

Marc knew he was nearing his target area holding Princess Iris. He could sense her closeness, but at the same time he could also sense her vibrations growing weaker. *"I must hurry and find her"*, he thought. *"She might be wounded, or in danger"*. His steps quickened. So far, he hadn't encountered any obstacles or opposition. The uniform was uncomfortably large on him, but he really hadn't had the time to choose the right size. Tootee was following silently. In his mind's eye, Marc saw that Princess Iris was on the move. He saw the distance closing between them.

Approaching an intersecting passage, he stopped and waited. When he heard footsteps approaching from the opposite direction, and saw a flicker of light far down the corridor, Marc stopped and composed himself with the knowledge that he was about to meet the enemy.

Two soldiers were approaching. Between them, they dragged the limp body of a young woman with long, black hair. Marc stepped out from the shadows and blocked the passage. "Guards, where are you taking this prisoner?" he asked authoritatively.

"Admiral's orders. We are to take her to him," replied one of the guards. "But who... ?"

Marc lifted his hand and said in a high, insistent voice, using the modulation of Light to influence the opponents.

"You are dismissed! I will conduct her personally to my Admiral."

"We are dismissed," echoed the guards. "Of course, Sargeant."

"You are good soldiers. You will be rewarded." added Marc, as he took control of the limp body.

"We will be rewarded," echoed the guards.

"Dismissed!" Marc waved a hand. "You may return to your post."

The guards saluted and turned, retreating down the passage. Marc struggled to prop Princess Iris on her feet. *"Now what?"* he thought. *"I need a quiet spot somewhere in order to revive her before we attempt to escape".*

Half carrying, half dragging Princess Iris, he stumbled over to a locker and peered inside. It was empty. Taking her in his arms, he stepped sideways through the opening and gently laid her on the floor inside, reaching back to press the button that would activate the door. Leaning over her, he felt for a pulse. It was weak and irregular, and her breathing was shallow. He wondered if she was drugged. Gently, he shook her once, twice. Nothing happened.

When he lifted her, the head lolled as though she were unconscious. Marc closed his eyes and concentrated. Her force field was weakening and growing more difficult to distinguish. He reached for her mind. *"Iris, don't leave me,"* he pleaded silently. *"I'm your friend. I've come to rescue you. Iris, can you hear me?"* Marc repeated his silent message over and over again. Finally, Iris stirred and opened her eyes.

"Who are you?" she whispered.

"I am Commander Marcus Galaxia. I came with an expedition from Carrandon to rescue you and free your people from Sadra's tyranny."

"So, you got our message." There was relief in her voice. "This means my brother's death was not in vain." She added softly, "He was killed while getting the message out of our system."

"Are you strong enough to walk?" asked Marc. "We have to move from here before we're found."

"Just give me a few moments," she whispered back and, closing her eyes, she took a series of deep breaths.

While Princess Iris was summoning her strength, Marc took advantage of the moment to take a good look at her. Tall and slender, she was an extremely beautiful young woman. At that moment, Iris opened her eyes and returned his gaze steadily. Her thick, dark hair fell to her waist and her aristocratic, aquiline features were blessed with shimmering blue eyes. *"What an unusual color,"* he thought. Her lids fluttered closed, as if she could read his thoughts and they made her self-conscious. He noted that her skin was very smooth and of the color of warm amber. She opened her eyes again.

"Now I feel stronger," she smiled at him.

Marc helped Iris to her feet and she stood, as tall as he, their eyes on the same level.

"Before we leave this ship, I must rescue my staff," she announced with determination.

"Where are they being held?" Marc thought he was

stretching his luck in going after more Hydrans at this point. Frankly, he'd prefer to retrace his trail with Princess Iris and put a suit on her, then get off this vessel and into his ship.

"I don't know how to direct you there. But I'll sense them as we near their cell." Iris, urged. "Please, let's go, quickly!"

"Okay," Marc took her hand. "Lead me to them." Then, as he was reaching for the door activator the air exploded with shots, shouts and running footsteps. "My friends are here," Marc said worriedly, "and they are in trouble."

*** 

Countess Liana felt herself falling at a dizzying speed, bumping and bouncing off the walls of the narrow ventilation shaft which was almost vertical in its descent. Each impact with the walls gave her yet another painful bruise, and these few seconds seemed like an eternity of fear and torment. Buck was falling, too. She caught glimpses of him in the space above her. She waved her arms, trying to catch hold of anything that might slow her fall, but the smooth walls of the shaft offered no resistance. The tunnel was narrowing now, and she was feeling claustrophobic. But despite imminent danger to herself, she couldn't think of anything but the danger to Reb.

*"Oh, I hope he got away safely",* she thought, as she fell further and further from her beloved. Something jerked at her side, again and again. She wondered what this new pain meant, but it was too dark to see anything now. Possibly there were rods protruding from the wall

of the shaft. Liana pictured her graceful home in the capital of Carrandon, and longed for its comforts and safety. But her reverie was interrupted by a sudden connection with a thick, slimy, substance. It was mud! And before she had time to think, it had closed over her head and filled her mouth and eyes. She couldn't scream for help, couldn't move. Her lungs were empty of oxygen and she was suffocating. Scenes of her life flashed through her mind with terrifying speed and Countess Liana realized that she was dying. Just before she lost consciousness, she thought about Reb.

Unit 4-2-N0 was busy with repairs to the *Golden Phoenix* and thus failed to notice the dark shapes of enemy soldiers surrounding the ship. They had exited the ship through the same service door that Reb and his party had used earlier, to enter the command battleship.

Repairs to the fire-damaged cargo department, were nearly completed and unit 4-2-N0 was in the midst of ventilating the ship when he detected someone trying to activate the door of the main hatch.

*"Oh, dear, I wonder how long the hatch door will hold?"* muttered Fortuno to himself. He ran a calculation in his electronic brain. It would take them about twenty minutes to breech security. "Goodness!" he spoke aloud, "What shall I do?" But no answer came back. He often talked out loud to himself when he was alone, especially when faced with a problem. "I wish Tootee were here to help me. I'm just not a fighter," he complained. "I am merely a liaison android and assistant to the Countess. I am not a hero!"

But Fortuno was first and foremost an electronic servant, and his programmed instructions were clear. He made certain everything was secured and then climbed into the artillery tower. Taking a seat behind the heavy cannon, he found he could see the interlopers very clearly. Quickly, he counted them. Twenty-seven in all, and all armed with high tech laser blasters. All the soldiers wore silver space suits and oxygen masks. And all were engaged busily at their task which was to break security and enter the *Phoenix*. Hard at work with laser cutters, ultrasonic probes and other technically advanced devices, they failed to notice the droid who was observing them from his ship.

*"Now, how am I supposed to shoot at them, when I am programmed not to harm a living thing, human or otherwise?"* Fortuno was in a quandry. *"Those humans contradict themselves so much sometimes. There is no logical connection between their ideals and their actions."* philosophized the droid, as he delayed his crucial decision. Aloud, he said "Well, I can't wait any longer. I shall assume those suited creatures to be robots, for the purpose of following my directive, just in case I should hit one."

He took careful aim and fired. A laser-gun held by one of the soldiers exploded harmlessly. Seconds later a large blaster held by three soldiers, who were melting a hinge on the *Phoenix's* main hatch, met the same fate. Surprise and confusion could be interpreted in the body language of the soldiers. Methodically, he aimed and fired until he had disarmed them, one by one. Meanwhile, many of the soldiers had retreated back into their ship, having suffered damage to their suits which threatened them with decompression.

"Ha!" he chortled gleefully. "I've done it!" he observed with satisfaction, as the last of the soldiers disappeared back into their battleship. What he failed to notice was the charge of explosives that still adhered to the hinges of the *Phoenix's* main hatch.

When the explosives detonated, the ship shook with such force that Fortuno was hurled to the floor. With some effort, he managed to regain his footing and hurried to the main control deck to check the damages.

The first code he entered activated a hydraulic seal on the emergency door between the main hatch and the inner passage, thus sealing off the escape of atmosphere from the ship. Just then, he observed the soldiers again emerging from their battleship to drift toward the *Golden Phoenix's* blown main hatch.

"Oh dear, oh dear," he lamented. "More trouble." I'll just have to lift off, out of reach, for now." he decided.

Taking his place in Reb's chair, he moved his hands over the computer console and activated the acceleration boosters. Within seconds, *Phoenix* had lifted from the surface of the battleship and was drifting in distant space, out of reach of the enemy. The surprised soldiers opened fire on the *Phoenix*, but it was well protected by the magnetic shield which Fortuno activated.

*"My goodness, that was close!"* thought Fortuno with a sigh. *"Crisis like this are going to cause me to short-circuit one day,"* he announced with asperity.

\*\*\*

Reb and Digger shot at their pursuers without hesitation. Not that they had an alternate choice, mind you. Their chances of survival were growing thinner by the second.

"Digger," yelled Reb over the noise of battle, "when

I give the sign, you throw an explosive into the passage on your right and hit the boards. After it detonates, get on your feet and run like the devil."

Reb and Digger thus aimed their hand explosives straight at the soldiers and scattered them. Reb took the left passage, Digger the right, and they ran with all the speed they could muster. Unknown to them, the two passages formed the spokes of a "Y" and they bowled each other over on impact, some moments later. While dusting off, they took stock of themselves. Reb's uniform and Digger's thick fur were singed and smelling acrid from the burns. But at least they were free from persecution for the moment.

"Shhhhh!" A sharp hiss in a side passage startled them and they stopped in their tracks. Stepping out from the shadows, Marc and Princess Iris were a sight for sore eyes.

"No time for introductions," urged Reb. "Let's get this show on the road. If we can reach the main controls, we can immobilize the ship before they can stop us." He moved forward and motioned for his friends to follow. Princess Iris fell into step behind Digger without comment. She was accustomed to fighting, after so many political skirmishes on Hydra V.

"Take this. You'll need it to defend yourself." Marc handed Iris his blaster.

She smiled at him gratefully and Marc's heart skipped a beat. He struggled to maintain a serious expression. After all, the situation could hardly be called romantic.

Little Tootee kept pace with the group, with some difficulty. His bulky little body wasn't exactly made for racing. But in no time he sensed they were close to the ship's reactors and he beeped the news to Marc.

Rounding a corner, they were confronted with a solid metal wall. There was no way forward. The soldiers had activated a door which slid into place like a wall, blocking the corridor. They could hear heavy footsteps on the other side. They were trapped. The way forward was blocked and the way back was full of soldiers.

"Tootee, can you override their circuits and activate this wall?" called Reb urgently. "Please try. Hurry!"

The little robot made straight for a control box, inserted a probe into an opening and buzzed away busily. Just then a group of soldiers appeared around the corner behind them and aimed their weapons.

"Everybody down!" Reb dived to the floor and fired his blaster at them on the way down. Everyone followed suit. Marc found himself under Princess Iris. He could feel the warmth of her body against his and he was grateful for the darkness, so nobody could see him blush. His days as a bashful graduate architect were long past, but Marc was having trouble controlling his emotions around this special lady.

"Hurry, Tootee," he urged his little pal. "We don't have all day here," he added. "My blaster is overheating."

The soldiers were advancing nearer. The wall Tootee was trying to manipulate was melted here and there from blaster shots, but still it did not budge. The smell from the weapons and scorched metal caused their nostrils to smart.

Suddenly, Tootee beeped triumphantly to Marc and the wall slid back to reveal the rest of the passage. Everyone scrambled through the opening as Reb cried, "Tootee, close it behind us!"

This was an easy task and Tootee had the wall back

in place instantly, leaving the frustrated soldiers on the other side.

"Tootee, lead us to the main reactor!" urged Reb. "Let's go!"

They trooped behind the little robot, up one passage and down another. Then without warning, a dark and powerful shape stepped from the shadows and blocked their way.

Marc froze in his tracks. The menacing figure reminded him of Emperor Drakkor. But this entity was even bigger, and the mask on its face was somehow different, somehow monstrous. Shiny black metal protected its body.

"It's a Sydhar!" whispered Princess Iris, in a trembling voice. She reached for Marc's hand. "Nothing can defeat them," she added fearfully.

The black nightmare just stood there, towering over them, silently blocking the passage. Its presence had a paralyzing effect on the small rebel group. Marc pulled himself together and, releasing his grip on Princess Iris's hand, stepped out in front of the others.

"No! Don't challenge him. He'll kill you!" Princess Iris cried out in vain.

Marc was dwarfed by the Sydhar. Stepping back, he activated his laser sword. Standing there, wielding his weapon, he seemed ridiculously small and impotent compared to this metal giant.

"Step aside. We have a message for your admiral and you must not delay us," commanded Marc somewhat shakily, trying to employ the commanding tone of voice which was part of his Jaira training. Strangely inarticulate rumblings emanated from the giant which perplexed the group until they realized he must be laughing!

The giant then outstretched a huge hand. In it he held an unusual looking device. The Sydhar flipped a switch with its thumb and the small band of revolutionaries was instantly crushed by massive waves of oppressive pressure which was collapsing their lungs. Marc felt as though the flesh had been ripped from his body and a compactor was crushing his bones. The pain expanded to the accompaniment of a high, nearly inaudible tone. *"An ultrasonic torture device,"* he thought with difficulty as his knees buckled under him.

Marc's laser sword was lying on the floor, forgotten. He was writhing in agony with the others, pain blurring his thoughts. He wanted to give in to the pain, to let himself sink into it and yield to the sweet relief of death. *"If the Sydhar increases the ultrasonic volume, we will all die."* This thought was followed by another. A message was feebly trying to come through. *"Shield... with Light... together!"* Marc realized Princess Iris was projecting to him. Yes. If they joined their efforts they might be able to free themselves! Marc forced his mind to clear, he forced himself to concentrate.

One glance at Iris told him she was straining to build herself a shield from pure Light. He followed her example, linking his mind with hers. He could see the product of their thought projections taking form, creating a spectral wall of flickering Light. They concentrated, focusing on their shield. It grew thicker and more opaque. They were all feeling relief now, from the crushing pressure. Princess Iris' face paled with effort. She was still weak from her previous ordeal and from the self-induced catatonic condition in which Marc had found her. Marc sensed her weakening. He reached for her hand and grasped it to strengthen the rapport between them. Reb and Digger were scrambling to their feet.

"Aim for the eyes," yelled Reb to Digger, as he tried to get a good shot at the Sydhar from behind the shield. Then he and the Prozoan took aim and fired simultaneously. The shots connected, the giant stumbled. Where his eyes had been, only smoking holes remained. Reb and Digger continued to fire until they were sure the menacing Sydhar was dead. The wall of Light was now dissipated. Marc and Iris leaned weakly against the wall, smiling their relief at each other, still holding hands:

"Iris, thank you for your assistance, you were a life saver. I never could have done it without you." He mopped his forehead with a metallic sleeve and looked at it in surprise, having forgotten what he was wearing. "You know, Iris," he went on. "I've never done that before. Didn't think it was possible. Never could have managed it alone." He squeezed her hand. "You are the first person to ever establish such a close mind rapport with me, aside from my Jaira teacher."

"We are all betazoids in my family," she replied proudly.

Reb was inspecting the fallen giant. Removing its glossy black helmet, he shook his head at what he saw. The Sydhar was a cyborg: half organic, half robot. Its electronic circuits were intermingled with living cells.

"Now I know why my command voice didn't work on him," said Marc. "I thought I was losing my powers."

"Let's get going," urged Reb. He motioned for Digger to assist him and pushed the corpse to one side. "I hope we never encounter a monstrosity like this again," he said with disgust. They all walked around the corpse and followed Tootee, who had been waiting down the passageway all the while.

# CHAPTER FOUR

Countess Liana tried to cough, and choked. The taste in her mouth was vile. She tried to open her eyes but could not. Then she realized someone had her by the back of the neck, gripping her gown, dragging her behind him.

*"Buck!"* she thought. She hoped it was Buck.

Buck was slogging through thigh-high mud, struggling to maintain his balance and his grip on the Countess. If he didn't get through this stuff pretty soon, and clear her breathing passages, she could asphyxiate on mud. Progress was slow. The mud was sloppy and slippery. It was too dark to see what lay ahead. The mud was also strangely clammy and cold. The smell was horrible.

Countess Liana tried to help, but her body wouldn't cooperate. She felt paralyzed, she opened her mouth to gasp for air but her throat was clogged with drying mud. She wanted to vomit. Her mind was still alive, though and it formed a thought which she hurled out with all the strength she could muster. *"Marc! Help!"*

A small yellow light glowed in the gloom to his left maybe two hundred feet down the gooey trough. Buck's breathing was laborious and his throat ached. His limbs were growing numb from the cold. He coached himself. *"Just a few steps more. You can do it."* He forced his tired body to make a last burst of effort and then took a step which rang metallically on solid ground.

Liana never knew when Buck laid her on the dry floor and rolled her onto her stomach to pound her back in an effort to loosen the wad of mud that blocked her oesophagus. She had lost consciousness again. Turning her head to the side, Buck inserted an exploring finger into her throat and saw that the blockage had moved forward. Sliding his finger along the side of her throat and behind the obstruction, he gently pulled until it slid forward. Grasping the wad of mud between forefinger and thumb, he eased it out of her mouth and gave Liana CPR to fill her lungs and get them working again. *"If she lives, she's going to have one helluva sore throat for a while",* he thought as he worked over the lifeless girl.

Well, he'd done all he could do for her. At least she was breathing now. He placed her limp form on a narrow ledge and, seating himself heavily beside her, waited for her to come around. The little yellow light didn't offer too much illumination, but in the semi-darkness Buck could see something move on Liana's body. Then he caught a movement on his own leg. He bent to take a closer look. Vampire leeches! They had attached themselves to the skin wherever their jumpsuits were torn from the fall. *"Ugh!"* He hated those things. They were black, about eight inches long, and growing fatter by the second as they gorged themselves on their victims' blood. Buck was feeling weak. He knew the leeches wouldn't let go until they had drunk their blood to the last drop. Only his fast action would save them.

He felt for his knife. He silently thanked the Light; it was still with him. He cut the first leech out of his leg, biting his lip in pain. It took him several minutes to cut away all the leeches on his body. Bleeding profusely from the many cuts he had given himself, he turned his attention to the Countess. *"Good, she still unconscious",* he thought, *"She won't feel the pain".* He set to work removing leeches from Liana's body as gently as possible. He left the leech's mandibles fastened within her flesh, removing only the engorged bodies. If they ever got out of this one, there would be time enough to have Tootee excise the remaining parts properly. He just couldn't bear to carve her up. Meanwhile, at least she would lose no more blood.

\*\*\*

Reb had a strange feeling nudging at the back of his mind. He wasn't a betazoid, but he had developed a strong emotional link with Liana and now he knew that she was in danger.

"Marc," he said. "I think Liana is in danger. I think she needs us. Can you tell me where she is?"

The young Jaira monk wrinkled his forehead with the effort. It was difficult to exert oneself physically and mentally at the same time. He scanned the ship and found nothing. As far as he was concerned, Liana was not aboard. This could not be! Reb had said she was with Buck in the ventilator shaft the last time he'd seen her! He tried again. Couldn't sense her life force. He felt panicky. *"Had they caught her? Killed her? Oh, no! Not his beloved twin! She couldn't be dead!"*

Reb was watching Marc closely. "What is it, Marc? What's wrong?"

"I can't find her!" Marc was nearly in tears.

"Try to find Buck. They were together." suggested Reb softly.

Marc made another mental scan of the ship. He searched for the familiar brain-wave patterns of his friend Buck. He found them, three levels below. Buck was okay. Then, he felt the presence of another being beside Buck. Liana! The vibration of her life force was very weak. He strained to amplify his reception. *"What could have happened to her?"* His scan did not provide the answer however, the distance between them was too great.

"She's alive!" he cried to Reb. "Liana is alive and she's with Buck! There is something wrong with her, though" he added worriedly.

"We have to find them before we disarm the reactor," Reb decided out loud. "Let's move it, people. Tootee, please locate the most direct route to the third level below. We'll follow you."

There were several routes running to higher and lower levels of the ship. They descended behind Tootee for two levels and stopped. Tootee could not locate access further downward. They searched the passage. It appeared to be solid wall. "Buck and Liana are directly below us," said Marc. "Tootee, please search the wall, it must contain a seamless door."

"Over there," pointed Princess Iris. "Use the ventilation exit."

They removed the small cover and peered into the darkness. Then Marc's eyes adjusted to the gloom and he saw two figures far below.

"Liana, Buck, are you all right?" Marc shouted.

"Just barely," Buck's voice came back. "Can you get us out of here before we rot?" He spoke with his usual sarcasm.

"We have no ropes and I see no way to scale the wall," shouted Reb. "Is Liana okay?"

There was no answer because Buck couldn't think what to say.

"Buck! Is Liana okay?" demanded Reb's voice in a louder tone.

"No." came the gruff reply. No details. "Just get us out of here, dammit!"

Reb turned to Marc. "Well, Jaira, we need a miracle at this point. Your sister must be badly wounded."

Marc braced himself for another effort and Princess Iris stepped in beside him. "I'll help," she whispered. Together they closed their eyes and set to work. They shuddered with the, effort. Levitating another being wasn't an easy task.

The inert body of Countess Liana rose slowly from her ledge and floated upward. Reb reached out and helped it through the ventilation access. "Liana! Sweet little Liana, what's happened to you?" Reb was distraught, bending over her wretched, lifeless mud-drenched form through which blood from her wounds was trickling, making little furrows. Reb brushed her hair away from her face tenderly and held her in his arms.

"Tootee, get over here and cauterize the Countess' wounds," he said, as Buck came floating through the access.

"Careful, Tootee," Buck added, "she's full of vampire leech mandibles which you must carefully extract before you cauterize."

4X-2T acknowledged the communication with a singsong of musical beeps.

Marc and Iris emerged from their trance and looked down in concern as Tootee worked quickly and efficiently to extract the leech mandibles and cauterize Liana's wounds. When Tootee was done, the Jaira and his friend joined hands again and focused on Liana, infusing her with their energy. She opened her eyes. Reb swam into focus.

"I thought I'd never see you again," she smiled. She looked around at her friends. "Thought I'd never see any of you, that is." Her eyes found the grimy Buck and she added. "Buck, I owe you my life. Later you must tell me all about our ordeal. I missed most of it, you know."

Buck softened considerably when he looked at her and his voice held nothing of its usual irony. "I know. Tell you what, Countess. When we're safely back on Carrandon, and you're strong again, we'll visit the Dream Vision Center together and I'll run it through for you on the big screen Hologenizer. How's that?"

"You've got a date, Buck. Thanks," she said softly.

*** 

Soldiers appeared, just then, at the opposite entrance to the dead-end corridor and Reb took command. "Marc, Iris, Buck, follow me! Digger, carry the princess and follow the others." He made for the staircase they had taken and paused to herd them all upward. "We're aiming for the upper level," he ordered. "I'll hold them off as long as I can, to give you a head start. Tootee, you stay with me. Now, move it, guys!"

The Prozoan cradled Liana like a child, in his huge furry arms, and hurried after his friends. Reb grabbed the Prozoan's weapon from his belt as he passed, and opened fire on the soldiers with a blaster in each hand, ducking into the stairwell to avoid the return fire.

The little band reached the upper level in short order and Reb raced up to join them, instructing Tootee to close and lock each hatch opening as they passed through.

"Now that we're all together," said Princess Iris. "I'd like to request that we rescue my servants and my own personal guard from their lockups. My guards are trained soldiers and will give us the backup we need in whatever has to be done." She looked inquiringly from Reb to Marc.

"Sounds good to me," said Reb. "Where exactly are they? Can you lead us to them?"

She nodded and started off. "We have to reach the seventh level. That's where the prisoners are kept. I'll show you the way."

Minutes later, they approached the prison section and Reb cautioned them to halt. "We'll need to overcome the guards before we can do any good," he said, scratching his tousled brown head. "Anybody got an idea?"

"Leave it to me," offered Marc.

"It's all yours, Jaira," grinned Reb.

"Here's my plan," said Marc. "I'm dressed like one of them, so I'll pretend Princess Iris is my prisoner. Tootee will come along, and the rest of you will wait in silence. At my signal you will rush in and attack. This way, we'll take them from both sides."

Princess Iris nodded and stepped forward. Marc held her hands crossed behind her back and pushed her along in front of him, with Tootee following at a discreet distance. The others hid in the shadows.

Marc assumed his air of command authority as he approached the armed guards to the prison section. Iris took on the cowered look of a victim reluctantly shuffling along.

"LAM-5XR. Admiral's personal guard, escorting prisoner back to cell," he improvised with a salute.

"We weren't informed about receiving a prisoner," the guard protested. "I'll have to check with... "

Marc lifted his hand and made a slight movement before the guard's eyes. "I'll escort the prisoner to her cell, personally," he said sternly. "Please show us the way, Captain." Marc wondered how the guard would react to being boosted in rank.

"Yes, sir. Follow me. This way, please," said the guard obediently as he opened the heavy gate.

Trailing behind them, just out of sight, Tootee made sure the gate couldn't be relocked, by sabotaging the tumblers. Then he whirred along after his master.

Stopping before a high, barred security door to one cell, the soldier opened it. "I'm sorry, but I have to do this," said Marc, giving a little chop to the back of the guard's neck and rendering him unconscious.

"My attendants are in here," said Iris, entering the darkened cell.

"Herme... Estri..." she called softly. Movement was felt near the far wall.

"My Princess...!" a small voice piped up, full of joy. "We are all right." Two small beings rose to their feet.

"Lony wasn't es lucky as we, though," said the second voice.

"I know," answered Princess Iris. "I'll treasure the memory of her heroism as long as I live. But we must leave her now, there is nothing we can do to bring her back. Follow me." Her voice was strong as she took her rightful position of command among her followers.

"Where is your personal guard?" asked Marc. "We must hurry."

They stopped before another door at the far end of the corridor. "Tootee, open it for us," commanded Marc. Tootee busied himself with the security code that locked the door. Then Marc heard shots and the sound of running feet back at the prison gate. "Our friends have been discovered," he whispered to Iris. "Hurry, Tootee. Hurry!"

The expression on Princess Iris' face told him she was trying to break the lock code mentally. He never found out whether it was she or the 4X unit who succeeded, but the door swung open soundlessly and Iris ran into the cell.

"Guards! You are freed! Rise and assume battle formation. There is no time to lose! Now, march!" Her commands galvanized the soldiers into instant action. About twenty-five beautiful young men and women filled the passage, fell into place behind their glorious commander and marched to the entrance. There, they easily crushed the small force of prison guards who had overtaken Reb, Liana and Digger. The fight was over nearly before it began and the group rearmed themselves with weapons taken off the fallen guards.

"That's better." grinned Reb. "Now let's see what we can do about the reactor. I can't wait to put an end to this flying piece of space junk!" Reb felt more cheerful and optimistic than he had since this expedition was organized.

\*\*\*

No one ever intruded on the Admiral. To interrupt him without being bidden meant death to the interloper. He was nearly ready to climax with his victim, and the beautiful, dark-haired, thirteen-year-old Hydran boy was screaming in pain.

"What the hell..." the Admiral snarled." Whoever has dared to breech my privacy will pay for this... "

His threat trailed off ineffectively. Digger's big hand reached out to grab him by the hair and swing him around to face his assailants. "Excuse the interruption, Admiral, but we have an account to settle with you." Princess Iris faced her enemy with an odd expression in her eyes which had turned dark with anger. "You are going to pay for my little brother's humiliation and slaughter." She drew her weapon.

"Iris, wait!" Reb broke in. "Before you kill him, I have a job for him to do for us. He can still be useful for a while. He grimaced at the Admiral, wriggling in Digger's grasp. "Cover your nakedness, scumbag." He spat with disgust, "You and I are taking a little trip to the bridge. Move it!" He gave the scaly green humanoid a kick. "Buck," he added as an afterthought, "calm that poor child and bring him along."

Surrounded as he was, the Admiral could not resist. Outside the door, they stepped over the body of a guard they had disabled on their way in. The officers on the bridge were a little surprised to see their Admiral half-dressed and surrounded by a ragged group of humans pointing weapons at him.

"One funny move on your part and we'll blow him into fragments," Reb informed the crew cheerfully. "Drop your weapons. Kick them over here. That's good."

The officers hurriedly disarmed themselves in jig time. "Now, resume your positions, gentlemen. That's right. Now," he instructed the Hydran partisans, "cuff them securely to their posts, just so they won't try anything. Good. Now, gentlemen, we have some questions for you." Reb turned to the Admiral. "How did you know where we were going to emerge from hyperspace, and how did you learn of our expedition?" He cocked the blaster's trigger.

The Admiral's eyes shifted around the room. He looked like an animal in a trap. "His Highness Ardano Ad Sadra gave us the coordinates. We were following his instructions. I have not been apprised of his source, he replied.

"Where is the Tyrant Sadra, now?" insisted Reb.

"In Janeera, of course," came the answer.

"What system of defence does Janeera employ and how many men does the Tyrant have stationed in the Capital?" broke in Marc.

"I can't tell you that. Any breech of our intelligence would mean death." The Admiral's green skin was turning violet with fear.

"It will also mean death if you refuse to tell. The difference being that this death will come much sooner," assured Reb.

"You won't get away with this... ," started the Admiral angrily.

"Just a moment, I have an idea." Buck was recovering from his ordeal and doing some creative thinking. He still looked like something the cat had dragged in, all covered with dried mud and smelling like excrement. "Point this big gun, here, at their sister ship," he pushed the gunnery officer's hand off his control board and worked at the console. "Like this." The sister ship now became the object of focus on the target screen. "Now, I'm going to count to ten. If we don't get an answer from the Admiral by the time I finish my count, you can say goodbye to your sister ship." There was a hard edge to his voice as he began his slow countdown. "Ten, nine, eight, seven, six, five, four, three... "The Admiral looked distinctly uncomfortable, but he counted on it being only a bluff. "Two... "His mouth remained shut. "One... "Buck looked around at the Admiral, who was beginning to smile in triumph, at having won the bluff, and smiled a little smile himself as he flipped the firing key.

The screen image exploded in a burst of flame. By now, the Admiral had turned deathly pale.

"This doesn't seem to be your day, does it, Admiral? You just lost half your army out there. I would suggest you try to be a little more cooperative in future, unless you are tired of living, yourself." Reb's voice was even paced and logical. His expression was almost gleeful.

The emergency alarm sounded in shrill blasts and they all looked at each other in astonishment. Then the speaker crackled and an urgent voice called out, "Officer Roonar to the bridge. Explosions from our sister ship have hurled pieces of fuselage into our power plant. Our reactor is damaged and leaking. We can't seal it off. A ripple effect has begun. We estimate you have ten minutes to evacuate the ship before detonation. We are awaiting the Admiral's instructions to evacuate personnel."

The revolutionaries looked at each other in alarm. Reb was cool. "Quick! Everyone, to the *Golden Phoenix*!" he shouted. "Follow me!"

Panic broke loose on the ship. Officers who were on the bridge were writhing and begging the Admiral to uncuff them. The revolutionaries and Hydrans raced at breakneck speed through the ship toward the emergency port's airlock, passing soldiers who were frantically trying to gather their belongings and get to the life boats. Nobody challenged them, fighting was out of the question, it was every soldier for himself.

Passages that had been formerly dark were now brightly illuminated with phosphorescent green light. Red emergency flashers were blinking their alarm, and casting a ghastly red glow against the green.

Laughing as they ran, Reb slapped Buck on the back. "You did it, you mud-ball, you're a genius! That's what I call killing two birds with one stone!"

"Hey, called Marc, ahead of them. "We can't go out like this! Follow me, I know where to find fresh suits." He led them to the storage room he had stumbled into when he came in, and everyone except Liana jumped into suitable space gear in a matter of seconds. Liana, still carried by Digger, had to be gently dressed by Princess Iris and her attendants.

"I'm going to take off in the *Star Wind,*" called Marc, leaving them to don their helmets, "and I'm taking Tootee with me. See you on Hydra V!" He raced around a corner as he spoke, and he and little Tootee were gone.

"We don't have much time," urged Reb. "Hurry, hurry," he panted to Iris, "my chronometer shows that we're going to blow sky high in four more minutes!"

Just then a voice came through the ship's communication system. "Four minutes and counting to detonation," it intoned, "Abandon ship, abandon ship, abandon ship." The voice was bereft of emotion, as only a computerized message could be at a time like this.

The little band of revolutionaries moved as fast as their legs would carry them.

"Three minutes to detonation," intoned the voice which came from nowhere.

"We're almost there!" Reb stumbled. They were all pushed to the far edge of their endurance. Reb was worn out, tired, breathless.

"Two minutes to detonation." They reached the airlock to the emergency hatch and crowded in like thirty-three sardines in a can. Nobody spoke while the airlock decompressed. Reb saw their worried faces and smiled to himself. Soon, this would be over. Another moment and they would be aboard the *Golden Phoenix*. Another moment after that and they would leap into the safety of hyperspace.

He opened the hatch door. The smile froze on his face. His brows knit together as he scanned the hull's surface! Where was the *Phoenix*?

It was gone! Reb could not believe his eyes. What had that bird-brained Fortuno done with his ship?

The pitiful cluster of guards and revolutionaries stood on the hull of the battleship, saying their prayers. Their only means of escape was gone. Reb looked out at the void of black, silent space and then back at the spot where his beloved ship had once stood. He turned to say goodbye to his friends. Death was imminent. It had all been for nothing.

# CHAPTER FIVE

The silence of space was broken only by Marc's breathing and the pounding of his heart, as he slid through the colorless void in his *Star Wind*. He and his robot, Tootee, were accelerating away from the enemy ship which would transform into an explosive ball any minute now. He knew nothing would survive the detonation of that ship's nuclear reactor plant. All aboard would be annihilated into miniscule particles destined to float in space for eternity.

Marc was worried about his friends. He wondered if they'd made it to the *Phoenix* in time. He scanned the space around him on his radar screen and picked up nothing. Not a trace of the *Golden Phoenix*. "*I should go back and make sure they got out of there okay*", he thought to himself.

"Tootee, what do you think?" he said out loud. "Should we risk going back? I don't see the *Phoenix* out here with us where it should be." He was answered with a shrill staccato of negative beeps from the agitated 4X-2T unit.

He sighed. "I guess you're right, Tootee. It would be

suicidal. But where are they? Where are Liana and Reb and Iris and the rest?" In spite of the alarm he felt for them, he smiled as a vision of the beautiful Hydran revolutionary leader overwhelmed his imagination.

Abruptly, the small V-wing was violently rocked in the shock wave of an explosion. His controls went wild, and the little craft spun off in aimless abandon with Marc slumped helplessly in his safety harness, and rapidly losing consciousness. Tootee was functioning, though, and he futilely signalled Marc with curious little bips, as a small lifeboat shot past the *Star Wind* with startling speed, guided by an expert pilot.

***

Reb's heart missed a beat. His stomach cramped and knotted itself into a frozen lump of fear which rose slowly to his throat. He had no time to speculate on what had happened to his ship.

Then he remembered. He pushed the audio switch on his helmet, "Quick, everybody," he barked, "I saw a lifeboat in the corridor parallel to this. Follow me!" And before the words were out of his mouth he was on the move, taking long weightless strides in magnetic boots across the battleship's uneven hull. *"Let it be there, it must be there!"* he thought as he ran. *"It must be... It is!"* As Reb entered the lifeboat he heard the computerized warning bleating, "...... thirty seconds to detonation, abandon ship, abandon ship."

The lifeboat was equipped to provide for twenty survivors, so it was a little crowded after everybody was aboard. Not everyone could buckle up for take-off, but they clung to whatever stationary object they could find, relieved to be alive. Reb was firing the rockets even as the hatch closed behind the last man, and it was at nearly full throttle that the lifeboat vaulted off the hull of its mother ship and into space. Reb had made many jack-rabbit take-offs in his time, especially during his former career as a space pilot where speed often meant the difference between freedom and capture. But this take-off had been the most desperate and reckless, ever.

Seconds after the lifeboat's successful leap into space the enemy ship exploded in a violent flash. The shock wave hit moments later and their lifeboat was thrust helplessly outward at a dizzying speed.

Reb was first to recover his senses. He looked around. Many of his passengers had slumped momentarily unconscious from the impact of the explosive shock wave. He moved a lever and began to pressurize the cabin.

*"Merciful Light, that was close!"* Reb thought as he relaxed behind the controls. *"Now what, in a thousand plagues, has Fortuno done with the Phoenix?"* He puzzled. *"He was given specific instructions. Where.... How...."* But his thoughts were forced back to the situation at hand. First things first. Placing the ship on autopilot, he checked the lifeboat for damages. Miraculously, there were none, all equipment and structural components were intact. Reb sighed, in approval and relief, as he returned to his console.

He surveyed the crew. Most of them were in poor shape, but Countess Liana and Buck were the worst. Liana was no longer unconscious, but she was very weak and her wounds were reopened and bleeding. Leaning over her poor, battered body with a worried expression, Reb found himself wishing mightily that they were inside the Phoenix where he could see that she was properly medicated in sick bay.

A light touch on his shoulder caused him to look up. Princess Iris, a great deal worse for the wear, had not lost her spirit. "Let me do what I can to make her comfortable." She wore an expression of compassion. "I have experience in the healing arts."

Leaning over the wounded countess, she closed her eyes in concentration and then reached out one slender hand which she held suspended over a large flesh wound on Liana's arm. At first, nothing happened. Then the bleeding slowed to a trickle, and stopped. Iris' face was drained of color from the exertion. The wound changed from red to pink, it closed. Reb looked on, mouth agape, as he witnessed a miracle of healing before his very eyes. The wound displayed a fresh cover of thin new skin; purple at first, because it was so thin it barely covered the raw flesh below. Then, as the skin developed more dermal layers the color changed from angry pink to pale pink to creamy ivory like the rest of her skin. There was no scar.

"Amazing," he murmured with appreciation. "You are a remarkable young woman, Iris."

"Thank you, Reb," she flashed a brilliant smile despite her obvious exhaustion. "You can help me, though. I want to clean some of this mud off the princess before I attend to her other wounds."

Together they worked in silence, cleaning Liana to the best of their makeshift ability with the supplies provided in the lifeboat's First Aid Kit. Meanwhile, the other passengers slowly regained strength and revived

54

spirits as they rested and shared the food and drink stored in the lifeboat's little galley. There wasn't much talk. The long stretch of battle and imprisonment had left them drained and subdued into quiet introspection.

\*\*\*

Fortuno looked in dismay at his master screen. Four enemy V-wings were still on the *Phoenix's* tail. They had been chasing him for the last half hour and he didn't know what to do to shake them. *"Oh, dear!"* He fluttered to himself, *"I'm just not a fighting android. I have no skills at this sort of thing. My programming is deficient in this area. Oh dear, oh dear."* But there was no one to hear him. Fortuno was on his own. *"It doesn't seem heroic, but all I can think of is to flee."* he justified himself to the air.

The *Phoenix* reverberated from a near hit. *"Oh my. This is not fair!"* Fortuno quivered in alarm. The V-wings were closing and he had no more time to lose. *"I wonder if I can do it?"* he wondered. A hyperspace jump was a complicated procedure even for an experienced pilot like Captain Reb. Fortuno seated himself at the ship's main computer console. *"Well"*, he thought, *"if I don't try, I'll never know. And it's the only thing can think of to do to shake these V-wings off my tail."*

Computing the possibilities, Fortuno began to lock in coordinates of the planned landing site on Hydra V. Another near hit shook the *Phoenix*. He must hurry! A minute later, everything was ready. Then, in astonishment, four enemy fighters witnessed the instantaneous disappearance of their target, without a trace.

Everything went smoothly for Fortuno once he achieved hyper speed. He was safely in hyperspace and had nothing to worry about any more. *"Well,"* he chortled happily, *"now that my pursuers are taken care of, I can get back to my repairs without any fear of interruption".* He clanked off his console chair and tottered back to the hold.

\*\*\*

Marc Galaxia shook his head and tried to refocus his eyes. It was a few minutes before he remembered what had happened. He felt a sharp pain in his shoulder and tried to shift his weight. It was then that his eyes registered the strange perspective he had on his cockpit. He realized that he had been thrown from his seat and his shoulder was being jabbed by the edge of the computer console. Every bone in his body ached.

"Uhhhh," he moaned, and thought, *"I'm alive, that's what matters."* He righted his position painfully and eased down into his seat. "Tootee," he called, "are you all right?"

Cheerful bips assured him his little friend was fine.

A quick check of the console also yielded good news. Marc stretched painfully and tried to relax. He wondered if Reb, Liana, Buck and their followers had survived the holocaust. Of course they had! He could feel their vibrations.

Sighing with relief, he set his coordinates for Hydra V and prepared his little ship for the jump into hyperspace. Now, with the ship on autopilot, all he needed to do was relax and think of something pleasant until he fell into a much needed sleep.

He smiled. *"What could possibly be nicer than the thought of reuniting with my friends and Princess Iris on Hydra V?"* he thought. *"And what could be more pleasant than the anticipation of being with Princess Iris?"* During their very brief acquaintance, Marc had become very fond of this exquisite, brave girl. He remembered how he had shared everything with his twin sister, Liana, for so many years, and how he had raged with jealousy when the day came that he had to share her with his best friend, Reb. He consoled himself with the knowledge that Liana had loved Reb Morningstar from the start, and that she was, after all, his twin sister. But now Princess Iris of Hydra V was moving into the center of his emotional universe.

One standard hour later Tootee woke him from his reverie with a staccato of alarm beeps. The ship was approaching Hydra's atmosphere. It was time to prepare for entry and landing.

***

*"Where in starblast is the Golden Phoenix?"* wondered Reb to himself for the hundredth time. He just wouldn't accept the thought that his beloved ship was lost.

"Don't worry," Countess Liana seemed to read his thoughts as she reached around and took his hand in hers. She was recovered from her wounds, showered and changed into fatigues she had found in a locker. Although her energy wasn't yet back to par, she was feeling almost back to normal as she rejoined her beloved Reb. "Cheer up, darling, I can sense Fortuno.

He's still functioning. And that means the *Phoenix* must be safe." After a long pause, she continued. "Our new Hydran friends are very efficient, wouldn't you say?" She stood in front of his console and spread her hands, looking adorable in her oversized jumpsuit with arms and legs all rolled up to accommodate her petite frame. "Look, I'm all healed!" She smiled like an angel. "You know, all the best medical treatment available on Carrandon would not have healed me like this. It seems our beautiful new friend has won her way into all our hearts." She pointed, "Look at Buck!"

Buck Salladian was deep in conversation with Princess Iris. They were sitting side by side on the opposite bulkhead of the crowded cabin, sharing refreshments. Buck's face displayed an emotion which was more than that of grateful patient to lady doctor. He was clearly feeling something more. Princess Iris seemed to be enjoying his company. Her eyes sparkled and she smiled often as she talked with enthusiasm. "Why don't we join them?" suggested Reb, taking Liana by the arm and signalling to Digger, who was seated nearby, to join them.

"Are we interrupting anything?" joked Reb.

"Oh, no. Not at all. Please find a spot to sit and join us." Iris motioned to her assistants, Estri and Herme, to clear space. "There are no words to express my gratitude to you all for saving my life and my honor, and for rescuing my people from their imprisonment," she blushed.

"You've accomplished quite a lot yourself, what with helping to save us all and healing Liana and Buck's wounds," countered Reb as he touched her arm reassuringly, "so I think we're just about even."

Noting that all eyes were on him, he continued. "Now, let me tell you all what our situation is at present. This small life craft can't make the jump to hyperspace, so we will proceed to Hydra V on standard drive. The trip will take about a week. I hate to waste the time, but we have no choice. I guess we should be happy we're alive and try not to demand too much from 'lady luck' right now." He turned to Iris again. "Princess Iris can make use of this time period by describing to us the history of political unrest on Hydra; how it began and what balance of control presently exists between the opponents. In other words, we need priming on precisely what to expect when we arrive on Hydra V"

Princess Iris looks extremely tired, but hearing her name, she snapped back to attention, suppressing her urgent need to rest, leaned back and began her story.

"Two centuries ago, my ancestors of the house of Odman were rulers of our entire star system, including Hydra V and our neighboring planet of Gandra. Sadra's people were then our neighbors and advisors. They were very close to the throne. Our two families coexisted in peace for centuries. Then, one hundred Hydran years ago, our year being half of the standard year, the Immen Sadra, grandfather to the current tyrannical ruler, killed the Hydran king and almost all of his family, ascending to the throne himself. Only the pregnant Hydran queen survived the slaughter, because she was absent from the capital at the time of the coup. She was my paternal grandmother. Upon her return to Hydra she was hidden by loyalists and soon after that she gave birth to my father."

She paused to take a sip of her drink, then continued. "I can't explain why Sadra's bloodline metamorphosed

59

into the cruel beings they are today. Hydrans are a very peaceful people, but it is said that even our blood carries a curse of evil genes, the latent genes of Urfee, the evil ones. It is our most dreaded fear that those genes could surface one day." Her voice caught, then trembled as she spoke. "Urfee was a beautiful but very cruel humanoid race which lived on Hydra V in the beginning of recorded time. They were constantly fighting among themselves and they almost destroyed Hydra in fiercely fought internal wars, two thousand standard years ago. The Urfee wars were so violent that they sunk all existing continents and ruined everything they had created. Legend says they still sleep in cryo-chambers deep in the beds of our oceans, and that one day they will awaken to bring destruction to our world. We fear the legend as we fear our own dormant genes which might one day awaken to turn us into savage beasts."

The expression of pain on Princess Iris' face and the vibration of fear was almost more than Liana could bear. She reached for Iris' hand and stroked it as the girl continued.

"Well, bringing my story up to the present day, my father had seven children who are now all dead except for me. All my brothers and sisters were killed by Sadra and his followers. Sadra resides in Janeera, the Capital city of Hydra, and also in Lamanda, his summer home, on the planet of Gandra. His army is mostly composed of Sydhars of the same type you met on the battleship. His personal guard consists of two thousand Sydhars who accompany him everywhere. I'm sure you'll believe me when I say that the Sydhars surpass any human race for sheer daring and cruelty. Sadra is also a betazoid, although he leans to the dark side of its application. That's probably how he knew where to find you when you emerged from hyperspace, that's how he would know you were coming. You say you carried my little statue on board. Well, it's keyed to me and emits the same vibrations that I do. Sadra probably picked up on those vibrations." She stopped for another sip of her drink.

"That answers one of my questions," Reb broke in. "Pardon my frankness, but the thought that we had been betrayed did cross my mind once or twice back there. Tell me what other surprises you think Sadra might have in store for us."

"Well, as far as I know, he employs a network of Hydran spies. They are planted all over the planet, ready to report to him any news of my whereabouts as well as pass along the name of anybody who is suspected of being associated with the rebellion. We must be extremely careful."

"Oh, great!" exclaimed Buck sarcastically. "That makes things all that much easier for us," he shot her a look of scorn.

"What are the rebel forces like? Can you give us numbers and locations?" asked Reb.

They talked long into the night. Sometime near morning, Countess Liana's head nestled onto Reb's shoulder and she drifted off to sleep in the crook of his muscular arm.

# CHAPTER SIX

Fortuno maintained his balance with great difficulty. Tottering around unsteadily on his metallic feet, he tried desperately to maintain a vertical position while he successfully landed the *Golden Phoenix* at the appointed place on Hydra V. Having completed Reb's ordered repairs to the ship, the silver android wondered what he could do next in view of the fact that he lacked any programmed orders suitable to his present situation. Activating the exterior scanners, he was rewarded with a view of water lapping slowly at the hull of the floating airship with hypnotic regularity. On the horizon there was nothing but ocean, endless ocean as far as the eye could see. The sun was high in the sky and the console recorded elevated surface temperatures outside, but none of this was of any interest to Fortuno.

"*Dear me, I should have stayed behind on Carrandon,*" he lamented plaintively. "*Water is just not my element, not my element at all,*" he sighed and placed his hands on his hips in exasperation. "*Everyone knows rust is the worst enemy an android can face. Oh dear, what shall I do now?*" He thought aloud nervously, rocking back and forth as he talked to himself. "*If only Master Marc and Tootee were here...*" The mapping screen confirmed that the nearest settlement was at least twenty standard miles from where he stood. Fortuno felt very lonely.

Then, just as he reached out to turn off the exterior scanners, he was startled to see a small head emerge from the waves. It appeared to be the head of a boy, perhaps twelve years old, with black hair and skin toasted a very dark brown. The boy was looking at the ship suspiciously and Fortuno detected a movement of lips. He switched on the two-way loudspeaker and called, "Yes? Boy, I am speaking to you. What are you doing out there in the water?"

The boy grew pale with fright at the sound of Fortuno's disembodied voice. Then he replied in a frightened stammer, "I... I... am wondering why you have invaded my family's fishing territory."

"Oh, you can speak Standard. Thank goodness!" exclaimed Fortuno excitedly. "Young man, you will never know how glad I am to see a sapient being at last! I really thought I'd just have to sit and rust away here in solitude. Do you have a vehicle that could transport me over the water and then could you conduct me to your village so that I may explain to your elders why I have come here?" Fortuno wasn't sure if this was correct protocol with these natives, but he had to start somewhere. "By the way, young man, I am a 4-2-N0 android unit from a distant star system; from Carrandon, in fact, have you heard of it?"

"Carrandon!" the boy's voice exclaimed with joy. "Carrandon! We have been waiting for your system to send aid for so long. Are you the only survivor aboard?"

"Survivor? Survivor?" Fortuno could not compute this question for a moment. "Oh, no! There are no other passengers on this ship, young man. Only myself. Oh, dear. This is so confusing."

The boy swam to the ship and climbed onto a projection. Fortuno could see that he was small and fine boned, his muscles strained taut against his bronzed skin. "My name is Vittor." he spoke. "You may call me Vit for short. I live in the village of Kaatra, nearby," he waved toward the starboard bow. "I was just inspecting our nets when I saw you crash into the sea. Where are your companions?"

"If they didn't arrive before me, they will be along shortly," Fortuno replied, as matter-of-factly as he could muster considering his insecurity over the encounter. "And I didn't crash, I splashed down!"

"Oh." Vit was looking at the ship curiously. "Could I come inside and look at your craft while we are waiting for your friends to arrive?" The boy was eager for discovery, like all children of the galaxies. He found *Golden Phoenix* both fascinating and intimidating at the same time.

"Oh, of course, of course," replied Fortuno, "I'll just release the starboard hatch for you. My instruments indicate your atmosphere is nearly identical with that which we maintain in the ship, so you are free to enter directly without undergoing decompression."

When the young boy was face to face with the shining android his eyes grew as wide as saucers and he grinned delightedly at his host.

"I welcome you aboard *Golden Phoenix*, young

man. But I am concerned over how to go about visiting your village?" Fortuno was impatient as ever to be getting on with things.

Vit had been gazing, open-mouthed, around the ship's cockpit. Now he reluctantly brought his attention back to his host. "Village? Oh, yes. We don't use vehicles for water travel, we swim! But I think you should get this ship away from this position and into hiding before a Sydhar spots it. They patrol these waters in their wave hoppers, but we never know when they'll come."

"Oh, my! I've heard about the Sydhars. Such brutes!" fluttered Fortuno. "What shall I do?"

"Can you lift off from the water and fly in that direction?," asked the boy as he pointed to their right. "And will you let me fly with you?"

"Of course, of course," Fortuno was in motion, busying himself with the controls. "Just hop up and belt yourself into that seat over there and keep still while I program a short-range flight plan."

The *Phoenix* lifted gracefully from its watery perch and Fortuno activated the drives. "We will be in your village of Kaatra within minutes," he nodded to the boy.

"Only a few minutes? In that case we'll arrive in time for the evening meal." Vic tried to sound casual as he tilted his head to one side and levelled an inquiring look at the silver droid. "But tell me, do all the inhabitants of Carrandon look as interesting as you?"

\*\*\*

It was past midnight when Marc's V-wing touched the waves in precisely the same spot the *Golden Phoenix* had touched down only hours earlier. He was disappointed when he didn't see the familiar outline of Reb's ship, for he had hoped his friends would be there before him. After checking external atmospheric conditions on his instrumentation panel, he opened the *Star Wind's* canopy and breathed deeply. The air smelled vaguely of salt and it was very refreshing. A moon was rising high against a marine-blue sky and it cast a dancing shimmer on the ocean, lending an unearthly enchanted aspect to the endless surface of the water upon which he bobbed. The gentle rocking of the *Star Wind*, as it floated from crest to crest on gentle swells, made Marc very drowsy. *"Guess I'll take a nap while I wait for the Phoenix to arrive"*, he decided, and made himself comfortable. He was drifting downward into slumber when a small, wet hand touched his cheek and startled him badly.

Leaping nearly out of his seat he looked wildly around in the darkness with unfocused, sleepy eyes, fumbling for his laser sword as he struggled to get his bearings. Slowly, his eyes focused. A petite, slender, long-haired girl was standing on one of the wings of his small craft, in the blue-black darkness.

"I didn't mean to frighten you," she said in a soft voice. "I bring you a welcome to Hydra from our people. We have been awaiting your arrival. Your silver messenger reached our capital earlier today and told us to wait here for you," she explained. The words tumbled out breathlessly, "I am Lady Tyla Voogu, daughter of Lord Voogu, the magistrate of my village." She looked about twenty years old, very pretty with long black hair falling to her hips and eyes that reflected the moonlight like those of an exotic animal.

Marc introduced himself, "I am Commander Marcus Galaxia, at your service."

"Nobody is sleeping tonight in my village because all are celebrating your arrival. If we hurry we'll get there in time for the best part of the evening, the meal of roasted giant eel," she urged.

"Okay, climb in and fasten your seatbelt. Can you give me the coordinates to your village?" Marc indicated the co-pilot's seat and turned on the engines. Tootee whirred softly in the rear of the cockpit.

"I am sorry, but I am not familiar with the term *coordinates*," Lady Tyla replied. However, I can point you in the right direction and guide you there."

"Very well, we'll go on manual pilot and take it slow," Marc agreed as they lifted off the undulating surface.

Moments later the lights of the village could be seen and Marc was astonished by the view which confronted him. An enormous tree rose from the ocean, its mammoth roots anchored in the ocean floor. Among its close-knit branches were colonies of human settlements. The sheer size of the tree was an overwhelming sight. It contained great halls at the conjunction of branches and sub-aquarian tunnels in its roots.

\*\*\*

By no stretch of the imagination did Marc believe a tree could grow this big. The village was illuminated by an eerie green light, as were the outer passageways and tunnels.

"What is that unusual green light?" he asked Lady Tyla curiously.

"We breed fireflies to provide us with light," explained the girl. "There are virtually millions of them, everywhere. You will understand that the use of fire for illumination would be very dangerous, and so we cultivate fireflies. Come, we're almost there." She pulled him toward the great hall.

Marc saw a huge room filled with dark haired people in a very festive mood. Apparently the shining Fortuno was the object of their celebration. He was on the podium, standing beside what appeared to be an impressive-looking chief.

Tyla led Marc to Lord Voogu's side. "We are honored by your presence," the chief spoke in a formal voice, inclining his head in greeting as he extended a hand and placed it on Marc's shoulder. "My people welcome you with open hearts. Our city is your city, our food is your food. You are welcome to everything we have. Will you join us now in this modest celebration of your arrival? You and your group are our only chance for liberation from Sadra's tyranny. But we can discuss this tomorrow when the remainder of your people arrive. Today, let's just enjoy good food, and sing and dance and be happy."

Marc couldn't help wondering why Fortuno had been sent as a messenger. *"Why are the others not here? Where have they taken the Phoenix? Why have they left the android behind?"* He might be a very able liaison officer, but it wasn't Fortuno's duty to attend functions on his own; his duty was to accompany Liana. *"I can't wait to get Fortuno alone and demand a few answers"*, he thought.

A long banquet table was set in the center of the

great hall, loaded with wonderous displays of food and drink. Marc was seated somewhere between Lord Voogu and Fortuno, beside Lady Tyla.

Excusing herself momentarily, Tyla disappeared somewhere inside the maze of the tree to change her wet clothes and dry her hair. Somebody passed a platter to Marc. It smelled of delicious smoked meat and tantalized his taste buds. He wondered if waiting for Lady Tyla to return was the polite thing to do, but his stomach overrode his good manners as he loaded up his plate and dug in.

Tyla rejoined Marc within minutes, looking fresh and dry and very pretty in a gossamer sea green dress, her neck draped with several strands of luminous pale green pearls. After a copious meal, accompanied by a strong, sweet liqueur which had been extracted and fermented from the fruit of the tree, everyone was in the mood to sing and dance.

A guest somewhere in the great hall began to sing a lilting, melodious song and before long everybody, with the exception of Marc and Fortuno, had joined in. It sounded a little like an old gospel song Marc had heard on a sociology tape recounting the history of African American people on the planet Earth. The song captivated him completely and he felt the Light mounting in the great hall. The words were repetitive and easy to catch on to. After a while Marc joined the chorus and sang along, feeling as one with the Hydran people. While the words were easy to imitate and intone, their meaning eluded his grasp, as the song was being sung in the ancient Hydran tongue. But he could guess at the spirituality of its meaning, it sang of a sharing of souls and a union in the Light.

Tyla moved next to Marc, her eyes glimmering mysteriously in the soft light. Behind her followed Lord Voogu. Placing an arm around her fragile shoulders he spoke. "Commander Galaxia, with your permission, I would like to appoint my daughter, Tyla, as your guide in the learning of our customs."

Tyla stretched out her hand invitingly. Marc took it in his and replied to the chief. "Of course, Sir. It will be my honor and pleasure. I will try to be an attentive student and I shall hope not to absorb too much of her time."

"Her time is your time, Commander Galaxia." The chief bowed his head slightly and walked away.

"Your father is very kind." Marc pressed Lady Tyla's hand and gently released it from his grasp. She reminded him of Iris. But she wasn't Iris. He wanted Iris to be his teacher. He hoped she would arrive soon. Meanwhile, he dared not refuse the magistrate's offer of Lady Tyla's services. To do so would be an unspeakable insult, he felt certain.

The singing had stopped and was replaced with the rythmic beating of a deep drum. At first the tempo had been regular and monotonous, but now it was increasing in tempo and tone as more drums were added. Marc was drawn by the hypnotic beat. He could feel a surge of excitement tingling along his spine. Something primordial stirred deep inside him and he felt the Light again. Taking the girl's hand again in his, he led her to the dance floor and began to move to the beat. All the people in the great hall followed suit and soon the floor was very crowded with couples.

Marc sensed that there was something very significant in this celebration. Although he couldn't put his finger on what was happening, he knew he had never felt like this before. The dance continued, the feeling intensified, and it was nearly dawn when he was finally ushered to quarters assigned to his exclusive use. It had been so long since he had last seen a real bed. He was asleep as soon as his head touched the pillow.

# CHAPTER SEVEN

Sometime around midday, Marc raised his head from the pillow and listened to the sound of splashing and children's laughter from just behind his bedroom wall. He stretched lazily and rubbed his eyes before looking around to inspect his surroundings. He was in a small chamber fitted with simple furnishings. Everything was made of wood; walls, chairs, wash basin and stand. Marc rose from his cot and splashed water on his face as he looked out the window. Several youngsters between six and twelve years of age were frolicking on the ocean. They skated around on the surface with the help of supports which looked something like the webbed feet of a reptile called *frog*, which he had seen in a video class on Earth Science.

It wasn't easy using the sea walkers, and every once in a while one of the youngsters would slip and plunge beneath the surface to the accompaniment of companionable laughter. Sunlight could not penetrate the density of the giant tree's foliage, so the light from fireflies, flitting about the walls and ceiling, provided a flickering illumination within. Just about the time Marc completed examining his surroundings, a curtain covering the entrance was lifted to admit Lady Tyla, carrying Marc's breakfast, of birds' eggs in fish stew, on a wooden tray.

Marc sat on a low chair and cautiously tasted the stew, while Lady Tyla described the plan for that day. "Your silver messenger, 4-2-N0, told us the rest of your party will be arriving soon, so our people are watching for them." She pronounced the android's name with great difficulty. "Meanwhile, both your ships have been well hidden from the eyes of intruders so that, even if the Sydhars come to inspect our village, they will find nothing to alert them to your presence, so long as you both keep out of sight. And that reminds me. We discovered a curious machine in the cockpit of your ship. It floats and emits light and sound effects that we do not comprehend. Did you wish to have this machine brought to you here?"

Marc had been watching her with a jumble of emotions as she talked. "*Two ships hidden? Then Fortuno had been alone! Why had he brought the ship to Hydra V without waiting for Reb and his crew? Where were Liana, Iris, Reb, Buck and Digger, not to mention that hoard of Hydran guards and servants? Jumpin' Jehosephats! Had they all blown up along with the enemy vessel?* He felt alarmed and panicky all at the same time. Using his Jaira training, he pulled himself together and concentrated on the one thing he could answer.

"Yes, Lady Tyla, the machine you speak of is an 4X-2T unit, a robot of advanced technology. It is very useful to me."

"Oh, do you mean like a secretary?"

"Well, yes, that's as good a description as any. I would appreciate having the unit brought to me at your earliest convenience, and I will also need to meet with the silver android whenever your father, Lord Voogu, can part with his company for a short time."

"I will be happy to have your robot unit brought to you at once, Commander Galaxia, and also the silver android. My father won't be requiring its presence today." She looked at him thoughtfully as if undecided about something and then asked. "Is this what's been bothering you? I've felt your vibrations of worry and anxiety since I met your ship. Have you been lonely for your mechanical friends?"

"No, my Lady. There have been other matters on my mind. But I will very much enjoy meeting with my, er... mechanical friends, as you called them, and I hope that what the silver android has to report will greatly ease my mind."

Tyla paused, her hand on the curtain. "I will go at once." Then she remembered something. "But wait. I came not only to bring your breakfast, but also to extend you an invitation from my father."

Marc brushed off a small spot of stew juice from his moisture repellant jumpsuit and stood at ease, with arms crossed, waiting for her next words.

"The morning sky blessed us with a triple rainbow today, and my father took it as an omen to good fishing. Shortly, he will sail with his fishing party far out to sea to catch the Ko'onu fish. It is a very big, flying fish and very difficult to catch. It is also a dangerous fish which can strike without warning and sever a hand with one bite."

"If the Ko'onu fish is so dangerous and difficult to

catch, why do your fishermen risk their lives for it?" Marc sensed she wasn't finished, but he couldn't help interrupting.

"Because it is delicious and considered a great delicacy for our table." She continued. "My father believes your presence on this fishing expedition would bring good luck. I am instructed to persuade you to go. Would you like to go?"

Marc didn't want to go. He hated the idea of being side-tracked into a fishing trip when all he could think of was talking to his friends Tootee and Fortuno. "Lady Tyla, I am honored by your father's invitation and I would like to go, but I am not physically equipped to hold my breath underwater the way the Hydrans can, and I am not a skilled swimmer."

"Oh, don't worry about that. My father is too old and rheumatic for such athletic feats. Whenever he goes fishing he takes a special launch which is built of wood and is relatively unsinkable." Her shiny face looked back at him in encouragement. His heart sank. He would have to go through with it, like it or not.

"Very well. I will accompany the fishing expedition with pleasure," he lied. "But first, do you think there is time for me to meet briefly with my friends?"

"Of course," Tyla was radiant with pleasure at the good news she would carry to her father. "I will give the order to have the robot brought to you and then I will rush home to tell father that you accept. When I return, I will bring the silver android with me, and I will ask my' father to delay his departure an additional hour so that you have time to take care of your own business first. Will this be sufficient?"

"Yes! Wonderful! That should do it." Marc suddenly felt better about everything. Once he had all his questions answered, perhaps he'd even enjoy the fishing experience, who knows?

Minutes went by. Marc strolled up and down a few pathways among the branches, smiling and nodding at the Hydrans who seemed thrilled by his presence. Then he returned to his quarters to sit by the window and watch the children at play until Lady Tyla reappeared in his doorway with Fortuno and a boy who was followed by Tootee.

"Hello again," she gestured at the silver droid next to her. "I have brought you your friends. I will return and take you to the boat in half an hour."

Tootee let loose with a cacophony of bips the moment the curtain fell behind Lady Tyla's retreating figure.

"I know, Tootee, it was stuffy and cramped in the *Star Wind*. And thank you for waiting so patiently, but I felt protocol was best served at the time by meeting the villagers alone."

"Yes, Tootee," a crisp voice broke in, "Master Marc is absolutely right. He followed the best protocol possible and you shouldn't complain so selfishly at being left out. You may be my friend, but you're a robot, not a human. And don't you forget it!"

"Fortuno, don't you dare scold little Tootee. You're as bossy as ever, I see." Marc shot a stern glance at the silver droid. "I am very glad to see you again, however. I have a great many questions for you. Shall we begin?"

"Yes, Master Marc. I suppose you want to know why Reb, Liana, Buck and Digger aren't with me."

"It occurred to me to ask you that, yes, Fortuno. Where are they." Marc spoke impatiently.

"Now you're getting me all flustered, Master Marc," Fortuno complained. "Which question do you want me to answer; where they are or why they're not with me?"

"Oh, for pity's sake, Fortuno, just go back to the beginning and tell me as briefly as possible what happened."

"Yes, Master Marc." And Fortuno launched into his story in great detail, uninterrupted by either Marc nor Tootee, who were both listening as if struck dumb by the history of that surprise attack, so eloquently described by the silver droid.

"Well, that tells me why you've arrived alone on Hydra V., but it doesn't begin to answer my concern for the whereabouts or safety of the others." Marc muttered half to himself.

"Can't you sense them, Master Marc?" inquired the worried droid.

"No. They're not orbiting Hydra, wherever they are." Marc was suddenly struck by a new thought. "But with the inventive Reb Morningstar as their leader, I'm certain they've found an ingenious solution to their plight." He smiled at his friends. "They'll all show up eventually, I'm sure of it. Meanwhile, I don't want to see either of you worrying."

Tyla appeared in the doorway once again, signalling her readiness to take Marc to the boat. He instructed Tootee to fill Fortuno in on the events that had taken place on the enemy battleship and left them together to await his return.

Marc strode along beside Lady Tyla, deep in

thought. Relieved as he had been to hear Fortuno's story and learn how the *Phoenix* had been saved, his concern for Liana, Iris, Reb, Buck, Digger and the rest had only increased. He forced himself to think about the fishing party. To begin with, he distrusted the sea. Having been raised in the desert he was not fond of large bodies of water. As if that weren't reason enough to decline the invitation, he thought about the legendary Ko'onu fish. Fishing for bloodthirsty sea creatures was not his idea of fun. But how could he say no to his host? *"What the heck"*, he thought. *"It looks like I have some time to kill. Might as well go, and try to enjoy myself"*.

Tyla tugged at his sleeve. "There's the boat. I see my father is already aboard."

"Great!" Marc grinned. "I'm ready to go!" He forced enthusiasm into his voice, hoping she wouldn't sense his lie.

\*\*\*

The boat was rocking dangerously on the swells, and Marc was afraid he was going to be sea-sick. The wild undulations didn't seem to bother the natives, who were cheerfully chatting to one another while seated on the deck. The sun was fierce and Marc could feel the redness of a bad sunburn inflaming his face and hands. Thank goodness he was otherwise covered with his insulated jumpsuit, but he hoped Lady Tyla would have a balm to spread on his crimson face and hands tonight when he returned. If he survived the day, that is.

The boat's single, strangely-shaped sail luffed in the wind. They had already sailed far from the village and only an endless expanse of ocean surrounded their flimsy craft.

The fishing party was led by Lord Voogu and consisted of about twenty young men and women. Once in a while, a few of them would jump overboard to cool off. They would swim around the boat and dive under it, laughing and playing in the sea. They seemed so carefree and happy that Marc found himself envying them their simple lifestyle. He had never seen such expert swimmers, and he watched them with the grudging admiration only a sand dweller could feel.

As if reading his thoughts, Tyla, seated next to him, said, "My people swim before they walk." Then she tilted her head back and laughed merrily. "Will you join me for a swim?" She jumped to her feet, taking his consent for granted.

"I am not properly dressed for swimming," he began.

"Oh, just strip to your briefs and jump in, no one will notice." She was dancing up and down, tugging at his jumpsuit zipper as she spoke.

Marc computed the situation rapidly and decided that obedience was the better part of valor. He did not have Fortuno around to advice on the best protocol in this situation, so... *"Better naked than rejected"*, he thought, as he stripped to his briefs.

"I'm not an experienced swimmer," he began again. But before she could reply the boat bounced on a large swell and he lost balance, falling into the water. Coming up for a breath of air, he shook his blond cowlick out of his eyes and looked for Lady Tyla. She was waving at him. She dived. He took a large lungful of air and imitated. The cold water closed over his head. He opened his eyes underwater and he was in a blue twilight full of schools of colorful fishes swirling all around. His lungs were bursting. He surfaced again, and Lady Tyla was at his side, urging him to chase her under and around the boat like the others. He did his best, but it taxed his aerobic capacity to the max and, after fifteen minutes of play, Marc managed to haul himself back onto the boat where he collapsed in exhaustion.

Suddenly the air was full of voices. "Ko'onu in sight," they chorused as young men and women jumped to their feet and took their positions. There was no time for Marc to recover his breath. Still gasping, he hove to his feet and got out of the way of the hands that were arranging a big net into an unusual wooden frame in the center of the vessel. Harpoons appeared, and another net was stretched out in the aft section of the vessel to provide shelter for the crew. Then someone thrust a harpoon into Marc's hand.

He looked at it, wondering if it was manual or automatic. Then he looked up and saw the Ko'onu. A school of them, in fact, leaping out of the water, maybe a hundred of them, in graceful arcing curves. They were coming straight toward the boat and as they neared he could see that they were about five feet long, with open mouths full of white, jagged teeth. They looked entirely capable of eating everything in their path, and Marc didn't like the thought one bit. His hand grasped the harpoon as he prepared for battle.

Meanwhile, the natives were showing no fear. They were ready for the fight. Lord Voogu gave the command, "Everybody into the shelter."

Ko'onu began leaping into the boat, their sharp teeth

gnashing away at anything they encountered as they floundered on deck. Marc imagined what it would feel like to be bitten by one of them and shuddered. The net which had been spread on the horizontal frame in the center of the boat was now hanging vertically. It was the catch net. Ko'onu were bouncing off the net and falling onto the deck, where they were stabbed by the natives wielding harpoons. In minutes it was all over.

The deck was drenched with fish blood. Marc walked over to take a closer look at the catch. To his dismay, he noted that the Ko'onu had something resembling hands where the caudal fins should have been. He shuddered involuntarily and vowed not to eat tonight. *"I'd feel like a cannibal,"* he thought.

\*\*\*

"We'll be landing in a few minutes, everybody, buckle up while we navigate atmospheric entry," announced Reb.

They were all relieved that their journey had come to an end. A week in the confining quarters of the lifeboat had tried everyone's patience. The Hydrans were looking positively elated and eager for a chance to go for a swim just as soon as the ship touched down.

Assured by Iris that atmospheric pressure was no problem, Reb pressed the release button which blew all the airlocks and laughed, along with Liana and Buck, as the Hydrans all jumped into the water and romped like homesick children. Digger groaned, "Ouuuuuuuu," in anguish at the thought of having to go in the water, and retreated to the cockpit where he slumped in a big furry huddle. Princess Iris looked longingly at the ocean, but restrained herself, while Liana tried to cover a distasteful expression but Buck grinned with delight at the thought of getting in some really good swimming.

Princess Iris addressed herself to Reb with a worried frown. "It is my suggestion that we try to make it to Kaatra, the tree village, before we're spotted by Sydhar patrols. Will this lifeboat move over water?"

"It'll be faster if we fly, Iris. Why don't you recall your people and we'll get underway?"

Minutes after the cumbersome lifecraft took off, it made another watery landing and was quickly concealed among low hanging branches of the huge tree, next to the *Golden Phoenix* and the *Star Wind*.

Reb blew the hatches again and their little party emerged to see the place that would be their home for the next few days. They looked upon the tree in amazement, and then they spied a familiar suit. It was the figure of Marcus Galaxia and they ran to greet him.

Liana was the first to reach her brother and their embrace was silent and fierce as they spoke in the language of emotion. Then Buck, Reb and Digger were all laughing and slapping each other on the back in greeting, while Princess Iris stood aside and waited her turn to extend her hand.

"Hey, Marc. You look like a native already," joked Buck in reference to Galaxia's sunburned face, "All you need to do is dye your hair black!

During his week in the tree village Marc had acquired a deep sunburned tan on his hands and face. Only his shock of sunny blond hair and clear blue-gray eyes separated him from his Hydran hosts.

Fortuno and Tootee had followed close behind Marc

and were also greeted with warmth by the happy band of newcomers.

"Fortuno! I saw the *Phoenix* when we docked. How and why did you get here by yourself?" Reb demanded of the silver droid.

"Master Reb, it is a very long story and with your kind permission I will relate it all to you later," replied Fortuno in his clipped diction. "I do venture to say, though, that I am glad the danger is past. I am a liaison android and not programmed to take part in battle skirmishes and dangerous adventures."

"Well, I'm sorry to disappoint you, my friend," Reb levelled a serious look at the droid, "but I think our adventures on Hydra V have hardly begun. I'm grateful to you for having brought the *Golden Phoenix* safely to Hydra V, and I look forward to your account of events. But I won't deny that it nearly gave me a heart attack when I rushed out of the battleship with all those people following, and found only empty space awaiting me."

Countess Liana diffused the potential skirmish between her lover and her droid with an interruption. "We have two days to rest in the village and then we must be on our way to Janeera," she said. "I wish we could stay on here a little longer, but time is of the essence."

\*\*\*

That evening, after a sumptuous banquet of welcome, they retired to the salon from which radiated the spokes of hallways to their sleeping quarters. Iris called for refreshments and asked everyone to make themselves comfortable. Then she suggested to Liana that they work out a plan of action. Once the business of planning their attack was out of the way, they could all take a well-earned, two-day rest.

Princess Iris started the ball rolling. "The distance from here to our floating capital takes a month to cross in a small boat, or a few days by wave hopper. As you will understand, it is difficult to calculate exact distances when there are few landmarks to relate to. However, your ships should only take a short time to fly to Janeera. The point is to arrive there unnoticed."

No one spoke. Everyone was trying to think how to make a spacecraft invisible.

"Your ships can travel underwater, can't they?" Iris volunteered hesitantly.

"No." said Reb. "But the *Golden Phoenix* is heavily armed and well shielded."

"The Sydhars' ultrasonic emitters can penetrate any energy shield with the exception of the Light," she said gravely.

"How many soldiers do we have?" asked Reb, changing the subject.

"Together with those we brought from the battleship, we can count on perhaps another thirty Hydrans from the village and another hundred from Itoomo. Itoomo is the big floating island where I was born and we have to stop there on our way to Janeera." A note of nostalgia crept into Iris' voice as she spoke of her home.

"Well, our army is small compared to the two thousand Sydhars who accompany the tyrant Sadra, isn't it?" Buck was disillusioned at the thought. "We'll be lucky to get within visual distance of Sadra's palace, let alone survive to overthrow him."

"Our only hope is to plan an attack that will catch him by surprise," offered Marc.

"Wait a minute," said Reb. "If Sadra is betazoid, he already knows we are here. So much for planning a surprise."

"We will all use our creative intelligence to put together a workable plan," said Princess Iris, smiling at Marc as she spoke. "I have heard that Countess Liana is a betazoid, too, but lacks training. "Isn't that correct?" she said, turning to Liana.

"I've never really had the time or opportunity to train," Liana replied regretfully.

"Well, in the next couple of days, I can give you some classes," offered Iris. "The success of our mission may depend on your help. And I can also sense a potential in you," she added, turning to Buck. "Would you mind taking lessons from me, too?" Her smile wiped out any doubts Buck might have had and he was quick to nod his assent. He and Princess Iris had become good friends during the long ride in the lifeboat.

"We'll start training tomorrow, then," said Iris. "But today the chief gave a long and exhausting celebration in our honor and I'm sure you're all as ready to retire as I am. So I'll say goodnight." She rose gracefully and turned into the hallway that led to her room.

Buck was on his feet and at Princess Iris' side in a flash. I believe we occupy adjoining quarters," he bowed gallantly and offered his arm. "May I walk with you?"

Iris flashed Buck a delighted smile and looped her hand through his bent arm. Marc's heart froze, his eyes flashed and his nerves buzzed with signals of jealousy.

As Buck and Iris retreated down the hall, everyone stretched and rose from their chairs, saying goodnight and heading for their rooms. The general bustle in the room masked an almost indistinguishable splash in the water just outside the window. A dark-skinned shape swam quickly out of sight and moved noiselessly towards his destination.

\*\*\*

Major Roold had heard enough. He had to get the message to the Sydhars as soon as possible. The Tyrant had promised to release his adored wife, Mona, from captivity, in return for information about the whereabouts of Princess Iris and her band of revolutionaries. Roold believed that what he had just overheard would buy his wife's freedom. He hated to sabotage Princess Iris. He was sympathetic to her cause. But he had no choice. He loved his wife more than anything on Hydra and he was ready to do whatever he had to do in order to get her back. He'd been told where to go to contact the Sydhars if he ever had any news. He pushed his small boat away from its moorings and sailed away into the darkness of the night.

# CHAPTER EIGHT

It was a beautiful, sunny day and the ocean unfolded like an endless sapphire carpet far below them. The *Phoenix* was approaching Itoomo, the artificial floating island which Iris called home. Everyone was in a good mood. Everyone, that is, except Reb. He'd just spotted a number of tiny dots moving across the surface of the ocean and he guessed they were wave hoppers.

"What's got you all scowly-faced, darling?" Liana was watching him quizzically.

He set his mouth in a grim line and pointed at the radar screen. "So much for our big surprise," he growled

Iris, hearing the exchange between Reb and Liana walked over to the console and peered at the screen. "Looks like the regular civic patrol, but it might be a good idea to circle the island, before we land, to see if there are more of them."

The island below them was in the shape of a figure eight, and was covered with abundant tropical vegetation.

"Have you ever seen the huge luminous pearls we cultivate here?" Princess Iris asked Liana. "They are valued very highly," she added with pride. "And there,"

87

she indicated another point on the map screen, "is where we have our algae plantation. We use it for food, to complement our diet of fish." Then she smiled and added, "This world would be really beautiful without Sadra and his Sydhars."

"That's why you sent for us," said Buck, "to make sure it gets that way."

"Leaping lizards!" exclaimed Reb. "It looks as though your island is completely surrounded by wave hoppers." They could see hundreds of tiny dots, on screen, in the waters around Itoomo.

"It would be very risky to land down there right now, don't you think?" Countess Liana turned to Iris as she spoke.

"They do seem to be expecting us," Iris replied in a thoughtful voice. "I believe we should alter our plan and land away from the island. From there, a few of us will swim to the shore, underwater, and fetch my soldiers. It will take a few days, though. They won't be able to all leave at once, as that would look suspicious." She looked around at everyone as if hoping for approval. They nodded, in unison, to urge her on. "My soldiers will leave Itoomo at night, on wave hoppers, ten to twenty at a time. In this way I can smuggle my forces out from under the Sydhar's very noses under blanket of darkness. Do you approve?"

"I can't think of anything better," Reb said. "I'll communicate this change of program to Marc at once."

The *Star Wind* was flying above them. The lifeboat, which had saved their lives, had been left hidden at Kaatra, the tree village.

"Take us there." She pointed to the map screen,

indicating a point twenty miles north of Itoomo. "The waves are always so high in that area that wave hoppers never attempt to patrol in the region. The only way the patrols could spot the *Golden Phoenix* there would be from the air."

They landed minutes later on swells that curled and frothed over troughs twenty feet deep. They were awed, if not a little afraid.

"Oh my," twittered Fortuno. "We will all get dreadfully seasick."

"Androids can't get seasick, you ninny," scoffed Buck.

"Yeah, that's a privilege reserved for humans," added Reb, trying to mask his own acute discomfort.

Marc landed the *Phoenix* and secured his ship before boarding, with Tootee in tow, to be with his friends. Laughing, he announced, "It is just a little bit bumpy out there. I was afraid I'd get sandwiched between the *Phoenix* and the *Star Wind* while I was anchoring her."

"Now that would definitely have put you between a rock and a hard place," Reb chuckled.

Iris selected eighteen soldiers to go with her. They began preparing for their long, difficult underwater swim, with deep breathing exercises. Then, each of them stripped from fatigues to reveal a bodysuit of rubber, and produced fins and gloves from their backpacks.

"That's what I call being ready for anything," laughed Marc.

"It is standard issue to all soldiers on Hydra," Iris returned. "We will dive to three meters below the trough, where the water is quiet, and we will swim at that level until we reach Bantuu Island, where we will surface and rest."

Buck moved across the cockpit and touched Iris on the shoulder. "I would like to accompany you," he said quietly.

"You're crazy! You can't handle that," exploded Reb. "Don't take him up on it, Iris, he'll never make it."

"How do you know?" growled Buck. "I'm a natural swimmer and in great condition. I think I'm the best judge of my abilities!"

"Buck," the soft, sensible voice of Countess Liana broke in, "you don't have a wetsuit or aeration equipment."

Iris ignored Liana's remark and looked deeply into his eyes. Buck gazed back at her unflinchingly. Finally, she said, "If this is your choice, yes, come along. One of the soldiers who will stay behind will remove his suit and fins and give them to you."

Iris pointed to a soldier having Buck's approximate weight and said, "You. Go into the nearest cabin with Minister Salladian and exchange your suit."

Marc's blood boiled and he took a stride toward Buck as if to challenge, but some inner warning stopped him and he sat down again, aiming a look that could kill at Buck's back.

Eventually, the hatch was opened and Iris' group jumped, one-by-one, into the boiling foam. "If we do not return within twenty days, proceed without us," Iris instructed, and then jumped into the ocean with Buck right behind her. The water closed over their heads and they were seen no more.

Those who remained behind in the *Phoenix* were lost in silent contemplation of the scene. Marc was struggling with feelings of jealousy, until he realized that even to think of joining Iris on her swim would be suicidal. Nevertheless his heart was heavy, for he had lost a chance to be with the girl of his dreams.

***

Buck was keeping up and showing good form, so far, although he had to surface to fill his lungs far more often than the Hydrans who were on their seventh mile and showing no strain. It was wonderful to be cutting through the aquamarine twilight at Princess Iris' side. He felt almost like a boy again. For all of his adult life he had cruised the galaxy, visiting nearly every star system that had been charted. Yet, he had always missed that youthful feeling of being so alive and so close to nature. Until today. Today he felt happy and, having a beautiful woman at his side only added to his excitement. Around them swam a group of highly skilled swimmers and divers, and they were accompanied by schools of fish in a myriad of exotic colors.

Then, without warning, a large shape joined the schools of fish. Large, perhaps seven to eight feet long, and of an elongated, sausage shape, it abruptly veered and turned to cut across their path.

Iris caught Buck's hand to get his attention and then began to sign to him. The Hydrans had developed a special sign language with which to communicate under water. Buck understood that the creature was an electric eel which emitted some kind of paralyzing energy and that she was warning him to stay away. He committed to memory the long, black, yellow-spotted fish for future reference.

Other dangers abounded in the ocean. They were eager to avoid contact with the Ko'onu fish whenever they surfaced to replenish their oxygen. The Ko'onu were surface feeders, and to encounter a pod of them could mean sure death for the swimmers. Each swimmer was armed with a long blade strapped to one leg, but such weapons were limited in their effectiveness. Buck marvelled at how they knew which way to swim in the directionless ocean. He noticed that every time he surfaced alongside Iris, she was studying the surface of the water intently. Perhaps she was guided by the flow of the surface currents, for each time she resurfaced she would choose the way without hesitation. *"I must remember to ask her about her directional instinct when we reach land,"* he thought.

After another mile or so Iris surfaced and floated on her back, resting and breathing deeply. Buck surfaced and floated next to her. She looked over at him and smiled, the droplets of water on her face and hair sparkled like diamonds. She never looked more beautiful. He took her hand. She didn't resist. Thus encouraged, Buck gave in to temptation. Drifting closer to Iris, he kissed her on the cheek. She hesitated, then turned her face to his and their lips met in a salty embrace. Buck's heart filled with joy. Did he sense a barely concealed passion behind her cool poise? He knew she was the most desirable woman he had ever known, he could afford to take his time, to wait for her to come to him.

Rested, they submerged again, and continued their swim. From time to time they saw gardens of needle sharp crystalline structures which swelled up from the depths and broke the surface. Transparent colonies of crystals poking out of the waves would refract the sunlight with an almost blinding brilliance. Iris explained to him, during a surface rest, that these were the remains of the infrastructure of the dreaded race of Urfee, and that Hydrans regarded the crystals with fear and trepidation, keeping a safe distance from them at all times.

*"An interesting phenomena"*, mused Buck to himself. *"Perhaps it bears looking into after we've ousted the Tyrant."*

The sun was low on the horizon now, and it was becoming difficult to see underwater. Buck guessed they might have another hour of light left. Although they needed the darkness as a cover as they drew close to the Sydhar's zone of patrol, they knew the danger they risked of unwittingly swimming into a pod of bloodthirsty Ko'onu.

Then, through the dusky twilight and into focus swam a large, vicious-looking creature. The end of its leathery scales formed spikes and it swam with a mouth, the size of *Phoenix's* hatch, filled with jagged teeth. Buck nearly gasped in alarm, then remembered he was underwater. He could not begin to guess at the creature's dimensions, but he had never seen anything so large. The nightmare was coming straight at him, he looked around for Iris and she signalled to him to fire his blaster and aim for the eyes. He would have laughed, if the situation had not been so dire. The monstrous creature was covered with eyes, or markings that looked like eyes, peering out from between the spiked scales. Which eye should he aim for?

Buck tried desperately to fight off the panic he felt and think of something sensible to do in this situation. There was no time to get out of the monster's way. He treaded water and took aim. The laser blaster burned a patch on the beast's left flank and it veered slightly, passing the group of Hydrans so closely that their wet suits were ripped in places by the spiked scales. Unable to avoid entering the monster's slipstream, they were thrown into concave spaces between the spikes and forced to helplessly ride along. The fish was moving at a dizzying speed and they saw it was diving for the base of one of the Urfee crystal clusters. Nearing the cluster, the fish passed so close to the crystals that Buck and Iris flattened themselves between the spikes for fear they would be crushed.

*"I think that this monster wants to shake us off, or rub us off, as the case may be,"* thought Buck. The other swimmers were lost from view and the water was turning midnight blue.

Buck became conscious of the pressure; he hoped his eardrums wouldn't blow. Then he saw the base of the colony, full of multi-shaped corals and other strange sea organisms that he could not identify.

Now the monster was trying to disengage his passengers on the sharp edges of a dark red coral bush that looked like it was painted with blood. Buck held his breath, feeling his chest expand dangerously and knew only a miracle could save him now. He needed desperately to resurface for air, but he was trapped between the spikey scales of a sea monster.

Buck flattened his body to the side of the fish, avoiding the coral, and Princess Iris did the same. Once, twice, three times the monster scraped his side against the coral. Then it seemed to give up. Two thick tentacles extruded from the sides of the huge mouth and Buck felt weak as he saw them snake along the fish's side and towards its captives. *"No doubt it's tired of playing and ready for a meal",* he decided.

One tentacle wound itself around Princess Iris' right hand, the other around Buck's ankle, and helplessly they were dragged towards the awful razor mouth. Buck saw Iris' panic. He knew he was going to suffocate if he didn't get to the surface, now!

He saw the eye. He remembered Iris' signal to go for the eye. *"This must be the one"* he thought, it was right in the center of its forehead. He drew his laser blaster and aimed. Princess Iris was being drawn into the beast's mouth. *"Oh, no!"* He flipped the barrel to full power and fired. The creature recoiled from the impact and spun off crazily into the darkness. Iris was limp and a bit stunned, but alive!

Her wrist was bleeding where the sea monster had held it in a death grip. Buck shuddered at the thought that she would have been in the stomach of that beast in another moment. It was too close a call. He caught Iris by the other arm and began to push toward the surface with forceful frog kicks. Within a minute, Iris was kicking too, and each was making rapid progress upward without the drag of the other's weight.

Surfacing and gulping for air all in the same motion, Buck was trembling with the tension of the battle and from sustaining his empty lungs. Iris swam over to him with an expression of great concern and patted him helplessly on his back as he gasped for air like a drowning person. Finally, his breathing and heart rate slowed and he was able to float and recover some strength. The other swimmers were nowhere in sight when Buck and Iris submerged for the final leg of their journey to the little island of Bantuu. He guessed the Hydran soldiers were following orders to stop for nothing, not even their missing leader.

# CHAPTER NINE

Impassively waiting around for other people to get their show on the road was not Reb's strong suit. The others on board the *Golden Phoenix* felt nervous and restless, too. Only Digerawicz was relaxed. In fact, he seemed to be hibernating.

Countess Liana tried to maintain concentration as she worked on a project with Fortuno, but she was hard pressed to stay focused. Marc meditated to free himself of his anxiety and jealousy over Iris and Buck and his concern over Iris' safety. For the first time in his life, he wished he was a strong swimmer, a water-baby like Iris.

One evening they gathered in the *Phoenix's* lounge, sipping a sweet nectar cocktail and making feeble attempts at conversation. It had been ten days since Iris departed for Itoomo with her entourage, and the crew of *Phoenix* was bored with the waiting. The constant rocking of the ship had become unbearable and tempers were frayed. All, save the snoozing Digger and the implacable android, were feeling edgy and irritable.

Reb cleared his throat to catch his companion's attention. "How about if we make a high altitude pass over Itoomo to see if we can see anything resembling a skirmish between Iris, her soldiers and the Sydhars? I know it sounds lame, but there must be something we can do besides waiting?"

"We are all impatient, darling," said Liana gently. And we're all eager for action. But we did give our word we would stay here and wait."

"What if Iris is in trouble?" asked Marc. "What if she needs our help?"

"I share your concern," replied the level-headed princess, "but we must adhere to our promise. We also agreed to wait for the soldiers to return, and then to proceed without Princess Iris if she should not return. And this is what we must do."

"I still want to go out and look for her," replied Marc stubbornly. "I could take the *Star Wind* and fly by night so the Sydhar patrols wouldn't spot me so readily."

Liana's voice rose in irritation. "Marc, there is no point in debating this with me, nor will you achieve anything by making clever suggestions.

We could easily mess this whole thing up if we arbitrarily alter Princess Iris' plan. It's her planet, it's her cause, and it's our duty to respect her wishes and to follow her orders." She turned away. "I have no more to say on the subject. Except that you must know as well as I do that Iris and Buck are safe wherever they are. If I can feel healthy vibrations from both of them, so you most surely must feel them, too." She turned back. "Why are you making such an issue of going after them? You've never been this anxious on other patrols!"

"No special reason." Marc felt suddenly ashamed. Of course he felt their vibrations and knew they were safe. *"That's the problem, not that they're not safe, but that they are together!"* He wasn't about to admit his jealousy was spurring him to her side just to break up whatever was happening between them before she got too attached to his rival.

"You forget I can tell when you're lying, Marc." Liana smiled with sudden tenderness. "I can also sense the vibrations of infatuation, my dear brother. However I won't press you to tell me until you're ready."

***

A strong tremor shook the *Phoenix*. "What was that?" Reb jumped to his feet and ran to the console to activate the scanners. A wall of water nearly three hundred feet high was moving across the surface of the sea.

"Tsunami!" yelled Reb. "It will sweep us along on its crest until it reaches a land mass and then dash us to smithereens against the shore." He was all business now. "Man your stations, everybody. Digger! Wake up, man. I need you!"

The Prozoan staggered groggily over to his station and waited for further orders. Reb activated the jets and engineered a lift just before the wave reached them. Hovering briefly, he then made certain there was not another wave in close pursuit, before lowering the *Phoenix* gently back onto a surprisingly flat sea.

"This planet certainly specializes in last-minute surprises," Reb grinned with relief. "That sure took our minds off our boredom, didn't it?" He turned to Liana. "Are you all right?" He put his arm around her and drew her close. She looked a little pale and shaken. Obviously she didn't live for danger the way Reb and her brother did.

"I'm fine," she replied, hugging him. "I'm just not used to having so much water around me. I can't swim at all, remember?" She was trying to make a joke of it, but it was easy to see she was intimidated.

One of the Hydran soldiers approached Reb. "The tsunami was almost certainly caused by a sub-oceanic temblor," he suggested. "We shouldn't have landed on the water just yet because there will be other waves to follow."

"How can you be sure?" Reb retorted in irritation. "We'll subject our ship to Sydhar detection if we hover at an elevation, you know."

"We are trained to read the pattern of ocean currents. This flat surface is just the calm before the storm."

"Can you all predict the weather like this?" asked Liana politely.

"Yes, even the children can do it. The sea is our mother. We know everything there is to know about her."

Reb frowned. "What else can you read from the currents?"

"We can tell how far it is to land, or how far to a floating island. We know when there is any alien disturbance on the water, such as the wave hoppers. And we know how many wave hoppers are there."

"That's amazing!" Liana encouraged the-man to continue. "How does this gift work?"

"When you drop a stone into the water, it causes a disturbance and creates its own whirlpool of currents. The same occurs with all types of interruptions to the normal ebb and flow. This activity is written all over the surface of the ocean for us to read," he said knowingly.

"Okay, then. Can you tell us if there are any enemy wave hoppers in the vicinity?" asked Marc.

The native looked at the video screen which displayed a moving image of the surrounding watery panorama. "There are about fifty of them disturbing the environment within close range," he replied. "They are moving in our direction," he answered with finality. Nobody doubted him.

"Can you say how soon they'll be visible on our scanners?" asked Reb.

"Yes," said the native, studying the water. "In perhaps ten minutes."

"Can you redirect us to this location if we leave?" Reb had obviously made a decision. "We can lift off and orbit while this tsunami does its thing, but we'll have to return to rendezvous with the party from Itoomo."

"I can redirect," replied the Hydran.

"Prepare for lift off and warp one acceleration," ordered Reb. The *Golden Phoenix* rose from the water's surface and shot upward in warp drive. In the blink of an eye the *Phoenix* had disappeared into the planet's heavy cloud cover. When the Sydhar wave hopper patrol came over the horizon they were disappointed to find no trace of the airship their leader had promised them was there. Perhaps Sadra was not a seer, after all.

\*\*\*

Buck and Princess Iris were closing in on Itoomo. Only the reefs now separated them from shore a mile away. They had stopped at Bantuu Island to rest, as planned, after their harrowing escapade, and had looked around for Iris' soldiers in vain. Obviously the Hydrans had already come and gone.

The few hours of sleep they had enjoyed on deserted and peaceful Bantuu, which restored their energies and renewed their spirits, now lingered in their memories as if they had merely imagined it. For the second half of their swim had taken its toll. They were feeling a thermal chill and nervous exhaustion mitigated by fasting from both food and water intake during the entire swim.

Despite their eagerness to reach Itoomo, which meant shelter, food and rest, they had to go slow now and be extra careful. For the hated Sydhars continually patrolled offshore on their wave hoppers. Buck's arms felt like lead; they moved rythmically through the shallow water with labored movements and surfaced every five minutes to re-oxygenate their lungs and check their position.

The moon cast an indifferent shimmer on the water as they surfaced no more than fifty yards from shore. Just then Iris heard a familiar sound, the splash, splash, splash of oncoming wave hoppers. They dove, hoping they had not been spotted yet. The sound of the wave hoppers' engines grew closer and then deafening as the Sydhars passed right over their heads.

Abruptly, inexplicably, Iris and Buck became entangled in a fishing net that caught them up from behind. Iris was dumbfounded at first. Who would be fishing at this time of night? Then she knew. Those blasted wave hoppers were trolling submerged nets behind them in the hopes of just such a catch.

Buck panicked. His strength was gone, his lungs were depleted and his rib cage ached with the effort he had already made. The thought crossed his mind that the Sydhars were expecting them and had probably been methodically dragging the shallow coastline waters for the past couple of days. It was black as ink in the night sea. Buck couldn't see a thing, but he could feel Iris thrashing around in the net nearby. He pulled the knife from its leg sheath and began to saw at the ropes that bound him in an ever tightening embrace. He hoped desperately that Iris had remembered her knife and was trying to cut herself free, as well.

She was. Her betazoid sensitivity had picked up on Buck's actions and she imitated and drew her own knife. The net was made of a strong organic fiber which didn't yield easily to their knives. The wave hoppers were towing them into shallower water now and there was a danger of being raked across the sharp coral heads.

Buck was almost too tired to saw at the rope. He wondered what would happen if he just gave up. Then he remembered the Hydran child in the admiral's cabin on the enemy ship and he shook his head violently to clear it and concentrate on the cutting. It was useless. He would have to come up with something else. The net was dragging them against outcroppings of lava now, and their bodies were feeling battered and bruised.

The water grew shallow and the wave hoppers slowed. In the pale glimmer of moonlight he could see Iris, and she was still conscious. He pushed his head through to the surface and breathed deeply, noting how the ropes that drew the net were attached to four wave hoppers.

If they could climb the net and inch along the tow rope, undetected, and switch to the other side, they'd be able to lower themselves into the water again on the outside of the net.

He motioned to Iris and they surfaced together under the net. He explained his plan. He whispered to Iris that the Sydhars would be conscious of their weight in the net, so they dared not let go until they were close enough to shore to race up to the vegetation line before the Sydhars realized their catch was gone. "We'll let them drag us along on the outside of their net until I tell you to jump free," Buck advised.

They began to climb towards the rim of the net, inching their way cautiously toward the backs of the Sydhars. Fortunately, the roar of the wave hoppers disguised any conversation they might have, and the constant bumping and jerking of the net against the uneven ocean terrain masked the tugging generated by their climbing efforts.

After what seemed like an eternity they were over the top and inching their way down the outer flank of the big net. Suddenly the net snagged on something. They felt it immediately, and knew it would be only moments before the wave hoppers were brought up short on the ropes' slack. They looked at each other, hearts in their throats. If the Sydhars turned back to untangle the net, they would be caught red-handed with no hope for escape!

Simultaneously they moved with instinct, scrambling frantically down the net towards the water. If they could reach the water there might be a chance to swim away before the Sydhars could detach the lines from their wave hoppers and circle back to free the net.

But they needn't have worried. For something happened just then that nobody counted on, least of all the Sydhars. Abruptly, all the slack was taken up in the lines and the wave hoppers were yanked violently on the end of their ropes. In an instantaneous loss of control, the wave hoppers spun on the water and cashed against each other in an explosive display of fireworks. The cyborgs were catapulted from their machines and sunk to the bottom, prevented by their sheer metallic weight from rising to the surface or swimming ashore. They were goners.

Buck and Iris exchanged surprised looks, then wasted no time in making for the shore and the vegetation line. Under cover of thick water reeds they sat for a few minutes to catch their breath and contemplate the serene night sea where only moments before they had been trapped.

Rising to her feet, Iris said, "Now, follow me and don't make a sound."

Still aching with exhaustion, shivering and chilled by the cool air, Buck followed her on stiff limbs. Together they plunged into the tropical foliage. The trees and shrubs were all illuminated by the faint green effervescence of fireflies, causing the scene to appear mysterious and beautiful.

As the distance closed between them and the settlement, the light became brighter and brighter until it was almost as bright as day, as the number of fireflies grew more dense. Iris stopped and listened carefully to the night for signs of danger. Buck stopped, wordlessly, and waited. Presently she made a sign that they could continue their walk, and they arrived at the settlement without further ado.

It was a small settlement of perhaps twenty-one dome-shaped residences that circled a big plaza, in the middle of which stood usual looking, circular temple.

Thousands of fireflies illuminated the area. Buck could clearly see the detail work on the pillars which stood in a circular formation, capped by a circlet of stone. The roof and walls were open to nature and in the center of the temple there was a dark reflection pool in which mirrored the pillars, the stars and the moon.

Walking across the plaza, Iris led him to the building with the biggest dome. They entered through the oval doorway and Buck guessed, from the sound of regular, deep breathing that this was some sort of dormitory. Iris crouched low, over one of the sleeping figures. The man raised his head and Buck recognized one of the soldiers they had rescued from the battleship.

"My Princess..." he whispered in reverence. "We thought... We all surfaced on Bantuu as planned, and waited there for two days, but you did not appear. Then we all swam here to Itoomo. Only Roold didn't make it. He was the only one missing when we walked ashore." He looked apologetic and when she said nothing he opened his mouth again to speak.

Iris cut him short. Placing a finger on her lips, she silenced the man and motioned to him that they were going. Then, moving deeper into the structure she led Buck to a small empty room with a thick woven mat on the floor. Lowering the curtain across the doorway to signal a need for privacy, she motioned for Buck to lay down on the mat and quickly moved to lay beside him. In another instant they were fast asleep in each others' arms.

***

The *Golden Phoenix* was safely orbiting Hydra. At this

distance its energy screen would deflect any detection devices and keep its presence secret. Two standard days had passed since they lifted off Hydra just in time to avoid the tsunami aftershock and the Sydhar patrol. But Reb was not concerned for the *Phoenix's* safety. He was anxious about Iris and her group. His radar screen indicated a flotilla of perhaps one hundred and fifty wave hoppers circling right over the spot where the *Phoenix* had been bobbing two days before; on the exact spot marked for rendezvous with Iris and her troops.

"Somehow, we must warn Iris before they get there," said Liana, sharing her partner's concern.

"I can go," volunteered Marc. "I'll take the *Star Wind* and fly at night. All I need are the coordinates to the settlement where her soldiers are housed."

"We don't have coordinates, remember?" Reb was sarcastic. "You'd have to fly by dead reckoning. I suggest you take one of the soldiers with you to act as navigator."

"Oh, Master Marc. Dont go!" Fortuno's voice had lost its composure. "Please, don't go! Your chances of finding them are not very good, while the possibility of your capture is paramount."

A shrill chorus of angry little bips interrupted Fortuno. "What? Tootee, are you serious?" The droid shook his shining head in disbelief. "Are you quite certain of this?"

A little trill of bips answered him. "Tootee must have a short circuit," he said apologetically to whoever would listen. "He is trying to convince us that he is picking up a strange electromagnetic frequency from the ocean floor." He pointed a metallic finger at the radar screen. "Right there." He indicated the precise location of the wave hopper patrol.

"That's strange," murmured Reb. "If there is an electromagnetic field down there, it isn't affecting *Phoenix's* computer at all." He looked doubtfully at the silver droid, then back at the console with surprise. "Wait! Our gyroscopes are going wild. Tootee is right, there is a powerful gravitational pull down there."

"How about if I fly down and use the cloud cover to conceal the *Star Wind* while I take more precise readings?" Marc asked, pulling on his helmet and boots and heading for the airlock as he spoke.

"Be careful," Countess Liana called after his retreating back.

Descending into the cloud cover over the area in question, Marc turned on the *Star Wind's* radar scanner. For a moment he thought he'd overshot his mark. He rechecked his coordinates. He was in the right place. Perhaps the instrumentation was disturbed by electromagnetic activity. He took a big chance, emerging from the cloud cover and exposing his ship to detection, but visual perception was the only thing he could rely on now.

Marc did a double take. He blinked again and looked down at the water. There was not Sydhar nor wave hopper in sight! The entire flotilla had vanished without a trace! "Reb," he spoke into his com-link in an awed voice, "unless these wave hopper double as underwater scooters, and those cyborgs are waterproof, I can't imagine where they've gone, but there's not a wave hopper anywhere down here."

"Stay cool." Reb sounded bewildered. "I'll ask our Hydran friend if he can sense them anywhere. Stand by."

# CHAPTER TEN

Moments later Reb's voice blasted out of the speaker excitedly. "Marc! Get back here! The Hydran sensed the presence of the Sydhar flotilla under the sea, drawn down into an electromagnetic vortex. You are in danger." His voice became urgent. "We don't know how powerful the field is, but we don't want to risk entanglement. Soon as you're back we're out of here..." The voice trailed off.

As he listened to Reb's voice, Marc realized his craft was circling in an unintended downward spiral. *"What on Mezzotrak is going on here?"* he thought as he flipped the communicator switch. Nothing. All communication was dead. Marc sensed a disturbance in the Light. His little craft spiralled downward, out of control. He was glad Tootee was back on the *Phoenix*. His thoughts drifted helplessly and it seemed that the *Star Wind* was in freefall for a long time before she sliced through the waves and penetrated the waves.

The vortex was sucking the *Star Wind* down, down, down. It felt surrealistic to be diving underwater in his ship. He knew it would be some time before all the oxygen was used up and he asphyxiated in his own cockpit. At least it was as impervious to the water as it was to the void of space. He had entered a dream-world not of his making and it was odd that he felt so peaceful... losing touch with reality, as if in the state of narcosis sometimes suffered by pearl divers.

As the *Star Wind* sank even deeper, the water turned from Aquamarine blue to black, and visibility was impossible. He didn't care. Iris' image floated into his mind and he smiled. Then she evaporated and the image of his teacher, Benja-Ko Menjoro, took her place.

"Marc..." his friend Ben was trying to tell him something.

Marc woke up. Hearing his name had jolted him back to reality.

His eyes were open, but the voice of his friend was still inside his head. "Marc, wake up! Call the Light! Save yourself... Hurry! Do it... Marc ..."

He rubbed his eyes and looked out through his canopy. It was as dark as space out there. No, wait. His eyes grew accustomed to the darkness and he saw strange luminous fish shapes moving through the water like mysterious phantoms.

Marc was shaken, and afraid. Then he remembered Master Benja-Ko's teachings and made a mighty effort to pull himself together. As the *Star Wind* was sucked deeper into the vortex, Marc forced himself to relax and enter trance state and recall the principles of levitation. He felt the Light flowing through him and he relaxed onto a deeper level. He visualized the *Star Wind* reversing direction. He visualized it floating upward, ever upward until it resurfaced.

Into his meditation crept the realization that his downward drift had stopped. He maintained the picture of *Star Wind* on the water's surface fixed in his mind. Slowly, slowly he felt the tiny ship begin to ascend.

Marc focused with intensity on the picture in his mind, the ship continued to rise. Then the surface tension broke and dissolved in ripples as Marc and the *Star Wind* emerged into the white overcast of the day. The brightness stung Marc's eyelids and he forced himself to wait a moment before opening his eyes. Then, in a flash, he lifted off the water in a last burst of effort to escape from this place while the Light was still strong within him.

"What in Andromeda's moons is going on now?" Reb did not like situations over which he had no control.

Liana stood behind him, patting him on the shoulder. "Relax, darling, Marc is alive."

A group of Hydrans stood uneasily to one side. "We wish to inform you that the electromagnetic vortex which has swallowed the flotilla, has now swallowed your friend, Commander Galaxia," one of them said nervously.

"What?" Reb was incredulous. "But, Liana, you just told me Marc is alive..."

"She is right," interrupted the Hydran before Liana could reply. "We believe there are Urfee devices still active on the ocean floor. This is the only explanation we have for the sudden disappearances like todays' occurrences." He looked at Liana, and then down at his boots shyly, "We hoped that our visitors from the stars could illuminate our knowledge with an explanation of this phenomenon."

Liana was not paying attention. Her mind was elsewhere. Her brother was summoning the Light, she felt it. Here was a chance to use the training Iris had given her. She turned away from the hub on the *Phoenix's* bridge and let her mind relax and reach out to Marc. The Light welled up within her and she commanded it to pull her brother out of the sea and back to her. She focused, saw the *Star Wind* in her mind. She drew it toward her and saw it steadily rise through the water, onto the water, into the air, through the ozone belt...

"Hey!" Reb's voice broke excitedly into her thoughts, accompanied by Tootee's little singsong of happy bips. "Marc has just docked! He's back!"

When Marc reappeared on the bridge, he was mobbed. Countess Liana was the last to greet him. She was not accustomed to using the Light and the effort had drained her, momentarily.

"I thought we'd never see you again, Master Marc!" exclaimed Fortuno.

"I knew we weren't rid of you, yet!" countered Liana in jest, as she gave him a tender embrace.    '

"Well, I thought we'd lost you this time, buddy!" interjected Reb with a huge smile of relief. "What do you think that was all about?"

"I can't say," Marc was still unnerved, although he was grateful to be back with his friends. "I've never encountered anything like it before. It sucks your mind as well as your ship. It leaves you powerless. It's hypnotic and terrifying." Marc was searching for the words to describe his experience. "Had I not been trained by the Jaira masters, I would not have been able to escape. I don't know how I managed to summon such

Light, but that's what pulled me up."

"I helped," said Liana proudly. "I was pulling, too."

"Well, Iris promised you, you could make the difference, and she was right!" said Reb and smiled proudly at his lady.

Digerawicz was swaying bashfully in the background, softly calling his pleasure to Marc.

"Thanks, Digger, I'm glad to see you again, too."

"Well, it's all over with now, pal." Reb gave Marc a playful shove. "When all this Sadra business is over with, the Democratic Senate will probably send an expedition over to study that electromagnetic phenomenon. Meanwhile, we're still faced with the challenge of notifying Iris and her troops.

"That's all decided," said Marc with conviction. "I'm going to take one of these Hydrans with me and fly to Itoomo as soon as it's dark. I'll take Tootee with me, too. He always comes in handy."

"I wish we could all go to Itoomo," Reb said wistfully. "This waiting around is getting on my nerves."

Liana touched his arm with a delicate hand. "I think it's best that Marc go as he planned," she cautioned.

"I guess that's the best way," Reb backed off, "but I am not the type to survive for long without some action."

Marc laughed. "Don't worry, friend, I have a feeling we'll have all the action we can handle before we see another sunset. Now let me put my gear in order and run an instrument check on the *Star Wind* before dinner. You know, I'm actually looking forward to this trip."

\*\*\*

Something heavy was sitting on Buck's chest, pressing hard. He couldn't breathe. Little drops of sweat beaded up on his forehead and he knew that the only way to break free of his nightmare was to force himself to wake up.

Slowly he fought his way back to reality and opened his eyes. But the nightmare didn't stop. His eyes slowly focused and came to rest on a huge boot planted right on his chest. The boot was attached to the body of a towering Sydhar. Buck sucked some air in through his nostrils and felt a piercing pain as his lungs fought in vain to expand. He turned his head. Iris was nowhere in sight. He wondered if they'd carried her off.

With great difficulty he forced the words out of his mouth, "Let me up, you bloody monster!" he growled. The foot retreated. Then a huge hand grabbed Buck by the collar and hoisted him to his feet as though he were a rag doll.

The Sydhar was heavily armed and clad in black, shiny armour. It stood over eight feet tall. Buck had a splitting headache and his muscles were stiff and sore from the long swim. This new twist was the straw that broke the camel's back. He wondered what to do.

"What did you do with my companion?" he asked gruffly.

His question went unanswered. Either the Sydhars did not speak Standard, or were programmed against communication with prisoners.

Then the colossus grasped him by the collar again and strode off, dragging him through the big dormitory he had seen the night before. Several bodies lay strewn on the floor, their necks broken. Iris was not one of them. Buck breathed a sigh of relief. Outside the residence several more Sydhars stood guard, and he counted ten more arranged between the pillars of the central temple with the reflecting pool.

Then he saw Countess Iris. She lay teetering on the rim of the reflecting pool, her long hair floating on the water, hands and feet tied and tethered by a long rope to one of the pillars.

Then, rippling movements in the pool caught his eye. It was the Ko'onu fish. Buck could not identify the species but he guessed they were killers, put there to frighten Countess Iris into submission. The sight of their snapping jaws made Buck's blood run cold. Her face was averted from the water, as she tried to inch away from the excited carnivores. A look of pure repugnance distorting her beautiful features.

With a mighty jerk, Buck wriggled free of the giant metallic hand that was holding him, leaving a piece of his wetsuit in its grasp, and raced toward the girl. Before the huge cyborg became aware Buck was missing, he had run through the pillars to kneel by her side. He reached for his knife. Surprisingly, it was still strapped to his leg! *"Either an oversight on the part of my guardian, or it's simply too paltry a weapon for these giants to concern themselves with,"* he thought.

The Sydhars drew their emitters as they advanced upon the defenceless couple. Buck quickly sliced through the ropes tying Iris' wrists and frantically slashed at the rope tethering her to the pillar. Hastily, she scrambled to a sitting position, tugging at the ropes on her ankles and trying to undo the knots. The Ko'onu swam excitedly in circles at the side of the pool where its dinner was sitting, snapping at the air viciously. Soon,

Iris knew, one or more Ko'onu would excitedly leap from the water and land on the marble terrace, snapping at anything in their path, severing whatever they encountered. Then they would flop about, slowly suffocating, and either flip back into the pool by sheer chance and live, or flop away from the water and die. She didn't want to be around when that happened.

Freeing her ankles at last, while Buck crouched, sizing up the giant fish warily, Iris jumped back from the pool's edge and looked at her friend with gratitude.

"We'd better find a way out of here before either the fish carves us up or the Sydhars break our necks!" she gasped.

"Is there any place we can hide if we can get past the Sydhars?" he asked in return.

A couple of the Sydhars were aiming their emitters. Buck flinched involuntarily with the anticipation of pain. One of the Sydhars came within firing range and hit Iris with a paralyzing blast. She buckled and toppled towards the water.

Buck reacted instinctively. Reaching out, he caught her by her long hair as she was falling. Jerking her off her feet, he pulled with a superhuman effort and flung her backwards with all his might. She landed with a soft cry, just as another blast caught Buck and caused him to roar with pain. He fell to his knees and covered her with his body, shielding her as well as he could from the excruciating rays.

Iris struggled to push him away, and stretched her hands to the skies in silent homage, then she folded them and knelt deep in thought.

Buck felt a tingle. She was communicating with him

through the Light! He remembered her lessons back in the tree village of Kaatra and put the brakes on his wild thoughts. It took an effort to calm himself and link his mind with hers, but he managed to find rapport.

Within moments a heavy vapour had formed on the surface of the reflection pool. Rapidly outward it spread, enveloping everything and everyone in its increasing density. Buck couldn't see the Sydhars, and he assumed the Sydhars couldn't see them, either. They heard the snappy sound which accompanied emissions from the Sydhars' weapons and realized the giants were firing, willy-nilly, into the fog.

They groped for each other and grasped hands. Their feet hardly touched the marble as they fled from the temple, hoping against hope that they would not blunder straight into a Sydhar in the opacity. Iris counted on her sensitivity to direct her through the gaps in the circle of Sydhar guards.

Hand in hand they ran from the village. The fog had expanded like a dense white blanket and was spreading out to sea, immobilizing all activity within its radius and causing the Sydhars' armored suits to clang and ring as they stumbled clumsily into each other in the haze.

Fortunately, Iris knew which way to go and she led him by the hand on a mad dash for the beach. Suddenly Buck hit something with his foot and nearly broke his toes. While he hopped around, muttering curses, Iris bent to examine the object.

"Buck!" she exclaimed, "A wave hopper! Let's drag it into the water." Forgetting his pain, he said, "You got it." Then grasping the lightweight alloy construction, he carried it effortlessly to the water as Iris tugged him forward by the arm.

Running the wave hopper into the surf they jumped in and Buck accelerated to top speed. They could hear the Sydhars lumbering along behind them in the white opacity, fumbling for their wave hoppers and ill-equipped for efficiency in a situation like this.

Protected by the fog, they sped out to sea. Iris studies the wave patterns for a moment, assessed the direction, and indicated to Buck that she wanted him to head for the rendezvous place where the *Phoenix* waited. They knew they had put enough distance between themselves and the wave hoppers to give them an edge. Setting the drive on autopilot, Buck took Iris into his arms and, tenderly brushing a wisp of silken hair out of her eyes, enfolded her in a long kiss. When they separated, no word was spoken. Standing side by side, their arms entwined around each other's waist, they knew they were destined to be together, always.

Tomorrow would be soon enough to contemplate their future together, however.

"Did you create this beautiful fog?" Buck voiced his suspicion for the first time.

"No, the Light created the fog. I simply called upon the Light and placed our order!" she twinkled at him.

Abruptly she frowned and appeared to be listening intently to something. Bristling visibly with anger, she announced that the Sydhars' wave hoppers were following at a miles' distance behind them. She estimated about a hundred of the giants were in hot pursuit.

"What do you suggest?" asked Buck. "Can we hide on Bantuu? We must be pretty close to the island now."

"No!" she cried in alarm. They will sense we're there

and surround us. There would be no escape. We must head directly for the *Golden Phoenix* and sacrifice my plan to collect the soldiers, for now."

"If we make it back to the *Phoenix*, where do we go from there?" Buck was feeling her disappointment. He seemed to be able to communicate with her on an extrasensory plane, today.

"We'll fly to Janeera and try to make the best we can with the people we have." The fog was lifting and Iris looked as though she was going to cry. Instead, she raised her face to the sun which was breaking through the clouds and closed her eyes.

Buck admired her beauty silently, and bent to kiss first one dewy eyelid, then the other. He wondered how an old pirate like himself could get so lucky?

Without even a cough of warning, the engine of the wave hopper hiccupped and died.

"What in blazes?" Buck had never felt as responsible for anyone as he did for Countess Iris, or so helpless to rescue anyone as he did right now. He busied himself with the ignition wiring, checking for trouble in the starter. Then, he peered at the gauges. Truth was, the machine had run out of fuel. He looked hopelessly at Iris and shrugged.

"Never mind," she soothed. "Our people have an assortment of hiding places for just such occasions. Pull on your flippers and follow me.

Buck could hear the drone of a hundred Sydhar wave hoppers closing on them, although they were not close enough yet to see more than the sun shining off their metallic armour in the distance.

Iris dove under the waves and Buck followed. Then

she had second thoughts and resurfaced long enough to swamp their wave hopper, watching it sink from sight. "They'll think we went down with the wave hopper, or that we're still far ahead of them and on our way to rendezvous with the *Phoenix*," she said in sign language to Buck as she joined him in the aquamarine depts.

\*\*\*

Iris led him almost straight down. The water grew darker as less light penetrated the blue twilight. Then his eyes were rewarded with the sight of a great, glimmering coral garden which seemed to be illuminated with phosphorescent single-celled plants of every description in all the colors of the rainbow. Iris swam directly for the coral gardens and it was then that Buck saw the openings to the tunnels and caves in the reef.

Following Iris into one of the tunnels, he was too busy 'trying to keep up with her to make any leisurely observation of his surroundings, apart from the fact that the water was turning back to aqua green as they made their way upward again. Suddenly she stood up, and he realized they were in the tidal pool of a reef cave. He stood up, too. There was oxygen here. Terrific! They could hide out here until Iris sensed it was safe to continue their swim.

Meanwhile, Iris had already climbed onto a ledge and removed her fins, hooking them back into place on her belt. Marc did the same, and they looked at each other and grinned.

"How do you like my underwater hideaway?" she asked laughingly. Before he could open his mouth, she jumped to her feet. "Come," she said, reaching for his hand, "I want to show you something."

Buck shook his head in amusement. He'd follow her anywhere, didn't she know that? They ducked through a narrow tunnel in the rock and Buck stopped in open-mouthed astonishment. He had never seen anything so wonderful in his life!

They never heard the deafening roar of the wave hoppers as a hundred Sydhars, led by the treasonous Major Roold who had intentionally abandoned his Hydran group at Bantuu, roared past on their way to a watery grave at the electromagnetic vortex where they thought their quarry would be found.

# Chapter Eleven

Marc had easily located Itoomo, with the help of his Hydran guide, and he was delighted to find the place shrouded in a dense white fog which perfectly occulted his activities. Circling the small island over and over again he and his Hydran guide tried in vain to sense the presence of Princess Iris or Buck, but came up with nothing.

Marc flipped his comlink switch to the *Phoenix*. "Liana! Reb! Bad news... I think. We've drawn a blank. Iris and Buck are not in Itoomo although my friend Rajaar, here, tells me about half of the soldiers who deployed for Itoomo are still there. Perhaps the others have started back for the rendezvous point, along with Iris and Buck."

Before Reb could reply, Marc's voice rasped out, "Great guns! Do you know what that would mean? They would all be sucked into that electromagnetic vortex on their wave hoppers! I'd better run over there and take a look. If they're still alive, I'll head them off."

"Be careful. Remember your last encounter with the vortex. We are still registering massive electromagnetic activity in that area!" Countess Liana's voice came back, sounding a little shrill.

"Don't worry, Sis. I can take care of myself. It's Iris and Buck that I'm worried about!"

"Call us when you spot them. We'll fly down and land on the water, so they can board." offered Reb.

"You got it. Signing off." Marc turned and banked, flying low towards the rendezvous coordinates.

\*\*\*

The setting sun casting a pink reflection on the billowing clouds, turned the sky an apple green and the sea to liquid gold. But Marc had no patience for the beauty of this foreign sunset. The ocean rolled below him with huge swells that made it difficult to see objects in the water. He wished Princess Iris was with him, and he pushed back the jealousy he felt about her friendship with Buck. After all, Buck was his friend, and an older friend than Princess Iris at that. He was suddenly overwhelmed with embarrassment for his ungenerous attitude. How could he permit himself these feelings of petty jealousy when his friends' lives were in danger? His first challenge was to find them. Thoughts of winning Iris' affection had zero priority right now. He was a disciplined Jaira and he would behave like one.

Rajaar tugged at Marc's suit just as Tootee sounded off, breaking into his master's reverie. "What is it?" Marc snapped at the little robot in annoyance. But Tootee was cheerfully unaffected by the vagaries of human mood and beeped his message anyway.

"A flotilla? Great! It must be Buck and Iris and her soldiers!" Marc exclaimed excitedly.

Rajaar looked at Marc and frowned. "No, Commander

Galaxia, this is a flotilla of Sydhars. They may be chasing Princess Iris and her companion, because I can sense she is down there somewhere. But she must have travelled over the horizon because I can't see her."

"The fog is dispersing," said Marc, "and the Sydhar patrol will be able to see us if they look up. Have they weapons which can reach this altitude?"

"No, Commander. Their emitters work only at point blank range. Besides, their wave hoppers make such a deafening sound that nothing we do would cause them to look up"

"Good. Then it doesn't matter if they do see us." Marc grinned at the thought of the Sydhars' frustration if they caught sight of the *Star Wind* and could do nothing about it. "We'll just zip on ahead of them and catch up to the Hydran soldiers and my friends. I can warn Buck about the vortex on his comlink."

"No need." replied Rajaar. "I do not sense a single soldier out here. I do not sense Princess Iris and your friend near the vortex. They are close to our present position and not ahead of the flotilla, but I do not understand why I can't spot them visually."

Marc put the *Star Wind* on autopilot and, while the little craft circled at a fixed altitude, leaned back and closed his eyes to enter an altered state.

He sensed Iris and Buck below the water, alive and well. The vibrations he received from them were those of joy and excitement. Tootee broke in on his concentration and he told the agitated little robot to calm down. "You broke my trance, Tootee. I know you're anxious for them, but that wasn't polite, you know."

Rajaar touched him on the arm just then to get his

attention and said, "Commander Galaxia, I, too have sensed they are under the sea. I know the area. If you can hover low enough for me to climb out on the wing and dive, I will find them and tell them it is safe to surface."

"But how can they stay under the water for so long?" Marc was totally unfamiliar with the waterborne talents of beings like Iris and Buck.

"I sense that they are in a volcanic undersea cave, and I know the area well. It is located among a sub-aquarian series of tunnels."

Marc flipped the comlink switch. "Reb! Liana! I believe Rajaar has sensed the position of Buck and Iris. They're hiding in a volcanic underwater cave. Rajaar says he can dive and fetch them, if you will bring the *Phoenix* down and land it here so they can board."

"Affirmative," replied Reb. "What is your status down there? Where are the soldiers? How about the Sydhar patrols?"

"Soldiers are still in Itoomo. A Sydhar flotilla is making it straight for the area of electromagnetic disturbance. Iris and Buck are together in the cave down below. There is a heavy cloud cover and a fog bank which completely envelopes Itoomo Island," Marc forecasted, adding. "We're descending to the water now, Rajaar is getting ready to make his dive."

"Give us your location, we're on our way," said Reb. "Stand by to compute our coordinates for re-entry, Fortuno," he added.

"Log us at thirty degrees West by one hundred fifty degrees North," Marc replied. "Rajaar has made the dive.

\*\*\*

"Iris, this is fantastic!" Buck found it difficult to control his enthusiasm. "We don't have anything like it on Carrandon. How was it built? Who was the architect?" He was full of excited admiration.

Iris laughed softly. This was her favorite hideaway. She would come to these tunnels when she wanted to think out a problem or just to be by herself.

The object of Buck's admiration was an ancient Urfee temple dedicated to the muses of the water. "Legend tells that an early Hydran priestess who inherited the temple, sometime after the extinction of the Urfees, controlled everything that lived in the sea. She could raise a storm or calm the tides. Of course, we do not have such power in this age," Iris laughed. "But this temple has other enchantments, too."

The temple certainly did have a fairy tale quality to it. The silvery paintings on the wall looked fresh despite centuries of neglect. Buck examined the carvings on the beautiful, translucent azure crystalline stone pillars and was amazed.

The mosaic floor was a masterpiece, too, representing scenes from the lives of the legendary deities; figures with a beauty beyond imagining. One portrait showed a slender, shapely female dressed in floating transparent veils and walking upon the water. Her hair, luminous and white, floated around her divine face like a halo. Her eyes were closed, and in the center of her forehead she wore a blue triangular stone, representing the third eye.

"This temple is very special to my people," confided Iris. "Couples who wish to wed come here to exchange vows of fidelity and to ask the gods for their blessings when they are betrothed. Following this they will lie together in this temple for one night to bond their destinies in marriage." She blushed and lowered her lashes.

"And if you loved me, would you be faithful and loyal?" Buck teased, as he boldly drew her towards him and kissed her on the lips.

"What impertinence!" She drew herself away from him regally, then relaxed and laughed. "Of course I would. Our people, once bonded, never betray their vows. On Hydra V, a marriage is forever and partners are loyal and loving up until death."

"Well! Perhaps you will consider visiting this place with me again, one day when we have fulfilled our mission here," smiled Buck, half in jest, as he gazed upon his lady with undisguised love.

"Perhaps," she smiled back. "There'll be plenty of time to think about it later." She tried to sound casual. "Come, we should enter the tunnel maze. Just in case the Sidhars saw us submerge and return to wait for us with nets covering our entrance, we can fool them and exit through the maze."

"I sure don't feel like being caught in one of those nets again," replied Buck. "Lead the way."

They left the temple through a small dark opening in the lava wall and soon they were groping their way along stone walls in utter blackness. The walls were clammy and the floor uneven, so their progress was slow. Then, the blackness turned into a gray-green twilight and they emerged into a cave with a wall of the same crystal material through which they could see a spectacular view of marine life. Thousands of multi-coloured fishes milled around, some bumping against the crystal as if trying to swim through. Iris laughed and then reached out to tickle the place where the underbelly of a large green water lizard was resting on the watery side of the crystal wall.

"How far do these tunnels go?" Buck was not in the mood to be playful. "How far can we travel before we surface again?"

"We could walk nearly to Janeera, if we wanted to," she replied, laughing at his look of astonishment. "This labyrinth of tunnels covers all of Hydra's ocean floor and many of them are still unexplored. Some were undoubtedly collapsed by earthquakes, and some were destroyed when the Urfees sunk their continents. It will take several generations for the Hydrans to complete mapping them all."

"Well, this is a great piece of news. We are out of the grasp of those blasted Sydhars and we can probably walk all the way to Janeera," said Buck. "The only thing is, we have no way to notify the *Phoenix* that we are safe and have been forced to make a change of plans."

"Use your comlink," she said simply. "Marc's right up there." She pointed directly overhead."

"Where?" asked Buck in disbelief.

"Overhead, in his little ship, of course..." she began. "Wait. I sense Rajaar has just dived into the water. We must go back and talk with him."

"Why didn't you tell me before that Marc was here?" He looked at her in disbelief.

"You didn't ask me," she replied teasingly. "Besides, the *Star Wind* arrived only moments ago."

\*\*\*

The thought that this assignment had more twists than a barber pole was foremost in Buck's mind as he reached inside his wetsuit for his comlink and turned it on.

"Marc! This is Buck. Princess Iris just informed me you are circling directly overhead."

"Buck. Glad you got in touch." came the reply. "A Hydran soldier named Rajaar came with me. He has just dived in to look for you two and bring you out. The *Phoenix* is going to be landing momentarily to take you aboard."

"Okay. But where is that flotilla of Sydhars?"

"Probably in Neptune's arms by now. I'll explain it to you later."

"Thanks, Marc. We'll meet Rajaar now and see you later on the *Phoenix*, okay? Over and out."

Buck dropped his comlink and let it swing from the cord on his neck as he hastened after Iris. Half running, half stumbling they went, back through the tunnel and into the clammy blackness that marked the entrance to the temple. They were elated to know they would find the faithful Rajaar waiting in the cave beyond.

Marc circled the *Star Wind* nervously as he waited for the Hydran to resurface with his friends. What was taking them so long? He couldn't help scanning the horizon continually for intruders in the form of Sydhar wave hoppers, but apparently that one flotilla was the only group that had been deployed to capture Iris and Buck, so far.

Then he saw the *Phoenix* as she came in for her splashdown and quickly completed a docking maneuver on her port side.

He flipped open his comlink and asked Reb to blow

a hatch so he could board.

Liana was waiting in the inner passage for him. "Congratulations!" She hugged her brother excitedly. "How did you find them?"

"I didn't, Rajaar did!" Marc replied. "Boy, am I glad he elected to come with me! I knew Buck and Iris were in the area somewhere, but I was way off about their location. You see, I thought they were somewhere ahead of the Sydhar patrol and heading for sure death in the vortex. It was Rajaar who accurately pinpointed their real location down in some ocean caves."

"Okay," interrupted Reb, who had caught the last of Marc's commentary as he and Liana entered the Phoenix's bridge, "my question is, how accurate is Rajaar's sensitivity. I mean, what if we've risked a landing for nothing?"

"Not to worry." chuckled Marc, "I spoke with Buck over the comlink. Princess Iris told him we were up above them and then Buck called me!"

"Are they injured?" asked Liana worriedly. "Can they swim up without assistance?"

"If they're uninjured, Rajaar will bring them up with him, and if they are injured, he'll carry them up one at a time. He's no fool," replied Marc soothingly to his sister. "Don't worry."

\*\*\*

Back in orbit, the fate of Iris' land based soldiers was temporarily forgotten in the joy of reunion. They had hastily exchanged stories and updated each other on events since their last meeting. Iris was elated to learn the Sydhar flotillas were meeting their maker in a watery vortex. "What an ironic twist of fate," she trilled jubilantly. "When Sadra detected the *Phoenix's* presence behind the waves, he must have broadcast that location to all his troops. If he still believes the *Phoenix* to be hiding there, then he will send his soldiers in, relay after relay when first flotilla, then another, and another don't return. And before word gets back to him that his metallic colossi are being sucked to a watery grave, he might well lose half his army!" She turned to Buck and there were golden flashes of happiness in her eyes. "Oh, I hope this works in our favor," she sighed. "Perhaps it will offset the loss of my men, although the vortex would have to swallow a couple of thousand Sydhars to even up our numbers."

Marc was not listening to the conversation. He was watching Iris and Buck and feeling their vibrations of affection as they stood conspicuously close to one another while they talked. He felt heartsick at the thought that his worst fears had come true about letting Buck go off with her.

Eventually Buck noticed Marc was behaving overly quiet and took it to mean he was offended at not having been given credit for their rescue. But before he could speak, Marc decided to go.

"Well, I've had a long day of it, people. I think I'll grab a few hours of shut-eye. Goodnight, all"

"Yeah, let's leave this couple alone to get their forty winks, too! added Reb jovially as he took Liana's hand and drew her from the room. "Goodnight," they called back as they left.

"Good night," said Marc, turning to leave.

"Good night, Marc, and thank you for finding us and engineering our return to the Phoenix. We owe it all to you!" Buck walked up behind him and gripped Marc's shoulder affectionately.

"Hey, my pleasure." Marc replied. "Just take care of that special lady for me," he added resignedly as he stepped through the door.

# CHAPTER TWELVE

They had all gathered in the lounge to exchange ideas and plan the next step in their campaign.

Reb directed his first question to the Hydran soldiers. "Can anyone tell me why Sadra doesn't maintain an air base on Itoomo?"

The small group of soldiers shuffled and looked at each other, then back at Reb with shrugs and negative nods of their heads.

He looked inquiringly at Princess Iris, who smiled and said. "I think our philosophy is to deal with actualities rather than to ask why. We deal with Sadra's tyranny, for instance, without analyzing his motives."

"Well, there is something strange about this planet," Reb complained. "I just can't put my finger on it, but something is bothering me. Things are not what they seem."

Liana smiled and patted his hand reassuringly and reached for her drink.

Reb was not in a mood to be put off. "What do you think, Digger?"

The Prozoan grimaced and made a face as if he were

tasting something sour. Then he threw his head back and roared loudly in agreement with his captain.

Just as Reb raised a bubbling green cocktail to his mouth, the *Golden Phoenix* shook violently as if in the grip of a giant hand. Reb dropped his glass, spilling its delicious contents all over the floor. Stepping forward, Reb slipped in the spilled liquid and fell. Liana fought to keep her balance by clinging to her chair. Digger's mane fell forward and covered his eyes. The others were in various stages of disarray.

"What in the Hills of Sharv has happened this time?" Reb scrambled to his feet.

"Virramota, the wind of death, the solar wind," offered Iris. This is only the beginning. We've got to leave orbit and descend into the planet's atmosphere while it rages."

Reb sprung into action, with Digerawicz right behind him. In a flash they were at the controls and everyone on the ship was strapped in for reentry and descent.

Inside Hydra V's atmosphere, Reb turned on his video scanners. Hydra's sky was unfriendly; the clouds were billowing and black, moving towards them at a terrifying speed. Although it was early afternoon the sky was dark and the horizon obscured. Far below, the ocean was boiling with white-capped waves as high as any they had ever seen. The ferocious solar wind was affecting the planet's weather, and Reb could tell they were in for a terrible electrical bombardment.

Then the lightning came. It raked through the bruised clouds and filled their scanning screen with a deadly violet light.

"Don't look at that light!" cried Rajaar behind him, as he threw an arm over his own face.

"Too late," murmured Reb, as he slid off his contour chair and slumped to the floor. They heard a loud crack as a bolt of lightning hit the ship, and the control panel went dark.

\*\*\*

For a long while, he lay in darkness. Then a single spark of consciousness emerged from the void like a faint star in the night sky.

*"I'm alive,"* he thought. But the thought was instantly overpowered by a landslide of pain that hit him like the sting of thousand silver needles behind his temples. He decided to let the head rest a bit longer and tried to grope around with his hands, instead. *"Where am I?"* He tried to remember what happened, but it was too painful to think. Then, in a flash, it came to him. *"The lightning!"* '

The textured surface under his fingertips felt just like the soft synthetic carpet which covered the *Phoenix's* floor. So that's where he was. On the floor. He forced his eyes to open. His eyelids felt as though they were hinged with rusty steel wires. It was dark, so dark he could see nothing at all. He crawled forward in the dark and felt around again with his hands. Not far ahead of him, he touched a delicate human hand and knew it was Liana.

"Liana, Liana... are you all right?" He crawled over to her and felt for her shoulders, sitting up and pulling her limp form into his arms.

"Reb..." her voice was weak. "What happened? I can't see a thing!"

"I know, darling," Reb hugged her gently. "It's so dark in here that I thought at first I was blind."

"Oh, Master Reb. How are we going to clean up this mess?" It was the metallically correct voice of Fortuno.

"Fortuno! Can you see in this darkness?"

"Darkness, Master Reb? It's as bright as day in here, now that the emergency lights have come back on!"

"Emergency lights?" Reb blinked his eyes, then rubbed them and opened them again. A cold finger of fear touched his heart. He was blind!

"Fortuno, please go to the lounge and make sure everyone is all right. Then bring Princess Iris to me." He scrambled to his feet, helping Liana to do the same, and holding on to each other for support.

"So! You looked at the light." It was the voice of Rajaar. We know that Virramota brings blindness, madness, sometimes death. I'm sorry no one warned you of it until too late."

"What caused this blindness? Is it permanent? Tell me how serious it is." asked Reb as he held down his feelings of panic.

"It depends on the individual exposure," replied Rajaar. "If the victim doesn't suffer too much intensity of light, he sometimes recovers vision after a week or so. Then again, sometimes the vision never returns at all."

"You're a great help," muttered Reb.

"Reb! What's wrong with you and Liana? Why are you both staring into space like that?" It was Marc, who had just arrived on the bridge.

"I looked at the video scanners and apparently my eyes were burned by the violet flash." Reb said.

"I was right behind him," offered Liana. "I got a

dose of it, too."

"Marc, until we know what my fate is going to be, you'll have to be my eyes. Please read the instruments and tell me where we are right now." Reb said in a voice of resignation.

"Sure, buddy. We are floating on the water's surface about twenty seven miles northeast of Itoomo. There is no major damage registering to the ship. All passengers are alive and well with the exception of yourself and Liana, although some of the soldiers are still unconscious from the impact they suffered upon crash landing.

"Fortuno." Reb called after the droid. "When did the storm abate?"

"Precisely two hours, seventeen minutes and forty-five seconds ago," replied the pristine voice of the droid.

"Digger, are you okay?" Reb turned his head in the direction of the co-pilot's chair. "Can you see?"

A pitiful, "Woooooo" indicated that the Prozoan was no better off than his captain.

"Well, Marc, it seems you and Buck will have to take over for now," said Reb. "Fortuno and Tootee will be your navigator and ship's engineer, in that order."

"Oh, goody!" exclaimed the silver droid. "Wait 'til I tell Tootee! What fun we'll have!" Then he stopped in embarrassment. "Oh, Master Reb, I'm sorry! I didn't mean that we would have fun at your expense. We all hope that your eyesight and that of the Countess' is restored quickly. We do, indeed," Fortuno stammered as he tottered off to look for Princess Iris, still talking to himself.

Marc took his sister by the arm, "While Rajaar goes to fetch Buck to the bridge, I'll steer you to your cabin so you can rest and place a cool compress on your eyes. Then, I'll see if Iris is feeling well enough to attend to you." As he led his sister from the bridge, Marc looked back at Reb and said. "Reb, when Rajaar returns, ask him to lead you to your cabin, too, right after you brief Buck on his duties."

"I'll be along later, Marc." Reb replied.

"When Iris comes, Liana, do as she says" Reb added as an afterthought. Then he turned again towards the co-pilot's chair. "Digger, wait right there. Don't try to move. I'll ask Rajaar to have a couple of the Hydran soldiers move you to your bunk as soon as he returns. We don't want you crashing around the ship on your own. And don't be frightened, Digger, this thing is only temporary, I promise you!"

"Oooooooo," came the Prozoan's soft, doubtful moan.

Just then Fortuno came bustling back onto the bridge. "Master Reb, Master Reb. Princess Iris says she will see you shortly, but I can't find Tootee anywhere!"

"OMG! Don't tell me Marc left his robot aboard the *Star Wind* again!" said Reb. "Fortuno, turn on the comlink and call him."

Fortuno did as he was told. "Master Reb. There is no reply, and our scanners do not indicate the presence of the *Star Wind* in her docking port. What shall I do, Master Reb?"

"Fetch Marc and tell him, Fortuno. The Star Wind must have been shaken loose when we crash landed. She's probably on the bottom of the ocean by now, with little Tootee aboard."

\*\*\*

Tootee rolled back and forth in the aft section of *Star Wind's* small cockpit, as the little craft bounced wildly on the waves. Tootee's bips of alarm were lost in the emptiness around him. He had been forced to watch helplessly as the *Star Wind* was torn from her moorings on the *Phoenix* and tossed into turbulent waters as the big ship fell toward the sea. The little droid had been calling his S O S, ever since, to no avail.

Abruptly, the V-wing craft ceased to rock and became stabilized. Tootee whirred over to the plexidome and peeped out. What he saw nearly caused him to doubt his electronic eyes.

The ocean had not ceased to roll past the little ship in enormous swells. The *Star Wind* was steadied by dozens of bodies with sleek, dark fur. They were lined up side by side, supporting the craft and balancing it on their backs. Their gleaming brown fur glistened in the sunlight and their big black eyes looked back at him in friendly rapport.

*"Mammalian creatures of the sea,"* Tootee ran a quick analysis. *"Friendly. Intelligence level is high."* A little mechanical arm slid out and opened the canopy so he could get a better look. All eyes were upon him, as the creatures seemed to be discussing and commenting among themselves.

Suddenly, a series of whistling beeps emanated from the largest of the creatures. It was a language Tootee could understand!

"Welcome, Brother! We are The Elders, known to the people of Hydra as the Brubit. We heard your call. We know you are in distress and we have come to help you. Soon your ship will be carried safely to a quiet island and there it will be placed upon the beach."

Tootee looked on impersonally as the creature continued. "You are the first visitor in more than a thousand years who can speak our language. We have been waiting in the depths of our ocean for your call. Today was our lucky day. You must be the leader from the cosmos that our ancient legends have predicted will come to lead the way to a magnificent destiny." The whistles and beeps were filled with emotion and, even as the creature spoke, the V-wing was smoothly navigated through choppy waters toward the island of Bantuu, borne aloft by his new friends.

But shock or surprise were not emotions that had been built into little Tootee's circuitry. He listened patiently until the furry creature appeared to have concluded his speech, and then logically replied.

"Many thanks for your kind assistance. But your assumption is in error. I am not a leader, I am a follower. Specifically, I am an 4X-2T electronic robot unit from the planet Carrandon and I am pledged into the service of my master, Commander Marcus Galaxia, the pilot of this airship. From my temporary position on the island of which you speak I will continue to broadcast my S O S at regular intervals until Master Marc hears my call. Please inform your companions, the next S O S they hear will not be meant to draw their attention."

"Oh," the Brubit sounded disappointed. "Well, we're glad to have been of help to you anyway. I will tell my friends not to respond to your calls for the rest of this day. But, if you ever are in need of assistance again, just whistle and we'll come."

The sun was high in the cloudless sky which followed

the storm. The sleek pelts of Tootee's rescuers glistened wetly in the brightness as they hoisted the *Star Wind* onto the beach of a little cove on Bantuu Island. Leaving Tootee to contemplate his next move, they returned to the mysterious depths which they called home.

# CHAPTER THIRTEEN

Iris appeared in the doorway of Liana's cabin just as Marc was pulling a thermal wrap up to the reclining Countess' chin.

"Reb sent me," she began.

"Yes." His pale eyes shone upon her like twin lamps of anguish. "I can't believe my sister is blind!"

"Rajaar told me they looked upon the lightning of the Virramota," she said. "I have seen this happen before."

"Is there anything you can do to help her?" He lifted his hands helplessly and then let them drop to his side.

Iris' dark eyes looked into his with compassion. "I'm not sure. I'd have to examine her, first, to sense the extent of the damage."

"Yes. Please put yourself at ease and get started right away," Marc responded with a frightened urgency in his voice. "I'll help you in any way I can."

"Very well then," she became brisk and business-like, "the sooner we get started, the better."

Princess Iris set to work. She entered a deep trance, holding her hands suspended over Liana's eyes. Her head dropped back and little beads of sweat pearled on her forehead. Her breath deepened and slowed as she reached out with her mind to explore the depth of Liana's injury. Marc moved behind Iris and placed his hands on her shoulders. Together they stood for countless minutes, letting the Light perform its healing magic.

Then Iris moved and opened her eyes, smiling up at Marc. "The nerve damage was not permanent. Liana's sight will be restored when she awakes from her sleep," she said. "Thank you for lending me your strength, my friend."

She looked so frail and beautiful, standing there in her simple gown and bare feet, that Marc had a sudden impulse to sweep her up in his arms and run away with her to some hidden place where they could forget all the strife and trouble of the recent past, in each other's arms.

"Now!" She was all business again. "Let's go and see what we can do for Captain Morningstar and the Prozoan."

"We'd better not hurry Reb while he's on the bridge. He's got something of a temper, you know. Rajaar will lead him here when he is ready." Marc cautioned his lovely friend. "Why don't we go visit the Prozoan in his berth, and check him out first?"

"Lead the way, then," she smilingly indicated the door with a wave of her hand.

They found the Prozoan in his berth, moaning softly in self pity, and Marc lent support while Iris re-entered her healing trance.

The session was brief. Opening her eyes she said, "The Prozoan's long fur must have given him considerable protection from the rays, because he was just temporarily affected. He would probably have been able to see before I healed him, if he'd bothered to open his eyes!"

Marc laughed. "Good old Digger!" He patted his

shaggy co-pilot on the back of his head. "Just take'it easy, Digger, and grab forty winks before you report back for duty on the bridge."

Iris joined Marc in his friendly joshing, her bell-like laughter tickling a primitive response deep inside him.

He remembered Reb. "Iris, let's see if Reb is in his cabin yet."

He was. Lying with an arm thrown over his face, and a grim expression about his mouth. "Reb. I want you to do your best to relax and think of something pleasant while I check you over. Please don't say or do anything to interrupt my healing trance. Instead, let me be the one to break my silence."

"Thank you, Iris." Reb's voice was flat and devoid of feeling.

This time, when Iris awoke from her healing trance she wore a sad expression. "I'm sorry to tell you, Reb, that you're not quite as lucky as the Countess. Exposure to the lightning rays and subsequent damage to the optical nerve was more severe. I will hold several healing sessions daily to see if your vision can be brought up to maximum strength, but I can't guarantee absolute recovery, Captain, you must understand."

Marc noticed that Iris' gaze was uneven and her lips trembled as she tried to break the news in an optimistic way. He saw that she was speaking with an enthusiasm she didn't feel. Marc touched her arm reassuringly. "Doubt is the first rung on the ladder to failure," he whispered in her ear.

"Reb," he spoke aloud. "If we all believe in the restoration of your sight, then it will most surely come true."

"He is right," added Iris. "Rest now, Captain Morningstar, and dream that your sight has been restored. Dream, and it will come to pass. We will leave you now and return in an hour for another healing."

\*\*\*

That evening, everyone gathered in the lounge, except for Reb, who was teaching himself to meditate. Countess Liana entered and smiled at them all out of newly healed eyes. "How fortunate I am to have a healer for a friend and a Jaira for a brother!" she trilled.

"Oh, I think Iris could have done it without me," Marc replied modestly.

He turned to gaze at the beautiful Hydran maiden as he spoke. She was breath-taking in a deep blue dress to match the color of her eyes. Then his smile froze and he felt as if his face would crack. For just as he turned his head he saw Buck's arm close around the Princess proudly, protectively, and intimately. He felt crestfallen as Iris snuggled closer in response.

"You have all endured many trials and tribulations for my cause," she said softly. "And I am very grateful to you. Considering the losses we have suffered and the setbacks which have occurred to foul our plans, I would not fault you for abandoning this mission and returning to Carrandon at once."

Marc was about to agree. After all, he had lost his precious *Star Wind* and his bosom buddy, Tootee, not to mention the Hydran Princess he admired and coveted, who was now in the arms of his friend.

"Well, I for one, do not agree." Buck's mellow voice

boomed out. "These people are counting on us, we can't let them down now! I think we should depart for the Capital just as soon as we can come up with a new plan," he added forcefully. "Iris hasn't elaborated the subject, but I know she's distraught over her father's imprisonment."

Liana bit her lip thoughtfully. "Yes, we should waste no time. We can fly to Janeera in an hour or so, but we are so short on manpower that we cannot hope to prevail against Sadra's two thousand Sydhar guards without a good plan and a lot of luck."

"Make that approximately one-thousand seven hundred and fifty Sydhars, thanks to the magnetic pull in that vortex." Buck chuckled wickedly, adding, "At present rate, it might take only another couple of weeks to lure them all into the electromagnetic graveyard. But what would we use for a decoy?"

"Let's get serious," suggested Liana, leveling a look at Buck to quiet him. "Can you diagram the Capital City of Janeera for us?" she asked Princess Iris, reaching for a sketching slate and handing it to her. They all leaned toward Iris and watched as she made a sketch of Janeera.

"Well! That's quite a large Capital you have, from the looks of it," exclaimed Marc. "I didn't expect it to be so big."

"It is a beautiful city," she replied with pride. "Sadra's palace is in its very core. Here." She pointed to a circular area from which streets radiated outward like the spokes of a wheel. "If we could land somewhere out of sight, we might be successful in disguising ourselves as servants and penetrate the palace one by one, to meet and regroup for a surprise attack."

"So far we haven't been too spectacular at surprising

Sadra. In fact, I think he's had a few surprises for us!" Buck was lapsing back into his usual cynicism.

"Yeah," Marc agreed reluctantly. "What we need is a good strategist among us."

"Never mind," Liana looked over at Iris with gratitude. "I owe Princess Iris a great deal. And I shall not cease to aid her in any way I can, while she is in need of our help."

Buck suddenly brightened. "Iris! How about the fog? Could you create it again? If we were able to enter the city under cover of dense fog, we would need no disguise and we would be able to gain entry to the palace. Even your soldiers would be invisible to the Sydhars."

Buck! That's a good idea! With four of us concentrating, we ought to be able to create a fog dense enough to cover a city of that size. It might be just the thing! What do you think?" Liana turned eagerly to Princess Iris with the question still on her lips.

"It's so good, I don't know why it never occurred to me before." Iris clasped Buck's big brown hand between her two small palms and squeezed it affectionately, looking up at him with pride. "Buck, you are a genius!"

Marc thought he saw a blush flood Buck's dark features. "Wait up there," he held his hand up with the palm out. "We haven't perfected the plan. But here's a thought that just occurred to me." He gestured as he spoke. "I propose that we program Fortuno to land the *Golden Phoenix* and let us off, then return to this orbit with the ship and wait in safety while we carry out our invasion. One of us can signal Fortuno on the comlink when we want him to come down and pick us up."

"Sounds good to me," offered Buck. "But what do

we do about Reb? He's in no shape to go with us."

It was Iris' turn to speak. "Reb has had three healing sessions with Marc helping. I will continue to do healings at two-hour intervals throughout the night, with Countess Liana and Commander Galaxia taking turns assisting me. By tomorrow we should definitely know what to expect." She folded her hands primly in her lap and looked around the room before she continued. "It is my wish that we wait to see if Captain Morningstar's eyesight will recover itself sufficiently for him to accompany us, because he has proven himself an amazingly versatile thinker in an emergency."

All heads nodded solemnly in unison. It was agreed.

***

His Supreme Highness Ardano Ad Sadra was reclining on soft cushions in his favorite orange chamber with a view to the west of the city. The pleadings of the slave girl being tortured in the courtyard below did not entertain him today. Usually this ritual put him in the mood to satisfy his demonic sensual pleasures, but not today. He waved a hand and the girl's Sydhar guardian quickly removed her battered and bleeding body from his master's sight, his metallic boots slipping in bright pools of blood on the marble courtyard floor.

The Tyrant turned to a slave who was fanning him with a tuutuu- bird plume. "Go, and summon Koh from the temple. I want to speak with him immediately!" he commanded.

"At once, Majesty," replied the slave as he ran for the door.

The Tyrant relaxed on his cushions. He was a dark, stocky creature with no redeeming features. His scaly head was distinguished only by two piercing black eyes. He reached for a goblet on a small jewel-encrusted table and drank deeply of the fermented ruby brew it contained.

*"If only I could capture her. She would make the loveliest conquest of all."* His bejewelled talons tightened around the goblet. *"I would..."* He thought of all the painful delights he would inflict upon the Princess Iris. But she had avoided his traps for so long that it was becoming harder and harder to imagine her in his grasp. Although he was obsessed with the idea of possessing this willowy maiden for his very own, he was secretly convinced that divine intervention would prevent him from destroying her as he had destroyed her family.

"How may I please you, My Lord?" His beautiful consort, Clevia, arrived to intrude on his reverie. She was a tall, regal creature with a dark, dazzling beauty. But her eyes, like those of her consort, were hard and cruel.

"Shall I summon Mona to entertain you?" Clevia was determined to catch her Lord's attention.

Sadra waved her away. "No, leave me." He turned away from her in a gesture she dared not ignore. As she departed she passed the high priest shuffling along the corridor. Shrugging, she threw a look of disdain at the bent figure and continued on her way.

"You called for me, Your Highness?"

It was amazing how this gnome knew he was needed before he could be called. "Yes, yes. You may approach your Lord." He beckoned the priest closer with a bejewelled talon.

Koh approached slowly. His gray robe dragged on

the marble floor, the hood covering his face, his body bent and gnarled with age. He stopped at the Tyrant's feet and bowed his head in reverence.

"My Lord. I am at your command. I have news. Rebel forces are going to approach the city. Their number is small and easily overthrown. But the oracle I consulted clearly spoke in their favor and this I do not understand."

"Give me specifics, Koh, or I will have you beaten. Specifically, when will they approach and specifically, where is Princess Iris?" Sadra held the quivering priest in an awful glare.

"The time of their approach has not been determined, but soon... soon." He trailed off thoughtfully as though listening to something no one else could hear. "Princess Iris... is reportedly in the company of a dark-skinned off-worlder. They were last seen on a stolen wave hopper heading for the landing place of their spacecraft beyond the waves. A flotilla of Sydhars was dispatched to intercept and return them to Itoomo."

The priest hesitated, as if doubtful that it was his place to say what he had to say next. "Your Highness, so that you may not suffer any harm as the result of the predicted battle, I humbly suggest to you that you depart for your summer residence in Gandra until this blows over."

Sadra brought his fist crashing to the little table and shattered it, scattering its contents and spilling his drink.

"Are you advising me to run away from that miserable number of stinking revolutionaries?" Sadra snarled and the priest shook with fear.

"Of course not. But, My Lord, the Oracle said... Master, we've never doubted the Oracle's wisdom. It predicts..." Koh hesitated for a split second and then rallied the courage to finish what he had begun. "It predicts... your death, Highness! You can avoid this fate if you leave Janeera at once."

"What? You dare to tell me I will die?" Sadra gave the little priest a withering look. "I am Sadra! I am immortal!"

"The stars are in opposition on your chart, Highness. Moreover, the configuration of Negaira in conjunction with Andradne in your Seventh House means nothing but trouble for you and your kingdom."

Sadra's rage subsided, but his eyes still glinted dangerously. He knew the predictions were always accurate. "How soon will they arrive?"

"Soon. Perhaps tomorrow at dawn, perhaps the next day at dawn. But soon," replied Koh.

"Bring me my personal viewer," ordered Sadra.   ,

The little priest approached a niche in the wall and drew aside a luminous curtain to expose an emerald crystal cube which shone with an inner luster of its own. Holding the object carefully between two withered hands, Koh carried it to his Master, placing it on his lap.

Sadra reached for the cube and held it before his eyes. Taking a deep breath, he relaxed on his cushions and gazed intently into the depths of the stone. Soon, images began to form within. Suddenly, Sadra gasped and Koh heard a sound that could only be the grinding of his royal teeth.

"So!" hissed the ruler. "She is befriended by the off-world ones." Another slow hiss escaped through his teeth. "I see her in the arms of the dark one. Shakrrrrrrr." he swore in a gutteral burst. Then, he abruptly shook with fear and nearly dropped the cube. What had unnerved him so? Koh took the cube from him and returned it to its perch in the niche.

"Very well," Sadra rasped. "Prepare for departure. We go at midnight. Alert the Sydhars. Prepare my updated data bank for transfer. Clevia will take care of all other details."

"Yes, Your Highness. Thank you, Your Highness," muttered Koh.

As the gnarled priest scuffled off to do his bidding, Sadra set his mouth in a grim line. "My name is not Ardano Ad Sadra if I don't devise for them such traps that they'll never get out of Janeera alive," he vowed.

# Chapter Fourteen

The *Phoenix* dropped out of the clouds and approached Janeera from the east, just before dawn. They had waited in suspense for forty eight standard hours while Iris and her assistants healed Han's eyes, and their need for action had grown stronger than their need for sleep.

The fabled city lay before them on the ship's huge video screen. Its graceful spires and arches were bathed in a pale pre-dawn light which cast no shadows and made the panorama look like a painting.

"Wow! I feel as though we are going to step into the stage setting for a fairy tale," Countess Liana murmured in a voice of awe.

"Well, Little Red Riding Hood. Don't get carried away with the fantasy, because there's a wolf down there who is filing his teeth while he waits for us, and he's very, very hungry." Reb chuckled as he pointed to the palace in the center of the Capital.

"Despite its evil ruler, Janeera is, indeed, a place of wonderment," Iris returned graciously. "I wish you could see it as it should be, filled with the joy of happy Hydrans at work and play."

"Save the thought." Reb turned his attention to the business of the day. "Can you indicate a spot where we can land, out of sight?" He turned to the Hydran leader who was watchfully riveted to the video screen. She was dressed for battle in a tight white coverall with laser blaster holstered to her belt. Reb thought she looked like a panther ready to spring on her prey. She looked beautiful and dangerous at the same time and, despite his deep love for Countess Liana, he couldn't help but be drawn to this exceptional woman.

*"If my heart were not resting in the palm of Liana's hand, I would most surely have the hots for Princess Iris",* he thought to himself. *"No wonder those two completely lost their heads over her."* He looked over at the glowing Buck and frustrated Marc.

Princess Iris was oblivious to his thoughts. She pointed to the far end of the floating island where a great dark patch could be seen. "Over there," she pointed. "That is where we hide our fishing fleet on the occasion of solar storms. The area should be deserted now." She shifted nervously from one foot to another as she studied the screen. "I have a feeling we have come here for nothing," she said. "I cannot sense the Sydhars. I cannot sense Sadra. There seems to be only a skeleton staff in the palace. I am sorry to have caused you all this inconvenience."

Indeed, the city lay quietly sleeping. There was no movement on the streets. The rising sun was glinting off the golden cupolas of a temple and casting a pale shimmer on the water.

"The silence of the city is unnerving," Reb agreed. "As a matter of fact, it's unreal. Doesn't it seem unnatural to you, somehow?" He turned to Marc.

"Yes. I sense something false about all this." Marc brushed his unruly cowlick away from his eyes and turned to Iris. "Do you think it might be a trap?"

"Yes. Considering whom we are dealing with, it is certainly a trap. But I sense my father is down there, so we must proceed at any cost." Her lovely eyes pleaded with Marc and the Countess.

"Let's land then," spoke Han. "I think we can forego the fog thing we were planning. Iris can't sense anyone down there but her father, so it looks like we don't need the fog cover. Let's take a vote on it now."

"I agree," said Liana.

"So do I," added Marc.

"Me, too," offered Buck.

"You're quite right, of course," said Iris.

"Oooooooo," added the Prozoan.

"Okay, let's take her down," ordered Han.

*** 

The area looked swampy and dark. Jungle crowded in on all sides. Princess Iris pointed toward a large, slimy platform floating in the muck.

"There it is. You can land right there," she cried.

Reb and Digger executed a perfect landing as faraway thunder sounded.

"Okay, everyone can disembark and wait on the platform." said Reb. "I'll join you in a few moments."

Everyone filed off the bridge in orderly fashion, preceded by Princess Iris, who headed off to organize her soldiers.

"Fortuno. This time I absolutely forbid you to fly the

*Phoenix* out of range. Your assignment is to take her up and orbit in safety until one of us calls you. Then you will descend to this very spot to pick us up. You will leave the comlink's switch open at all times, so that you can receive orders from any one of us at any time. Moreover, you are not to distract yourself with running the Countess' programs or performing any other tasks. Is this absolutely clear?"

"Yes, Master Reb," Fortuno fluttered." Of course you can count on me to do just as you say. Just so long as I am not expected to defend the ship in battle. I am not programmed to fight, Master Reb."

"Just stay within range and let me know if anything unusual occurs. I will advise you what to do."

"Oh, yes, Master Reb."

"Fine. Keep the exterior video scanners on until you lift off. You may fire your engines as soon as we are well out of range."

"Goodbye, Master Reb. Good luck to you all. And don't let anything happen to the Countess." Fortuno sounded almost weepy.

Reb stepped down onto the slippery platform and joined his small band of revolutionaries.

"Okay, everybody ashore so Fortuno can return this ship to orbit!"

*** 

The shore was farther off than it looked from the ship and the dark, foul-smelling water was chest deep. Bubbles of gas broke at the surface once in a while, releasing a revolting smell of rotten eggs. Marc was glad his suit was waterproof. He held his laser sword ready in case he met some unfriendly swamp creatures on the way. The bottom was slippery and the water was thick with algae so the going was slow. Countess Liana clung to Reb's arm for balance, and Princess Iris pulled Buck along by the hand, silently leading the expedition shoreward. The Prozoan was not faring as well as the others. His thick fur was matted with seaweed and its soaking weight made each step a strenuous effort. Iris' handful of soldiers brought up the rear. Occasionally the silence was broken by grunts and splashes, as they slowly made their way to shore.

Suddenly a scream ripped through the humid air, followed by desparate splashing.

"Stop!" Reb barked in alarm.

The creatures that emerged from the murky water were awesome in size. Their appearance was so nightmarish as to bring nausea to those who were forced to look upon them. Liana thought she would throw up. As if reading her thought, the monster closest to her pushed an eyeless face with huge gaping nostrils in her direction and barred its twisted teeth. "Ugh. Marc! Do something!"

"If we use our blasters on these critters, we'll wake the whole city," whispered Reb.

"Scarracs!" breathed Princess Iris, her face blanched with abhorrence.

"I can use my laser sword," offered Marc.

"Hurry up!" urged Buck. "They could kill us with their smell alone!"

Marc swung at a monster when as Buck cried out. One Scarrac had just closed its toothy mouth around his blaster. "Over here!"

"Princess Iris recovered her poise and swung into

action. "Yes, Marc, you push them back with your laser sword. The rest of you help me to draw a ring of Light around ourselves, keeping it between us and the Scarracs!"

She closed her eyes and a phosphorescent ball of Light materialized in front of where she stood. She pushed it with her mind and it began to scribe a glowing line around them. The others, seeing it take form, concentrated to give it more life, more substance.

When the Light had travelled half its circle, a Scarrac suddenly charged at Digger from the unlit side. Marc's laser sword moved in response and he decapitated the beast in mid-step.

Then Reb gasped as a giant hand grasped his leg and pulled him under. He tried to call out but only managed to swallow a mouthful of fetid water as he went under. Countess Liana shrieked as she groped under the surface. "Iris, Hurry! Reb is in danger!"

Iris' concentration never wavered. The circle of Light was completed moments later.

A silvery webbing gradually materialized out of the circle of Light, extending below and above the water in a shining barrier against evil. Marc holstered his laser sword and shifted his concentration to Iris, helping her to maintain the protective curtain.

The monsters were in pain, they shrunk from the curtain of Light in fear, their tentacles retracting as if burned by the energy. Digger howled in relief while Reb Morningstar burst from the water blinking with disbelief.

"Well, the Princess and the Jaira have done it again!" he hollered happily. "I guess I'll try to stay on your good sides for a while longer. You guys sure do come in handy!"

"Reb, we're still surrounded, in case you haven't noticed," Liana said in a tone of reproach.

"Hey, with the Princess and the Jaira ringing us with protective Light, not to mention you, my love, so obviously choked up over me drowning a minute ago, what do I have to fear?" he parried.

"Oh, Reb. Forgive me. I'm just upset over these Scarrac creatures. I didn't mean to snap at you!" she felt suddenly ashamed.

"Well, see that you don't do it again, my muddy little friend," he said as he suddenly hefted her into his arms and kissed her slime covered face.

"Reb! Don't! How can you kiss me looking like this?"

"Well, Your Exalted Muddiness, I've tasted better, but I'll take you however you come!" He looked at her with uncommon passion.

"Hey, watch it! Men stronger than you have ended up in shotgun weddings, and they began with a look like you just gave me, my love!"

"Hmmm. An interesting thought," Reb mused. "But not appropriate at this moment. We've still got these creatures menacing us and Iris looks like she's going to electrocute herself if she has to keep this curtain going much longer.

"You've got a point there, Reb."

*"What do we do next?"* Marc asked Princess Iris telepathically, so as not to break her concentration.

"We'll just have to maintain our protective curtain around us as we make for the shore," she replied calmly. "I'll need the help from every one of you, as we walk ashore," she added in an audible voice, "I haven't the strength to maintain this curtain much longer by myself."

Concentrating on maintaining the curtain of energy, they resumed their laborious walk, slogging along the bottom until they reached the shore without further incident, leaving the Scarracs behind, hungry and disappointed.

"We'd better find another landing place for Fortuno when he picks us up." Reb was serious. "I, for one, am not returning to that filthy swamp again!"

A few steps from that awful cesspool they came upon the sheds of the fishermen, draped with drying nets. Exhausted by their unexpectedly difficult journey through the swamp, they entered a shed to rest up for their long walk to the palace.

\*\*\*

The *Golden Phoenix* was safely back in orbit around Hydra V and Fortuno was tidying up the remains of scattered belongings left by the crew. He tottered to and fro, quietly humming to himself. Then he heard the sound. Dit Dit Dit — Dot Dot Dot — Dit Dit Dit; Dit Dit Dit — Dot Dot Dot — Dit Dit Dit, over and over again, faintly, as if coming from the bridge.

Fortuno hurried to the ship's console and paused. Why, it was a message of S O S! He located the coordinates and tuned in his receiver. Those bips sounded awfully familiar. If he didn't know better, he might think it was Tootee signalling. But he dared not reply. He computed the probability that the evil Sydhars were beaming up an S O S in order to lure the *Phoenix* into contact and thus discover its location.

He turned to leave the bridge again. The noise was

very irritating, but he had promised Master Reb he would keep the comlink open. Just then the message altered. To his surprise and joy the message beeped, "S O S *Phoenix*, this is *Star Wind,* S O S, come in *Phoenix*. Over."

"Tootee!" Fortuno called excitedly. "Where are you? I am receiving your message, my friend. I am alone on the *Golden Phoenix* and I am in charge of the ship."

A series of equally excited bips responded.

"On Bantuu Island? In the *Star Wind*? Oh, Master Marc will be so happy. Are you in any danger of being discovered? No? Very well, I shall call Master Marc's comlink and relay your message. Hang in there, Tootee. I feel certain that help will soon be on the way."

# CHAPTER FIFTEEN

It was late afternoon and Princess Iris sat in the company of her soldiers around a campfire. On second glance, Marc saw that it wasn't a campfire at all, but a small firey ball hovering just off the floor, at which they were all warming their hands. Iris' powers never ceased to amaze him. Just being around her was an education.

Marc looked around and saw that Liana was curled in Reb's arms, and Reb was resting his head against the wall, eyes closed. Buck seemed to be dozing, as well, twitching in his nap as if he was having a fistfight.

Marc rose to his feet, stretching. He noticed that Iris was holding her hands away from the fire and it took him a few minutes to accustom his eyes to the light to see that she was bent over the sleeping form of the Prozoan. She finished and looked up, sensing Marc's presence.

"He'll be fine. That gash made by the Scarrac was pretty nasty, but he'll be fine. It'll take a while for the fur to regrow over that bald spot, though." She pointed to the newly healed shoulder.

Marc nodded. Suddenly his leg muscles felt stiff. He decided to take a walk outside the huts and moved past the fire, motioning to Princess Iris that all was well and not to disturb herself. Outside, the evening promised to be clear and cold. Marc was glad of his insulated suit, but he was forced to breathe into his cupped hands to keep them warm.

A light touch on his shoulder caused him to jump in alarm. "Oh, Marc, I am sorry!" Iris whispered. "I'm always startling you, aren't I?"

Marc was pleased she had found him. "That's okay," he laughed. "I just get lost in thought sometimes, that's all." He looked at her thin dress and bare feet and grew alarmed. "Iris! You'll freeze to death in this chill air. I'll walk you back to the hut at once."

"Don't worry, Marc," she winked. "We Hydrans are cold-blooded and not bothered by temperatures that would cause a thermal chill to many off-worlders. I am dressed very comfortably, as a matter of fact."

"Very well, then, if you're sure. Would you like to walk with me?"

"Yes. Let's take this path, it leads along the waterfront and is seldom patrolled by the Sydhars."

At first they walked along side by side, somewhat formally. Then Marc offered Iris his hand to help her descend a short flight of steps, and somehow their hands remained joined after that. Marc felt shivers of hope run up and down his spine.

"Iris. I know it's none of my business, but there's something I want to ask you." Marc braced himself for the answer. Good, bad or indifferent, he had to know if there was anything really serious between Iris and Buck. He needed to know if he still stood a chance...

"Yes, Marc?" She turned a face of serene innocence

toward him.

"It's personal, Iris. So, if you object to my asking, just tell me to mind my own business...." He was interrupted in mid-sentence by a beep from his comlink. Reaching inside his suit he pulled it out and flipped up the cover.

"Marc Galaxia here, go ahead."

"Master Marc, this is Fortuno aboard the *Phoenix*. I have some wonderful news. Your *Star Wind* is safe. It is stranded in a sandy cove on Bantuu Island according to Tootee, who is still aboard."

Marc found it hard to speak. He gulped several times and opened and closed his mouth but nothing came out.

"Master Marc, Master Marc! Are you there?" came Fortuno's insistent singsong over the comlink.

"Yes, Fortuno. Thank you for this welcome message." He turned to Iris. "This has caught me completely by surprise. I thought for sure my ship had gone down with Tootee aboard. He made a sudden decision and pressed the comlink switch. "Fortuno, I'm signing off until I've had a chance to discuss this situation with Reb and Liana. Stand by for further orders. Out."

*** 

When they returned to the hut, everyone was awake. Liana was chewing on a concentrated food cube and making faces. "I wish the manufacturers were forced to eat this stuff themselves," she grimaced. "Then, perhaps they'd be more considerate of the consumer's taste buds."

"It's not my favourite thing, either, but it'll have to

do for now," Reb replied unsympathetically.

"I swear your taste is all in your left foot!" Liana wrinkled her nose. "You wouldn't know good food if it sang you a lullaby!"

Reb ignored her. "How're you doing, Digger?" The Prozoan wooooed cheerfully that he was feeling fine.

Marc stood in the doorway during this exchange, bursting to tell his news. But he forced himself to stand still until everyone turned to look at him. "You'll never guess what just happened!" He couldn't hold it any longer. "Fortuno called me to say he has been in communication with Tootee, aboard my *Star Wind*. Can you believe it?"

Reb jumped to his feet, ready for action, nearly knocking Liana over. "What! Where?"

"Don't get too excited. That's what I wanted to talk to you about.

Tootee and the V-wing are beached on Bantuu Island. At this point I could use some suggestions about how to get them out of there."

"Well, we could tell Tootee to sit tight until we complete this mission and then we could take you to Bantuu in the *Phoenix.*" suggested Buck.

"Not a good idea," interjected Iris. "What if there are Sydhars out on patrol who spot the *Star Wind* on Bantuu? That would be the last time you'd see it. They would sink it for sure!"

The Prozoan howled at the thought.

"Well, obviously *Star Wind* should be rescued without delay," concluded Liana. "But how?"

"Fortuno has proven his ability to handle the *Phoenix*," said Reb. "Tootee can provide him with a homing coordinates to guide the *Phoenix* down on Bantuu. Then, through comlink assistance, you can instruct Tootee to fly the *Star Wind* high enough to put her back into her docking port. Once they're back in orbit, Tootee can return to the *Phoenix* and keep Fortuno company."

"An excellent idea!" Marc exclaimed. "Reb, you communicate your orders to Fortuno and ask him to open communication to the *Star Wind* for me and put me through to Tootee when you're done. I'll stand by."

All thoughts of the palace or their mission was forgotten during the next hour, as Reb and Marc took turns directing their electronic friends in the rescue maneuver while everyone in the hut listened in rapt silence, hardly daring to breathe.

Then it was done. With defence shields up, the *Phoenix* landed on Bantuu and Fortuno worked in perfect coordination with his little pal, Tootee, to complete the re-docking of the *Star Wind*. Then, smoothly and swiftly, Fortuno whisked the *Phoenix* back to its orbit in space.

Everyone around the campfire was jubilant. They felt this was a good omen. They knew the Light would never let them down.

*** 

It was sundown when Iris politely asked if they were all sufficiently rested and nourished. "Just as your rescue of the *Star Wind* was aided by cover of darkness, so I believe our mission to enter the palace will be less noticeable by night." Suddenly she stiffened and doused her firelight. "Quiet! I hear the footsteps of Sydhar guards. They must have returned just now from patrol. Their barracks are nearby."

The small band of revolutionaries crouched in absolute silence as they heard the metallic footsteps of Sydhars clanging along the walkway. Closer and closer rang the fearsome sound. Nobody dared to breathe as six of the metal giants stomped past their shed, the floor reverberating with their weight.

"They're gone!" whispered Iris. "Come, we must move on. Rajaar will lead the soldiers to the palace up that street to the left, and I will lead all of you up the street to the right. Remember," she hissed in the dark, "the streets are cobbled, so take off your boots and carry them. And no talking, or we'll rouse the residents from their evening meal."

The cobblestones were so cold it was like walking on ice. At first they crept along, led by Princess Iris, darting from shadow to shadow on the twilight street. Then, the deserted street gave them courage and one by one they began to walk in the open, still not speaking, their heads on a swivel. It was a war of nerves, watching for Sydhars who might surprise them before Iris could warn of their evil presence.

The walk seemed interminable. Eventually the palace came into sight. Their steps quickened, despite the steep climb ahead of them, in anticipation of the adventure ahead.

***

The passage was dank and musty. They had reached the

base of the castle and met up with Rajaar and the soldiers after an almost miraculous avoidance of discovery by the Sydhars. Iris had immediately dispatched soldiers to check all entrances and now they stepped inside the only open door they had been able to find.

Inching their way along, in single file, they were struck by the oppressively increasing temperature of the air. Then a red light became visible in the gloom. It was coming from the recycling chamber and glowed with a demonic intensity. A few meters further ahead they found themselves in an eerie room bathed with the light of dancing flames.

In the center of the room stood a monstrously large recycling furnace with its sharp blades squeaking as they labored to turn in the large mixing vat. Occasionally, the sound of a crushing stone or other objects would interrupt the monotony. The tired group of revolutionaries stopped by the huge furnace, breathing heavily from their long climb, wiping the sweat from their brows.

"Sydhars are coming," called Princess Iris. "They will be here any minute."

"Too late to run for cover," replied Reb. "We're going to have to fight them."

Now they could hear the heavy thud of the Sydhars' boots as they came along the passageway. One shining black helmet appeared, followed by another, and another.

They readied their blasters. Iris bit her lip nervously. They opened fire. The cyborgs aimed their emitters but found no visible targets, since the revolutionaries were hiding behind the machinery.

The Sydhars pressed forward. The rocky walls of the recycling chamber captured the heat from the emitters and blasters and the room was beginning to feel like a living furnace. The revolutionaries retreated slowly toward an exit in the rear of the chamber. Marc held back as the others inched their way to the door, and joined Iris' soldiers in an uneven battle with their opponents. Countess Liana was exhausted from her swamp ordeal and the long climb to the palace. Reb was trying to lend support to her while firing unevenly at the enemy. Buck and Iris were valiantly firing at the massive cyborgs, but they clearly needed some backup.

"Digger! Take Liana and head for that exit. Wait for us on the other side." commanded Reb. "Hurry!" He turned back to the battle.

Marc was cornered between two opponents, his back to the recycling machine. Just as Reb headed into the fray, blaster firing on full beam, Princess Iris sensed Marc's desperation and decided to use her powers. Reaching out with her mind, she scooped a handful of molten rocks from the furnace and flung them at the helmets of the Sydhars. The onlookers were rewarded with the smell of burning flesh and shorting circuits. Again she hurled the molten rocks, and again, and again! The Sydhars were slowed enough that Marc was able to cut one of them down. But then another Sydhar had Marc by the throat and was lifting him into the vat with the terrible mixing blades. It would slice his body to shreds!

Countess Liana saw what had happened to Marc just as Digger picked her up. She wriggled out of his arms and ran back towards her brother. The Sydhar saw her coming. He held Marc in one hand, dangling him over the mixer and, with the other hand, he swatted at Liana as if she were a fly. She fell to the floor like a rag doll.

Marc's eyes were bulging and his face was red with the effort of struggling. With a mighty heave, he jerked himself out of the giant's grasp and dove for the floor. The Sydhar lost its balance and fell forward into the mixer. The blades rotated slowly, grinding everything in their wake. Marc picked himself off the floor, feeling for bruises, then cringed as the sound of crushed metal and bone signified the end of his captor.

A fast head count told Iris that she had lost some soldiers, but she also noted there were only a few Sydhars left. The tide seemed to have turned in their favor. With a last mighty effort, she reached out with her mind and bombarded the remaining Sydhars with molten rocks. "Hurry, everyone! Through the exit, and bolt it behind you!" she cried as she led the way.

Reb was at Liana's side in a flash, with Digger close behind. "Blast it, Digger!" growled Reb. If you'd done as you were told, she'd be on the other side of that door now. And she'd be conscious!"

The Prozoan howled with the humiliation of suffering Reb's angry outburst as he stood helplessly by.

Reb felt for Liana's pulse, making sure she was only unconscious, and lifted her into Digger's waiting arms. "Come on! Let's beat it!" Reb said as they raced for the exit.

# CHAPTER SIXTEEN

Sadra was reclining comfortably on his lounger, watching every move the little band of revolutionaries made in the palace through his closed-circuit video.

"My Lord, are you amused by the show?" Clevia looked at him from under half-closed lids. She looked more beautiful than usual, resting next to him on a low couch and sipping from a pearl-encrusted chalice.

"Absolutely! Now that we've warmed them up with their little adventure in the Recycling Chamber, I can't wait 'til they get the message I left for them!" His eyes were bugging out with excitement and his lower lip trembled the way it always did when he was up to no good.

"Highness, it seems such a waste to destroy a beautiful body like hers," she pointed to the figure of Princess Iris in the viewer. "I can think of several things I could do with her, if you deliver her to me alive." Clevia gave him a provocative look and smiled her cruel smile.

"We shall see what we shall see," replied Sadra. "I still have a few surprises in store for our friends. Surprises they may have just a little difficulty coping with," he laughed coldly.

"But you will think about giving her to me, for a little present, My Lord," she cooed, gazing at him coyly from her narrowed eyes.

"Ah, Clevia. Don't press me. If she ever arrives on Lamanda, perhaps I may let you have her to play with, after I'm done with her. Of course, this is with the proviso that there's anything left of her by then. He threw back his scaly head and his demonic laughter echoed back and forth through his chambers.

Even Clevia, who was used to the moods of her husband and master, felt an unpleasant chill run up and down her spine.

***

The off-worlders ran through twists and turns of passageways and stairs, led by Iris, with her guards bringing up the rear. Then, finally, they arrived at the throne room. The chamber was huge and well lighted with multi-tiered chandeliers. A red carpet stretched from the portals to the foot of the black marble throne. At first they thought the room was empty. Then they saw it, a white, bloodless corpse lying to one side of the throne, between two vertical columns, bound hand and foot. As they neared the throne they could see from his wrinkled skin that the body was that of an old man. And then Marc saw that the corpse was headless.

Suddenly Iris paled as if all the blood had drained from her body, and she ran to the headless corpse. Throwing herself upon it, her long hair covered her face as her body shook with heavy sobs.

"Could it be?" Marc whispered unbelievingly. "Was

that her father?"

The group approached the throne cautiously and quietly, coming to a halt a few steps from the grieving young woman. Unexpectedly, a low male voice rang though the silence. It came from somewhere behind the throne, from a concealed speaker.

"I WELCOME PRINCESS IRIS AND HER COMPANIONS TO JANEERA. IT IS WITH REGRET THAT I COULD NOT BE PRESENT TO GREET YOU PERSONALLY, BUT I HAVE LEFT YOU A LITTLE GIFT WHICH I HOPE YOU WILL ENJOY. UNFORTUNATELY I HAD TO TAKE THE HEAD WITH ME TO KEEP IT AMONG MY TROPHIES."

The message ended with the sound of insane laughter which filled the chamber and reverberated with frightening intensity.

Countess Liana could not bear it. She ran from the room with her hands covering her mouth to stop the rising well of nausea. The others turned and followed. Buck tugged at Iris' prostrate form until she rose and wordlessly followed him.

\*\*\*

It was just before dawn. The city was still asleep when the discouraged band of revolutionaries wandered out into the early morning light. From the palace, Reb had spied the royal gardens and called up instructions to Fortuno to land there and pick them up.

Rounding the base of the castle, they heard a Sydhar detachment marching toward them. Silently, they began to run. Reb hoped the ship would be waiting when they got to the garden. Princess Iris was running ahead with her small band of soldiers. She hadn't uttered a single word since the discovery of her father's corpse. Her lips were set in a thin line and she seemed lost in thought. No one could think of something appropriate to say to her in the face of such an abhorrent turn of events.

"By my calculations, we must be nearly there," said Reb, to encourage his friends. No one replied. They ran dispiritedly, each one alone with his thoughts.

They rounded a privet hedge and there it was, the *Golden Phoenix!* In less than a minute they were aboard and Reb and Digger were at their posts on the bridge.

"Here we go," called Reb. "We'll retreat into orbit and regroup from there."

A group of Sydhars ran out on the lawn, firing their emitters at the retreating airship. They were still firing stupidly at the *Golden Phoenix* long after it had disappeared from sight.

\*\*\*

The silence of deep space provided a healing balm for the shattered nerves of the crew after all they had endured in Janeera. The watery blue surface of Hydra was retreating on their optic screen as they settled comfortably in the lounge for refreshments and small talk.

"This mission has been far more interesting than I envisioned when I agreed to come along," began Buck Salladian. He cast Princess Iris a long, loving look. But she was impervious to Buck's innuendo, sitting there so pale and melancholy. Yet the tragedy she had suffered somehow made her face more luminous and beautiful than ever. Her long lashes cast butterfly shadows upon her cheeks. Deep in thought, she hardly took any notice of the conversation around her.

"I'm just grateful that we are safely away from Hydra V at last," sighed Liana. "I feared on more than one occasion that I was living my final hour." She remembered the enemy encounter and shivered.

Reb Morningstar stretched out on a couch and sipped away at his favorite drink. "Well, my Countess, now that you're assured you'll go on living for a while longer, how about following through on that marriage proposal you made?"

Countess Liana turned crimson with embarrassment and looked at Reb in bewilderment.

"Don't tell me that you don't remember proposing to me? In the swamp, remember?" He was teasing good naturedly. "I've been waiting for it for a long time, shotgun or otherwise. Thought you'd never ask!"

Liana suddenly realized he was teasing, and relaxed visibly.

"I never asked before, because I was afraid you'd accept!" She turned the joke against him. They both laughed.

Marc and Digger were playing holo-game. Howls of optimism and groans of defeat signified that it was a good game for Digger.

Fortuno saw that the game was not going well for Marc and tried to be helpful. "Shall I assist you in the next game, Master Marc? It's terrible to see you lose at holo-game, time after time."

"No thanks, Fortuno, I can manage." scowled Marc. "Tell you what, though, you can take my place for the next game. I quit!" He leaned back and yawned expansively.

"Iris!" Marc cut into her meditation and jolted her head around as if she'd been slapped. "Iris, tell us something about Gandra. I think we should know more about what we are getting into this time."

"Not that her briefing helped us on Hydra V," interjected Buck, "but what the heck!"

Iris looked blankly at Buck for a second and then nodded at Marc. Rearranging her gown, she composed herself on the lounge and began.

"Well, Gandra is almost twice the size of Hydra V, and it's closer to the sun, therefore it's much hotter. Gandra was entirely covered by ocean at one time but, due partly to Urfee practices of manipulating the atomic structure of matter and partly to evaporation, it is now hardly more than a rocky desert. The heat in Gandra is so intense that life forms cannot exist on the surface of the planet, and the inhabitants live in floating cities which offer a controlled climate and modern comforts. Remains of once splendid Urfee cities are now ruins definitely worth seeing, some structures are still erect as their architecture has far surpassed our own. It is said there are enormous treasures of science, culture and material wealth to be found among the ruins.

"Tell us more about the material treasures," Reb's eyes shone with the thought of getting rich on this junket.

"Those Urfee archaeological sites sure sound like the place to go," Buck added with enthusiasm.

"Well, I would like to hear more about their scientific and cultural treasures," Liana put in firmly. "Perhaps we could discover something there of true importance to our New Democracy.

The Prozoan and Fortuno were hard at their holo-game, and the lights were soft and mellow, putting everyone in the mood for an armchair journey to the cities of the ancients. Iris sipped her drink as she pondered the subject thoughtfully for a few moments, then she continued her story.

"The legendary Urfee Capital of Lotifaar is said to be located in the southern latitudes of Gandra. Lotifaar is in the hottest and most inhospitable part of the planet. The Urfee are believed to have mastered the Light in all her ramifications and are said to have been ultimately destroyed by it."

"Why?" asked Marc.

"Because they had a wicked strain running through the bloodline. They eventually activated the Dark Side of the Light and it destroyed them." She looked at Marc. "I'm not sure if all of you will understand this, but Marc will. As a trained Jaira he knows the laws of the Light." For the first time since her sad discovery in the throne room, Iris seemed like her animated old self again.

"What I'm trying to say is, with their minds alone the Urfee could control and shape the elements according to their will, for good or evil. Their white marble palaces have no known equal in our galaxy, perhaps even in the whole universe. Silver, gold and nal were all used by the Urfee in everyday utensils, especially the latter which surpassed all other metals in beauty and value. Their favorite gemstone was *teiral*, a bluish stone believed to be sentient, and which is so far beyond our comprehension and ability to achieve. Although other races have tried and failed to communicate with this alien intelligence of *teiral*, the Urfees were apparently successful in doing so, even living in symbiosis with it, inserting it into their bodies, as a third eye, or into their navels. The gem is rare and priceless. Legend tells of many palaces in Lotifaar brimming with it."

Iris looked at Reb, then at Buck. "I can see that this story is exciting your interest too much, and I do not want you to abandon our mission in order to go treasure hunting instead, so we will pass on to another subject. I will now tell you that Urfee scientific and cultural developments would probably be difficult for you to understand in the light of your own technology. Their sculptures were of such beauty that it is hard to believe a humanoid race could reach such perfection. The same applies to their music. Recently, some ancient recordings were discovered in one of the underground tunnels, and our scientists are now working to understand how to reconstruct this precious and unique art form. I have heard some of those recordings myself and, believe me, the music is heavenly!" Iris smiled with delight at the memory. "So, you see, not all aspects of Urfeean civilization was bad. In fact, much of it was truly admirable."

Countess Liana's cheeks were flushed with excitement. "Do you think I could obtain a sample of the music to take back with me to the Senate? It would give them the biggest thrill since the fall of the Old Order. Imagine how human and nonhumans alike could benefit from this archaeological find!"

Marc nodded in agreement with his sister. "Princess Iris, tell us of their advancements in science?"

"They were said to have mastered the transference of matter. This is something which neither our scientists, nor yours, have solved as yet. The Urfees were said to have been able to hop from planet to planet instantaneously through the use of sophisticated teleporters."

"Makes us sound bloody primitive, doesn't it, having to travel around in these metal cans?" snorted Reb, somewhat testily.

"Calm yourself, Reb," advised Liana. "Don't take things so personally. The first step to greatness lies in one's ability to admit his own insignificance." Then she added thoughtfully, "This is a discovery of enormous importance to all the nations of the New Democracy. I wish I could spend some time investigating these archaeological sites when our mission is completed."

"Yes! I invite you as my personal guest." volunteered Iris. "But first we must land on Gandra and enter the city of Lamanda. I will not rest until Sadra has been vanquished and made to pay for his cruelties and injustices to my people." Her voice suddenly had a hard, bitter edge to it.

"Meanwhile, it's time we all turned in for a rest," Buck stretched, yawned and rose to take his leave.

"Yeah," said Reb. "Let's get it while we can."

That night they all dreamed vividly of the fascinating Urfee civilization, while Fortuno and Digger stood watch and enjoyed endless holo-game rematches.

If an alarm bell goes off in the middle of the night, far out in space, it means trouble. On this occasion the ship had entered a shower of meteorites so thick that the ship's computer couldn't deal with it.

Reb and Digger switched to manual and for an hour they maneuvered the ship carefully through debris of rock sometimes as small as an egg and sometimes as large as a small moon. Fortunately, *Golden Phoenix* pulled through with some scratches and dents, hardly the worse for the experience.

"Luck still rides on our shoulders," said Reb. By now, everyone was clustered on the bridge, save the soldiers, worried for the safety of the ship.

"If you ask me, we're pressing our luck!" snorted Buck, as he turned and headed back to his berth, adding as a sort of afterthought, "This region of the galaxy has a bad reputation."

"What do you mean? What dangers are forecast for travellers?" Liana wasn't going to let Buck escape so easily.

"It has a reputation for magnetic disturbances, treacherous energy fields, and black holes, to name a few," Buck was serious, despite his penchant for sarcasm.

"Sounds like fun," said Marc, "especially for the pilot and captain of this ship. "Digger, we'll all have to keep our eyes open."

And so they did.

But that didn't exempt them from mines seeded in space by Sadra's forces. One of the mines exploded a gun-torrent and severely crippled one of *Phoenix's* cannons. Placing the navigation system on autopilot, and bringing up the protective force shield around the ship, Reb and Digger set to work making repairs. Reb knew their cannons would prove advantageous in a future confrontation, and he dared not risk having any one of them out of commission. Their repairs took several days and afforded the passengers and crew a well-deserved rest.

Repairs completed, Reb and Digger returned to the bridge and noted, with great amazement, that their coordinates were not the same as those previously keyed into autopilot. It was almost as if they drifted to another part of space pulled by some unseen, unknown force. Reb could not explain this anomaly. "I don't believe it! I'm seeing it but I don't believe it!" He double checked the reading and then called Buck to the bridge to show him.

"What do you make of this, Buck?"

"I told you, this sector is tricky," Buck offered little consolation to his bewildered friend. "I wish we could ditch this whole trip and get out of here," he added. "Something tells me I'm going to regret coming along on this escapade."

"We could stall around for a few days with our engines off, and see where this strange magnetic tide will pull us," Reb suggested.

"That sounds like a reasonable and scientific approach," affirmed Liana, who had entered the bridge while the men were conversing. "Anyway, I can use the extra time this delay will afford me to improve my skills and take up where Iris left off on my training. As Marc knows, training with the Light demands peace of mind and absolute concentration. Iris tells me that we must prepare for a fight, and this will draw upon much more than just our skill in firing blasters.

"Go, then! You too, Buck." urged Reb. "I still have some work to do here and then I'll shut down the engines. I'll see you at dinner."

After they left, Reb sat staring for a long while at the computer screen with a gravely troubled expression.

# CHAPTER SEVENTEEN

During the following week, the position of the ship shifted again, and again, in a disturbing and unexplained manner. Reb had stopped all engines several days prior, in order to monitor the direction of their drift. There seemed to be an invisible web of energy slowly drawing the *Golden Phoenix* towards its nucleus. The electronic star maps indicated a large black hole in space in the direction of their drift. Reb decided it was time to get underway again. He set his coordinates for Gandra.

The trip had been relatively uneventful and they were only a day away from Gandra when their complacence was shattered. First one blip appeared on the Phoenix's radar screen, then another and another until the vast armada, sent by Sadra to greet them, overwhelmed the projection screen.

"Well, lookee here. We have a reception committee," scowled Reb. "I vote we put her in hyperdrive and head back to Carrandon, pronto"

Princess Iris looked at him in disbelief. "You can't be serious!" she said tearfully. "You can't turn your back on the Hydran people now!"

"Don't worry, Iris, he's got a weird sense of humor." Liana jumped in quickly to smooth things over before Reb's big mouth got him into trouble.

"Well, if we're going to proceed on course, we'd better man the battle stations and get ourselves ready to return their little greeting," growled Reb. "Buck, please instruct Iris' soldiers on operation of the gun turrents and wake Marc up so he can take over one of the main cannons. You, of course, will take the other."

Everyone took their positions and waited. The fleet was still some distance off and approaching slowly.

"Do you have a plan?" Liana whispered to Reb.

"Sure I have a plan," he replied heartily. She sensed the lie. And she knew him well enough to know he was banking equally on his skill as a pilot and on the speed of his ship.

"Reb, you can't lie to me," Liana scolded. "There must be something we can do, short of jumping for hyperspace and running away. Princess Iris and her people are counting on us!"

"Liana," his voice betrayed a high degree of anxiety, "I have given the battle instructions because you and Iris are determined to face this enemy, but we're gonna be destroyed if we try to tough this one out. I warn you!"

Princess Iris spoke out. "Reb, Marc, Liana! Sadra is not with his fleet. I cannot sense his presence there."

"Just the same, we're going to have a busy day," Marc grimaced, seating himself behind the console which controlled the cannons on the right.

Suddenly the screen filled with tiny dots, as hundreds of small fighter craft were disgorged from the bowels of their carrier ships.

"Wow! Willya look at that!" Reb yelled.

"Subtract one, for whatever it's worth," Marc scored a hit.

"Looks like we've stirred up a hornet's nest," added Buck.

"What's a hornet's nest?" asked Marc.

"Never mind, here they come again! Buck barked.

"Reb, you are right, we cannot possibly win this fight," Liana's face was pale with concern. "We'll be massacred!"

"Let's make a run for it then," said Reb, "Break right through their flanks and head for Gandra's airspace."

"Then they'll really have us where they want us! We'll be sitting ducks!" Buck snapped.

"Buck, if you have a better idea, please share it with us," Liana snapped back.

"Calm down, Liana," Reb took charge of his panicky crew. "I suggest we do the honorable thing and retreat. We can leap into hyperspace and hope that they don't try to follow, and return to Gandra as soon as they all go home."

"Well, we'd better decide in a hurry. These babies aren't going to play tag with us for long," yelled Buck.

"Let's do it, then," Countess Liana spoke with finality. She was getting goose-bumps looking at the sheer size of that fleet.

Digger's wild howl pierced the cockpit together with the sound of crushing metal and the whistling sound of escaping atmosphere. The *Golden Phoenix* had taken a bad hit.

"Masks on, everybody!" Reb commanded them. "We've taken a direct hit! Tootee! Check for damage and see what can be done to seal off the tear in the hull.

Meanwhile, we have to make our hyperspace jump, fast. Here we go!" He punched up hyperdrive on his console. Nothing happened. His hands moved frantically over the console as he swore loudly in dismay.

"Just what we needed!" Reb kicked the computer console in frustration. The air inside the bridge was growing thinner.

Tootee and Fortuno reported just then that the hole in the hull was too big for emergency repairs.

"Then shut the passage hatch to that section and seal it off, quick!" Reb commanded. Tootee and Fortuno retreated in a hurry to carry out the order, sealing off the damaged area. Slowly the air stabilized and pressurization returned to normal.

"Man, that was close," sighed Reb. "How're you doing there, kid?" he yelled to Marc.

"As well as can be expected, thanks." replied Marc.

"Good, just hang in there until I get the engines working on this flying junkyard," Reb yelled back. "Buck, how goes it with you?"

"Fantastic! Never had so much fun. Like shooting fish in a barrel." the words were thick with sarcasm.

"Keep up the good work, everybody, we'll get out of this somehow!" Reb encouraged his crew.

It was getting warm on the bridge. Digger's thick fur was matting with sweat.

"We're in hot water, for sure," said Reb. "Digger, are our deflector shields up full force?"

The Prozoan grunted his affirmation.

"Yeeeee-ha!" Marc had just hit a carrier ship and exploded it into a zillion space particles.

The fighters had formed a dense ring around the

*Golden Phoenix* and seemed to be more interested in herding the rebel ship towards some unknown destination than they were in doing battle.

"What's going on here?" Reb suspected some evil plot.

"I think they are herding us into a trap." Iris spoke up.

"Do you sense anything else about this setup that might be helpful?" asked Reb nervously.

"No, nothing else. Only that their intent is not to blow up this ship, but to capture us alive."

"Jaira. What do you sense?"

"Oh come on, Reb, give me a break!" Marc was short tempered. "How much time have I had to contemplate our fate? These controls are burning my fingertips because my panel is overheating. You should do something about your cooling system."

"Touchy, touchy!" said Reb. "How about if we discuss ship maintenance at another time? Right now all I'm worried about is saving my ass!"

Digger's howl informed him that they couldn't maintain the deflector shields any longer. "Great! So what else is new?" Reb was at his wit's end.

Liana looked on, exasperated and frustrated with the situation, unable to help.

Reb glanced at the viewing screen and nearly rubbed his eyes in astonishment. He looked again. There were no fighters in front of them. In fact, there was nothing in front of them! Not a single star twinkled in the inky space. "What is this? Don't tell me we are headed for a black hole!"

"Certainly looks like one to me," said Buck helpfully.

"So! That's their trap," Iris was breathless, everything was clear and she understood Sadra's evil scheme now.

"If we fall into this hole, not even the Light will come to our rescue," said Reb disconsolately.

"Cut that out!" Marc had lost patience. "It's not over until it's over, my friend!"

"No wonder they call this sector the galactic graveyard," whispered Liana.

"Yes, holes like this one have earned this sector a real friendly reputation," sneered Buck.

"I had a nightmare like this, once." Countess Liana spoke in a strangled tone.

"Well, sweetheart, this nightmare is real." Reb was on the verge of losing control. The engines were of no use. They were being inexorably drawn into the terror of this blackness.

"The gravity reading of that hole shows a density of 1,200 kg/m3," Fortuno could never resist reciting statistics.

"We are helpless," cried Iris.

Marc composed himself for meditation.

"How can you be so bloody calm at a moment like this ...?" Reb began angrily. But he was abruptly silenced when the power plant died, the navigational sensors went blank and the ship went into a slow roll. Buck opened his arms to Iris and they stood, entwined, ready to die together.

Digger was a pitiful sight to behold. His long fur was matted and wet, his big body was squashed against the wall where he had slumped. He cowered in fear, a low whine issuing from somewhere in the hindermost reaches of his wide, hairy throat.

\*\*\*

Ardano Ad Sadra was in an expansive mood. According to all reports from his fleet commander, things were going extremely well.

"My Liege, you are looking very well today!" Clevia walked into the chamber followed by a Sydhar who was dragging a twin Hydran child by each hand. "I have brought you a little amusement to help you while away. See? I found a boy and girl for us to play with!" She laughed wickedly.

"Clevia, my sweet, you have outdone yourself! What plan do you have for them?" Sadra was filing his talons as he reclined in comfort.

"Well, My Lord, I thought that we might ask the Sydhar to loan us his emitter for a while." Her look was provocative. "Then, I'm sure we could take turns persuading these children to put on a little show for us."

"An excellent idea, my sweet. And if they survive the game?" Sadra's eyes positively twinkled with ghoulish glee.

"Why, Your Highness, I thought that if they survived the game we could separate them afterward for a little private fun."

Sadra's wicked laughter sent an unexpected chill through Clevia. "Naturally, my dear. I love it when you're evil. The girl will be yours and the boy will be mine, agreed?"

"Agreed. Let's get started," she held out her hand to the Sydhar. "Unholster your emitter and release those children, then go and guard the entrance to see that we are not disturbed."

The Sydhar hesitated, looking at the Tyrant for confirmation. Sadra gave the cyborg a curt nod. The colossus lifted his huge hands and sent the dangling children sprawling at the foot of the huge lounge, before stomping out of the salon. As the children clung to each other, sobbing fearfully, the Tyrant smiled down at his consort with an evil leer.

"What an enjoyable way to pass the time while we await the arrival of our main course." He chuckled at Clevia and a trickle of saliva ran down his neck.

"Main course?" she was puzzled. "But, My Liege, I did not arrange for other entertainment, only these two!" she cried, suddenly fearful of Sadra's wrath.

"Relax, my little serpent, I am referring to the arrival of the delectable Princess Iris and her friends. Oh, what fun we are going to have with them!"

"Yes! Oh, yes! I can hardly wait!" Clevia breathed a sigh of relief and beckoned to the cringing Hydran twins. "Come here, my darlings, we will just help you out of those ugly gowns, first." She winked at Lord Sadra, adding, "You undress the girl, My Lord, and let me begin with the boy. Later, we will switch as agreed."

*\*\**

It took only a minute for the black hole to swallow them, but to the minds of the *Phoenix's* crew it seemed like an eternity. Then the ship was sucked into that chasm in space, rolling helplessly like a small toy in an ocean whirlpool.

Abruptly, the ship's power plant roared back to life and a huge, dark, coppery globe appeared on their screen. The hairs bristled on the back of Reb's neck. What could that be? Could it be the cause of the heavy gravitational pull? Yes, there was an ultra-heavy iron planet hidden in the black hole, waiting for them like a spider spinning its web? The planet's ruddy, pockmarked surface was coming into clear focus on the newly functioning monitor as the *Golden Phoenix* fell towards its surface with terrifying speed.

Reb Morningstar and his rebel crew tensed and braced themselves for the impact.

# Chapter Eighteen

When Marc regained consciousness he thought, *"So this what death is like"*. He felt disembodied and free-floating in a dark void. Yet it was a good feeling. Warm and comfortable, like returning to his mother's womb. He did not regret being dead. In fact, he was glad. Life was nothing but pain and trouble. Who needed it? He wondered if he would be reunited with his father and his old friend and teacher Benja-Ko Menjoro.

He wondered where his body was and tried to stretch, he couldn't move! Then reality slowly invaded his quiet universe with the sounds and smells of his surroundings.

*"Oh, no!"* he thought unhappily, *"I'm still alive, after all"*.

There was the sound of water dripping somewhere nearby. Then an acrid smell of burning wires assailed his nostrils and he screwed up his face. Then, in a flash, he remembered everything... the black hole, the Iron Planet, the fall. Then he thought of Liana, Iris, Reb and the others. *"What has happened to them?"*

He tried to get up. Something very big and very

heavy was weighing him down. His rib cage felt like it was in a trash compactor. After a few moments of unsuccessful struggling, he decided to call upon the Light to free himself. Then he entered into a struggle that sapped every remaining bit of strength from him. Finally, the weight moved off him, reluctantly, and Marc scrambled to his feet. His body felt like it weighed many hundreds of pounds and every movement required an enormous effort.

*"The gravity of this planet must be horrendous",* he thought. Any physical effort seemed to sap his strength so much that he had no energy left over for thinking. Groping in the dark, he felt familiar objects that told him he was on the *Phoenix's* bridge. He lowered himself to the floor, where his body felt more comfortable, and crawled around slowly, calling his sister's name.

Then he found her. He sensed it was she, the minute his hand touched her cheek. He wished it wasn't so blasted dark in there. Groping, he traced her outline. She lay on her back, arms outstretched, lips parted, breathing irregular and labored. Marc slapped her gently on the cheeks, trying to revive her. Soon, she stirred.

"Marc, I sense it's you! Why is it so dark in here? Did we make it?"

"Yes!" Marc almost laughed, he was so happy to find his sister alive.

"Try to move. I'll help. It's a major accomplishment to move around in this gravity." He tugged at his sister's arm. "I hope you have no broken bones."

A few moments later they were crawling side by side, searching for the rest of the crew. They found Iris and Buck together, just regaining consciousness. They, too, seemed to have escaped with little damage, save for a few cuts and bruises.

"Where is Reb?" Liana's voice rang out in the heavy silence that pervaded the bridge.

"Whoa!" Marc stumbled over Digger's hairy leg and almost fell on him. A familiar howl greeted him and another assured him that the Prozoan was fine.

Reb was found under a fallen console unit, badly wounded and unconscious. Moving through the ship, like blind people who were familiar with their surroundings, they managed to carry Reb's limp body to his cabin and lay him out on the bed. His pulse was weak. Liana would not leave his side.

"Try to get some auxiliary lights turned on in here, Marc," she breathed laboriously. And get this gravitational field neutralized"

"I'll find Tootee and get him to help me," Marc said reassuringly. "I don't know about the gravity, but you'll have lights in no time. Just hang on."

"Iris! Can you do something to help Reb?" Liana's voice was begging. "We can't just let him die. I'll pay you back, somehow. I'll be in your debt as long as I live. Just help me to save him, now." There were tears in her eyes.

"I don't feel very strong right now, but I'll do what I can." Iris sat down on the bed next to Reb and passed her hand over his body to determine the extent of his injuries. Her diagnosis must have been pretty serious, as demonstrated by her troubled expression.

"Several of his ribs are broken," she began, "one lung is punctured and he has internal bleeding. Actually, his broken legs are minor problems, compared to the rest." As she was speaking, the lights came on.

"Oh, no!" Liana was tearful. "Can you heal him?"

"Liana, I can help him if you and Marc lend me your strength," she said. "But I don't think I can heal him by myself, I feel so weak."

They went to work. An hour later they were rewarded when Reb opened his eyes and smiled. Then he grimaced with pain because his ribs were so tender.

"Welcome back to the land of the living!" Buck lolled in the doorway and boomed his greeting with unaccustomed cheer.

"I'm glad to be back," he rolled his eyes. "What about the ship? Has anyone checked for damage?"

"I have Tootee and Fortuno working on it now. Don't worry about a thing, I'll take care of it and report back to you later."

"Doctor Iris says you'll be confined to your bed for a few days, darling," said Liana, stroking his brow.

"You're a lucky dog, Reb, with an exquisite healer and a knockout nurse looking after you." Buck indicated the two ladies. "What a way to go!"

"Get some rest now, Captain, I'll be back to do another healing in an hour or so." said Princess Iris, "I will leave you alone with Liana now and help the men to check out the ship." She threaded her hands through Marc and Buck's arms and gently nudged them out of the cabin.

The *Golden Phoenix* looked like it had been trashed in a wild party. Cheerful beeps announced the arrival of Tootee.

Buck bestowed a friendly smile on the little robot. "Boy, I'm glad to see that you are still in one piece. We need a complete report on damages." He disengaged from Iris' grasp. "Let's see if the lounge is habitable. Iris, why don't you see to your soldiers while Marc and I inventory the damages. We'll meet you later in the lounge."

A cascade of excited bips fell upon Marc's ears. "What? Where is he?" he replied. "Lead me to him, Tootee."

"Buck," he added, "I'll meet you in the lounge in a few minutes."

They rounded a corner and there, in the dimness, lay a pile of silver scrap metal. "Oh, Fortuno," cried Marc. "You poor thing!" The silver droid was in very poor shape.

"Master Marc," the poor droid's head was sitting beside his foot. "I knew it, I knew I should never have come on this trip," complained the droid. "I have suffered the most unspeakable indignities..." his voice trembled and broke off. Apparently his voice unit had suffered a short.

"Don't worry, buddy, I'll fix you up again. You'll be as good as new when I get through with you." Marc picked a limb up from the floor. "Just switch off for now, Fortuno, while I check out the overall damage and get repairs started on the ship, then I'll get back to you."

"Hurry, Master Marc! Please!" I just hate being in so many pieces. It's so distracting," Fortuno cried after him.

Marc decided to detour onto the bridge. The scene which confronted him was anything but encouraging. Loose cables lay in a tangle all over the place and shattered instrumentation panels were tossed around making the area look like an obstacle course. Priceless energy crystals were scrunched and shattered under his boots as he picked his way gingerly to the main console.

"Jehosephats! We're never going to be able to repair this mess!" Buck Salladian's voice cut through Marc's thoughts, echoing his own fears. "The lounge is usable, though, if only because most of the furniture is bolted down. But this place could use some maid service."

The island computer console was turned over and some of the panels were broken.

"Give me a hand with this," Marc chose this as the likeliest place to begin. Gravity was working against them, and moving around was no easy task, let alone lifting the equipment. Marc and Buck struggled for a few moments. Then Marc got irritated and called on the Light to wrench the console back into position.

"Now, let's see if this thing has any life left in it," Marc said, as he turned it on and keyed in some instructions. A display screen flashed some red, blue and gold light sequences and then died.

"Looks as though we'll have to run some probes and do a manual analysis," he concluded.

"I'll do it." offered Buck. "Why don't you coax Digger off the floor there and have him help you put Fortuno back together while Tootee gives you an analysis of other damages. And don't forget we promised to meet Iris in the lounge. If you see her, let her know where I am, will you?"

"Sure." Replied Marc. "Thanks. And, if you get the scanners going, please check and see if the *Star Wind* is still in her docking port. I sure hope we didn't lose her!"

\*\*\*

Marc and Digger carried Fortuno's parts into engineering control and began their task of piecing the silver droid back together. Tootee found his master and quietly began his rundown. The extent of damages to the *Golden*

*Phoenix* turned out to be a very depressing list, causing Digger to bawl in distress.

"We're faced with a pretty mess!" muttered Reb, trying to sort out the circuitry under Fortuno's breastplate. "Hand me a driver, Digger. No, Digger! That's his left leg, it goes on the other side!"

"My stars, what happened to your silver messenger?" Iris had found them, at last.

"He's going to be okay," Marc frowned. "Just needs a little soldering and reassembly." He looked at her over his shoulder, "How are your men?"

"Just fine. They were all strapped in to their sleepers and withstood the impact with no casualties. I have assigned them to cleaning up the rubble on the ship. Where would you like them to place the broken items?"

"Use the cargo bay." suggested Marc. "And I almost forgot, Buck asked me to tell you he is working on a console unit on the bridge. He might appreciate a helping hand."

"I'll send Rajaar to him." she replied. "But now I must return to Reb and Liana and do another healing."

\*\*\*

Buck and Rajaar had performed a near-miracle with the damaged computer system in order to get it functioning again. First, they keyed in the readings to correct the imbalance in the ship's internal gravity field. Then, they sent out soil and air probes which they ran through manual analysis. Finally they were satisfied that the atmosphere and soil of the planet were not deadly, and that organic life was present in various phases of evolution.

"A person wearing a light suit and filter mask could probably live out there," Buck said thoughtfully.

"Fortuno, now that you're in one piece again, would you like to run some further analysis for us?" Liana had taken a brief trip to the bridge while Reb slept.

"Yes, Countess, I am always delighted to serve you." It was odd to hear Fortuno replying so pleasantly when under such circumstances he was usually complaining to everyone within earshot.

"Fortuno, I fear you have fused a resistor in your personality sector, but we'll leave it that way for now. It's a refreshing change." Liana threw the droid an ironic look.

Buck and Marc got the scanners working and brought up the picture on their monitor. The *Golden Phoenix* had suffered a crash landing on a wide red plateau. In the distance to the right sharp cliffs stood outlined in the twilight. The scene was unearthly, and unfriendly.

"This is like a scene from a bad dream," mumbled Buck.

Marc had the discomfiting sensation that danger, in the form of an unknown beast, lingered outside in readiness to strike. He caught a slight movement in the low rocky ridge to the left of the ship and his body stiffened involuntarily. Standing motionless, he watched the screen intently for a long time. Then he relaxed his shoulders and sighed.

"I must be imagining things." he said aloud to himself. "I thought I saw something out there." He turned his attention to the repair of another panel.

"You know, we're all lucky to be alive," offered Buck, as if counting his blessings.

"Yes, we are," said Liana, "and we will deal with

whatever difficulties we encounter on this planet to the best of our ability. I am just very thankful that the power plant has been turned on. As long as we remain in the ship, in our own balanced environment, we will be unaffected by that awful gravitational force. You know," she added, "we are really very, very fortunate. The Light has never left us, despite our fears to the contrary."

"Well, Sis," said Marc, "I hope Reb recovers quickly. We have some heavy repairs to make which only he is qualified to supervise. Even with Reb's help, I figure it'll take a month to get this old jalopy fully functioning again."

"If there's any work to do outside, it'll be the worst month of my life," grumbled Buck.

"Fortuno, do you have readings which indicate the presence of intelligent life forms out there?" Princess Iris was thinking ahead.

"Our instrumentation is limited in scope at this time, therefore we are getting readings only on amoeba and other simple organisms, Princess Iris," came the retort.

"Oh, dear. I have a strange sensation that something frightening is lurking out there," she hugged herself as she spoke. "Marc, do you sense anything out there?"

"I'm sorry to say I do, Iris" he replied. Sis? How about you?"

"Yes. But it could be my imagination." Liana tried to pass it off. "We're probably all shook up and just a little spooked."

"No you're not." The voice was unexpectedly forceful. Buck looked positively more sure of himself than they had ever seen him. "There is something out there, and it is hungry. I sense it very strongly. I sense it in a primitive way." He looked at Princess Iris, surprised. "You were right, Princess, I do have sensitivity."

"Well, perhaps you're right. I, for one, have never been in such a depressing place," Iris added. "What's on the agenda for us?"

"About a months' worth of repairs to equipment," the young Jaira raised his eyes from the equipment he was repairing. This Iron Planet is not charted on our star maps. If we can overcome our fears, we might also use our time here doing a geological survey."

Digger, who was busy untangling twisted cables, gave out a howl of alarm and pointed a huge hairy arm at the screen.

"What is it, Digger," Marc asked, straining his eyes. "I can't see a thing out there."

But there was something. Crouched under cover of the rock formation two shapes, breathing laboriously, watched the alien ship with curiosity.

\*\*\*

Reb tossed and turned in a cold sweat. He was burning up. Liana was busy changing his compress while wishing with all her might that his fever would peak and recede.

Reb was hallucinating. He was in a small, dark chamber with a low ceiling where he could make out several shapes gathered around a large red, glowing globe. Reb could just make out their faces in the pulsating crimson glow and a terrified moan escaped his parched lips. The figures lifted their heads as if startled by this alien sound. They turned and spotted him. Their eyes burned like red hot coals and their gaze seemed to burn through Reb's brain. He screamed. The dark forms nodded their heads together as if discussing something among themselves. The glow from the red globe was growing brighter, casting a flaming light on their inhuman countenances. Suddenly Reb froze in horror. He saw that the ghastly red globe was a lamp which hovered over a table bearing the lifeless form of Countess Liana. The entities turned and moved towards him. They grew closer and closer, reaching their hands out for him. He wanted to run, but his legs were paralyzed. He felt their cold, bony hands touching him. He screamed, and screamed...

\*\*\*

"Yes, Tootee. I know night is coming, and we must return to the *Golden Phoenix*, soon." Marc was impatient with the intermittent reminders his robot was bipping. He looked through the windscreen of his Jet-Sled. "I think I saw something just behind those rocks. It won't take us very long to check it out, Tootee, and then I promise we'll go straight back to the ship. The Jet-Sled was cumbersome to pilot against the heavy gravitational pull, and Marc was reconnoitring the area with great difficulty.

Everything looked strange and alien in this landscape. Marc had to use infra-red visors to pierce the dim twilight. Moreover, currents of strong wind were buffeting the Jet-Sled from both sides. He knew the night storms were not far away.

As he navigated his way around the outcropping of rocks, Marc's thoughts drifted to Reb Morningstar. His friend was making a slow recovery from his injuries, under the tender care of Liana and Iris. He was glad the ladies had remained safely aboard the ship with Fortuno, while Buck and Digger did reconnaissance of the western range, using another Jet-Sled.

Marc hoped his friends had completed their mission and were safely back aboard the *Phoenix* right now, making everything secure for the nightly storms which ravaged the planet. But he knew Tootee was nagging at him because they would not raise the protective shields until Marc was back aboard. He felt an unpleasant shiver as he remembered the ferocity of those nightly storms. The ship always shook and creaked with the strain of withstanding the storms, and everyone within found it impossible to sleep through the racket until dawn, when the winds would finally cease to blow at gale force.

*"I hope we can leave this planet soon. I have a precognition of something unpleasant here. It's nagging at the back of my mind and I can't quite put my finger on it,"* he puzzled to himself.

He turned on his spotlight. There was an unnatural looking formation of rocks only meters away. Marc maneuverer his Jet-Sled closer to investigate. Suddenly he felt a jolt to his sled and it tipped out of control. Before Marc could react, he was falling below ground level, spinning through the air crazily as the gravity pulled him down. His last remembrance was of searing pain as the Jet-Sled crashed and jettisoned him to the floor.

\*\*\*

Buck and Digger were on their way back to the *Golden Phoenix* when they spotted a long, cigar-shaped object pointing at the sky, a little to the north of the cliffs. The strange shape was located in what looked to be an ancient volcanic crater.

"Let's move in closer and take a look," said Buck. Digger howled in protest, pointing to the sky.

"Don't worry, we'll get back in time to escape the storm," Buck brushed off the objection. "Marc will be back on the ship by now, making everything secure, Digger. When we get back, there won't be anything left to do except raise the shields."

Digger howled again in disagreement.

"That sure looks like a ship from some earlier period of space travel," Buck mused. "We have one something like it in our space museum on Carrandon."

Digger grunted unhappily.

"So, you think this place has very unpleasant vibrations, do you? Buck asked, as they approached the silvery, elegant shape.

"Seems like they made a perfect landing, with no problems. I can't see any signs of damage." Buck signalled to Digger and stopped his Jet-Sled. Dismounting, he walked slowly to the ship. The hatch was wide open.

"I don't like this," Buck unholstered his blaster. The wind was growing cold. It blew around them and almost knocked them to the ground. Buck pointed at the metallic plaque inserted over the gaping entrance. He read slowly from an ancient scroll. "This ship dates back to the Old Order. It goes back to before the Cyber Wars," he exclaimed.

"I wish Marc and the others were here to see this," he was forgetting the time element in the excitement of this discovery. They entered the ship. The corridor was very narrow and the air was musty. There were dark stains on the floor which were barely visible by the light of his torch. Yet there was no sign of a fight having taken place.

*"I wonder what happened to the crew?"* he thought. They reached the control room. There were dark stains on the floor here, too, but no sign of a struggle. In fact, everything seemed in perfect order, as if it had only landed yesterday. Buck played with the console and a bright light blinked on in the ceiling, almost blinding them.

Buck found the ship's log. He turned it on. The wide screen lit up and a pretty young woman appeared. Her voice was melodious.

"This is Olinda Ray, starfleet commander aboard *Space Eagle* from the Bollan system," she introduced herself. "We have made a forced landing on this uncharted planet. Repairs are underway and technically there have been no setbacks. But we are losing crew in an unexplained manner. Yesterday, Captain Val Lantana left with a group of five crew members on reconnaissance. They have not returned. We have reason to believe they may have been killed during the night when they were caught up in the fierce wind storms that rage every evening. Today, four others went in search of yesterday's party and this search party has not returned. There is something...." She interrupted herself to turn her attention to something in back of her. "I'll get back to this in a moment. I've got a situation here..."

The screen went blank. Buck continued to stare at it for a long while, wondering if Commander Ray would return. No such luck.

"Let's get out of here, Digger," he spoke finally. "This place gives me the creeps." He hefted his blaster, ready to use it on anything that moved. Running heavily through the small ship they made a quick exit and were relieved to see the Jet-Sled outside where they left it.

Jumping into the machine as if he were chased by demons, Buck pressed the ignition button. Nothing happened. They looked at each other and Buck punched ignition again. Nothing. He swore and knelt to examine the ignition coil. It was gone.

The wind was howling now. In another half hour they would be in the skirt of the storm.

"We'll have to find shelter, Digger. We can't stay out here tonight."

The Prozoan hooted his affirmation.

"Hey, let's get away from this ghost ship, Digger. Do you have any ideas?"

The Prozoan howled as he pointed to the cliffs.

"You're right. There's probably a network of caves over there. Let's make a run for it." He took off at a sluggish sprint, slowed by the gravity, with the Prozoan thundering along after him.

# Chapter Nineteen

Countess Liana was pacing back and forth in her cabin. Fortuno tried to pace with her, but he wasn't quite as quick. As a result they always ended up stepping on each other's toes.

"Cut that out, Fortuno," Liana snapped with irritation. *"They should be back by now. What has taken them so long?"*

Reb Morningstar gazed out from under heavy lids. His eyes shone feverishly, but he was conscious.

"Isn't it time for another healing?" He asked weakly. "Where is Iris?

"She's glued to the exterior scanner, looking for the men to return. They're out on reconnaissance right now," she replied. "Fortuno, please fetch Princess Iris for another healing."

"Yes, Countess," replied Fortuno, and added, "May I give you a reading on the storm levels before I go? Winds outside the ship have reached gale force and it is time to activate our energy shields for the night."

*"I wonder what has detained them?"* Liana said, again, to herself.

"Fortuno, let's hold off on the shields as long as we can, and meanwhile please fetch Princess Iris here."

In the darkness outside, the great wind stirred from its sleep like an awakening giant. Small stones, sand and debris were whipped around in the gusting gale which would soon gather force like a hurricane, destroying everything in its path.

Princess Iris appeared and apologetically went to work on another healing session.

Fortuno broke into Liana's concentration. "Countess, may I suggest that we delay not a moment longer in putting up our shields? We really can't afford to wait any longer. The winds are reaching hurricane force..." He stopped in surprise and dodged a flying object. It was Countess Liana's shoe! Reb tried to rise on the bed, but he grew dizzy and fell back almost immediately.

"How rude!" Fortuno recovered his dignity. "Countess Liana, I cannot tolerate such inappropriate treatment. I am not attempting to interfere with your activities here, I am performing my job!"

"Cool down, Fortuno," snapped Liana. "Iris, you'll have to do this one without me." She rose from her knees and bolted from the room, with Fortuno close behind.

Turning on the exterior scanners to infra-red she squinted to see if her brother and friends were in view. They were not. Then she was surprised to see formations of sparkling violet lights moving far out over the plateau. She thought she saw strange spectral shapes floating gracefully in the wind. Tiny lights sparkled along their bodies and they had what looked like tentacles waving around.

Liana was reminded of some sea creatures she had seen in books long ago. She watched them as though mesmerized. Suddenly she realized something familiar about them. The lights! It was the same kind of energy she had seen during the Virramota on Hydra. She tried to avert her eyes, but the fascination with these creatures was too strong. They were floating closer, swaying in the wind with beautiful, but deadly, fluidity.

She sensed that she must not look but she was fascinated in a morbid sort of way. Her mind fuzzed over. She couldn't remember what she had meant to do. She made one last, strenuous effort to break free of this hypnotic trance that had her body feeling numb and helpless. One of the creatures drifted against the ship and reached out a tentacle to explore the camera. Liana punched the button that activated the shields. It was her last act before falling to the floor in oblivion.

*\*\**

Marc lay on a hard surface and something sharp was poking his body.

"Booloo, booloo, booloo," he heard the sound somewhere off to his right.

"Booloo, booloo, boolooooooo," answered something to the left.

He opened his eyes and saw that he was being probed with a long spear. Two shapes crouched over him. He sensed that they were more curious than hostile. Marc stretched up his hand and gently pushed the spear aside. The creatures jumped up and exchanged rapid sounds of conversation. Marc stood up. The Booloo's, he named them for the sound they made, were small, about four feet tall. They were dressed in dark robes and the exposed parts of their bodies were covered with thick, grey fur. Their shiny round eyes were watching Marc with fear. Curiosity, however, must have been stronger because they didn't run away. Their whiskers were twitching with anticipation. Marc wanted to laugh.

He stretched out a hand towards them, palms up, to show that he was holding no weapon. "See, little guys? I mean you no harm!

Their long ears, peeking out from under their hoods, twitched in response. Then they were pulling at his pants and jacket, pointing to the sky which was visible far above their heads.

"Okay," said Marc. "I'm coming. Just let me get Tootee out of this mess, first."

The pile of junk which had once been a Jet-Sled still held its passenger in the rear of the compartment. With the help of his Booloo friends Marc pried the 4X unit out from the ruined Jet-Sled and dusted him off. A cheerful trill of bips reassured him that his little companion was fine.

It was time to take cover. The Booloo led Marc and Tootee to a tunnel. Once inside, they sealed the entrance with rocks, cutting themselves off from the world outside. Marc could hear the wind howling and whistling wildly through the rocks as it gained in power.

Leading Marc and Tootee through the tunnel to a small cave, they lit a fire and busied themselves with preparations for supper. Soon there was a stew bubbling and filling the cave with good aromas. Marc realized that he was hungry. After all, he hadn't eaten a thing since breakfast. They all ate heartily and then stretched out beside the fire for a snooze.

\*\*\*

Buck was afraid he wasn't going to make it to the cave. He was out of breath and his legs were aching from the climb. His heart was pounding so heavily he thought it would jump out of his chest.

"Ooooh, Digger, running in this gravity should be forbidden," he gasped.

The Prozoan pushed him forward. There was only a little way to go. Occasionally he saw zig zags of lightning slash through the darkness to cast an eerie light on the unearthly scenery. They were only a few hundred yards away from the cliffs when a twister swooped down on them, ready to swallow them up. Its column stretched up as far as the eye could see and it was tearing up everything in its path.

Buck could hardly force his legs to move. Digger was pushing him, then dragging him to the cliffs. They saw a cave opening and Digger dragged the stumbling Buck to the opening, giving him a shove and diving for shelter himself. Together, they crawled behind a large stone slab. Buck hoped they weren't disturbing any sleeping inhabitants, such as venomous reptiles.

Luck was with them. The Prozoan went to work covering the opening to their crevice with boulders while Buck lay propped against the wall, fighting to regain his breath. By the time his heart had slowed and his breathing returned to normal the winds were blowing outside with a gale force so blustery that the cave trembled.

\*\*\*

"I thought I'd never see you alive again!" Iris hugged Buck

with all her might as tears of relief rolled down her cheeks.

"For a while there, I thought so, too. Right, Digger?"

The Prozoan hooted his accord.

"I will do what I can to restore your strength, but first I must recharge my own batteries from the last healing session with Reb," she smiled tenderly at Buck.

"Marc was out all night, too," Liana joined in excitedly. "He arrived back at the ship early this morning with a couple of little friends in tow. He is in the lounge with them now, and Fortuno is acting as interpreter." She sighed with relief. "We stand to learn a great deal about this planet from the Booloo, that's Marc's name for them."

"How's Reb," Buck glanced at the Prozoan as he directed his question at Iris, knowing Digger was burning with curiosity.

"Recovering. He walked around very briefly this morning." Iris glanced at her friend. "But half the credit for his recovery goes to the princess. She has remained with Reb day and night.

"Liana, did you have white hair yesterday? I don't remember you being that blonde at the temples." Buck gestured as he spoke.

"I kept the shield down too long last night and experienced a strange phenomenon which blinded me for a few hours and altered the chemistry of my hair," Liana replied a little uncomfortably.

"Oh? Want to tell me about it?"

"Later, perhaps. Right now I'd like us all to join Fortuno, Marc and his Booloo friends in the lounge and see what they have to tell us."

\*\*\*

When they entered the lounge, the young Jaira looked tiredly at them. "I've been trying to explain to them how our Jet-Sleds work. They want to fix my broken sled and keep it."

"Good, they can have mine, too," offered Buck offhandedly. "It stalled over by the cliffs and Digger and I had to walk back without it."

They noticed that Fortuno was carrying on a very animated conversation with the two Booloo, and exchanged glances which communicated a mutual decision to leave well enough alone for now. Liana beckoned to Marc and gestured to the others to scatter, leaving Fortuno in the company of his new friends.

***

Days passed and everyone settled into a routine of repair and maintenance. Reb Morningstar was well on his way to recovery, but Iris was limiting his hours on the bridge, to conserve his strength since he tired easily.

Under Reb's expert supervision, repairs to the *Golden Phoenix* were moving along much faster than expected. The crew was infused with optimism over the thought of a prompt ETD from this inhospitable planet. The strain of having to work on the exterior under the increased gravity was very tiring and slow going for the Hydran soldiers, who had volunteered to do welding repairs to the hull. Even the strongest among them hastened to his bunk right after dinner to rest up for the next day's work detail. The gravitational pull was working its deleterious effects on everybody. Even those who never left the ship felt tired all the time.

It was after another such day that the rebel band gathered in the ship's dining room for a hearty meal.

"I never really appreciated the beauty of my home planet until I arrived here," Iris spoke slowly, and there was a note of nostalgia in her voice. The handful of soldiers seated at the far end of the mess table nodded solemnly in agreement. She looked at them and recited, *"the rainbows, the sunsets, the aquamarine of the ocean, the reflection of the moonlight, the luminous groves..."* she was far away, daydreaming now.

Buck put his arm around her and squeezed gently. "I promise to take you there as soon as we finish our business on Gandra," he whispered into her shell-like ear.

Marc glanced at them with envy. Reb Morningstar looked over at the couple and then grinned, reaching for Liana's hand.

"Carrandon seems like a beautiful place, too, compared to this ugly iron planet!" he said.

Outside, the night storm raged, occasionally shaking the *Phoenix* and causing tremors of fear to run through the crew. Their power plant was working full bore to provide an energy shield that was strong and durable, but still they felt insecure.

"How long do you estimate it will take us to complete the repairs and have all systems go?" asked Princess Iris.

"Something like two more weeks should do it." Reb hated to be pinned down. He personally wished they could take off in the morning. "Please be assured I'll have us all out of here as soon as I possibly can," he added. "I'm not enjoying myself down here any more than the rest of you."

Liana sensed Reb's mood and quickly changed the

subject. "Fortuno," she called.

"Yes, Countess." the silver droid hobbled in on slightly battered feet.

"Tell us more about the Booloo," she commanded. "They are the only intelligent life form we have contacted on this planet, and we'd all like to hear what you've learned."

"Indeed, Countess, they are very interesting. I've been studying them closely and have come to some very interesting conclusions. Fortuno tilted his head to one side as he spoke, and moved his arms in punctuation.

"The Booloo are a very peaceful race. Unless disturbed or threatened, they would never fight. Their skills lie in precision manual work. They do not possess the ability to think in the abstract, though. Their diet consists mostly of the fungus which grows in their underground caves and tunnels."

"Do they have any natural enemies? Marc posed the question while absently stroking his laser sword.

"Yes. They have told me of the City of Lost Ships, far to the north where a vicious race of beings reside. The descriptions of this other race is so confusing that I hesitate to try to describe them for you."

"Why confusing?" asked Liana.

"Well, one Booloo says this race is tall and dark and act with cool premeditation, the other says they are short in stature, and impulsive."

"I'll take the *Star Wind* and fly over to check out the City of Lost Ships tomorrow," Marc offered. "Can you obtain the coordinates from the Booloo for me, Fortuno?"

"I will program them into Tootee tonight," came the

reply.

"The name of the city is a real winner," shuddered Reb. "Are you sure you want to go? I mean, why look for trouble if trouble isn't looking for you?"

"Yes! Oh, Master Marc, he's right," Fortuno's circuits had been rebuilt and he was back in form. "Listen to Captain Morningstar. Don't go. This is a terrible place. The Booloo say it is a place of evil. Oh, Master Marc, I would never forgive myself if I gave you the coordinates that take you to your death.

"I'll be careful," answered the young Jaira with finality.

"Oh, my. Oh, my. What have I done? I shouldn't have mentioned the City of Lost Ships. It's all my fault," Fortuno cried.

"Fortuno, do you think one of the Booloo might be willing to go along as my guide?"

"I doubt it very much, Master Marc. The Booloo fear that place more than anything else on their planet; more than the storms and more than the night fliers that blinded Countess Liana," Fortuno replied without hesitation.

"Well then, why don't you come along? I might need an interpreter? Marc was teasing now.

"Oh, Master Marc! Countess! Please tell him I must remain here," pleaded Fortuno. "I am merely a liaison droid, I am not an adventurer."

"You are a very cowardly droid, at that," laughed the princess. "Don't worry, Fortuno, we do need you here."

"Yes indeed," affirmed Fortuno. "Besides, who will take care of Reb and Countess Liana if I am not here?"

Marc laughed. "Okay, Fortuno, you're off the hook!"

# CHAPTER TWENTY

Marc and the *Star Wind* were flying low over rugged terrain to the north of the Iron Planet. According to his chronometer it was early morning, but you'd never know it if you went by the light in the sky, since there was so little illumination on this dark world. In fact, there wasn't much difference between daytime on this planet and night time under a full moon back on Hydra V., although his infrared visors helped a little. He was disappointed when neither of his Booloo acquaintances had been willing to join him, but he had little Tootee, and he was thankful for that much, anyway.

Marc was fairly bristling with anticipation. If what Fortuno said was true, The City of Lost Ships could not be expected to welcome him in friendship. Were they really so vicious and evil? He couldn't help wondering how long the *Golden Phoenix* would escape detection. He wished Reb or Buck were with him, or better yet, Princess Iris. He thought of her longingly, then he pushed such impractical thoughts out of his mind. Everyone aboard the *Phoenix* was busy with their own priorities, and this was his. He switched his thoughts back to the mission at hand.

Every movement was frustratingly slow and difficult in this ponderous gravitational pull. He longed for the day this ordeal would end and they would pull free of the Iron Planet, so he could fly his craft without feeling the crushing oppression of his own weight. He sighed heavily, and cheerful beeps signalled the reception of his involuntary signal of distress from the rear of the cockpit.

"Thanks for the vote of sympathy, Tootee." he called over his shoulder. "I guess feeling sorry for myself won't solve anything, will it?"

A sharp, rugged line of cliffs became visible on the northern horizon. "That doesn't look like a good place for a city, Tootee," he commented to the robot, "What do you think?" A contradictory trill of bips told him that's exactly where he'd find The City of Lost Ships.

"Well, the inhabitants must be hooked on dramatic scenery," he said aloud as he pushed forward on the throttle and climbed to a higher elevation to avoid hitting one of the peaks. Looking down, he saw huge craters gaping between the cliffs. His instruments revealed an exterior temperature of 15°C.

As *Star Wind* approached the area roughly indicated by the Booloos, Marc caught sight of a long, arrowlike starship pointing at the sky. Its nose glinted dully in the dim light. Marc flew lower to get a better look and gasped when the city suddenly came into view. In the largest crater he had seen so far, thousands of starships of every shape and size imaginable and in all stages of disarray were parked neatly in their cosmic graveyard. Some looked fresh and new, as if they'd only landed yesterday. Others were badly corroded and appeared to have crashed and burned. Those metallic corpses stood like silent warnings to the young Jaira.

He wondered what kind of beings would live in such a place, as he circled the eerie city slowly. There was no signs of life, so he decided they must live underground. He looked for a place to land, figuring the best place to hide his ship would be right out in the open, among all the other exhibits. Landing on the fringe of the graveyard, he parked the *Star Wind* in the deep shadow of a high, overhanging cliff, where its presence was hardly visible, let alone suspicious.

"Tootee," he called softly, "wheel yourself over here and let's go! And keep all your sensors activated. I'm counting on you to keep us out of trouble." He felt for his laser sword and his blaster, both were sheathed on his hip. Laboriously, Marc climbed to the ground and waited for Tootee to catch up. The gravity was not helping. Then they set out to explore.

Marc lost track of all time. It was slow going over rough terrain due to increased weight. Often, they would find themselves at a dead-end with their way blocked by huge boulders with razor-sharp edges. Then they would be forced to turn back and retrace their steps until they found an opening. But the wonderland of star ships towering around them was an irresistible lure that pulled Marc from one to another in turn.

He readily identified a dish-shaped ship from the Roddan system, which was located on the far side of the Galaxy from their present position. The ship was corroded and she lay on her side, her stabilizers having been damaged during the crash landing. Marc was tempted to enter and investigate, but decided otherwise when his inner sense told him this would be unwise.

To his left he identified another craft, an egg-shaped ship from Cassedia. It had been a passenger star ship. He wondered silently what had become of all aboard when she went down.

Tootee's sharp beeps rang out in the still air and he spun, startled, to see a huge ball-shaped satellite right before him. He knew they built such satellites on Osima, the huge star cluster that took the shape of a horseshoe, close to the center of the Galaxy.

"Wow!" he whispered to Tootee. "I've never seen one of those up close before." Tootee softly beeped back. It was a perfectly round globe with hundreds of sharp spikes sticking out of the main body and placed close together. Its color was a brilliant blue.

"The beings that built this certainly had their good points." He chuckled at his own *entendre*. Even in the dim light the shape glowed as though possessing some sort of inner phosphorescence.

Slowly, Marc made his way forward. He saw cigar, saucer and X- shapes, as well as other indescribable configurations. All the while, a growing uneasiness was overtaking him, edging out the excitement he was feeling at seeing this marvellous display. He sensed someone, or something, was watching him. Gripping his laser sword for reassurance, he looked around apprehensively. Nothing moved. Yet the uncomfortable feeling persisted, and grew in intensity until he felt that a thousand eyes were upon him. He drew his blaster and stood poised for action.

His skin prickled and crawled. He felt an unreasonable sensation of fear. He tensed. Suddenly, shadowy beings stepped out from behind every object and moved forward stealthily to surround him.

Marc stood motionless, his weapons wavering, repulsed and sickened by what he beheld. The residents of this city were not unlike the star ships around them. They were relics, originally healthy, beautiful beings which nature created in all her universal glory, were now all twisted and deformed by the terrible gravity of this world. Marc was uncertain whether to find them terrifying or pitiful.

The approach of these demented-looking beings was not friendly. They advanced, holding weapons, and Marc knew better than to try to reason with them. Closer they crawled, limped and hobbled, insanity glinting in their eyes. Marc cocked the firing pin on his blaster and wished something would happen so that he didn't have to fire first. But he couldn't let them get close enough to clutch at him with their deadly tentacles and long, bony limbs.

Tootee's beep of alarm came simultaneous with a piercing blow to the back of the head. The blaster slipped from his hand as he sank to the ground. His captors closed in around him.

\*\*\*

After passing an interminably sleepless night, Buck, Iris and Digger took a Jet-Sled and went out in search of Marc, but not before having a difficult scene with Reb, who needed strong persuasion to stay with Liana aboard the *Phoenix*.

"Reb, you still haven't fully recovered and besides, if we don't return who will get this ship out of here? Liana's safety is in your hands," Buck had argued successfully.

"And we must get back to warn the Senate," added Liana.

"Okay," sighed Reb. "You three just see that you take it easy and don't do anything foolish. I still can't believe that anything bad has happened to the kid," he trailed off muttering to himself.

"By Jet-Sled, it should take us several days to reach The City of Lost Ships," theorized Buck. "Fortuno, take good care of your mistress and Master Reb, you hear?"

"Of course," piped up the android. "It will be my pleasure."

"Digger," Reb broke in. "You look after those two. I want them back safe and sound." The Prozoan howled a reassuring reply.

"Go then, before I recover my sanity and keep you both here," ordered Reb.

*** 

They'd been travelling all day without incident, speeding over the rough terrain on a course bearing due north. Now evening was falling and they knew it was time to seek a place to take shelter for the night.

"Let's take cover in those rocks over there!" Buck pointed at an impressive outcropping of stone. Princess Iris nodded and moved closer to him, as though seeking protection and warmth.

"Makes one feel like a character out of a stone age melodrama," laughed Buck. "Shelter for the night in a rock cave beside a roaring fire with an exotic captive woman by my side. Very romantic, except that we have to worry about hurricanes and flying monsters. What do you think?" He put his arm around her slender waist and drew her closer.

Iris closed her eyes demurely and said nothing.

"When we return to Hydra let's take a nice long vacation, just the two of us," he said, kissing her temple. She snuggled closer and they stood like that for a moment, forgetting about everything except each other.

"I hope it is soon," she whispered. "I miss my beautiful world so much. I never knew just how much it meant to me until now."

"You almost make me jealous," smiled Buck. "I wonder if I can compete with a whole planet for first place in your affections?"

"Don't worry, Buck, there's room in my heart for both of you," she laughed up at his handsome face. "I'll take you for a moonlight swim, to my favorite place, a little temple under the sea," she said dreamily. "Remember?" The look on her face told him that, in her imagination, she was already there. "We could...."

The sled halted with a jolt and brought them back to reality. They blinked as if awakening from a dream and looked around. The big, hairy Prozoan had already disembarked and gone off in search of a place to take cover for the night.

Buck jumped from the sled and reached for Iris' hand, helping her to alight. Then the Prozoan returned to shrug his hopelessness at finding nothing suitable for them.

"Let's pitch the steel tent we brought," suggested Buck. "We can wedge in between the rock formations and secure it with tethers. Hopefully the winds won't shred it if we get it set up right."

First, they secured the Jet-Sled and then set to work on their tent. Then, using the freeze-dry and space cube food they'd brought, Iris prepared their meal.

While they were eating their supper the hurricane winds grew stronger and buffeted the steel tent as if trying to get inside. Outside, the creatures came. Borne by the winds, dancing on the air currents, they searched for prey. Inside the tent slept the two humans, dreaming of blue water and sparkling rainbows, while the Prozoan stayed on watch. After all, the humans needed their nightly rest and Digger could hibernate to catch up on his sleep when they got back to the *Phoenix*.

\*\*\*

"You're in an uncommonly good mood, today, My Lord," said Clevia. Sadra was leaning over his jewel encrusted table where the glowing viewer rested. "Anything interesting happening on Gandra?" she asked, not really expecting a reply. She looked very exotic and seductive in a golden dress that clung to her shapely form like a second skin, leaving little to the imagination. Sadra didn't even turn to look at her.

"Yes." he finally spoke. "I am having a good day." He never took his eyes off the viewer. "Our little band of troublemakers won't escape me this time, my dear. I have pinned them to the Iron Planet and they still haven't discovered they'll never be able to take off, because they haven't completed repairs to their ship, or tried to fly." He rippled his scaly neck and laughed mockingly.

Clevia moved closer and hesitated. She was never quite sure when he would turn on her and lash out viciously because she had taken one liberty too many. His moods were so fickle.

"Come!" he leered. "Look for yourself. Look how

helpless and pathetic those creatures are, running around trying to save one another. They don't realize they are just another addition to my museum of space junk!" He pointed a thick, clawed finger at the viewer.

Clevia moved closer, nodding encouragement, urging him wordlessly to tell her his plan.

"I have given my subjects precise instructions. They know how to dispose of the revolutionaries." He drooled in anticipation. "Only that one," he jabbed his finger at the picture of Iris with such force that the light wavered and the picture dimmed, "She will be saved for me! The others are expendable. My subjects can have their fun with all but the girl."

Suddenly he grew impatient with the dim picture on the viewer screen and picked the cube up, shaking it violently as he uttered a stream of oaths. The picture faltered, then died completely.

"Summon Koh, immediately," he ordered Clevia. "One day he will pay dearly for these power failures." He threw the viewer back on the table in disgust. "Now it will probably take that fool all night to recharge its energy. And I cannot monitor Gandra without it!"

Clevia could see his mood was turning ugly. She must think of something quickly to divert his attention. "My Lord, I know! I'll bring Mona here to dance for us. We haven't played with her in many moons, you know. She will have grown lonely for you, Master," her face contorted with voyeuristic lust as she spoke.

At his nod, she left the room. Minutes later, two hulking Sydhars rolled in the cage. Inside stood a very pretty, slender girl with long black hair and violet eyes. She was entirely naked. A wild, haunted, animal fear was clearly visible in her expression and, when she saw Sadra, she fell to her knees and stretched out her hands in supplication.

"My Lord," she cried in a high melodic voice, "inflict whatever pain you wish upon me, but give me news of my husband, Major Roold, I beg of you!" She lowered her head.

"How touching," sneered Sadra. "So! you plead for news of your husband. I may consider your request." He got up and walked over to the cage, unfastening the door. "Come out, my dear. Come closer." He lifted her chin with one hand and caressed her bare breast with the other. "Let's see." he murmured. "What are you prepared to do to persuade me to reunite you with your husband?"

"Anything, My Lord, anything..." she whimpered softly, tears of shame and humiliation rolling down her face.

***

Far below the surface of the Iron Planet, in a low-ceilinged chamber, gathered a group of hooded beings. They were coal black with blazing yellow eyes, and they were intent upon the globe of their communication unit. Their master, Lord Sadra was transmitting his orders.

The communications globe cast a ruby glow over their faces and it would be hard to imagine a more evil-looking group. The air in the chamber was hot and stuffy, and that's the way they liked it. Its fetid heat somewhat resembled the climate of their half-forgotten home on the planet Voodan. Of Voodan only myths, not memories, remained to entertain these descendants on the Iron Planet.

Their leader turned off the communication unit and relaxed, letting his mind drift nostalgically for a moment. They were all sentenced to remain here for eternity, caught in an awful web of magnetic energy from which no star ship could escape the pull of gravity. A small craft could fly, but it could never escape the gravitational atmosphere of the planet. Either it could return to the planet's surface or forever remain in orbit.

Disobedience never crossed his mind. That's why he was the leader. His loyalty to the Tyrant was unwavering. But sometimes he caught himself daydreaming and wondering what it would like to be free... to travel to the stars... Enough! He looked around at the group. They all nodded in agreement. He switched on the communicator and spoke.

"Yes, My Lord. We will send an expedition immediately. You can be assured that we will bring Princess Iris Odman back here at once. You can send your ship to pick her up and she will be ready. We will switch off the tractor beam when you signal that your ship has arrived at the coordinates. May the powers of darkness serve you always." He lowered his head heavily and switched off the communicator again, throwing the chamber into complete obscurity.

As their eyes adjusted to the blackness, they began to glow with an eerie yellow light which pierced the gloom. Then their eyes flickered, as they spoke to one another in little flashes and nuances of eye-light, practicing an almost-forgotten Voodan language which was known only to the nobility of that planet.     .

\*\*\*

Three days had passed since Marc's disappearance, and two days since Buck and Iris had left with Digger to look for him. Countess Liana was weary. She brushed her hair off her forehead with irritation as she looked at the dozens of Booloos working under her supervision on one of the *Phoenix's* generators. She had to be everywhere at once, guiding her workers, correcting them, and this high gravity had a depressing effect on her. No matter. She had to get the generator functioning again and that was that.

Liana sensed that her brother was alive, and she despaired that she could not help him. She wished Princess Iris had remained with the ship. That gifted Hydran Princess had helped them so much in times past.

*"And to think, in the beginning, how jealous I was of her"*, Liana bit her lip in concern for her friend.

The temperature was dropping. She pulled her jacket close and fastened it. Then she leaned back against a boulder as she watched her group of grey furred helpers begin the reassembly. As she watched, her mind drifted away again. She thought of Reb and a warm smile formed on her lips, easing the lines of tension in her face. He was so good to her. They worked in alternate shifts.

And Reb was resting now that she'd taken over.

*"When we get back to Carrandon..."*, the thought was interrupted by a sound behind her and she turned to see what it was. But before she had completed her turn a thick net fell over her head and shoulders, both blinding and suffocating her at the same time. It tightened. She couldn't move. She screamed for help, but only a small choking sound came out. She thought, *"this net must be drugged..."* and then everything turned to darkness.

# CHAPTER TWENTY-ONE

Reb opened his eyes and immediately he knew something was wrong. Very wrong! Fortuno was tugging the sleeve of his shirt and calling his name with urgency. Alarmed, he sat up. "What is it, Fortuno?" He tried to look controlled, though the hair was standing on the back of his neck in fear. "Don't tell me something has happened to Liana!" He was on his feet and running before the droid could respond.

At the open hatch he stopped short, surprised at the scene that greeted him. The Booloos were all gone, pieces of machinery lay in a chaotic mess all over the ground. There was no sign of Liana, anywhere.

Reb drew his blaster and emerged from the ship cautiously. He checked the area, looking for signs of a struggle or some other clue, but it was impossible to detect anything on the rocky ground. Nearing the big boulder at the edge of the camp he thought he smelled something familiar. He stopped, took a deep breath through his nostrils, analyzing the odor carefully.

*"Yes! It was A.V.R., a paralyzing drug used in the Old Order. Someone had used it to kidnap Liana!"* He forced himself to think clearly.

228

"*Where could they have taken her? Probably to The City of Lost Ships,*" he concluded. He pondered a plan of action and then raced back to the ship to find the droid, who was tottering uneasily in the hatchway, peering out nervously to see what he could see.

"Fortuno! Call the soldiers! Have them search the entire area for clues!" Reb was beside himself with worry. "After that, prepare the Jet-Sled for travel. Load up as many explosives and weapons as the thing can carry! Blasters, grenades, thermal detonators, the works. Ask Rajaar to help you. Go on!" he yelled.

The soldiers combed the area for clues and found nothing. When Fortuno had the Jet-Sled ready, Reb checked it out. Satisfied that all was in order, he said, "You will stay here and guard the ship. And you'd better guard it well! He looked sternly at Fortuno. "Close all exits, raise the shields and remain inside with the soldiers at all times." Reb repeated the order to make sure there was no mistake. "Do you understand me, Fortuno? Remain inside all the time! I don't want anything to happen to my ship!"

"Oh, Master Reb, don't leave me alone again to guard the ship! I don't want to be in charge! Nights in this awful place give me the *willies*!" Fortuno wailed. "What shall I do if the Booloos return to work?"

"Stay inside and shield yourself. And don't get any funny ideas about taking off, because the ship is not flight-ready."

"Master Reb, I strongly recommend that you remain here with me," Fortuno began. "The odds in favor of your locating Liana alive in that morbid city are...."

"Cool it, Tin Man!" Reb snapped. "Your mistress has

been abducted and I am going to find her and bring her back and that's all there is to it! So just cancel your calculations and help me load this extra case of explosives."

Reb rechecked the supplies, thinking, *I'm going to give them a display of fireworks they will never forget!*

\*\*\*

Iris, Buck and Digger were nearing the outskirts of The City of Lost Ships.

"It looks spooky," commented Buck, leaning out of the Jet-Sled in order to get a better view. "Yes. It looks like a cemetery, rather than a city," he glowered.

"I agree." replied Iris. "It surely doesn't look very inviting," she added, a note of dismay in her voice.

"Inviting!" exclaimed Buck. "You wouldn't find me within a light year of this graveyard of it weren't for Marc. Do you still sense him, Iris? I sure hope nothing's happened to harm him."

"He is alive. That much I can guarantee, but that is all I know." replied the Princess.

"Okay! Let's find him then, and get out of here!" boomed Buck energetically.

"It might not be that simple," said Iris. She pointed at a wide path between the wrecks. Strange sickly-looking creatures were moving around down there, walking, hopping, crawling or dragging their twisted bodies along.

"I hope they haven't seen us," Iris whispered involuntarily, although they were still too far away for anyone to overhear. "We'll have to hide the Jet-Sled."

They found a good place among the rocks on the

outskirts and left the Jet-Sled there, camouflaging it with a covering of stones so that it was almost impossible to detect.

"Let's keep our distance and circumnavigate the periphery of the city on foot, to get our bearings and see what we can observe of the inhabitants," suggested Buck.

Iris and Digger nodded in agreement and they set off, with Buck in the lead and Digger bringing up the rear. In places where the rock cover didn't offer enough protection they were forced to inch along on their bellies to avoid being spotted.

*\*\**

They noticed that some kind of commotion was being made by the city dwellers, but there was no apparent cause.

"It looks like there is an entrance to an underground city over there," she pointed to a plaza in the center of the graveyard of ships where a crowd of the creatures were gathering. She closed her eyes and stood motionless for a few moments. Then, opening her eyes, she added, "Marc is below ground, beneath the plaza, far, far below. Perhaps seven or eight levels." She looked plaintively at Buck. "How are we ever going to get him out of there?" She sighed heavily, certain that their mission was going to be difficult, if not impossible.

"Well," replied Buck. "Why don't we begin by looking for another way to enter the underground city?" He adjusted his blaster and turned to the Prozoan. "Digger, if this was a Prozoan expedition, how would you tackle the problem of going underground without going near the plaza?"

"Wooooooo! Wau wau, grrrrrumppph, ayiiiiiihooooo! the Prozoan hooted in response. Buck quickly covered the Prozoan's mouth with his hand to silence him.

"Shhhhh! Silence, my friend," whispered Buck. "We don't want to attract any attention, remember?"

Digger didn't mind being gagged. He had an idea, which he explained in low howls, the Prozoan's version of a whisper.

"Digger says we should look for ventilation outlets," Buck translated for Princess Iris. "Sounds good to me," he added, clapping Digger on one shoulder in a congratulatory way.

Unfortunately, ventilation openings were few and well concealed. It took them more than an hour to find the first one. It was uncomfortably narrow for Digger, but they had no choice. Buck lowered himself into the dark tube, first. The darkness swallowed him up. Iris felt a cold shiver of fear as she saw him disappear, but she followed without hesitation. Last to enter was the Prozoan, howling painfully as he squeezed his bulky body into the tube, wishing he had never mentioned ventilation systems in the first place.

They moved downward slowly and with difficulty, disturbing the sleep of some small, unidentified animals which ran away in panic, uttering shrill squeaking sounds.

*"Could they be rats?"* thought Buck. *"Not very fitting company for a Minister of Arts and his Princess, but invaders can't be choosy"*. He reminded himself sarcastically as he inched his way along.

He reached a triple fork in the tunnel. "Iris, this tube divides into three, which way should we go?"

"Take the middle one," came her muffled reply.

Something flew at Buck, striking him in the

forehead with leathery wings.

*"Must be bats,"* he thought. His stomach turned. He hated bats. He felt tired, his muscles ached and his eyes were itching and watery.

Suddenly a strong current of air hit them from below with such a gust that they actually felt themselves being blown backwards out of the ventilation tube. They groped in the dark for something to cling to, but the sides of the tube were slick. Slowly, and with terrifying finality, they were spun up and out of the ventilation shaft.

Not until they were pushed out of the mouth of the shaft did they realize it was a different tube than the one they'd entered. Landing hard, they rolled and scrambled to their feet.

Buck was first to react. In an instant he drew his blaster from its holster and fired at the first line of beings he saw. They dropped their weapons and fell to the ground, charred by his plasma beam, only to be replaced by another row of creatures.

Princess Iris stood back to back with Buck, firing her blaster at the crowd. Digger opened his mouth and roared a terrifying war cry before lunging at the squirming mass of inhumanity before him. Step by step, the trio drove back the crowd.

The air was overheating from the plasma discharges and it was hard to breathe. What were left of their attackers, some few dozens of the sickly-looking creatures, jabbered orders back and forth and reconverged upon the trio, trying to press them into a corner from which there would be no escape.

"We must break through their flanks!" cried Buck. His blaster was overheated and the distance between the revolutionaries and their attackers was getting shorter. Buck broke out in a sweat of fear.

"Iris, do you think you could call on the Light by yourself? His teeth were clenched, his blaster was singeing his hand. "I can't hold them off for more than another minute."

\*\*\*

She nodded that she would try. Closing her eyes, she began building a shielding wall of Light, in her mind, separating them from their enemy. Leaning against Digger for support, she focused all her concentration on this work. Slowly, a shimmering, bluish wall of Light materialized before them. The creatures, who had never seen such a phenomenon in all their existence, dropped their weapons and fled in panic.

Buck sagged to the ground, dropping his blaster and throwing his head back to take some deep breaths. He turned his head and winced, then smiled at Iris, who was just emerging from her trance.

"With a girl like you at my side, I really have nothing to fear, have I?"

She smiled back.

\*\*\*

Marc opened his eyes. He was surrounded by a grey vapour that was impenetrable in its opacity. It was so thick, he could sense its density as quite substantial. He got up. The odd thing about it was, the fog was also under his feet. He appeared to be standing on it, although it felt solid and he had no fear of falling through.

*"Strange,"* he thought, *"very strange indeed"*. It was like walking around on clouds. He felt light-hearted and carefree. But there was something unnatural about this whole scene which wouldn't allow him to relax and enjoy. Then he remembered. His heavily drugged body was lying on the stone floor in the dungeons of The City of Lost Ships.

*"Am I dreaming this?"* he asked himself as he looked around curiously. *"What is going on?"*

And then he saw the Light. It was so brilliant that he narrowed his eyes, but he still couldn't look directly at it, and it seemed to be drawing him into its center with a gentle force that Marc couldn't resist. *"Is this a concentration of the purest form of the Light?* he wondered, trying to analyze the phenomenon. He moved closer. An incredible power emanated from the center of the Light, a power of positive radiance. He was very close now. He felt a desire to bathe in the light, to become one with it, and to forget everything else as he merged into endless bliss.

Then he heard a voice. Someone was calling his name. He turned back, reluctantly. He had been so close to experiencing true joy that he was irritated at this interruption. Then he recognized the voice. It was Liana! He looked around and saw her, running toward him, dressed in work coveralls, her long hair flowing, the fog parting before her.

"How did you get here? Why have you come?" he asked stupidly.

"Oh, Marc, I'm so glad I found you!" She threw her arms around him and hugged him with joy. "I was so worried." She kissed him on the cheek and hugged him again. Tears of happiness shone in her eyes.

"Where are we?" she asked, suddenly all business.

"I can't tell you where exactly we are, but I can tell you what probably happened to you," he said, realizing suddenly that she must have been drugged and snatched, too, else she wouldn't be here.

"Yes, tell me. What?"

"You have been captured, drugged and brought to the City of Lost Ships. At least, that's where I was when I passed out," he replied. "Now, it's your turn. Tell me everything."

"Okay. When you didn't return to the *Phoenix* in two days, Buck and Iris took Digger and a Jet-Sled and headed for the City to look for you. I stayed behind with Reb to supervise the round-the-clock repair detail on the reactor. While I was supervising the Booloos, and Reb was sleeping, I was drugged with A.V.R. and carried off. During the trip they kept me drugged and blindfolded. When we arrived at our destination, they put me in a small cell and drugged me again. And that's all I know." She paused and then asked, "Is A.V.R. a mind-altering drug? I didn't know it had those properties, yet I feel I am hallucinating?" There was a note of fear in her voice.

"I'm not sure." he replied. "I think we're probably okay and just experiencing out-of-body travel in the realm where crude matter doesn't exist. It's the dimension of free Light. I feel it all around us. I can sense its power, can't you?"

"Yes. But I wouldn't mind if it were a little warmer in here," she complained.

"Tell me, Liana, did your captors hurt you physically?"

"I heard them talking once when I awoke. They have orders not to," she said.

"That's interesting. Sounds like they have plans for you." Marc was clearly troubled. "We must prepare ourselves, somehow. We must not become the pawns of beings who wish to use us for some evil purpose."

"What do you suggest?" she asked. Have you thought of a way to penetrate the thick cell walls and escape from this dungeon?"

"Yes. As a matter of fact, I have an idea or two," he responded modestly. "We can use astral travel to spy on them, look for the best way out and be everywhere without being seen. In this manner we will take full advantage of our present situation."

"Lead the way, brother," she gave him a little push. "I can't wait to see Reb's face when I tell him!"

Together, they drifted through the underground city, learning all its secrets.

*\*\**

Reb Morningstar was speeding northward with his Jet-Sled's throttle at full power. He was loaded with arms and past caring about whatever dangers he might encounter. His only thought was to rescue Liana, Marc and his crew.

Night was falling, but he elected to press on for as long as he could. The winds were growing stronger and he braced himself against the console. The' weight of his blaster holstered securely at his belt felt reassuring. He pressed forward at full throttle with steely determination as darkness descended upon the landscape of the Iron Planet.

*"I understand that nothing can withstand these nightly storms,"* thought, *"and soon I'll find out if that's true"*. He was glad of his infra-red visors which allowed

him to see his surroundings.

His thoughts drifted to Liana. He wondered if she was alive, if she was all right, if he would ever see her again.

*"Oh, boy, if she could only hear this sentimental journey of mine,"* he thought, and smiled.

Danger was not new to Reb. All his life he had been jumping out of the pan and into the fire, attempting the impossible and succeeding. He hoped luck would ride with him, just one more time...

A sudden jolt threw him off balance. A strong blast of the impending hurricane rocked the sled as if it were only a frail toy.

Reb strapped himself into the seat. The belt fit tightly around his chest. Black clouds billowed overhead and paced across the sky with terrifying speed. Ghastly purple lightning exploded once in a while, bathing the alien landscape in an eerie glow. On the horizon Reb noticed sparkling violet lights moving and he knew he could expect a visit from the flying monsters very soon. He slid the Jet-Sled's canopy shut and made sure it was sealed. The defence shields on these small vehicles weren't very strong, but he activated them anyway. Some protection was going to be better than none!

Reb maneuvered his Jet-Sled so that the gusts of wind were at his back as he tacked across the planet's surface. Fortunately, the heavy load of ammunition helped to weigh the craft down against the vicious buffeting of gale-force winds.

The sparkling violet lights drew closer and closer. He knew he couldn't look at them directly, knew all too well what would happen if he did, knew that their energy could paralyze and blind him. They were close enough that his skin was already tingling.

*"I wish there was a way to capture one of these creatures, he thought. Our scientists back on Carrandon would be very excited over them. If only they weren't so deadly, they would be considered beautiful"*. They flew with unsurpassed grace, their movements so harmonious that Reb involuntarily glanced at them for a few seconds, through his visor, momentarily forgetting about the danger. In that moment he saw one of them attack. It drew its body together and formed a round ball of light which was hurled at its victim with startling speed. The unfortunate victim was a small animal hiding among the rocks. Reb scratched his head in amazement, thankful that the visor had protected his vision during that moment of carelessness.

*"Wow!"* he thought. *"To escape a frontal attack I'd have to propel myself at more than the speed of light"*. Then he caught sight of a Booloo. He recognized it, lumbering across the landscape, desperately trying to avoid capture. He directed his Jet-Sled towards the creature, cutting it off. It pulled up short.

He opened the door. "Hop in, little fellow!" he cried, as he reached out and grasped a fistful of fur and yanked the terrified creature towards him. When the Booloo was inside the Jet-Sled, Reb reached around it and closed the door just as three balls of light flung themselves at the opening, veering off in a split second when they were met by a solid door. The little Booloo rolled about helplessly in the sled. Colliding with the cases of ammunition, it hit its head and slumped to the floor where it remained, flat and unmoving.

"Hey, little critter, it's all right!" Reb laughed, touching the Booloo gently with the tip of his boot.

"Come on, stop that! You are safe! Reb was losing patience with the cowering creature. He pushed it a little more roughly and a pair of round button-eyes opened and gazed at him in pure fear.

"That's better," laughed Reb. "Now get up and see if you can be of some use to me, here."

The creature scrambled to its feet, its grey fur still standing on end with fright. Its ears quivered nervously. The Booloo scratched its head and sniffed the air suspiciously.

"Well, I've found myself a fine little adjutant," he grinned. He sat the Booloo behind the small cannon he had fitted the Jet-Sled with before leaving the ship. "Let's see if you can operate that," he said. "When you see one of those flying things coming too close, just press this," Reb pointed to the firing button. At that moment a strong gust of wind almost overturned the Jet-Sled.

"You man your station, and I'll take care of mine!" Reb shouted as he grabbed for the controls just in time to right the Jet-Sled and prevent a catastrophe.

The night seemed interminable as Reb and the Booloo sped across the great plain in search of The City of Lost Ships, their engine labouring against the awful magnetic pull of the Iron Planet.

The little creature cringed every time one of the balls of light bounced off the defence shield, and forgot to fire at it. Reb found himself tugging at the Booloo, repeatedly pointing out the fact that it had a weapon and should use it against the flying night terrors, until finally the little critter got used to the idea and began to enjoy itself as it picked off the demons as though they were rolling ducks in a shooting gallery. Reb marvelled how the black-irised, red eyeballs of the little Booloo were completely impervious to the violet flashes. He decided he couldn't have hired a more appropriate gunner.

# CHAPTER TWENTY-TWO

Buck, Iris and Digger descended to the fifth underground level. The inhabitants of The City of Lost Ships had heard the alarm and now every member of this society was searching for them.

"Are you all right?" Buck asked Iris, supporting her as she stumbled and forced herself to continue moving against the terrible gravity.

"I'm fine," she smiled at him weakly. "I was just thinking about the population here. What a strange collection of genetic crossbreeding there must have been to product such a weird variety!"

"Weird is right! Degenerate is more like it," he added.

"They are so twisted, both physically and mentally," she continued. "They must have interbred many species from different star systems."

"Well, whatever occurred, the final result is ghoulish, if you ask me." Buck definitely didn't go for them at all. "What do you think, Digger?" He looked back at the Prozoan who was lumbering along.

Digger howled, leaving no doubt in Buck's mind that the Prozoan wasn't attracted to them, either.

They found themselves in a passage that led to the place Marc was being held, according to Princess Iris' psychic scan. Or was it? There was a whole maze of passages branching off to their left and right. It was so confusing that only someone trained in the extrasensory directional gift of the Light could avoid becoming hopelessly lost.

An explosion somewhere down the passage ahead of them announced the presence of the enemy. But when they arrived at that spot with blasters drawn for action, they found the passage collapsed with piles of rocks blocking their way.

"We've got to go around this obstruction," Buck decided.

They turned into a side passage and there was another explosion. This time it was so close it collapsed the passage where they walked, almost burying them under falling rocks.

"This is a planned ambush," cried Buck. "They want us to run us around in here like rats in a trap and then pick us off one by one!" He grabbed Iris by the arm. "Hurry, we must outwit them!" They took another passage, but the same thing happened there, and in the next two as well. They were trapped. There was no way out. All exits were sealed with fallen rocks.

"Blast! What do we do, now?" Buck was breathing heavily. Princess Iris brushed a strand of hair from her cheek.

"Give me a minute to rest and then let me examine this place with my special senses to see if there's any way out that is not immediately apparent to us," she said. Then she closed her eyes and went into a light trance.

"A psychic has her own way of doing things," Buck winked at Digger. "Let's have a snack while we wait." He handed the Prozoan a cube of concentrated emergency food and began chewing on another.

A strange noise permeated their silence. It was coming from within the stone wall itself. Buck stopped chewing and choked on his mouthful when the stone wall suddenly broke open right before his eyes and something shiny jumped at them from the opening. He raised his blaster and shot at it without thinking, then shook Iris violently to bring her out of her trance. She did not respond. Her head lolled uselessly.

"Wake up, Iris!" he yelled. "Look! They have creatures here who can drill right through solid rock with their bodies! Iris!" She opened her eyes. Buck pointed at the floor. The remains of a strange alien life form lay there. Digger howled in terror. The noise was back! It came from all directions at once. Buck caught Iris' hand and squeezed it as they exchanged glances.

The floor burst open and they leaped to one side just in time to avoid a horrible mouth with teeth sharper than knives, sharp enough to cut through stone as if it were made of jello. Buck fried it with his blaster. Another one broke through the wall at their backs and chewed a patch of Digger's thick fur right off his mane before Buck fried it.

The one that burst through the ceiling almost did them in. It came so unexpectedly that Buck almost missed it. It hung from its hole in the ceiling, it's flexible, scaled body undulating, it's horrible armoured mouth searching for prey. The deadly blades passed only inches away from Princess Iris, they would have shredded her into little pieces. She screamed and Buck took aim, but only nicked it. With a strange, squealing sound the thing retreated into his hole.

"It's still alive!" cried Buck, firing into the hole again and again.

Princess Iris tugged at his sleeve, "We have to get out of here, quick!" she cried. "This entire place will collapse any minute now." She looked around and then pointed, "This way! We can crawl through one of these holes! They must lead somewhere. There is no other way out!"

They had no choice. The hole she indicated wasn't very wide, but they managed to squeeze into it and inch their way forward, away from their trap. Digger was having difficulties, as usual. But the fear of being buried alive gave him the motivation to push his way through. Soon they heard a rumbling noise and felt the stone around them tremble. The passage they had just been in was crumbling, and buried in the rubble were the remains of the stone cutting beasts.

\*\*\*

Like everything else in The City of Lost Ships, the droids were rusting and had been stored in disuse for a very long time. Tootee had been deactivated and placed in storage too, together with other robots and androids from alien star systems.

Tootee had mastered the art of self-activation a long time ago. So he turned himself back on, looked around and beeped in amazement. Some of the shapes that surrounded him surpassed even his encyclopedic knowledge about artificial life forms. Many of the droids were broken and had obviously been out of commission for several centuries. Tootee whistled. A huge metallic spider was standing in the middle of the storage room, its thin limbs blocking Tootee's way. He rolled around it.

The room was pretty big, and it took him a while to locate the exit. The thick, metal gate was closed. Tootee rolled closer and examined it. The mechanism was unfamiliar, but he decided to try to open it, anyway. Just as he stretched out a probe to insert into the lock, the door sprung open. Tootee froze. Two black-skinned beings, robed and hooded, entered. They moved in jumps rather than normal walking, their eyes gleaming a brilliant yellow in the dark. They didn't even notice Tootee's little shape by the door.

"Where is it?" One of them spoke to the other with a unique form of communication. Tootee could easily translate the flashes of their eyes. "It appears to have been borrowed, without permission, by one of our brothers. We will all be punished for this. How will I explain this disappearance to the Tyrant?"

"It was here only yesterday," answered the other. "I checked on it personally."

"Well, it's not here now." The Leader spoke with reproach.

Tootee took advantage of their confusion and rolled quietly past them in the darkness and disappeared down a long, obscure passageway.

***

Marc was awakening from his nightmare. His head was splitting. His throat felt so dry that he didn't try to utter a sound. His eyes were glued shut with salty sweat and he had trouble opening them. He felt the hardness of stone under his cramped body, but he didn't care about physical discomfort. He remembered everything. He knew there was still some of the drug in his system, he felt it. But he could think clearly in spite of it. He tried to swallow and licked his parched lips. He could hardly contain his excitement. In his out-of-body travels he had penetrated the most important secret on this planet, a thing he and his companions on the *Phoenix* had never dreamed existed.

It was a neutron reactor, in the bowels of the City. He knew it was the source of the web of gravity that stretched far out into space. And he knew it was the reason star ships couldn't leave the planet, and it was also the force that snatched ships from space and drew them into an early grave.

Marc now understood why they were having so much trouble with their own engine repairs, and he understood the phenomenon that had caused them to drift off course in space. Reb had been at a loss to explain the effect, but Marc could tell him, now.

*"The neutron reactor must be destroyed!"* he thought with determination. He tried to sit up. His hands felt weak and shaky. He was irritated by the heavy density of his body and he was fed-up with being so clumsy.

The Light was very strong within him now. Realizing this, he decided to heal himself before he ventured forth. He closed his eyes and let the stream of the healing force flow through him, restoring and regenerating him, nourishing every cell. When he felt one hundred percent again, he jumped easily to his feet and looked around. His cell was so small there was hardly enough room to turn around. Unexpectedly, the door to his cell opened and two robed beings entered.

"Amazing how quickly he has recovered," said the Leader with his eyes. "We'll have to drug him again," he advised.

"I'll see to it," replied the other, groping for something in the pocket of his robe. He found what he was looking for, and drew out a small syringe full of bluish liquid. Marc paled with fear seeing that he is going to be knocked unconscious again with that powerful drug.

*"I have to keep them from injecting me,"* he thought feverishly. *"I have to stop them."* His mind raced. He knew that his opponents were armed and that any physical resistance was pointless. The syringe was moving towards him. There was no time to lose. He waved his hand in front of the glowing eyes. "It is not necessary to drug the prisoner," he spoke with firm command in his voice he learned in the Jaira training.

"It is not necessary to drug," said the robed figure holding the syringe as it turned and repeated the message to the Leader. The syringe disappeared back into the folds of its robe.

Marc waved his hand again, before the Leader's face. "The prisoner must be released," he spoke firmly in his tone of command.

"Release the prisoner," the Leader ordered its companion.

Marc sighed with relief. He knew his grip on their minds wouldn't last very long. He had to act fast. He turned to one of them. "Give me your syringe," he ordered. The syringe was handed over to him obediently.

The Leader, emerging from Marc's control,

struggled briefly when Marc injected him. Moments later both beings were laying on the floor in a drug-induced slumber.

Marc shut the door to his prison cell and ran down a passageway which led to the lowest level and the neutron reactor.

\*\*\*

Reb Morningstar and his little Booloo friend survived two nerve-wracking nights as they moved north without stopping. His eyes were as red as the little Booloo's from lack of sleep, but he pushed exhaustion out of his thoughts and focused on the terrain ahead.

They were approaching the City. He could tell from the strange shapes of spacecraft pointing at the sky. The Booloo sitting behind the cannon was visibly shaken. He sat alert, ears up, whiskers trembling.

"Well, where is everybody," said Reb, mostly for the sake of hearing a human voice. "Not that I expected a warm welcome, but..." Then he saw the movement and paused in mid-sentence. He was only mildly surprised by the weird look of the degenerated inhabitants of The City of Lost Ships, and deduced that these residents lived underground.

"Okay, little fellow. Are you ready for some action?" he asked the trembling Booloo. The creature shook his head vigorously in denial. Reb ignored it.

"Let's go for it, then!" He hit a button and the Jet-Sled jumped forward, heading straight for the enemy. Reb and the Booloo were armed to their teeth. The city dwellers were so astonished by the sudden appearance of the Jet-Sled that they offered no resistance. Reb swept through their midst with the beam of his blaster, just in case they changed their minds. He couldn't afford to take chances. He had to impress them with his weaponry before they got ideas. A few of his opponents reached for their weapons and were turned into charcoal before they could take aim.

Reb stopped the Jet-Sled near an underground stairway. He strapped on his backpack arsenal and jumped out, motioning to the Booloo to do the same. The ramp spiralled downward and together they moved forward with blasters cocked.

On the first level they encountered an organized resistance. News of their arrival had obviously spread quickly, and dozens of pale denizens were gathered under the dominance of a coal black, robed and hooded being who ordered them to open fire as soon as the intruders came into sight.

"Time for the fireworks!" yelled Reb, as he threw several grenades into the crowd. Whatever was left of them after the explosions were cut down with the beam of his blaster. The Booloo was doing a pretty good job securing his back, and it was obvious the critter had completely forgotten its fear in the excitement. In fact, Reb noted its face had acquired a fierce, warlike expression. He stifled a laugh as he gazed at that furious countenance which only moments before had looked so cuddly, innocent and fearful.

"Let's descend," commanded Reb. The second level was both dark and quiet. "Nobody here," he said jauntily. Just then the air exploded in fire which formed a ring all around them. The Booloo cried out in alarm.

Reb didn't lose his head. Grabbing his furry companion by the scruff of the neck he bolted through the ring of fire. Flames engulfed him for a moment and he smelled his hair singe. On the other side, he slapped at the Booloo's fur until the little burning patches were doused. Fortunately, only Reb's eyebrows and hair had singed, thanks to the fabric of his clothing which was resistant to all the elements.

Dropping the Booloo, he set his blaster at full power and swept the area in its beam. Nothing could be seen in that darkness, but he could hear the sound of falling bodies as the beam swept through the unseen foe and exterminated them one by one.

Down the ramp they moved, deeper into the underground. Reb wasn't Light sensitive but somehow he had the feeling Liana was down here. He remembered Marc having once tried to teach him some basics.

*"Let your intuition guide you,"* he'd instructed. *"Listen to your feelings."* Now, Reb did just that.

The entrance to the third level was barred by a solid metal door. *"It would use up the charge in my blaster to melt this,"* he thought. *"There must be some other way,"* he thought. Then a grin slowly spread over his face, indicating he had an idea. Motioning to the Booloo to be quiet, they stood there in silence for a couple of minutes. Then Reb stepped forward and knocked on the door. Nothing happened. He waited a few moments and then knocked again, a little louder. Still no reaction from within. He tried something else. Retreating a few yards, he ran to the door, trying to make as much clatter as possible with his feet. "Open up," he cried. "They are coming! Open up quickly!"

He thought he heard movement on the other side of the door. Something creaked and it swung open just a few inches. A curious eye peered out from the other side. That was all Reb wanted. He slipped a booted foot into the space before the creature could slam it shut and aimed his blaster at the eye. Having thus satisfied the curiosity of the nowly-charred being, he pushed open the door. The way ahead was clear.

"The saying goes, in order to open a door, all you have to do is knock!" Reb laughed. "But I didn't believe it until now."

The Booloo licked its narrow lips with a long tongue, indicating thirst.

"Here, take a drink, you earned it," Reb handed him a flask. He never expected the fearful, rabbit-like creature to stand up with him and fight like this one did.

He looked at the little critter with admiration. Then noticed it was still drinking. "Hey! Hey! Leave some for me!" He grabbed the flask just in time to save the last few swigs for himself. Then he wiped his forehead, smearing some sooty marks there into an intricate mosaic.

The Booloo gestulated pointing at his forehead. He touched it again, curiously, then looked at his hand. It was smeared with soot.

"Those black beings will think I'm one of them!" he laughed. "Can't flash my eyes like that, though. Wrong color eyes, too. No, I guess it wouldn't work." He took a last swig and threw the flask aside. "Time to go forth and conquer another level!" he ordered.

But the fourth level was devoid of population. The fifth, however, almost cost him his life. They were waiting for Reb. And they were well prepared. They opened fire as soon as Reb and the Booloo began their descent. There was nowhere to hide from the blaze. Reb was glad they were using rather antiquated weapons. He ordered the Booloo to hit the dirt and gave one of the most terrible war cries he could muster. Then he leapt towards the enemy, sweeping the area with his blaster and twirling as he advanced. After several spins he grew very dizzy and staggered around for a few moments while his head cleared. Then he saw that the devastation had been total. Nothing had survived, except for the little Booloo who was still flattened to the floor. Piles of charred bodies were everywhere.

"Oh boy, that was a close one," he hollered. "On your feet, little critter. We gotta move along." The Booloo scrambled to its feet and they moved forward together.

Reb's intuition was driving him downward. After another brief skirmish on the sixth level, the seventh was quiet. Reb decided to explore it a little. Choosing a dark passage to his right, they walked carefully along it, ears perked, ready to fire at any moment. "It doesn't look like any city I've ever seen," whispered Reb. "It's so gloomy and depressing in the dark." The Booloo, native to the Iron Planet, had probably seen worse and looked on impassively.

This passage apparently serviced a dormitory for the residents, with many doorless openings up and down its length. "There's nothing for us, here," he decided, aloud, after prowling the corridor for a few minutes. "Let's go back." he ordered.

As they were turning around, a familiar beep stopped Reb in his tracks. He wheeled around. "Tootee!" he called. A whole orchestra of beeps responded, as the small bulky robot rolled out of the gloom.

Reb was so happy to find Tootee undamaged, that he

felt like hugging it. The Booloo was a different matter. It sniffed the metallic body and looked at it suspiciously. Tootee beeped a salutation at the Booloo, blinking and flashing its electronic eyes. After a few moments, they apparently reached some kind of understanding and the Booloo accepted the presence of the robot without further incident.

"Okay, men, let's go!" Reb called to his troops as he headed for the ramp again. "No time for social interchange, men, step lightly." There was a playful lilt to his voice.

The eighth level also appeared to be abandoned, but there was an aura of danger there, as though something was lying in wait.

"I'm not sure I want to explore this level," remarked Reb, hesitantly trying to penetrate the darkness with this keen eyes. The Booloo also sensed danger. Its fur was all on end and it looked like a fuzzy grey ball. Its ears were flattened to the sides of its head and its whiskers stretched out like antennas set to receive signals of danger.

Tootee was unmoved. His programming did not include instinctive perception. The trio stood there for a few seconds, poised at the landing to the eighth level, uncertain what to do. Suddenly a wave of excruciating pain hit Reb, accompanied by an incomprehensible vibration in the air. *"Ultrasonic weapons!"* And he'd thought everything they had was archaic!

He tried not to lose his grip on his blaster as he fell to his knees. He swept the area with its beam, he was determined not to sell his life too cheaply. A cry from the little Booloo told him it had been hit, and a thud told him the critter had dropped its blaster. He looked, and saw the furry little thing writhing in agony. Just then Reb took another hit; his vision blurred and he fell, knowing he'd be unconscious in a matter of minutes. *"What a stupid way to die,"* he thought. He blinked and strained to see, but his eyes would not focus. *"How can I die, and leave Liana in their hands?"* Tears welled in his eyes.

Something was intruding into his thoughts. A few seconds later he realized it was Tootee. Beeps... A message... A flash of hope! He tried to focus, strained to stay awake.

"Tootee! Where are they? Search! Scan! Destroy! commanded Reb through clenched teeth.

Tootee obediently scanned the area with his sensors and soon, triumphant beeps were accompanied by a deadly beam that shot out from a laser mount on Tootee's body. Whatever was out there in the darkness gave a smothered cry, and the sudden ebb of ultrasonic energy told Reb it had been disabled.

"Good shot, Tootee!" Reb exclaimed. He scrambled to his feet, massaging his aching body. *"Blast! That ultrasonic weapon sure plays havoc with my nervous system!"*

Picking up the terrified Booloo, he propped it against a wall and turned back to Tootee.

"Listen, little buddy, I want you to tell me if you can find Marc and Countess Liana."

To his surprise, a cacophony of beeps affirmed the challenge. Reb listened, unbelieving.

"Are you certain of this?" he asked. "I can't believe my luck! Let's go, troops," he commanded. According to the information Tootee provided, Countess Liana was only one level below.

# CHAPTER TWENTY-THREE

The rock walls vibrated all around them. They could hear more of the stone drillers coming, the sharp blades cutting the stone. And there was another sound. The animals seemed to be breathing laboriously as they churned their way through solid rock. One was close by. Iris, Buck and Digger froze in their tunnel.

*"In seconds, maybe a minute, this primitive creature might turn us into minced meat,"* thought Buck in anger and desperation. He had never felt so helpless. He hit the rock wall with a fist and then gasped with pain. Digger also sensed the danger and was battling with his own fears. The situation was nerve-wracking and seemed hopeless.

"Iris! Is there anything you can do to get us out of this mess?" Buck pleaded with her, knowing full well that only supernatural intervention could save them from a horrible fate.

"This is a very difficult situation," she replied. Accustomed to open spaces, Iris was fighting claustrophobia. She had the impression that she was about to suffocate. She tried to concentrate, to get a hold of herself. Concentrate... concentrate... She tried to ignore the lack of oxygen in her lungs.

The stone-boring animal was very close now. Already they could hear the cracking of the rock wall of their tunnel. Small stones were showered upon them and dust filled their nostrils. They coughed and choked as they continued to inch along.

"Iris!" It was a final, desperate plea from the man she loved.

Rock began to crumble all around them. The noise was deafening, and labored breathing could be heard only yards away.

Buck stared, transfixed, at the place where the bladed mouth would emerge from the rock to take their lives. He was drenched with sweat. He perceived everything in slow motion and with a terrible clarity. Then a wave of nausea twisted his stomach. He saw the movement in the rock, the blades... He wished he could lose consciousness before that awful mouth reached his body and cut through it. He closed his eyes. He couldn't bear to see it happen.

Suddenly, the noise stopped. The animal sighed heavily and was quiet. Buck opened his eyes and could hardly believe what he saw.

"Iris! My sweet girl. You did it again! You really did!" he reached back to grasp her hand and give it a squeeze of thanks. But there was no hand reaching for his. Iris didn't answer. She had passed out from the depletion of energy expended to win this battle for their lives.

***

"Idiots!" screamed the Tyrant. "Cretins! Imbeciles!" he yelled. He smashed his fist down on the table. "You have the wrong girl! Exterminate her at once and deliver Princess Iris Odman!"

Sadra was shouting commands into his communications unit. "I want Iris! Get her or you are all dead!" he threatened. "I'll destroy the whole blasted planet if you don't deliver her to my ship by tomorrow," he ordered with a snarl. "See that you don't fail me this time," he cut the transmission. His eyes were shining dangerously and his breathing was rapid. Clevia knew better than to go near him when he was in a rage.

From a safer distance across the table, she asked, "What would please My Lord today?"

"Bring me half a dozen slaves. Or better still, take them to the arena. Order the turrons prepared. I want to see the slaves torn to pieces by the turrons. I want blood!" he cried.

Clevia wasn't at all sure if it would also be her blood that would be spilled tonight.

*** 

Reb knew that Liana was only yards away on the other side of the heavy metal door. He also knew that she was in danger. He drew his blaster and fired at the gate, using his weapon on maximum power. The lock smoked and melted. He kept his finger on the trigger, the hole in the metal door was growing bigger. Through it, he could see a red glowing globe hovering in mid-air and a cluster of hooded shapes that turned their heads to watch his work. Their eyes burned like the yellow tip of a flame. He shivered. He remembered this chamber from somewhere... remembered the touch of bony fingers on his body...

The hooded beings nodded their heads together in a somehow familiar gesture, as if discussing this unexpected intrusion. Reb knew that Liana was laying on a stone slab below the red globe, even though he couldn't see her yet. He also knew she would die if he didn't hurry.

He cursed softly, his blaster had exhausted its charge. He dropped it and grabbed the other blaster from the Booloo's paws. The hole in the door was big enough to have melted the entire lock. He kicked it with his foot and it swung open.

The beings surrounded a slab upon which she lay unconscious. He could see the outline of her pale, unmoving shape. For a moment he thought they had already killed her, but he pushed this thought away. *"How could it be! This was the scene in my delirium! She must be alive!"*

One of the hooded ones produced a long thin rod from the folds of its robe and twisted it gently until it lit up. It glowed a deadly red. The hooded one lowered the rod, almost touching Liana's forehead.

"Nooooo!" shouted Reb in an inhuman shriek as he was galvanized into action. He fired on the enemy with sweeping strokes of his blaster, carefully avoiding the slab on which Liana lay.

The hooded ones fell, one by one, charred and lifeless, their gleaming yellow eyes the last thing to die.

The hovering globe aimed a red laser beam at Reb. He jumped to one side to avoid the attack. The globe acted as if it had an intelligence of its own, swooping at Reb with agility and speed. It was sneaky, and fast! Reb shot and missed several times. Then, from behind, he heard several timid beeps and then saw a ray of white light hit the globe. The object shattered into a million sparks which rained to the floor like a fireworks display. Thank goodness for Tootee and his built-in defence system!

Reb ran to the slab and covered Liana with his body to protect her from the falling shower of sparks. She stirred, and opened her eyes woozily. "Reb?" she smiled a wobbly smile. "I knew you would come, darling!" She murmured in a voice so low that Reb had to strain to hear.

"Hush, Liana. Don't talk. Everything is fine, my love. I'm with you now." He gathered her into his arms and rocked her like a child, She fell asleep with her head on his shoulder, smiling and dreaming a lovely dream.

This is how Marc found them minutes later as he turned the landing on his way down the spiral ramp. Tootee was so overjoyed to see his master that he filled the chamber with a song of beeps which was used only for special occasions.

"Reb! Tootee! How did you find her? I'm so glad you came!" Marc strode over to them with a smile as luminescent as a sunrise.

"Marc! I'm glad to see you alive and well!" Reb spoke softly, so as not to awaken Liana. "I thought we'd lost you for good. What did they do to you. Are you all right?" he asked, looking at his friend's bruised face and torn suit.

"I'm in great shape. But you don't look so glamorous yourself, you know," Marc laughed. "I wish I had a mirror!" He looked at Liana curled in Reb's arms. "I see your princely kisses have lost their power to waken the sleeping Countess." His tone was light, but his expression was worried. He moved closer and examined her with his psychic sense, projecting his mind outward and letting it travel through her body to determine if she suffered any internal damage. She lay, in Reb's arms, as innocent as a child.

Sighing thankfully, Marc stepped back. "She's only drugged. Let me see if I can bring her out of her stupor." He went to work and after a while she opened her eyes again, shaking her head as if to clear her mind.

"Ooooh, I have a splitting headache," she complained. Marc touched her temples with his fingertips and stroked her lightly for a few seconds. "Better now?" he asked.

She blinked and smiled. "The pain's all gone!" She jumped out of Reb's embrace and laced her fingers through her hair, brushing it back. "Now, we must go and destroy the reactor," she announced impulsively.

"What reactor?" asked Reb. "Am I missing something here?" Marc explained all about their out-of-body discovery.

"Do you think your trance information is reliable?" Reb asked in a doubtful voice.

"I think we should go and find out," Marc replied with finality.

Thus, the small band of revolutionaries disappeared down the dark passages of the lowest level of The City of Lost Ships, in search of the reactor.

\*\*\*

Buck reached the other end of the rock tunnel and climbed out, helping Iris out after him. Then, together they tugged at Digger until he was free of the small opening. Iris was gasping for breath. The chamber they were in wasn't very big, but anything was better than the narrow tunnel where they'd almost lost their lives.

"I thought we'd never make it," said Buck with relief. "You okay, Digger?"

The giant, shaggy Prozoan seemed to be in poor shape. He was shaking himself violently, trying to dislodge the dust and small stones that were caught in his long fur. He responded with a long, low moan.

"Any idea where we might be?" Buck turned to Princess Iris, who was recovering her composure. Her face was pale and drawn but her eyes shone through with strength and determination.

*"What an unusual woman she is!"* thought Buck as he gazed on her with affection.

"We must be on the eighth or ninth level underground," she answered after a while. "I can sense that Marc, and yes, Liana, are not too far from here. Reb is here, too, as well as another being. I am picking up the vibrations from four warm blooded beings somewhere on this level. I think we should find them," she concluded, adjusting her blaster and shaking the dust from her coveralls.

"Will you act as our guide?" Buck looked at her with admiration.

"Yes," she answered simply. "Follow me."

Every five minutes Iris had to stop long enough to examine with her mind's eye the location of the others and be certain they were going in the right direction.

"There is a strange pulsation in the Light," whispered Iris in the darkness. "It's as if a huge heart were beating somewhere down here. I wonder what could it be?" A note of fear crept into her voice.

"I wish I had the answers," replied Buck, "but I am not sensitive in the realm of the Light."

"It is such a powerful pulsation," Iris said with dismay. "Somehow frightening," her voice dropped to a nearly inaudible pitch. "It comes from over there," she pointed to a passageway leading to the unknown.

"Well, if the pulsation is so strong, Marc and Liana must have detected it, too," reasoned Buck, "and they have probably gone to see what is causing it. So let's walk in the direction of the pulsation and we will probably find our friends."

As they crept stealthily along dark, empty corridors, nothing interfered with their forward progress. The pulsation became audible as they grew nearer. Even Buck could hear it clearly, a mysterious, powerful beat. Buck's heart started pounding in unison with the pulsation. He felt exhilarated and scared at the same time. The red light at the end of the passage cast a coppery glow on Iris' lovely face. Buck gripped his blaster in anticipation, and Digger howled.

Tootee's whistle answered back at Digger! Buck stumbled and wiped the sweat from his forehead. He knew they were only yards away from that demonic pulsation, and he knew, at least, that Tootee was nearby. He narrowed his eyes against the red light, which was becoming too bright to look at directly.

At the end of the corridor they stood on the threshold of a huge chamber. The intensity of the light was so strong that they were forced to cover their eyes and, peeking out from between their fingers, accustom themselves to it a bit at a time. It seemed as though someone had captured the sun and released it to shine down here, thousands of meters beneath the surface of the Iron Planet.

When their eyes adjusted a little more, they could see several dark, robed and hooded figures moving around a huge, bright globe. The temperature in the chamber was incredibly high. "Can you tell me where Marc might be?" Buck whispered into Iris' ear.

"He is nearby," she whispered back. "I can't tell exactly where. The light and the vibration are interfering with my sensibilities. I can't concentrate."

Buck looked from Iris to Digger and they all looked at the glowing globe. Then something touched Buck on the shoulder. He tensed. Iris and Digger were on either side of him. He gripped his blaster, drew it and spun around.

"Take it easy," laughed Marc.

"This place can really make you jumpy, can't it!" added Reb, just a step behind him.

Buck relaxed and greeted his friends. After a few minutes of exchanging greetings and stories, they got back to the business at hand. Marc explained that the huge globe was a powerful reactor that produced an invisible energy field which reached far out into space. They agreed that in order to lift off from the Iron Planet, they would have to destroy the reactor. A plan was formed, ingenious in its simplicity.

A warning alarm pierced the air, ringing with lingering intensity, signalling that their presence had been discovered. They noticed more of the dark shapes running around the reactor, their numbers increasing with every second.

"How do they control this globe? There must be a control post somewhere around here." Marc was thinking aloud.

"They're coming," cried Liana, pressing back against the stone wall. The hooded figures gathered into a half-circle and pressed forward, trying to surround the group of revolutionaries. Brilliant yellow eyes in coal black faces peeped out from under their hoods. Their rod-like weapons were drawn. There was no time to lose.

Reb waved at the little Booloo who was trying to hide behind the humans. "Unload your pack! Get out the grenades!" He turned to Buck, "Help me get this thing unstrapped, it's full of goodies."

The ammo was quickly distributed among the group. "On three, pull your pins and throw your grenades!" Reb yelled. "Three!"

Leaning over Tootee, Marc murmured something in a low voice. The robot separated himself from the group and rolled off on its mission. Their robed opponents were very nervy. One of them saw the bulky little robot rolling away from the group and shot at it. Tootee met the enemy charge halfway with his own laser beam and instantly the dark shape fell to the ground lifelessly smoking. Tootee rolled on, continuously scanning the big chamber with his sensors. Finally, he found what he sought and beeped a triumphant message back to Marc.

The control post had been located. Tootee had orders to destroy everything that stood in his way, and so he did. The robed figure watching over the control board slid to the ground, pierced by Tootee's laser, as did his two assistants, when they tried to stop the robot.

Tootee rolled over to the control board and examined it with his probes. Soon, he knew what had to be done. Inserting a long probe into the circuit, he reprogrammed the control unit and then withdrew and retreated back to the group of humans as fast as he could, beeping and whistling all the way.

Marc knew they didn't have much time before the chain reaction Tootee started would destroy the globe-reactor and the entire city with it. He knew the reactor's explosion would have a ripple effect that would spread a wave of destruction, destroying everything in its wake. Tootee beeped his calculation that the Iron Planet would self-destruct within forty-eight hours. He knew he'd done a good job and he was satisfied.

*** 

They heard the first explosion when they were on the third level. A wave of hot air hit them and slightly singed their skin. Cracks appeared in the rocky walls and big boulders began to fall from place. The ground shook with the force of detonation and they realized in that instant that the magnetic web had been weakened. Their limbs moved freely as they ran for their lives. Running was easy now, almost effortless, compared to the oppressive gravity they'd been accustomed to in the last few weeks.

Digger loped along with giant strides, carrying Countess Liana under one arm and the shaking Booloo under the other. Tootee was making his own way with considerable difficulty, continually having to detour and roll around rocks and other obstacles in his path. Reb, Marc and Buck led the group, with Iris close behind. Up the circular ramp they fled, floor by floor.

A low rumbling sound filled the passages. They reached the second level as the rocky walls surrounding them vibrated with violent shudders. They felt the ramp breaking up. Far below them flames licked the walls. Marc felt as though his lungs were filling up with the searing smoke and he could hardly breathe. His heart was pounding so fast that he was certain it would burst if he held his breath another minute longer.

Princess Iris was running just behind him and suddenly fell on her side, having been hit by a falling rock. She moaned, tried to get up, couldn't. A narrow stream of blood was trickling from her temple. Marc forgot his bursting lungs and turned to aid the fallen girl. He caught her by the arms and began to drag her towards the exit. Buck came up from behind and hoisted her on his muscular shoulders, relieving Marc of the burden. Just then the ramp developed a fissure and was rent in two. Marc was trapped on the opposite side from his companions and his way forward was cut off. Flames and volcanic dust spewed upwards through the fissure as though the planet were about to erupt. There was only one thing to do. He had to jump through the fire, to the other side. Retreating a little way, in order to gain some speed, he ran for the edge and jumped. He almost made it. His foot slipped on the opposite ledge and he fell, clinging to the precipice by his fingertips.

Reb was quick to react. He reached down and grasped Marc's wrists, pulling him up in one rapid motion. Just in time, too. A major explosion rattled their teeth and sent the flames leaping out of the abyss.

"Thanks, buddy, I owe you one!" panted Marc as they jumped back from the flames.

Buck leapt out on the surface of the entrance foyer and ran for the door, followed by Marc. Almost simultaneously, Reb and Digger emerged from the ramp with little Tootee whistling as he followed them out.

# CHAPTER TWENTY-FOUR

An impenetrable barricade of fallen rocks closed the exit from the foyer to the outside world. Reb swore. Digger stood uncertainly, then released Liana and the Booloo from his grasp. Marc stumbled, then recovered his balance. Buck lowered Princess Iris gently to the polished stone floor. They had reached the end of their endurance, and they sensed that only the Light could release them from this rocky tomb.

Marc had a job to do. He tried to relax, a difficult accomplishment under the circumstances. The ground shook and stones were raining down around their heads. Marc forced himself to concentrate. It took enormous effort, but Ben Menjoro had taught him long, long ago how to let the Light flow through him. The calm that filled him was like a healing balm. He probed the thickness of the stone barrier with his mind. Then he gasped as he perceived how thick it was.

*"Am I strong enough to levitate this wall?"* he wondered as his calm became disturbed with doubt. Then he remembered the words of his master and teacher, Benja-Ko.

*"Size matters not, only in your mind the difference is. You don't believe, that's why fail you!* Marc determinedly wiped the thoughts of doubt from his mind. He felt the Light building and growing stronger within him.

"Hurry, Marc!" He could hear his sister cry out, but he ignored the distractions and interferences from the outside world. Slowly, methodically, he started levitating the rocks which blocked his way. Suddenly he felt he wasn't alone in this. He felt another presence close to him, helping him, lending him strength. Iris? The thought almost caused him to lose his grip on a large boulder.

Now the work seemed easier. Marc felt almost happy. He always felt uplifted like this when working with Iris. He couldn't help himself, even though he knew her heart belonged to another. The sky became visible through a small opening in the wall.

*"Just a few more rocks and we will be free,"* he thought, making one final effort. Another explosion rocked the place. The ceiling cracked in half and caved in on them. Flames were bursting through the cracks everywhere.

They all jumped for the newly created opening and scrambled to freedom. Liana and the Booloo were easily lifted through by Digger. Then Buck helped Iris to the other side and squeezed his own tall body through with difficulty. Reb followed and, once on the other side, ran for his Jet-Sled, waving for everybody to follow him. The underground city was collapsing so fast that Marc was afraid for a moment he wasn't going to make it.

Then Digger got stuck. "Hurry, Digger!" Marc was

pushing the Prozoan from behind with all his remaining strength. Digger was panicked and howling pitifully. He couldn't budge. The fire was licking at Marc's heels and blood was trickling down his face from the numerous cuts he had sustained from the rock falls.

Sensing that physical effort would be of no avail, he called upon the Light again. Wrestling a big chunk of rock out of the opening, he widened the exit and the Prozoan scrambled out, howling joyously. Marc followed, the cooler air from outside felt refreshing and welcome on his burning cheeks. He drew a deep breath and was running to join the others on the Jet-Sled when smothered bips stopped him cold in his tracks.

"Tootee!" He raced back. Disregarding his own safety, Marc jumped back through the opening. Fire was raging inside. Weak beeps were emanating from a pile of rocks several feet high. "Oh, no!" moaned Marc. "He's been buried under a rock slide." He started throwing off the rocks furiously and slowly, the bulky little robot emerged from the pile. His metal body was so hot that Marc couldn't touch it. Tootee wasted no time as he made for the escape hatch with all the speed he could muster. A split second after Marc followed Tootee through the hole, the whole place collapsed inward, leaving only a huge crater in the ground. Dancing flames were all that was left of The City of Lost Ships.

*** 

How to get everyone back to the *Golden Phoenix* was a problem. The Jet-Sleds would take two days under normal conditions, possibly longer with a heavier payload of passengers. And the planet was due to destruct before then. Marc presented the solution.

"Buck, why don't you take Princess Iris and Digger, Tootee and the Booloo with you in the Jet-Sled and head out onto the plain? I'll fly Reb and my sister back to the *Phoenix* and then come back for you and Iris on my second trip. I'll be able to spot you and land easily on the plain, and you'll be at a safe distance in case this place blows up!"

"Where will I sit?" demanded Liana. "There are only two seats, in the *Star Wind*, remember?"

"I figure you're small enough to sit curled up in back of the cockpit, where Tootee usually rides. Reb is too big for that, he'll have to ride in the co-pilot's seat."

"Oh, great! Ain't it wonderful to be small!" Liana crooned sarcastically, with no appreciation for the urgency of the moment.

"Quit bitching, Sis. It won't take more than a half hour to get you home to the ship. You can handle being cramped for half an hour, can't you?" Marc snapped.

She was instantly contrite. "Yes. I'm sorry, Marc. I guess this situation has gotten on my nerves."

Marc, his sister and Reb ran for the *Star Wind*. Then, true to his word, Marc landed beside the *Phoenix* a half hour later and waited for his passengers to disembark. Then he was airborne again to look for the Jet-Sled and pick up Buck and Iris.

***

The silver droid saw them coming and lowered the shields and blew the main hatch so they could board.

"Mistress Liana, Master Reb! How good it is to see you again. Where are the others?"

"They'll be along soon. Marc is ferrying us two by two because the sleds are too slow." Reb offered.

"Too slow, Master Reb? I don't understand." Fortuno insisted.

"You'll hear about it later, Fortuno," interjected Countess Liana. "Right now I want you to help me. We have to get this ship ready for flight. We'll need some additional manpower, too, Call the soldiers."

"My goodness! This is obviously no time for chitchat," chimed in the talkative droid. "Let's get to work, by all means!"

"Liana, please have Fortuno help you format our flight program. We must leave the planet's surface in precisely thirteen hours, fifteen minutes and ten seconds if we are to achieve warp drive before this graveyard blows itself to kingdom come!"

\*\*\*

Marc found the Jet-Sled without difficulty and quickly boarded Buck and Iris. Iris assumed a crouch position in the rear of the cockpit without protest. Digger was left to cruise along in the Jet-Sled containing Tootee and the Booloo until Marc got back.

Landing beside the *Phoenix*, Marc waited for his passengers to disembark and then was airborne in another minute.

Iris' handful of soldiers were waiting outside the *Phoenix* to greet their leader and it was a happy reunion indeed. Iris and Buck joined Reb and Liana in the flight preparations, while the soldiers were dispatched outside to work on the disabled engine and Fortuno was excused from his duties with Liana in order to go outside and supervise them.

This was the first time the silver droid had ventured outside the ship, his metallic composition having been too susceptible to the magnetic pull of the planet to permit him to venture outside the ship before. Now, free from the awful gravity, he tottered around happily, chattering orders at the soldiers as they picked up the scattered parts that had lain on the ground since the Booloos had abandoned their work, and began the task of reassembling the engine.

Marc landed beside the Jet-Sled one last time and was happy to note it had made good time across the plain now that it was travelling at full power, unhampered by an excessive gravitational pull. Digger helped him throw what was left of the ammo from several open crates into one single crate. Then they loaded it along with another sealed crate into the cargo area of the *Star Wind*, along with the small Booloo. Then, Tootee sat at his usual spot in back of the cockpit and Digger rode as co-pilot for the final trip home to the *Phoenix*. Marc thought it was unfortunate they had to leave two perfectly good sleds to be destroyed with the planet, but there was no time to worry about such insignificant losses.

This time, Marc landed the *Star Wind* in *Golden Phoenix's* docking port and Marc secured it carefully before unloading the cases of ammunition. Digger easily hefted the two crates and the trio walked aboard.

Reb met them in the open airlock and was pleased that they'd thought to bring along the remaining ammo.

They both followed Digger to the supplies locker. "I'll just do a quick inventory of what we've got left, since Fortuno is overseeing exterior repairs." Reb said, unlatching the first crate. While he was counting out grenades and thermal detonators something rattled the other sealed crate with a violence that made their eyes open in startled surprise.

Marc was already unlatching it when Reb restrained him, saying, "Wait. We don't know what's in there. Let's screen it first."

"I'm receiving very negative vibrations from it, whatever it is," muttered Marc.

Reb ran the scanner over the box and its heat-sensitive beam picked up a living form inside. "From the shape, I would say it's one of those night flying critters," he said. "Let's get it into a compressor bottle and place it in a cryo chamber, to take it back to Carrandon."

"How will we get it into the bottle?" asked Marc.

"Same way it got into the crate. We drill a small hole and put the neck of the bottle against it. The thing will squeeze through the same way it squeezed into the crate, thinking it's escaping, except that once it's in the bottle, we can seal it while we transport it back home!"

"Will it live in that way? Won't it use up all its oxygen and die?"

"Probably." Reb agreed. "Well, it sounded like a good idea at the time." Then he brightened. "Tell you what. We'll get it sealed into the bottle and then ask Fortuno to calculate its needs. If need be, we can run an oxygen line into the bottle. How's that?"

"Sounds good to me. I'll get the bottle and the drill, Reb. You stay with this thing to make sure it doesn't leave before I get back." Marc shouted to Digger to go fetch an empty compressor bottle and ran outside to confer with Fortuno who promptly provided him with a pneumatic mini-drill.

Reb and Marc donned their infra-red visors and set to work. They cut the hole and quickly placed the mouth of the bottle against it. The little creature slid through the opening and plopped into the bottle, instantly curling itself into a ball of light which bounced off the sides of the bottle in a frenzy to escape.

"Let's have Digger put this baby in the lab. Our scientists are going to be very excited over it, if we can get it back alive! They'll have a lot of fun learning about its source of energy, for one thing. Look at it zip around!" Reb laughed.

"Digger, put on your visors and get in here," called Marc on his communicator. The Prozoan did, and came loping back to the locker.

"Take this exhibit to the lab and spray the outside of the bottle with liquid photogrey so that anyone can observe the little fellow without visors and not burn their eyes."

"Wooooooo." the Prozoan agreed, and left with the bottle.

\*\*\*

Not five hours had gone by when Reb realized the *Phoenix* would never be ready for take-off within the allotted time. The engine needed a lot more work before it would function at all. Fortuno was giving hourly reaffirmations of the nuclear ripple effect that would disintegrate the planet in another twenty six hours.

"There must be a way to get this scrap heap in the air!" exclaimed Reb. He smashed his fist against the engine that was causing the problem. "I can't believe we've destroyed a powerful energy web only to discover that we are trapped in the wake of its own self-destruction."

"This is ridiculous!" grumbled Buck. "Seems we've been digging our own grave all this time, and we didn't know it."

"Let us continue with the repairs to that engine." Liana observed soberly. "If nothing else, it'll will keep our minds off our misery!"

Everybody knew Liana was right. The hours were dragging by. Everything aboard ship was in readiness. There was nothing to do but rewire, and solder, and bolt, and weld the disabled engine.

Then Fortuno announced it was T-minus five hours and counting. Their efforts had been in vain. They'd done everything right, but the engine would not fire. It appeared they were stranded on the surface of a planet that was going to die, and they along with it.

"I simply can't accept it!" Reb was overwrought. "Marc, call on Benja-Ko! Find us a solution, or we'll all die!"

Marc looked over at Iris. Theoretically the Light could lift this ship, but how high? He was reluctant to try it alone. The very idea of trying to levitate a star ship into space made him dizzy.

He closed his eyes and relaxed. The face of Benja-Ko appeared in his mind.

*"No! Not different from any other levitation. Think not of the weight. Relative is weight. Think not of size.*

*Relative is size. Remember you training. Believe!"* Marc remembered his Jaira training. He also remembered levitating the *Star Wind* out of that magnetic bog as though it had happened yesterday.

He opened his eyes. "I will need help from all of you. Except for Reb and Digger, that is." He assumed command. "I still have time to prepare you to levitate this ship. Every iota of your energy will be concentrated toward this achievement. You all have some experience with the Light and you know what I mean. We will gather in the lounge in five minutes and practice our relaxation techniques. We will limber up our minds with the levitation of small things in order to gain confidence. And in no time we will be levitating the ship!"

\*\*\*

Only one hour remained in the safe time frame they had in which to exit the planet. At Reb's request, Fortuno had conferred with the Booloo. The little creature had become very fond of Reb and, when it understood that the planet was about to self-destruct, eagerly agreed to remain aboard the ship and return with them to Carrandon.

"All the more reason to lift this flying junkyard off the planet," exclaimed Reb. "We'll be the talk of Carrandon with the specimens we're bringing back!"

Digger threw his head back and howled his indifference.

"Hey, Digger, what's the problem? You gotta go for the glory, you know?" grinned Reb. "Have faith, Digger. Isn't that what Marc says?"

\*\*\*

Marc, Liana, Buck and Iris entered the bridge, sat, and strapped themselves into their chairs. "My soldiers are in position," said Iris.

"Reb, broadcast the order." said Marc. "We are ready for takeoff. Have the droid, robot and Booloo take their positions, now!"

Reb did as his commander asked. A hush fell over the bridge.

"Now, relax, everybody." Marc said. "Do just as we've practiced. Don't let your thoughts drift. The ship is all you can see in your imagination. When we have a firm image of the ship, we will count to ten. Then we will lift. When the ship is off the ground we will push. Once we have pushed the Phoenix into orbit, Reb can fire his remaining good engine to hyper-drive and move us out to a safe distance in space."

The Jaira closed his eyes and the others followed suit. Within minutes they had all achieved a trance state. The energy gathered, grew, felt like a tangible thing. Reb and Digger closed their eyes and imagined the ship being lifted too. Every little bit would help.

The Light gathered above the ship and pulled until the *Phoenix* had levitated just off the ground. Then the Light enveloped the ship, pulling from above, pushing from below, moving it higher and higher. Their old campsite grew fainter and more distant, until the curve of the planet's horizon came up over *Phoenix's* starboard bow. Higher and higher she floated until she passed through the atmospheric shroud and entered orbit.

Reb felt the ship moving. He opened his eyes and saw that the group was not conscious in this realm. He poked Digger and indicated that it was time to go to work. He punched a button and his panel lit up. He checked his altitude and waited until orbit was achieved, then fired the remaining engine. Reviving to hyper-drive, the ship accelerated and shot out into space. They were already several light years away when their star chart registered a bright new star in the firmament. The Iron Planet had ceased to exist.

# CHAPTER TWENTY-FIVE

The heat was so intense that they could breathe only with great difficulty. The torrid air was vibrating in waves of heat, distorting their vision of the terrain on which they stood. A fine film of red sand covered everything, including the *Phoenix*. It was in their hair, on their eyelashes, in the cracks between their fingers and toes and under the perspiration soaked coveralls that they wore.

They had reached Gandra several hours earlier, with only one engine firing, and landed without incident on the smooth surface of the red desert. Their location was north of the floating, airborne city of Lamanda, seat of the court of Sadra the Tyrant. Through a pure stroke of genius, Fortuno had found the reason the reassembled engine wouldn't ignite. During their travel through space, en route to Gandra, Reb had ordered Fortuno to run a complete systems' check on the *Phoenix's* computerized circuitry and eventually located a relay circuit board, which had fused, causing the engine failure.

While the space ship rested on Gandra's surface the engine housing was unbolted and brought aboard the *Phoenix*, in order to avoid contamination with the sifting red sand, while Tootee and Fortuno repaired and tested the electrical relays. This gave everyone a chance to stretch their legs and visit some nearby caves on their remaining three Jet-Sleds. The petroglyphs were fascinating, but they were unfortunately not the caves containing the precious mineral Iris had spoken of. "This planet doesn't look all that much different from the Iron Planet, except that it's a lot sandier," said Reb. "I guess I've had enough adventures on barren planets to last me a lifetime or two." They all agreed heartily, especially Iris, who was desperately longing for a swim. There was much rejoicing when the *Phoenix* was finally given the green light, and they could look forward to completing their mission.

"The sooner we get to it, the sooner we go home!" announced Buck heartily, as everyone looked at him with mixed emotions.

They held a meeting of all the crew and soldiers and after much discussion over lunch in the ship's lounge, they formed a plan. They would leave that very day.

It was decided that Marc would take the *Star Wind* on a night mission. Flying low, with Iris as his navigator, he would slip in under Sadra's surveillance system and reconnoiter Lamanda, while the *Golden Phoenix* circled in orbit, well out of the Tyrant's range of detection.

Marc helped Iris into the cockpit and ran a routine check on its controls. Everything was in order. He saw Iris gazing at the horizon, transfixed, and paused at his work for a minute to look out the transparent canopy at a splendid sunset. "I think this is the most spectacular sunset I've ever seen," he acknowledged. A huge ball of crimson hung in the sky, just above the horizon, bathing the desert floor in gold, purple and amaranth.

"Whatever else might be wrong with this place, its sunsets are not one of them," he said with a smile. "Reminds me a little of Argalon, my home," he added, a hint of nostalgia in his voice.

"You chose an interesting moment to make nostalgic observations," Iris smiled in return. "We have a serious mission ahead of us, nevertheless, so perhaps we should think about getting underway."

Marc cast one last look at the setting orb and kicked over the engine. He adjusted the headpiece to his comset. "*Star Wind* to *Phoenix,* we are at T-minus thirty seconds. Stand by for takeoff. I'll keep in touch."

"Okay *Star Wind*," came back Reb's voice. "*Phoenix* will be in orbit before you're halfway there!"

\*\*\*

Koh's lifeless form sank to the floor. Clevia ducked behind a pillar, keeping out of sight of Sadra, who was in a demonic rage the likes of which she had never seen.

"Fools!" he screamed. "All I have for subjects is fools! You let them destroy my Iron Planet and get away with it!" He grabbed his precious jewel-encrusted chalice and crushed it in one hand, dropping the remains in disgust. His fingers were cut and blood was dripped off his talons, but he didn't take any notice. The towering, armoured Sydhar leader stood before him in silent obedience, his head bowed. The cyborg's half-organic, half-cybernetic compositions were programmed to know no fear, thus the giant remained unmoved in the knowlege of the cataclysmic destruc-tion of the Iron Planet.

"Surround them! I demand their capture!" ordered

the Tyrant. "Bring them all to me alive! I wish to observe them at close range and try to find out what makes them so invincible. I want to know why they have survived every test of death I have prepared for them!"

The Sydhar spoke. "Our surveillance network informs me that they are in our atmosphere at this time My Lord. Shall I set traps for them in case they try to land on Lamanda?"

"Yes! Do it!" cried Sadra. "When they have been captured, place them in the prison cells that we reserve for high security guests. Give them the special treatment. By the time I decide to see them, I want to find them in a humble, cooperative mood. Do you understand?"

"Yes, Master. I understand. It will be done as you command." The Sydhar bowed and backed out of the room.

"And see to it that you do not fail me this time!" Sadra yelled after him.

Easing his stocky body down onto the cushions, Sadra closed his eyes. He was very tired after all the excitement of losing his Iron Planet, not to mention The City of Lost Ships, which he considered to be his most prized museum of space technology. Behind closed lids he began to fantasize images of Iris and her companions, subjected to his cruel games, shedding blood, walking in fire... He opened his eyes again.

"Clevia, come here. Where are you? I know you're in here somewhere, Clevia dear!" It was a bad sign when he called her dear. The last time he had called her that, she'd spent two weeks in her bed recovering from the battering she'd taken. She reappeared quickly before he had to look for her.

"Yes, my Lord? I was just resting between the

pillars, looking at our exquisite sunset." She tried to hide her fear.

"Order the Sydhars to bring Mona's cage here. No, wait! I am bored with her. Come closer, Clevia. I keep forgetting how beautiful you are." She moved forward obediently and he put his hand on her shoulder and squeezed until it hurt. Clevia bit her lower lip in pain. He hooked a talon into the shoulder strap of her beautiful emerald gown and yanked. It slipped from her body, leaving her exposed and helpless.

Sadra drew a small, thin laser knife from his belt and began caressing her skin with its deadly tip. She winced with pain and held her breath. A few drops of blood appeared on her beautiful neck and full breasts as he traced lines with the blade, and she sighed and closed her eyes. She'd always known she would one day die at the hands of her cruel consort. She knew all consorts before her had met this fate. She wondered if this day was to be the last day of her life.

*** 

The *Star Wind* flew low over the desert as darkness fell. Wearing infra-red visors made everything as clear as day. Marc leaned back, letting the automatic pilot take over. He was thinking about their impending confrontation with the Tyrant. He thought about the paltry number of their party compared to the massive force of Sydhars which were stationed here. Marc knew he had the Light on his side, but still the fight promised to be very uneven. Princess Iris was silent, lost in her own thoughts. She knew her father's brain was somewhere on Lamanda, and she felt its vibrations strongly. Or thought she did. The sensations were so intense, she often wondered if she was imagining it. Was she losing her mind?

Marc looked down at the sea of sand below. A few shining stars twinkled on the horizon. He suddenly wished he'd brought Tootee along. He missed the little guy somewhat. The night hunters were out, searching for food. Nothing special was going on.

Marc had already turned his attention back to the console when he glimpsed something ahead in the dark. Adjusting his visor, he looked again. It was a city! Its countless lights, white copulas and spires were coming into full view. Marc blinked. "It's impossible!" he said aloud to Iris. "Lamanda is still an hour away."

Iris leaned forward, peering intently at the image.

"What is it?" Marc asked.

"Something is wrong." she replied thoughtfully. "Unless they changed the city's location, it shouldn't be here."

"Let's fly around it and check it out. It might be a trap." said Marc. "Could it be an illusion, or a mirage?"

"I don't understand this," said Iris nervously. "I sense nothing. Only emptiness."

They could see it more clearly now. The huge towers, the gravitational stabilizers all around the edges, the multi-color lights. Abruptly, a voice in his head screamed a warning. Suddenly the V-wing's red alert lights were blinking alarmingly.

"Iris! We are caught in a tractor beam!" Marc checked his console. "It's drawing us towards that city, or whatever it is. We can't break free! How could I be so stupid?" He hit his head with his fist in frustration.

Just then a flotilla of enemy fighters sprung from behind the city and flew straight at the *Star Wind*.

"Take evasive action!" cried Iris.

"Too late! There's no time. They've got us." Marc yelled back.

Enemy fighters were surrounding them. The illusion of the city began to fade and the dispersing fog gave Marc a clear picture of what really lay ahead. A huge battleship hovered where the city lights had shone only a moment ago. Now the V-wing was falling toward it, caught helplessly in the tractor beam of the big ship, unable to break free. The circle of fighters closed around *Star Wind* and Marc was overheating its engines in a futile attempt to break out of the tractor's grip. His mind was racing, only seconds separated them from being swallowed up by the battleship.

His throat was dry. He tried to speak to Iris but his voice was gone. Iris was shaking him by the shoulders, shouting, but Marc couldn't understand a word. The battleship was looming so large it filled his vision. His control board went dead, deactivated by the enemy as easily as though it were a child's toy.

Marc realized they were beyond escape. He swallowed with great difficulty, sweat pouring off his temples. Iris tapped him on the shoulder. She was composed in spite of the tragic situation at hand. He felt ashamed of himself. She smiled at him. He smiled back, feeling almost happy that she was with him. He decided to meet his fate with a tranquillity Benja-Ko would be proud of.

The *Star Wind* glided gently into the docking port of the huge battleship. Marc could see hundreds of fully armed Sydhar guards waiting for them to disembark.

"This is a nice mess I've gotten us into," said Marc through clenched teeth.

He put up a good fight, but his laser sword wasn't enough to fend off the Sydhars that came at him from all sides. Now, bruised and aching, he stumbled along between the guards who were dragging him into the cell block.

"I never thought we would be defeated so easily," murmured Iris from behind.

"I guess we thought we were invincible." Marc said. "If I hadn't panicked and froze, I could have called the *Phoenix* for help."

They were tossed into an austere metal room and watched as the guards retreated and swung the heavy door shut with a clang.

"Well," murmured Iris, as she dusted herself off and pulled herself to a sitting position on the cot. "The situation is difficult, but we might still turn it to our advantage."

"Right," replied Marc sarcastically, "any minute now we'll mutiny and take over this battleship and fly it to Lamanda where we'll destroy the Tyrant with a couple of thermal bombs!"

"I'm serious, Marc." she pulled him up beside her and brushed his cheek with concern. "We are not going to Lamanda the way we planned, but we are going there. We will undoubtedly have an audience with Sadra, and isn't that what we wanted?"

"Well, you must forgive me for being a wet blanket, but this isn't exactly what I had in mind," Marc responded in a dour tone.

"Wait 'til you see the city, though, Marc!" she enthused. "When you look at it, it will be hard for you to imagine it as the home of such an evil ruler. In our culture there are legends about this floating marvel." She closed her eyes and a wonderous expression came over her face as though she were remembering her childhood again.

Marc put his arm around her and kissed her gently on the cheek. "When we conquer Sadra and his army, this city will be your playground once again," he said, looking at her tenderly.

She turned her head and looked deep into his eyes. He wanted to kiss her on the mouth, to crush her frail dark beauty in a passionate embrace. But a Jaira is an honorable man, and Iris was Buck's girl now.

"... and before all else, I must solve the mystery of my father's missing head, Marc. I don't know what is the matter with me... don't know what I am sensing." He realized she had been speaking to him. Then a cold look came into her eyes.

"Excuse me, I can't imagine what got into me for a moment. I keep thinking my father is still alive. I can sense him. I feel he is not too far from us." She looked at him quizzically. "I hope you don't think I've lost my sanity, but the feeling of his presence is growing stronger and stronger with each minute."

"Of course I don't think you're crazy, Iris. But you've been through a great deal..." his thought trailed off as he rocked her gently back and forth in the crook of his arm.

\*\*\*

The *Phoenix* orbited Gandra for a time, with the communications open and waiting for a message from Marc. When none came, Reb grew increasingly preoccupied. Finally, Liana sensed that Marc and Iris were greatly stressed and in danger. With Buck's help, she persuaded Reb to take the *Phoenix* down to Lamanda and see if they could fly close enough for her to communicate telepathically with Marc. Unfortunately, the *Phoenix* was lured towards the same mirage, and caught helplessly in that same awful tractor beam.

"Oh, no! Reb cursed under his breath. "We can probably escape from this tractor, but it will be at the risk of burning out our power plant! Blast!" He pointed at the screen. "How about that, Liana? The city was only a hallucinogenic disguise for their battleship! What fools we are! If I'd suspected a trap, I'd have travelled with shields up!"

"Let's go to three-quarters power and see if we can shake them," suggested Buck.

"Digger, you heard the man, fire the boosters to three-quarters thrust power and take evasive action," ordered Reb.

Several minutes went by as the *Golden Phoenix* shuddered uselessly as it tried to jerk free of the restraining tractor beam. Then the Prozoan roared loudly and Fortuno made his report.

"Master Reb, I'm afraid your instrumentation is showing an overheating status. It's moving into yellow alert, Master Reb. It is advisable to cut your engines at once!" Fortuno's voice rose in panic.

"Chill out, Fortuno, the Captain knows what he's doing..." Liana spoke urgently. "Reb, I sense Marc and Iris are in that battleship. We have come to exactly the right place to rescue them. If we don't fight the tractor, it will pull us in."

"Okay, I'm game. Digger, cut all engines!" Reb hollered. An abrupt silence followed as Digger powered down.

"Reb, when we disembark, let's leave Fortuno and Tootee aboard to secure the ship. The Booloo can stay on board too, if it pleases. Ask Fortuno to talk to it," Liana suggested, and turned to Buck.

"Salladian, do me a favor and alert the soldiers. We're about to be taken prisoners by the battleship. Have them leave all their arms behind, since they're probably going to be stripped of them, anyway."

Buck took off at a fast stride and Reb turned to Liana. "No arms? Hey, that's a bird-brained suggestion if ever I heard one, Countess. My idea is that we follow the soldiers out and let them exit the ship, blasting our way through as many of those cyborgs as we can, on the way."

"Those Sydhars can paralyze us in an instant, Reb, and you know it," she snapped back at him. "But go ahead, turkey, arm the soldiers and enter the battleship with blazers blasting away, don't let this bird-brain stop you!"

Reb laughed at her spunk and called to Buck as he re-entered the bridge, "Change of plans, Buck. We're going to let the soldiers lead the way with weapons blazing, while we try to make a run for it. Maybe one of us can get to the battleship's control room and take over."

"Sounds like a lame idea to me, Reb, but you're the Captain!" retorted Buck, "I'll tell the soldiers to arm themselves.

"Liana, you tell Fortuno that after we leave, he's to pressure-seal the ship as soon as the last man's off. I don't want those Sydhar creeps to stomp around in here and trash my instrumentation."

\*\*\*

The soldiers made a good showing of it, storming off the ship after it was secured in its landing port. Several dozens of the cyborgs were cut down by blaster fire for every Hydran who fell. They were well trained, and valiant, just as Iris had claimed. But the Sydhars outnumbered them a hundred to one, and ultimately the revolutionaries were defeated.

Stunned in one shoulder, and suffering the dreaded paralysis from emitter fire, Reb saw the foolishness of his ways. Throwing down his weapon, he looked around at his ragged crew and at the soldiers lying dead or wounded. Next to go would surely be one of them. He couldn't have Liana's death on his hands, much less Buck or Digger.

Smiling ruefully at the cyborgs, Reb put his hands on top of his head cooperatively while motioning to the others to do the same. They were thus marched off to a cell block and locked up.

"What a mess!" snorted Salladian. "That's the last time I'll let you lead me into battle, Captain! I wonder how many of Iris' soldiers will stay alive to tell the tale?"

"Buck, Reb did what he felt was required under the circumstances. It was a bad call, but we all goof up now and again." Suddenly Liana was protective of her man. "Fortunately, the little Booloo chose to remain with Fortuno and Tootee, aboard the relative safety of the *Golden Phoenix*. I'm so glad they weren't with us!"

"You'll excuse me if I'm more worried about the four of us than I am about the soldiers or the Booloo," said Reb. "In the event everyone has been so busy blaming me that you've failed to notice, we're locked up, our blasters are gone, and we're not anywhere closer to finding Reb and Iris!"

"Calm yourself," Liana replied with a stern look at him. "How can I transmit with you losing control and disturbing my concentration? I'm still very new to working with the Light, you know."

"Yeah, give the little lady a chance," Buck intervened. "There's nothing either of us brilliant strategists can do right now, so we might as well conserve our strength and see what happens."

"Okay, Your Highness," Reb gave Liana a little bow. "You heard the man. Do your thing. Send your mind forth and find your brother."

Liana sat on a cot with her legs crossed and her back to the wall and counted herself silently into a trance, the way Iris had taught.

Reb lowered his voice and spoke to the Prozoan and Buck. "I've never had much liking for crowded places." He tried to pace but couldn't do it without tripping over the Prozoan's long legs. He looked around. There was obviously no way out. He wondered where they were being taken and why they had not yet been beaten or paralyzed by the Sydhars.

"I think we're being saved for something," he began.

"Yeah. No doubt for someone's dinner!" Buck was in no mood to talk. Reb lapsed into silence and no one spoke for a long time.

Liana opened her eyes. "I have good news and bad news," she said. "The good news is that Marc and Iris are unharmed. The bad news is that they are also imprisoned in a cell and Iris thinks we will all be taken to Lamanda as prisoners of the Tyrant."

"Might as well grab forty winks until we get there, then," said Buck dryly. "Will you join me in a nap, Sir?" He poked the Prozoan playfully and leaned against him, closing his eyes.

\*\*\*

They felt the ship land with a jolt. "We're on Lamanda, I know it!" said Iris breathlessly.

An escort of Sydhar guards marched up to the cell and waited while it was opened. Marc and Iris were roughly pushed out into the passage and the guards changed formation so that Marc and Iris were forced to walk along between them. Four Sydhars marched in front and four in back. Marc felt for his laser sword and then remembered they had taken it away, along with his and Iris' blasters. Ceremoniously they were marched out onto a great ramp and the lights of the city almost blinded them after the many hours in a dark prison cell.

Lamanda was impressive, all right. Marc saw that the real city was far more beautiful than the illusion that had trapped them earlier. The city was a rainbow of lights twinkling in a sea of darkness as the disc-shaped island floated majestically on the night sky. A few clouds drifted above them, descending from time to time like a gossamer veil.

\*\*\*

At last, they were marched into the very heart of the enemy fortress. After descending a long, lighted tunnel, they were taken to another cell, a large one, and pushed inside unceremoniously. The heavy door swung shut with frightening finality.

Then it abruptly opened again to admit the rest of the human prisoners.

"Liana! I'm sorry you were captured too, but we were very glad to learn of your presence," Marc walked over and hugged his sister, clapping Reb on the bicep.

Buck moved to Iris and took her in his arms without a sound, crushing her in his protective embrace.

"Cut it out, you two!" Reb said gruffly. "This isn't a honeymoon hotel, you know."

"Don't be insensitive, Dear," chided Liana. "He's just jumpy because we're in it up to our necks again," she apologized.

The revolutionaries settled into a gloomy quiet. No sound penetrated the walls of their windowless cell. Iris and Buck sat side by side, holding hands. Liana and Reb were trying to pace and constantly bumped into each other, not to mention other people's feet and Digger's legs.

# Chapter Twenty-Six

Marc willed himself to remain calm. He stood by the cell door, arms folded, eyes closed, and meditated. Opening his eyes slowly as if awakening from a dream, he looked around.

"I can sense the Tyrant's presence very close to us," he said to nobody in particular. "Since the death of Emperor Drakkor, I've never sensed another entity so cold and cruel. His vile goal is to destroy everything in the universe that is positive and good. Perhaps there is truth to the Urfee legend about an evil legacy. I don't mean to offend you, Iris. But I'm wondering if latent genes were awakened to evil in that individual and if they could awaken again in another of his kind."

Marc shifted his weight and placed his hands on his hips and said, "Instead of using up our energies on pointless frustrations, we must build our strength and be ready for whatever challenges confront us. I sense the final confrontation is close. We will need to be strong because the only weapon we have against him is the Light."

Liana and Reb stopped pacing and turned to look at Marc with interest. "Do you have a plan?" asked Reb hopefully.

"Yes. I want to use this time to train all of you in using the Light. Especially you, Reb. Our success or failure may depend on the strength of one man more or less. We can't afford not to train you!"

Hope died in Reb's eyes. "I doubt you can make a magician out of me," he said. "But I'm willing to do whatever you say."

Marc sat on a narrow bench against one wall. "Okay," he said. "In order to perceive the Light you have to relax very deeply. Don't try to see it or hear it. Let yourself feel it all around you and even inside you. You can generate and store a big supply of this force inside your own body and use it for healing purposes or to accomplish levitation, not to mention materializing objects in order to confuse or influence others. Reb was watching him intently. He continued.

"The Light can supply you with everything you need for survival. Light, food, protection, etc., so long as you learn how to cooperate with it. Your mind is the key. With your mind you can shape the Light to do your bidding and make so-called miracles happen. However, be aware that there is no such thing as a miracle. Everything occurs according to the laws governing the Light. These laws are known only to the Jairas and to a few wise men in this universe."

Everybody was listening to him intently now. Marc licked his dry lips and said. "Liana, come forward, please." he gestured and waited until she was beside him. "I would like to teach you all something practical which I will demonstrate at the same time. So sit beside me and relax. Tell me what you most desire at this moment?" he asked his sister.

"Oh, there are dozens of things I could think of, but I believe I'll ask for a zeppel because they're so delicious." She looked at Iris. "Perhaps you are familiar with this fruit. It grows on Carrandon."

"Very good." said Marc approvingly. Everyone can do this exercise with me. Pick your own favorite fruit." He looked around at their rapt faces. "Now close your eyes and relax. Go deeper into relaxation... Deeper." A few seconds passed and Liana breathed deeply and slowly, a peaceful expression adorning her pale face.

"Good. Now, in your imagination I want you to picture your favorite, delicious, juicy fruit. Build the picture until it is perfect in every detail. Concentrate on that picture. Don't let it out of focus in your mind. See its color, feel its texture and remember its smell. Taste the sweet-tart flavor on your tongue. The final result depends on your accuracy at this point. The quality of your fruit will depend on the quality of your work. Hold the image firmly in your mind. Now project it outward. Stretch out your hands. Imagine that you are holding the fruit in the palms of your hands. They all stretched out their hands, palms up.

"Very good!" said Marc. "Now recall the image of your fruit and fill that image with the Light. Charge it with the Light."

A few seconds passed in complete silence. "Okay, people, open your eyes, now!" he commanded.

They did as he suggested and the little cell filled with assorted murmurs and gasps. On Liana's palm rested a delicious, red zeppel. On Iris' palm was a grape-like orange cluster of crikkos. Reb sat, open-mouthed, as he gazed in disbelief at his own banana-like tucorfo. And Digger howled and dropped his branch of eucapapas buds in surprise, as if it had burned him. Marc laughed. "Eat hearty, my friends. You've all just performed your first 'miracle'."

"What fun!" giggled Liana, sinking her teeth into the tasty fruit. "Want a bite?" she asked, handing it proudly to Marc.

\*\*\*

Marc tossed violently on his cot. He was suffocating, gasping for air, unable to pull enough of the precious element into his lungs. Something heavy was weighing him down, crushing his chest. He felt hot and faint. He inhaled in gasps and he was in a void. His lungs ached and were close to bursting.

Suddenly an excruciating pain invaded his body. He was paralyzed! He felt the flesh torn from his bones. He was dying. His hair stood on end in horror. He looked for his friends. They were writhing on the floor in convulsions.

The pain clouded his thoughts. He couldn't think straight. Then, in a flash it came to him. He understood everything. They were being tortured. He could sense the ultrasound waves that caused this incredible pain. The oxygen must have been sucked from their small room.

*"What can I do? I must do something!"* Marc thought helplessly. He saw Princess Iris lying a foot away. There was blood on her lips from where she bit into them in pain. Her eyes were open wide and glowed with such a deep blue that they almost looked black. Pain distorted her beautiful face.

Marc couldn't bear to see her suffer like this. Then, before he could begin to build a shield of Light around her, he gasped in horror as her flesh began to part, exposing bloody tissue and bones. Her beautiful face crumbled and disintegrated. Marc saw the panic and despair in her eyes just before they started to shrivel, too. He was too terrified to scream. He couldn't make a sound. He looked down in disbelief as the flesh began to peel from his own bones.

*"If I have to die. I will die with dignity. But not like this…"* he pleaded silently. *"Benja-Ko… help me, not like this!"*

His companions were suffering the same ordeal. Somebody was screaming. Marc felt sick. He closed his eyes. He couldn't look any more. He was going to throw up. Another wave of pain crushed his chest and he passed out with relief.

\*\*\*

The first thing Marc noticed when he woke up was that he was breathing without restriction. Then he realized he was not in pain. He passed his hands along his arms and across his chest. He was in one piece! His skin felt cool and smooth. He opened his eyes in disbelief. He was as undamaged as if nothing had happened at all.

*"Another illusion?"* thought Marc, as he remembered the vision of Lamanda.

He sat up and looked around. His friends were still out cold. Princess Iris lay on the floor with arms outstretched as if begging for help. Her lips were slightly parted, her breathing uneven and feverish. Marc leaned over her and brushed away the locks of dark hair falling across her face.

*"Why do I always fall in love with the wrong woman?"* Marc thought sadly. Iris stirred and opened her eyes, which were still darkened with fright and fever. Marc caressed her hair and propped her up into a sitting position. She looked at him with a haunted expression and a tear rolled out of one eye and down her cheek.

"It was only a bad dream," he whispered. She sighed, closed her eyes and went back to sleep as peacefully as a little child.

Several days went by and each day there was a session of psychological torture to endure. The revolutionaries' strength and determination was slowly breaking down.

"When will they take us to Sadra?" asked Iris impatiently.

"Yeah, we're not much of a threat to him in our present state." added Reb ironically. "How can we hope to overthrow him and defeat his army of Sydhars with our bare hands?"

"Stay cool, Reb. This is no time for a fight." Marc warned. "Our only chance lies in the Light and in our unity."

As he was speaking, the door of their cell sprung open noiselessly. A dozen Sydhars surrounded them with weapons pointed at their heads, almost touching their temples. The revolutionaries knew this was no time to try to make a move for freedom, so they offered no resistance.

They didn't have far to walk. In the next rotunda stood a large cage made of some transparent material. They were herded into the cage by the Sydhars, who secured the door behind them. Through the transparent walls of the cage, the revolutionaries could see the Sydhar's activity and it seemed as though they were preparing for something.

"What are they up to?" whispered Liana.

Marc shivered, he sensed something unpleasant was coming, but he couldn't guess what it might be. Countess Liana took his hand and squeezed it empathetically. He could feel her trembling.

"I don't know whether I can take much more of this," she murmured in a small choked voice. "Why don't they just kill us and get it over with?"

"I think their objective is to humiliate us, first," replied Marc sadly. "Let's try not to give them that satisfaction."

Countess Liana sighed with resignation.

"There is no way to break through the wall of this cage without my blaster," growled Reb, as he examined their new prison.

"What are they waiting for?" snarled Buck.

"I don't like any of this," growled Reb.

The Sydhar guards, meanwhile, stood motionless around the cage, never taking their eyes off the prisoners.

"What are you staring at?" yelled Buck, yielding suddenly to the pressure and smashing his fist against the transparent wall.

A faint noise reached their ears that reminded them of the buzzing of a thousand bees in the hive. Princess Iris grew as pale as a sheet and her warm amber skin turned ashen. "Flesh-devouring insects! I know their buzz!" she cried. The noise was getting stronger.

"Tell me about the insects," demanded Marc as he shook her to get her attention. She appeared to be convulsing with fear. "There must be some way to fight them," he pleaded and looked at her hopefully.

She gained control of herself. "Perhaps with the

Light," she stopped. The first of the buzzing insects entered through slotted openings in the back of the cage. "They drill into the living flesh and devour it so fast that it only takes minutes to reduce the victim to a skeleton," she whispered.

"Let's build ourselves a shield with the Light," suggested Marc hurriedly. The insects were already buzzing around their heads, the air thickening with more of them every second. The whole place resonated with their buzzing and Digger howled in fear.

"We have to be efficient about this," whispered Marc. "I have never cared much for the idea of being eaten alive." He dodged a large insect that flew straight at his face.

Countess Liana gasped and cried out in alarm as a dozen of the things landed on her exposed arm. She shook her arm frantically, but the insects wouldn't let go. The situation was obviously critical.

\*\*\*

Behind the row of Sydhars stood Ardano Ad Sadra with a smug look of satisfaction on his face. He observed his victims' reactions carefully, taking great pleasure in the thought of their suffering and death.

The revolutionaries stood, back to back, in a circle, swatting at the flying insects and trying to hold them at bay. Thin trickles of blood were already streaming from Iris' and Buck's necks, faces and arms. Any exposed area of flesh was a prime target for the insects. Then Countess Liana fell to her knees, covering her face with her hands. Reb Morningstar fell upon her, in an attempt to shield her with his own body. He was clearly taking

304

the brunt of the attack.

It was then that Sadra observed a bluish-white cupola of shimmering light growing stronger around the unfortunate prisoners. The insects couldn't seem to penetrate it. Sadra lifted his hand and gave a signal.

"That's enough for today," he commanded. "I don't want them killed just yet. They might be more entertaining than I thought. And, of course, there is my unfinished business with Princess Iris." He laughed unpleasantly.

"Come, my dear," he turned to Clevia. She was dressed in a gown that entirely covered her arms and shoulders to hide the wounds and bruises her consort had inflicted on her the other night. Half way to the exit, Sadra turned back. "Prepare our guests for the Arena," he shouted. The chief officer of the Sydhars bowed his head in mute obedience.

\*\*\*

The Arena was more like an enormous stadium. Tiers of seats surrounded the field and most of them were already occupied. Everyone was waiting for the Tyrant and his court to arrive.

Ardano Ad Sadra was late, and the audience was growing impatient. The performers on stage below tried in vain to entertain the waiting crowd, but their efforts were ignored. The rabble began whistling and stamping their feet in unison, creating an incredible noise. They wanted the main event, and they wanted it now!

When Sadra finally appeared on the scene, borne aloft on his elaborate throne, the noise died abruptly. Every one of his subjects feared the Tyrant, and even the bravest among them dared do nothing to displease him.

The Tyrant clapped his hands, giving a sign to the Sydhars to let the games begin. A small door at the far end of the Arena opened, and Marc, Reb, Buck and Digger were pushed out into the field. It was very bright and they stood there for a moment, blinking and trying to accustom their eyes.

Marc, Reb, and Buck were all outfitted with shiny golden armour- plate and Marc was given his laser sword. Reb and Buck had been equipped with ancient swords and the Prozoan had only his bare hands.

"Sadra must be a collector of antiques," commented Buck, looking at his sword curiously.

"I'm afraid everyone will be disappointed with my lack of jousting skills," remarked Reb as he looked at the crowd who were applauding wildly. "Looks like we're the top draw attraction," he added.

Marc wondered what they had done with Liana and Iris. He scanned the bleachers to see if they were in the crowd.

A rumbling noise was heard just then and a large gate on the other side of the Arena was thrown open. The audience screamed with delight. Seven huge, dark, hairy beasts emerged onto the lighted field, to the roar of the crowd. They were disoriented by the brightness of the stadium lights and beat their hooves on the sandy ground, as they lowered their horned heads and flexed their wide wings.

Two of the largest of the beasts carried Countess Liana and Iris strapped to their backs. Liana was sobbing with humiliation and Iris was trying unsuccessfully to preserve her dignity. She flashed a telepathic message to Marc.

"Those beasts are called turrons, and they are

deadly." he relayed the message to his companions. "We must rescue the ladies before they are shaken off and stomped or gored to death."

Just then the turrons noticed the group of men at the far end of the Arena and charged at full speed. Marc drew his laser sword and Reb and Buck readied themselves for defence with their archaic swords.

The turrons attacked. Their wings beat wildly as they thrust themselves into the group of revolutionaries with a blood-curdling war cry. The audience went wild. The attackers were so fast that Marc barely managed to stop the onslaught just inches from his head.

Reb fell to the ground and rolled away to avoid the curved horns. Buck wasn't so fortunate. He was knocked off balance by the beat of a powerful wing and quickly scrambled back onto his feet, blood gushing from a wound in his shoulder. The crowd roared.

Digger howled and grabbed a turron by the wing, dragging it to the ground. But the beast righted itself easily and shook off its attacker. Digger was undeterred, however, and got another stronghold on the wing. The beast lifted the wing and Digger sailed into the air, making an attempt to jump onto the turron's back. The turron was bucking and slashing at him with his sharp horns, but Digger would not give up. He clung stubbornly to the beast and hefted his hairy body to a mounted position on the turron's back.

Marc, meanwhile, managed to sweep one of the beasts with a clean blow of his laser sword that cut off its hooved feet. The turron fell with an awful groan, then beat its powerful wings and flew to the attack again.

Another turron, carrying Countess Liana on its back,

was hovering above Marc's head. Liana let out a sharp cry as the turron dropped like a stone toward its intended victim. Marc managed to leap aside in the nick of time, simultaneously slicing the first turron in half with his laser sword.

Reb Morningstar took full advantage of the situation. The moment Liana's mount touched the ground he jumped astride it, landing behind Liana. The applause and hoots from the crowd were deafening. Reb squeezed the beast with his knees and put a protective arm around Liana.

Digger was also emerging victorious from his struggle with the turron. In spite of the incredible strength of the beast, Digger had managed to ride it, bucking, to exhaustion.

Buck was in trouble. He fell to the ground again and again as one of the mighty turrons bucked and kicked him down each time he tried to stand up.

Princess Iris had pretty well succumbed to her role as victim until she saw Buck's plight and remembered herself and her powers. She projected her mind into the core of the brain of the beast that carried her and, under her influence, it flew down and viciously attacked the turron that was mutilating Buck. The fight between the two turrons was violent and to the death. Iris clung to her mount, directing it with her mind, and did not relax until her beast had fatally wounded the other with a bite to the throat.

The dying turron gave a mighty roar and rolled its eyes upwards as it sunk lifelessly to the ground. The Arena resounded with wild applause. Iris gave a victory cry of her own and directed her turron to attack its next opponent. Although exhausted by Digger's ride, it still fought back valiantly until it succumbed to another death bite to the throat.

That left four. Buck collected himself despite the ache in his ribs and fought, back to back with Reb, slashing at the circling airborne beasts. Marc's laser sword was losing its charge and the light within was growing smaller and weaker. He decided to follow Iris' example. The turrons' primitive minds were easy to influence. *"Why didn't I think of this earlier?"* Marc admonished himself. *"Iris has found the solution! We don't need to fight these beasts! All we need to do is control their minds and turn them against each other!"*

Looking up, he said. "Great work, Iris. Now, let's see if I can give you a hand."

With his mind, he brought one of the beasts down and made it lay on the sand. Then he did the same with another, and another until all of the four remaining turrons were on the ground with their wings folded quietly. Reb and Liana dismounted, and Buck limped over to take Iris' hand and help her down, as Marc knelt beside one of the beasts and scratched it behind one ear.

The audience was whipped into a frenzy. Screaming. Clapping. Stomping their feet. The noise was overpowering. Then they began leaving their seats and running toward the victors.

"You see? And you thought you had no aptitude for this stuff!" Marc cried to Reb. "They're crazy about us! They both laughed with relief.

# CHAPTER TWENTY-SEVEN

Sadra paced his chamber angrily. "This is the first time in the history of my reign that something like this has occurred!" he yelled with outrage. "And once is enough! I'll put an end to their cleverness. Bring them to me, at once!"

The Sydhar guard moved quickly to carry out Sadra's orders. The Tyrant felt as though he had received an unpardonable insult. His plan to humiliate the rebel group in front of his subjects had failed. Instead of ending up defeated and humbled by the experience, they had emerged triumphant and victorious. Sadra could never forgive them for that.

"I'll show them who has the last word on this planet," he mumbled coldly as he tightened his fists. Dangerous glints shone in his evil eyes. "I will create another surprise for them. And what a surprise! Once I extract the information I seek from them, they will join all the others." The Tyrant's lips twisted in a cruel grimace as he seated himself on his throne and waited.

The door to his chamber opened and the prisoners were brought in. Disarmed, with dirty faces and torn clothing, and smeared with dirt and blood, they didn't look very brave. A cordon of Sydhars marched in formation around them, weapons drawn, ready to paralyze the whole bunch of them at the first suspicious move.

Sadra motioned and the revolutionaries were pushed closer to the throne.

"Welcome to Lamanda, my dear guests," he began expansively in a hearty voice. "I certainly have admired your courage in coming here. Just yourselves and a handful of inept soldiers hoping to overthrow me and my powerful army. Very brave, but very foolish."

He looked keenly at Iris. "And you, my dear Princess, must be the leader of this unfortunate escapade. I have looked forward to meeting you for a very long time. You are not nearly as beautiful as your reputation promises, you know. Perhaps all you need is to bathe and dress, and anoint yourself with perfume and jewels, then you may live up to your legend. But right now, my dear, you look like something the turrons dragged in!" He threw his head back and laughed heartily.

"My soldiers...?" she hesitated.

"Your paltry collection of soldiers were either mortally wounded or imprisoned on the battleship, my dear. Except for my favourite informer, Major Roold who was the unfortunate victim of a catastrophe at sea that killed one hundred of my best cyborgs. But we are deviating from the point of your visit."

He settled back and composed himself complacently. "To get to the point and tell you why I have brought you here. There is some information I would like you to share with me, Princess Iris. Your family has sacrificed much, in fact they have sacrificed themselves one by one, to protect the Secret of Hydra and guard it from me. Now I

311

am ready to hear it from your own lips."

"I will never tell. You are an impostor! I am the true ruler of this realm, succeeding in my father's place," she answered defiantly.

"Come, come, my dear. I can ask the Sydhars to punish you until you give in, you know. Would you like another session with their emitters?"

"You can kill me as you have killed my family," she haughtily replied. "But I will never reveal the Secret that is entrusted to me."

"Oh, I think you will," Sadra replied, wearing something akin to a smile. "I can be very persuasive at times." He chuckled softly and winked at her. "I have a very special surprise for you, my dear. And I also have something to show you that very few people, apart from my closest confidants, know about. I promise you will be impressed."

Sadra rose from his throne. "If you wish to cooperate with me of your own free will, after seeing my surprise, I will be very appreciative. I may even free your soldiers so that they might return to their families on Hydra. Follow me." He grasped Princess Iris by the elbow and steered her towards the door, indicating to the Sydhars that they were to escort the other prisoners, and follow.

"You deceive yourself, Ardano Ad Sadra, if you think I could ever be persuaded to cooperate with the likes of you," she hissed at him in disgust. The Tyrant squeezed her elbow and she bit her lip and winced with pain. But she walked proudly, her head held high.

\*\*\*

They entered a large chamber illuminated with brilliant lights. At first it seemed empty. Only a wide, black console stood in the middle of the room. But then they noticed the walls were covered with thousands of small illuminated balls mounted tightly next to one another and connected with multi-coloured cables. Each ball seemed to bear an engraving, which they weren't close enough to read.

"Do you know what this is?" asked the Tyrant with a proud smile. "This is the largest Brain Bank computer in the galaxy. It is millions of times more efficient than any electronic device ever invented. It gives me a power over my star system that will eventually extend to the New Democracy and beyond. Look!" he cried, as he punched a button on the console.

\*\*\*

The silver balls lit up and became transparent. Their contents were thus exposed to view. Within the balls, thousands of human and more highly evolved non-human brains lay captive, imprisoned in the silvery cells in which they floated in an organic liquid life support system.

"They are alive, and they are working for me day and night. This is the most powerful Brain Bank ever devised," he repeated proudly.

The group of revolutionaries stood in horrified awe, too overcome to speak.

"He is insane," Princess Iris finally whispered.

"Don't make a rash judgement, my dear," the Tyrant said. "One of these brains may be of special interest to you." He waved for them to follow and walked to a portion of the vast wall.

313

"Step along, my dear. I invite you to read the inscription on this particular cell."

She leaned forward and obediently read aloud.

"King Handor of the noble house of Odman of Hydra V.," she began to stammer and looked as if she might faint. But suddenly she turned on Sadra with clenched fists. "You will pay for this, and for every other evil thing you have ever done, with your own life!" she whispered in a voice filled with such hate that the Tyrant involuntarily took a step back.

But Iris was too shattered by this revelation to summon the Light. She hid her face in her hands and wept. "Father!" she cried. "I will avenge your murder. You won't be this despicable tyrant's helpless pawn for much longer!"

The brain of King Handor Odman recognized a familiar brainwave, and knew it was his daughter. He used the only power to communicate that he had left. He spoke to her telepathically.

Iris, said his thought impulse.

*"Don't concern yourself about me. I am beyond saving. But together we can destroy him. Be patient, my daughter. Keep the Secret."*

Iris lowered her hands and lifted her face. She gazed, transfixed at what remained of her beloved father. The color flowed back into her face. She turned and smiled at the Tyrant. All her anger and frustration were transformed into a powerful charge of the Light which could kill a normal being. But she knew Sadra was all too familiar with negative charges of the Light, and was not surprised when he caught it in his own field and reversed its flow.

Then the Tyrant laughed and waved a signal to the

Sydhars to intervene, and the giants obediently fired their weapons, immobilizing the revolutionaries. Two of them grasped Iris and suspended her between them.

"You have made a very unwise and foolish move, my dear," said the Tyrant with false blandness. "And now you will tell me the Secret so jealously guarded by your family." He lifted her chin and tilted her face up to his.

"I would rather die," Princess Iris hissed back at him violently.

"That can be arranged, my dear," replied Sadra in the same congenial tone. "Or perhaps we could dispose of this beautiful body of yours and add your brain to my magnificent collection." He waved his hand expansively around the room. "I do have a few cells still vacant and I could easily accommodate all six of you."

He threw the stunned revolutionaries a cursory glance. "And so, my dear Princess, it is really in your best interests to become more talkative."

She opened her mouth to speak, her face twisted into an expression of darkest loathing.

"No! Wait!" Sadra cut her off. "I want you to be in full possession of the details before you decide." He squeezed her chin painfully. Her eyes shone out of her pale face like two pools of molten lava. In the brief silence that followed, only the heavy breathing of the excited Tyrant could be heard.

"My dear, I also host many other members of your illustrious family. Here is your little brother, Orlan, and your elder sister, Negari. She was of great service to me during the past few years." He laughed an evil cackle. "She was a good sport, that girl. When she was still in her physical body, we had lots of fun together."

Marc was regaining the feeling in his limbs. Because his perception had remained sharp during his period of paralysis, he knew the Tyrant was humiliating Iris in an attempt to bring her to the breaking point. When she lost interest in life, when she no longer cared about anything, then he would extract her Secret.

Marc read terror in the girl's eyes and he sensed she would not withstand much more of Sandra's macabre taunting. He realized he was still in love with Iris, and would do anything, even sacrifice his own life, to save her.

He closed his eyes and reached out with his mind, touching her. She was feeling great confusion, panic and shame, in place of her usual pride and self-composure. He was aware of the paralyzing power the Sydhars had over his body, so he didn't entertain the thought of attempting any physical confrontation at this time.       .

Voicelessly, with his thoughts, he called out to the princess. *"Iris! Iris! Hear me!*

*I have a plan. Try to buy us some more time. Play along with the Tyrant for now ... "*

He repeated his message over and over again. At last, a spark of understanding came into her eyes. She blinked once, and looked at him. *"Yes. Time"*, was all he heard telepathically in reply.

"My dear Princess," the Tyrant coaxed, "how can I persuade you to change your mind?" A cruel smile accompanied his next words. "Perhaps I should switch off the life support systems to the brains of your family members?" He dropped his hand to the console and rested one talon lightly upon the numbered key controlling her father's nutrient bath. "We can start with your father. But first, let me demonstrate." He moved his finger to another

316

key and cancelled the nutrient bath to a random storage cell. The lights in one of the balls went out and bubbles of oxygen escaped from the clear liquid in which rested the brain. The red light immediately began blinking, alerting maintenance to attend to the dying unit.

"One of your friends will be elected to replace the brain I have just wasted in this demonstration." The Tyrant cast a scornful glance at the rebel group, "I promise you that! Now, let's do the same with your dear father."

"Stop!" cried Iris. "I'll tell you everything! I'll share the Secret! Just give me a little time to recover my composure. This ordeal has been very tiring. I'll tell you tomorrow."

Sadra's face lit up with anticipation. "I knew you'd come to your senses! I told you I could be very persuasive." He laughed good humouredly. "Okay, I'll give you until tomorrow. Prepare yourself. I will send a guard for you."

The Tyrant was suddenly bored with this charade. "Take them back to their cell, and hose the filthy creatures down!" he ordered, and the Sydhar guard began dragging their captives out of the room.

\*\*\*

Tootee was growing restless inside the *Phoenix*. He had waited and waited for the return of his Jaira master while rolling about and tolerating the incessant chatter of the silver droid. Spontaneously, he decided to leave.

Despite the protests of Fortuno, he waited until it was time to change the guard and quickly unsealed the ship and blew a small hatch on the underside. Down he rolled to the ramp below and into a long corridor illuminated with greenish light. The corridor was barred at its end by a solid metal gate. Tootee inserted his probe into the security plug and manipulated the combination. A few seconds passed and the door opened to admit him.

"Well, well! What's this?" rung a voice from above. "I thought you had secured this passage, Rom?"

Tootee faced a group of Sydhar guards on the other side of the gate. They almost blocked the passage with their massive bulk. He knew the only chance of escape was speed. He rolled through their legs so fast that he broke his own lifetime speed record. Down the passage he sped, blinking all his lights.

The Sydhars galvanized themselves into action, and a crazy chase began. Tootee, beeping wildly, rolled forward in a zigzag line, impervious to beams from the enemy weapons. Occasionally, he would rotate one of his laser guns and shoot back, eliminating a Sydhar.

Trying to lose his pursuers, Tootee took a few sharp turns and attempted to disappear down one of the dark side passages. But the Sydhars weren't easy to shake. The little robot had already exhausted his repertoire of tricks, and the enemy was still on his tail.

Making a ninety degree turn into one dark passage on his left, he was immediately attracted to a niche in the wall where some repair trolleys and other equipment had been left. Just what he needed! He rolled into the niche and hid behind a piece of machinery. Heavy footsteps lumbered past and grew distant. Eventually only silence surrounded the robot. He emerged from his hiding place, beeping cheerfully, and rolled towards the center of the city where his sensors told him his master was being held. Once inside the palace ramparts, he encountered no more resistance, although his presence raised more than a few eyebrows as he rolled steadily towards the place his sensors indicated.

***

Buck rocked Iris in his arms, like a child. She was crying forlornly, her delicate body shaking with sobs.

"It's okay, my love," he soothed her with gentle words. Slowly, she began to calm down.

"I'm with you, Iris. We're all with you," said Marc.

She dried her eyes and looked at Marc with hope. "Did I receive your message correctly?" she asked plaintively. "Did you mean that you have thought of a plan?"

Everybody looked at Marc expectantly.

"Well, sort of..." he said hesitantly. "I'm not sure it will work, but it might be our only chance, unless someone else comes up with something better." The revolutionaries looked at each other, but nobody had any ideas whatsoever.

"Well," Marc cleared his throat. "Sadra's life support computer must control all the systems of this city, such as its gravity field, power, air, the works. So if Iris could establish a mental rapport with her father and other members of her family, perhaps we could all link up to sabotage Lamanda's power system. In the confusion, we could escape. In fact, the Tyrant might be easier to deal with if we could gain control over some part of his empire here."

"This could probably be done," Princess Iris replied thoughtfully. "We might be able to extract some important information about the computer through a mental linkup," she agreed. "But I will need your help." She looked around at the group.

"We will put all the muscle into it that we've got," Reb replied. "When can we start?"

"It will take me a while to establish perfect rapport with all the members of my family," she said. "At least I've learned of my father's whereabouts," she added. "I couldn't help thinking I was going mad when I kept sensing him near me."

Buck reached for her hand. "Mad or sane, I'll be here for you whenever you need me," he said.

She gave Buck a brief smile and continued. "I'm ready to start immediately. Stand by." In seconds she had achieved a state of deep relaxation. Her mind searched for a familiar presence. Yes, there he was... her father! And close to him were Orlan and Negari.

*"We have been waiting for you, daughter, King Handor spoke into her mind. We knew you would come."* Tears slipped out from under Iris' closed lids. She'd longed to hear her father's voice once again, but not like this... not like this! She set aside her emotional pain and regret. There was a vitally important job to be done. Their very lives depended on her mission's success. There was no place here for sentimentality. And, besides, she knew her father would grow impatient with her pity. He was a very proud man.

Iris swept her mind of its clutter and her reception immediately became crisp and clear. She transmitted Marc's plan.

*"Yes, together we can destroy the Tyrant and his army, she heard her father say. Be forewarned that you*

*and your friends may be sacrificed, but what must be done must be done."*

"Father! We don't have much time. I will be called to Sadra's chambers to confess our Secret tomorrow!"

*"I know. I heard. Now pay close attention, my daughter. Here is what I would have you do."*

# Chapter Twenty-Eight

The night dragged on and on. Marc had insomnia. He rolled from side to side restlessly on the hard floor of his prison cell. Tomorrow would be the final confrontation. Tomorrow they would either destroy the Tyrant or be destroyed by him. Marc had been close to death many times, but on this occasion he felt particularly apprehensive about their chances for success. He hoped their plan would work.

*"If not"*, he thought, *"my brain will float for eternity in a silver cell while my body turns to dust"*.

He hugged himself for reassurance that he was still alive. He wondered what the big Secret was that had cost Iris' whole family their lives.

*"Why hasn't she told us about it? Doesn't she trust us, after all we have been through to help her"?* He sighed. *"If only she had fallen in love with me, instead of with Buck..."*

He let his mind wander and old memories flooded back. The years on Argalon, meeting Liana, fighting against The Old Order, against the Emperor Drakkor...

Suddenly he heard the voice of his father.

*"Marc, beware! Beware of the Dark Force! Remember my example. Remember that every time you turn to the Dark Force, it will turn right back on you and seek to destroy you. When that happens, it will be too late. You will have to pay the price. Don't let hatred overcome you. Your negative feelings will activate the Dark Force within you. Remember all this when you face your greatest test tomorrow!* The voice was faded away.

Marc reached out with his mind. Searching.

*"Father! Father!"* he called. But there was no reply. Suddenly he felt lonely, and vulnerable. He opened his eyes. Digger was observing him with compassion. Marc crept over to the Prozoan and leaned his head on his furry friend. Together they slept for the few hours that remained until dawn.

\*\*\*

Sadra's audience chamber was lighted and decorated festively. A crowd of courtiers had been invited for the occasion. The Tyrant sat upon his throne dressed in a black uniform which was heavily embroidered with gold. Below him reclined his consort, Princess Clevia, on her own divan, resplendent in a shimmering violet gown. A huge, tawny spotted desert pumard lay at her feet, its collar adorned with multi-coloured crystal spikes.

A double ring of royal guards separated the ruling couple from the courtiers. Below, in the courtyard, the palace slaves were drawn by curiosity. Among them was the beautiful Mona, naked, and tethered to a Sydhar guard by a golden collar and leash.

The great doors clanged open. The prisoners were

dragged in, looking tired and disheveled. They were thrown at the feet of the throne.

"I trust you passed the night well, my dear Princess Iris," said the evil one. "And," he lied "I naturally wish the same for your companions. "Are you ready to reveal your Secret to me at last? I do hope you haven't changed your mind. That would be most unfortunate for your friends and family, because I really have my heart set on hearing your revelation." He looked at Iris chillingly and her skin crawled, causing her to give an involuntary shudder.

Princess Iris braced herself. She was now in continuous, simultaneous rapport with all the members of her family. She lifted her head proudly and look straight into the Tyrant's eyes. Silently, they gazed at each other for a few moments, sizing up the other's strength.

"Yes. I am ready," she replied in a grave tone.

"Good! Please proceed. We are all eager to hear it."

"My Lord. I cannot share the Secret with all these spectators. Once I have passed the Secret to you, it will be for you alone to enjoy. Surely you do not wish to share such an important and powerful knowledge with your people, after waiting so long to possess it yourself?"

"I agree, Princess Iris. Of course, you are right!" He turned to the leader of his royal Sydhar guard. "Out! All of you! And take my courtiers with you!"

"And would you give such power of knowledge to your consort that she may one day use it against you?" Iris challenged him.

"No, my dear. It is for us alone to share," he cackled an evil laugh. "Clevia, leave us!" Clevia threw Iris a withering look, and left.

"My Lord," Iris said. "You have promised to add the

brains of my companions to your collection in the silver cells on this very day. Therefore I beg of you. Allow them to hear the Secret which they have fought so valiantly to protect. They will carry it with them to their grave."

"Why, my dear. I had no idea you had such potential for mischief! Yes! Let us satisfy them before we add them to the Brain Bank." He nodded at her shrewdly. "I think, my dear, that you will be even more fun than your sister was. Perhaps you will receive the honor of ruling as my next consort!" Sadra drooled at the thought.

Iris ignored his last remark. She looked around to make certain the audience chamber was empty except for her group of silent, meditating revolutionaries sitting on the floor.

"Our Secret has been carefully guarded for many generations on Hydra V. It guards an incredible power connected to our Urfee legacy." Her voice was cool and controlled. "Under certain circumstances this knowledge enables us to become extremely powerful. Almost invincible." She observed the vein throbbing in Sadra's temple. He was growing very excited with greed at the thought of possessing even greater power.

*"Good,"* she thought. *"Soon I will have him eating from my hand".* She paused, to let her words take full effect on the Tyrant, then continued.

"We know how to harness and transform energies. For instance, at this very moment I could reverse your planet's gravity field, or create a meteor bombardment. What would happen to Lamanda then, Your Lordship? Or, I could explode all your power systems. Would you like a small demonstration?" she asked, her voice devoid of emotion.

Sadra was torn between fear and disbelief. He leaned back on his throne and laughed.

"Really, my child. Do you expect me to believe all this? How naive you are! Please proceed with your demonstration. Be my guest!" he continued to chuckle derisively.

Iris closed her eyes. All the lights went out. Outside the chamber, cries of consternation rang out in the darkness. The revolutionaries could hear the sound of running metallic cyborg feet and the cries of the courtiers, who had been waiting in the antichamber, as they pushed and stepped on one another in confusion.

\*\*\*

The great doors opened a few feet and a small bulky form rolled through the wedge. It whistled a greeting to Marc.

"Tootee!" cried Marc. "What are you doing here?"

Tootee rolled over to the revolutionaries at high speed and beeped his happy explanation. Marc wanted to hug him, but they had all agreed to remain motionless so as not to alarm the Tyrant.

"I don't know how you did it, but I'm very glad you're here," Marc whispered, as he cautiously rose to a kneeling position. He looked to see if the Tyrant had noticed, but Sadra was glaring at Iris with a venomous look that excluded everything else. "Listen, Tootee, here's what I want you to do." He leaned into the robot and gave the instructions in a very soft voice.

When the lights came back on a few moments later, Tootee was gone, heading for the *Phoenix* and the *Star Wind*. Marc had dispatched him to prepare the V-wing for takeoff and to tell Fortuno to do the same for the *Golden Phoenix*.

\*\*\*

Sadra continued to observe Iris in deadly silence. He stared at her like a snake that was hypnotizing its prey before it struck. Princess Iris stifled a shiver under his penetrating gaze. To avoid his eyes, she looked over at the group of revolutionaries scattered in various positions of semi-recline on the marble floor. Her gaze swept past her friends and out onto the courtyard, where a beautiful girl was collared and leashed to a Sydhar guard.

"Mona!" She recognized the girl and a question was answered in her mind. "So it was Roold who betrayed me! Sadra has held her hostage in order to manipulate my loyal soldier."

Mona received the telepathic communication of Princess Iris and covered her eyes. Roold was drowned! She couldn't control her sobs. She would have sagged to the ground, if it weren't for the collar holding her in the tight grip of her Sydhar chaperone. Iris felt a wave of pity for the poor girl. But she forced her attention back to Sadra.

"You will not distract yourself from me again," he bellowed. "I command that you continue your explanation of the Secret power."

"Shall I continue my demonstration with an interruption to your gravity field?" she asked charmingly.

"How dare you threaten me!" the Tyrant bellowed furiously, jumping off his throne. "Guards! Guards" he ran to the chamber door. "Get in here! Seize them all! Fire at will! Shoot to kill the Hydran traitor!"

The royal Sydhar guard rushed in and opened fire. Marc realized that a split second separated Iris from death. Without thinking, he struck out at the cyborgs with a deadly charge of the Dark Force. The guards scattered and fell, dropping their weapons. Then Marc struck down the guard who had grasped him, and another who was holding the struggling Buck Salladian.

A tremor passed through the palace. Lights flickered and dimmed. Marc strode to where Iris had fallen and checked her pulse. She was badly stunned, but very much alive.

Explosions could be heard nearby as the palace continued to shudder. Sadra was dashing in and out of the chamber doors and shouting into the courtyard at the amazed courtiers and servants who had collected there. "Arm yourselves! Kill them all!" He scrambled to collect the ultrasonic weapons from the fallen guards and tossed them into the crowd.

*"Oh, no!"* Marc wondered why his rebel band had not been first to retrieve the ultrasonic weapons and looked to see his friends collapsed and reeling from emissions that had stunned and paralyzed them. He closed his eyes and made rapport with Iris. She and her disembodied family members were building a ring of power. Marc joined them. The lights in the chamber went out and he heard confusion breaking out again in the corridors. Then he heard a platoon of Sydhars clanging along the ramps leading to the palace and heard the cries of courtiers and servants as they were trampled underfoot.

Countess Liana, sensing heavy mental activity in the room, joined her thoughts with Marc and Iris. The Light was building. Marc felt his sister enter the ring, and then

Buck and Reb. They were good students. He knew that the Light must not escape their control, or it would turn into the Dark Force and destroy everything, cause a terrible holocaust that would most likely destroy Lamanda completely, turning its beauty to dust. He felt a stab of fear. Never before had he wielded such a powerful force. Then he felt a powerful grip on his shoulder and pain, as the Tyrant's talons pierced his flesh.

"You will never escape me!" hissed the evil voice.

Marc struggled to free himself of the Tyrant's powerful grip.

*"If only I had my laser sword"*, he thought. Sadra moved his grip from Marc's shoulder to his throat and began to squeeze hard. Marc was suffocating. He dropped his concentration from Iris' circle and summoned his laser sword to him with a mighty thrust of his mind. As it flew into his hand he felt the simultaneous loosening of the Tyrant's grip and opened his eyes in surprise to see a Hydran girl standing over the body, holding a bloody knife. She kicked at the inert form with her bare toes.

"He deserved to die," she whispered. "He has tortured and raped me and sent my husband to a watery grave. Death is too good for him!"

The floor continued to shake. Marc looked around. Everyone was concentrating on the ring of power and had not yet noticed that the Tyrant was dead. He must intervene. The power must be reduced. But how? Unexpectly he heard his father's voice in his head.

*"Marc, beware! The Dark Force has been awakened. It will destroy this place. You can't control it now. It's too late. Run! If you want to live, Son. Run!"*

Marc was bathed in sweat. He mopped at his forehead. The air was different, wavering and trembling as if there was a heat inversion. An acrid smell rose from the floor. Marc knew something dreadful was about to occur. He shook Iris, to bring her out of her trance. Her head lolled, but she soon opened her eyes and tried to focus on him.

"Marc! What? Leave me alone..." she began to mumble.

"The Dark Force is unleashed," cried Marc, shaking her roughly. "We must run for the ship! This place is going to blow up any minute now. Tell your father!"

She looked at him uncomprehendingly. Then the light of consciousness came back into her eyes. She whirled around. "Rouse the others! I have to save my father and the rest!"

"No! There is no time for that!" he yelled, waking up each of his friends in turn.

"Reb! Buck! Digger! Liana! Follow me! Quick! He shouted as he grabbed Iris by the hand and ran for the tunnels that led to the docking port. Countess Liana grabbed Mona by her bare wrist and tugged her along.

"Marc, let me go to my father! I have to save him," Iris pleaded, resisting him every step of the way.

Marc held her hand in a firm grip as he pulled her along. "You won't save him, Iris! We'll die if we don't take off immediately!" he shouted out of breath. "There's no time to lose!"

More explosions rocked the city. Marc figured they came from the power plant. The floor tilted at a strange angle, as if one side of the floating city was higher than the other. Yes, it was tilting to one side, and the slant was growing more pronounced with every minute. They began to slip and slide as they ran.

Suddenly Iris wrenched herself free from Marc's grasp as they passed the corridor to the Brain Bank.

"Iris, come back, you'll die in there! cried Liana. "Reb, do something or we'll lose her."

"No, Reb. I'll try to save her." He anticipated the response.

"Don't argue. You must reach the *Phoenix* and get these people to safety! I have the Light in me. We'll make it." Iris disappeared from sight while he paused to shout at Morningstar.

"You take the others back to the *Phoenix* and get underway without us. Buck, fly the *Star Wind* to the garden of this palace and circle until you can land and pick us up." Marc yelled as he veered off down the passage toward the brain bank.

Mona tried to hang back, but she was pushed along by Digger as the group ran, slipping and sliding toward their ship.

"It's getting harder and harder to navigate on this slope," panted Liana. "I only hope Lamanda doesn't break up before we reach the *Phoenix*."

"We're close!" cried Reb. Just then the floor slipped from under their feet and they fell to their knees, sliding along at a mad pace. Thankfully, the slide was brief, and the floor stabilized itself at a forty-five degree angle from horizontal. Now they were partly running on the walls, with the smell of thick smoke and burning acrylic filling the air.

Buck coughed, his eyes watered and itched. The others weren't too much better off. Luckily, they were entering the docking area and they could see that the *Phoenix* was still in her resting place.

Reb flipped his comm-link open. "Fortuno, come in. This is Captain Morningstar. Lower your shields and blow the main hatch. We are coming aboard."

"Yes, Master Reb. Oh, I am so glad you're back!" came the excited reply. Oddly, there wasn't a cyborg to be seen anywhere down here.

Without warning the ramp gave way and a fissure opened in the construction, as a strong gust of wind knocked the rebel group off their feet and scattered them. Liana felt herself being blown along and grabbed desperately for a handhold to keep from falling into the gaping chasm. Buck braced himself just in time to avoid going over the edge and looked down to see the rusty surface of Gandra through a rent in the clouds. Clearly the city was breaking up and he caught sight of giant sections hurtling to the planet's surface.

Reb grabbed Liana by the seat of the pants just in time to save her from toppling over the edge. The wind whistled in his ears and nearly deafened him.

"Fortuno! Start the engines. Lower the boarding ramp." Reb barked, as he tucked Liana under his arm and ran for the ship. "Digger, grab Mona and get aboard!" Wasting no time on pleasantries, he made a mad dash for the hatch opening and dropped Countess Liana into the astonished Fortuno's metallic embrace.

\*\*\*

Marc found Iris tugging at the silver cell of her father, frantically trying to disengage it from its resting place.

"Iris, don't be crazy! You can't keep that cell alive once its disconnected from its power source." Marc tried to pull her away as he spoke.

"That's what you think, Commander Galaxia!" Her voice was frosty and determined.

*"That's what I get for arguing with a lady when her mind is made up"*, he thought and shrugged.

"Okay, Princess Iris," he returned the formality. "We don't have any time to waste. So I suggest you retrieve your father's brain and say goodbye to the rest of your family, because we'll die if we fool around in here one minute longer." He moved to the control unit. "I don't think you can disengage the cell until the power source is turned off, so here we go." He found the number on the board corresponding to the number on the silver cell and pushed.

"Yes!" Iris called. "I have it! Let's go."

"This way," he put his arm around her and tugged at her to move quickly as she cradled the silver cell in her arms. "Come on, Iris! We've got to run. If that thing is going to slow you down so much, you'll have to leave it behind."

"I will not!" she shouted angrily. It was the first time he had ever heard her lash out and it startled him.

Just then the floor tilted out of control and they slid the rest of the way down the passage that normally led up to the palace gardens. Tumbling out into the brightness, Marc looked to see where Iris was. Miraculously, she was on her feet, serenely cradling the silver cell in her arms. Even more amazingly, the thing looked as though it had never been disconnected from its life support at all.

But there was no time to contemplate the state of the

silver cell. Marc jumped to his feet just as the city righted itself to an angle of forty-five degrees and looked around for the *Star Wind*. He knew that if his friends did not reach the *Golden Phoenix* in time, there would be no Buck and no V-wing to rescue them, and all their heroism would have been for nothing.

The gardens wavered and shuddered before their eyes, and then the ground began to break up. Iris and Marc looked at each other frantically, fully expecting they would be thrown off this floating nightmare at any moment. Obviously the gravitational stabilizers were holding up fairly well, but the city was breaking up from the explosions and shock waves.

Marc sent a thought to his father.

*"You were right, father. We have unleashed the Dark Force and it is destroying us. But am I alone to blame?* He desperately felt the need for absolution from guilt in these final moments of his life. *"Benja-Ko! What say you?"*

No reply came.

Just then a familiar sound graced his ears, and he turned around to see the *Star Wind* zoom up and make a low pass, banking and returning to land nearby.

"Yaaaaay!" Marc cried like a schoolboy who'd just won a prize. In a twinkling they were aboard and Marc had to repress an urge to hug Buck Salladian, as he swung Iris into the back of the cockpit with her precious charge.

As they lifted off and accelerated upward, they saw the city break into countless pieces and drop to the planet's surface. It was a spectacular sight, and a sad one. He punched the com-link on his console.

"*Star Wind* to *Phoenix*. *Star Wind* to *Phoenix*. Rescue

is complete. We are in flight. Send your coordinates from orbit so that we may rendezvous a.s.a.p. I'm just dying for a shower and a change of clothes!"

"Please refrain from using the word *dying*," Buck remarked drolly. "Personally, I could use a stiff drink!"

Laughter from the bridge of the *Phoenix* came floating back. "Roger, *Star Wind*, coordinates are on their way from Fortuno. Keep this channel open. Over and out."

\*\*\*

Marc secured the *Star Wind* in its usual docking port on the *Golden Phoenix* and, after wriggling into spacesuits with some difficulty, the trio boarded the starship at last.

In the airlock, Marc turned and clapped Salladian on the arm, shaking his hand energetically. "Buck, I want to thank you for coming back for us. Just let me freshen up and I'll buy you that drink!"

Iris headed for the Lab with her precious cargo, as Reb set course for Hydra V, and Marc thought about the shower he'd promised himself.

"Iris, wait," he called, as he ran to catch up with her. "What I'm curious about is how you've managed to keep your father's nutrient bath fresh during our little escapade. We all saw what happened when the Tyrant disengaged the power supply to one cell."

Iris turned to him with a smile and patted her precious cargo as she replied. "Why Marc, you surprise me in your *naiveté*!"

"I'm serious, Iris," he persisted. "How did you do it?"

"With the help of the Light, of course!" She laughed as she walked away.

# CHAPTER TWENTY-NINE

As they came in for a landing, thousands of shimmering lights illuminated the Island of Itoomo. The cold phosphorescent green of the fireflies mixed with the golden light of torches to create an intricate, lustrous mosaic.

Traditionally, many people of the galaxy made an annual pilgrimage to Hydra V to celebrate Life. But this year, the celebration held special meaning for the natives. King Handor's cerebrum was now a living shrine which would be kept eternally alive and from whence counsel could be sought by Princess Iris or her successors whenever a mental link was desired.

The victory over Sadra and the end of his long tyranny meant peace and freedom for the inhabitants of this watery world, at long last, and the natives had prepared for weeks of feasting, dancing and celebrating.

The revolutionary group of offworlders who had contributed so greatly to the overthrow of tyranny were receiving a special Hydran welcome as well. The *Golden Phoenix* was nearly obscured by the tiers of flowering strands with which it was decorated, and thousands of fireflies illuminated the exterior of the starship with their

336

eerie green light, lending it a fairytale quality.

Countess Liana sat on the edge of the temple's reflecting pool, dangling her feet in the cool water, which was now freed of bloodthirsty Ko'onu. For her, as for the families of those heroic Hydran soldiers, the joy of celebration was marred with mourning. She would never forget those brave men who had accompanied them with patience and willing hands for so long, only to perish in battle with the Sydhars, or in their cells when the Tyrant's battleship exploded on Lamanda.

Reb knelt down and trailed his fingers in the reflective surface that looked like a pool of liquid silver in the soft starlight.

"It's so beautiful here on Hydra," said Liana dreamily, "I'll be sorry to leave."

"Would you be willing to give up your seat on the Senate, along with your power and influence, to live here in tranquillity?" Reb asked with a note of curiosity in his voice, sitting beside her and linking his arm around her waist affectionately.

Liana was gowned in a beautifully draped garment of white, her long, blonde hair falling gracefully to her waist. She had never looked more beautiful in all the years he'd known her.

"No." she responded with slow, measured words. "I couldn't do that. My work on the Senate is more important than my own preference for lifestyle or planetary location." She looked at him and then lowered her head in resignation. "There is so much to do... They need me on Carrandon. It isn't so bad there, after all..."

"Hey, you two. Why so down-in-the-mouth?" laughed Buck. "I've never seen such long faces on two people who haven't got a care in the world!" Then his jovial expression changed to one of concern. "What's wrong?"

"Nothing, really," replied Reb Morningstar. "My Countess can't stop thinking about her administrative responsibilities long enough to party, that's all." He winked at Buck.

As if guessing their thoughts, Buck replied, "I can imagine you're feeling reluctant to leave this wonder-world. So I would like to remind you of the invitation that you've all received from the new government, to drop by any time you're in the mood for a swim."

"Yeah, thanks." replied Reb. "If we ever get tired of the pressures back on Carrandon, we won't hesitate to head for a vacation by the sea."

"Buck! Aren't you planning on coming back with us?" asked Liana with concern.

"I thought I'd hang around here a while longer," he answered lightly. "The ruler of Hydra V has asked me to assist her with the formation of a new government," he explained.

"Well, we all have to follow our private destinies...," Liana began, and stopped short in surprise.

A tall pilgrim had surprised her as he stepped from the shadows and walked over to the temple pool. He was dressed in the costume of a distant planet, and his long coarse-looking brown robe looked out of place in this balmy place. He stood, facing Liana, for a few minutes. She tried to peer into his face but the dark hood obscured his features. Then he spoke.

"I am Brother Raffe O'Gornon from the White Brotherhood of R'Bragno," he said by way of introduction. "Kindly excuse the interruption, but I was drawn here by a whirlpool of tension which caused a disturbance to the otherwise placid Light in this city. He turned and moved his gaze from Liana, to Reb, to Buck, and back to Liana again.

"Don't they teach you, in your brotherhood, that staring at a Countess in such a rude manner is highly inconsiderate?" she demanded indignantly of the robed monk, as she turned her back and made as if to leave.

To everyone's great surprise, the pilgrim laughed lightly as though he were unaffected by the countess' sarcasm.

"Sorry, Countess, I didn't mean to offend you." he apologized. "I was only studying the pattern of your aura. It is very unusual. Have you undergone any training in use of the Light?" he inquired gently. His voice was the voice of a young man, and his hands, which were visible, were a golden bronze.

Liana felt an inexplicable feeling of empathy towards this monk and she smiled as she turned back.

"No, not really," she replied. "But my brother Marc was trained as a Jaira by the master Benja-Ko Menjoro.

"I sincerely hope I'll have a chance to meet him while I'm here," said the monk. "Perhaps you would consider visiting me on my home planet of R'Bragno? My order provides what might be considered the best training in this field available in the whole galaxy," he added proudly. "We trained Princess Iris, and I think the results speak for themselves."

"The existence of your order is unknown to our New Democracy," Liana said. "Only a very few people have had proper training and can use the Light safely. And I know it would be of great advantage to the New Democracy to have a few chosen people trained in the Light. Perhaps we can arrange a cultural exchange program between your people and mine. Naturally, Captain Morningstar and I would lead the first delegation." Countess Liana was really warming to the idea.

"I will present your proposal the next time I confer with my superiors," responded the monk. "And presently you will be informed of our decision."

"How? When?" Liana asked all in a rush.

The monk laughed again. "How impatient you are" he commented. "You must gain more control over your emotions."

Countess Liana didn't like being criticized by the stranger, and she was getting ready to hurl a disagreeable retort when Princess Iris Odman strolled into the temple garden, followed by her servants Herme and Estri, and a new girl who replaced the unfortunate Lony.

The Hydran monarch, now ruler of the system, looked breathtakingly beautiful and truly regal in her glittering aquamarine dress decorated with pearls and gathered at the waist by a wide belt which was encrusted with gems. On Iris' neck was a circlet of teiral stones which shone with a mysterious inner light. Her cascade of black hair was held back with a royal tiara which was also studded with priceless teiral stones. Buck sighed at the sight of her. How could he ever think himself worthy of a creature such as this?

"Ah. I see you have met Brother Raffe," she smiled and placed her delicate hand on his shoulder. "Brother Raffe was my teacher and, thanks to his teachings, I am still alive today. She swept the little group with a pleasant glance and stopped at Countess Liana. "But thanks to you and your friends, the people of my planet have regained their peace and freedom. Our gratitude cannot be adequately expressed in words."

"It was a worthy cause, and we were glad to rid the universe of that terrible tyrant," Liana smiled back.

"Just the same, I would like to send a little gift to the New Democratic Senate. We are a poor and underdeveloped nation, so I can't shower you with riches, but I have something you might like. If you will all walk with me, I will show you now."

Iris led them into one of the buildings surrounding the temple and entered its dark interior. Then her royal highness clapped her hands and the room filled with light. In the center of the room, on a crystal pedestal, stood a ring of sculpted figurines of unusual beauty. There were seven of them, three male and four female. So exquisitely were they sculpted that they seemed to come alive before the viewer's eyes.

Liana, Reb and Buck moved towards the display, speechless with awe. At last Liana cleared her throat and ventured a comment. "Iris, are you implying that you wish to give us these priceless treasures?"

"Yes! I hope your Senate will accept these sculptures as a token of gratitude and appreciation from the Hydran people and their monarch. They were found by an archaeological expedition to one of our subsea tunnels and were most certainly created by the extinct Urfee culture. Is it not difficult to imagine that such beauty could be created by a civilization which was at the same time so evil?"

She moved gracefully to the side of the room where she indicated a piece of furniture containing many labelled drawers. Here you will also find recordings of Urfee music, poetry and literary achievements discovered by our scientists on Gandra. Through the use of your advanced technology scientists in the New Democracy may learn much that we have still not discovered from these artifacts."

She reached into another drawer and gently withdrew a necklace and pendant made of three teiral gemstones masterfully set into hammered nal. The blue of the gemstones glinted with a mysterious inner light and prismed into a thousand brilliant sparkles. Princess Iris fastened the necklace around Liana's neck and the princess' excitement glistened in her eyes. Countess Liana was overcome and for a moment, she couldn't speak. Finally, she gave in to the emotion of the moment and threw protocol out the window as her arms went around the Hydran ruler and they embraced unceremoniously, like two royal sisters.

\*\*\*

It was late. Marc had gone for a stroll to work off his big supper and now he was sitting on a bench by the seawall, gazing at the brilliantly lighted boats and canoes which were lying at sea anchor in the deep waters of the bay. Thousands of fireflies adorned the masts and riggings of the festively adorned boats upon which happy fisherfolk laughed and danced to celebrate their joyous freedom from Tyranny.

Marc looked up at the stars and was suddenly swept by a feeling of great loneliness. Tootee, trailing along for the stroll, detected Marc's melancholia and whistled cheerfully to the accompaniment of his blinking lights, in an attempt to cheer his master up. But Marc took no notice. In his mind he was rehearsing his farewell to Princess Iris, the woman of his dreams. Soon, he knew, their group would board the *Golden Phoenix* and return to Carrandon, leaving the new ruler of Hydra V behind with her people.

He knew Buck was planning to stay on Hydra, too, and again he wished he'd been the one Countess Iris had chosen. So deeply was he submerged in his thoughts that he didn't sense the intruder. She came up behind him and stood silently, looking thoughtfully at the ocean. Finally, she spoke.

"I can feel your love and your sorrow," she whispered after what seemed like an eternity of silence. A tear rolled down her cheek.

Marc jumped, startled, and looked around, surprised.

"We are all betazoids on Hydra, although only a few are telepathic, like Her Highness," explained Tyla. "Didn't you know that?"

Marc didn't reply. Suddenly he felt very, very tired.

"I had hoped you and your friends would stay on as our guests for a while, because my father would like to take you fishing, again," she whispered. But now that Iris and Minister Salladian have found each other, I guess you have little motivation to stay ..." She stopped.

The partying on the boats had died down to a faint musical hum, and only the lapping of the waves and the singing of reptilian lagarticcas could be heard. Tootee rolled towards the seawall and stopped as though watching the ocean, beeping and whistling gently.

Then Marc detected a movement in the water.

*"Could it be a Hydran, out on a nightly swim?"* It

was just beyond where the little robot stood. Marc strained his eyes and peered into the dark water.

"Marc, I'm sorry if I spoke out of turn ..." began Tyla.

Ignoring her words, Marc placed a hand on the girl's shoulder and urged her to be quiet. Now he saw several big, dark shapes in the water, their short fur glistening wetly in the moonlight. He moved closer. He felt no sense of danger. The Light was undisturbed by negative vibrations and the visitors' eyes shone with surprising intelligence. Marc counted about a dozen of them. One of them, who was larger than the others, moved closer to the breakwater and uttered a series of whistles and sharp sounds.

To Marc's astonishment, Tootee responded enthusiastically.

"Tootee! You're talking to them!" he was utterly amazed. Tootee's beeps assured him that his rotund 4X unit was greeting old friends.

"Do you see that?" He turned to Lady Tyla excitedly. "Tootee has actually established friendly contact with an unknown alien intelligence," he exclaimed.

"They are not unknown to me," Tyla replied calmly. "They are Brubits, the keepers of the Secret."

"The Secret?" he repeated. "Can you tell me something about the Secret that they guard?" Before she could reply, Tootee signalled something in the other language that Marc couldn't understand.

Marc turned urgently to the girl and asked, "Can you tell me what the Brubit said?"

"No." said Tyla. "We don't speak their language. That's why they've been successful at keeping the Secret." She looked at the blonde, handsome Jaira with unabashed longing.

"Lady Tyla." Marc pushed back the tingle of attraction he felt as he saw her eyes brimming with romance. "Stop looking at me like that. This is important. Hurry to the village and bring me the silver android as quickly as you can. He is skilled in almost every known language in the universe."

"Wonderful! What a help that will be! But you must relax your formality and simply call me Tyla," she laughed as she turned and ran towards the village.

Marc was so nervous about this discovery that his hands trembled as he listened uncomprehendingly to the conversation between Tootee and the Brubit leader. He was overcome by that excited feeling one gets when he know he has stumbled upon some important discovery, even though he doesn't know quite what it means.

Before too long Tyla came walking back, with the silver droid following close behind.

"Yes, Master Marc. How may I be of service? This young woman tells me you require my expert services as a translator!" Fortuno was full of self-importance, as usual.

"Yes, Fortuno. I need your services as a translator. Now stop chattering at me and listen to what Tootee and the Brubit are saying to each other, and store every single word of their conversation in your memory. Then, at first opportunity, introduce yourself to the leader and ask who and what they are and where they come from. Most importantly, ask it to tell you the Secret, of which they are reputed to be the guardians."

"At once, Master Marc," replied the droid dutifully. He edged closer to the seawall and cocked his head to listen and record the prolonged exchange of beeps and whistles passing back and forth between Tootee and the Brubit.

Marc rocked on his heels impatiently as he waited for the exchange to end. Tyla stood silently by, not daring to say anything to interrupt the scene. The Brubits were very close to the wall, now and their big bodies were clearly visible in the clear, shallow water.

By the time Fortuno had completed his conversation with the creatures, Marc could hardly contain his impatience. "Quickly! Interpret what they said, Fortuno."

"Master Marc! This is quite incredible!" the droid exclaimed. "What a fantastic discovery!"

"Oh, get on with it, Fortuno! Tell me at once!" Marc ordered anxiously. "Who are they?"

"Very well, Master Marc. They call themselves The Elders. They are also known as The Keepers of the Secret. They were created as a result of a genetic experiment carried out by the ancient Urfees before they turned to the Dark Force and became evil.

"According to these intelligent mammalian entities, Master Marc, when the old, wise Urfees saw that they would be overthrown by the followers of the Dark Force, they created this race of Elders. Then the wise men of the clan recorded and programmed all of their knowledge and wisdom into coded language and locked it into the Elder's DNA makeup.

When the Dark Force won out over the Light, the Elders were forced to retreat into the depths of the ocean and wait there for a millennium while carrying the Secret knowledge deep within the core of their very being. There, they have waited for the day when the people of this planet would turn to the guidance of the Light and for a leader who could comprehend their complicated language. Among the people of Hydra V, only the royal family of Odman is blessed with the ability to communicate with the Elders, and now that Iris is Queen, the Secret will be shared."

Fortuno paused to record another short interchange between the Brubit and Tootee. Then he resumed his account, "Occasionally, the Elders have rescued swimmers in trouble or given aid to fisherfolk, without betraying their true character, but otherwise they have lived reclusively for centuries. The local people called them Brubits after Brubit Droog, the first Hydran fisherman to be rescued from the jaws of a Ko'onu by one of the Elders."

Fortuno paused again to record more beeps and whistles being exchanged between the Brubits and Tootee. Marc's ear was becoming accustomed to their speech patterns and their language sounded oddly musical to his ears.

"They say," continued Fortuno, "that now that the inhabitants of Hydra have overthrown the evil Sadra and destroyed his court, they are ready to pass along their wisdom for the benefit of all sapient life in this star system."

Marc came to attention and brushed the sand off his pants. The magnitude of this discovery was almost intimidating. He looked at Tyla. "Lady Tyla, Princess Iris should hear this at once," he said. "Please locate her and tell her I have something very important to present to her and she must lose no time in coming to the seawall."

"Yes, Count Galaxia, I will bring her at once." Tyla was obviously peeved as she tossed back her long mane of hair and departed for the temple on swiftly running feet.

Marc shrugged off his shirt and boots and entered the water. The Brubits clustered around him, touching him gently with their wet noses and flippers as they probed and jostled him. He stretched his hands out and stroked their wet fur. It felt soft and silken, like the most luxurious of exotic pelts.

\*\*\*

Before long, Tyla found Princess Iris walking with a strange offworlder monk in the royal gardens. When Brother Raffe heard the news, he lowered his hood and raised his eyebrows in question. "Would you invite an old teacher along on this momentous occasion?"

"I am honored, always, by your company." she responded with a slight bow. "But we must pick up our skirts and follow Lady Tyla at a run. We don't want to keep Commander Galaxia waiting!"

# Epilogue

The boat was rocking dangerously. The sun was high in the sky and reflected on the water like liquid gold. Fortuno was having trouble keeping his footing. He bumped against the sides of the boat, making small dents in his silver metallic chassis.

"Oh dear, I'm afraid it wasn't such a good idea to take me along on this expedition," he complained. "Goodness knows how I fear water and get dizzy with this awful rocking sensation. Oh my! What shall I do? I don't want to be here at all! We are so far from the shore, I can't even get my bearings," he grumbled.

"Oh, come on, Fortuno. It's beautiful out here." said the young boy who was working on his net. "Just look around you!"

Fortuno looked at the ocean disdainfully, then back at the boy with no empathy whatsoever.

"Soon, I'll sing my call to the fish," said the boy. "Then you can help me throw out my net."

"Vittor!" Fortuno had reached the end of his endurance. "Take me back to the shore at once!"

The boy just laughed.

"Please, Vittor. I'll give you the spare remote com-link unit you admired so much, if you'll take me back to *terra firma* right away."

The boy chewed his lip and looked shrewdly at the droid.

"Okay. But first I have to catch something for tonight's feast," he said. "There will be lots of food and singing and dancing. Oh, Fortuno, you don't know how good it is to be alive now that we can do as we please without worrying about the Sydhar patrols. Maybe one day I will even train to fly to the stars in a ship like yours." The boy's eyes shone with a desire for adventure typical of his age.

"I'll ask Master Marc if he can recommend you for enrollment at the flight academy on Carrandon," Fortuno suggested helpfully, temporarily forgetting his discomfort.

"You will?" exclaimed the boy with great excitement. "Oh, Fortuno, do you think I could come along with you on your return to Carrandon? Could I? What do you think Commander Galaxia would say?"

"Well, all I can say is I'll ask Master Marc. It is certainly a prospect worth considering. But... only if you take me back to shore right away," responded Fortuno with finality.

"Okay." the boy decided without hesitation. "Perhaps the other boats will catch enough fish for everyone. But remember, you promised!"

\*\*\*

The murmuring of the waterfall mingled with the voices

of celebrating Hydrans. Somebody sang a few bars of a popular celebration song and several other voices followed. Mats were spread on the grass and people were eating, talking and laughing. They were festively dressed and their hair was festooned with flowers and gems. Food was plentiful for this occasion. There were fish dishes, seafood and fruit. The locally made wine was delicious. Lyrical sounds emanated from the strange-looking stringed instruments they played.

Princess Iris and her group of offworlder guests occupied the place of honor in a beautifully lighted and decorated gazebo. Brother Raffe, the pilgrim from R'Bragno was also invited to join the festivities. Herme, Estri and the new girl, Zava, were serving Iris and her guests on beautiful crystal ware.

It was the final day of the celebration. Tomorrow, all Hydrans would return to their respective islands and, three days after that, the *Phoenix* would set course for Carrandon.

Everyone was a little sad over the impending departure of the offworlder revolutionaries. Having almost lost their lives here, on their earlier visit, they now relaxed in the company of good friends, and one had even found love.

The sound of drums wafted in on the breeze. The beat pulsated and became more intense. Soon it seemed to mingle with their heartbeats and excitement filled the hearts of Hydrans and offworlders alike.

Marc felt the power rising and recalled a celebration on Kaatra, the tree village, many months ago. The tempo was growing more primitive. Princess Iris rose to her feet and motioned for her friends to do the same. She started swaying her hips gently to the sound of the music. Her eyes glistened with joy. She leaned her head backward and her lips parted. Her hair fell to her waist. She held out her arms and Buck came into them without hesitation, the teachings of his own culture easily allowing him to imitate her movements and sway with her as if they were one.

Marc felt an intense flow of power through his mind and body. He felt as one with the rest of the group, as one with all human and nonhuman beings, as one with nature, with the universe itself.

He noticed that Iris shimmered with light as she danced. It emanated from within and surrounded her like a halo. Similar but less intense light radiated from Countess Liana as well. Marc stretched out his hands and saw that they, too glowed mysteriously. He had the impression that he was transparent and this didn't bother him at all. After all, it was the last night of the celebration of Life, and he'd encountered stranger phenomena in his travels.

Looking around, he spied Lady Tyla sitting somewhat forlornly by herself in a small lighted grove. So lost in thought was she that she failed to notice Marc's approach. Gently, he reached down and silently drew her into his embrace while swaying to the pulsating music. She moved to his rhythm as if she were a part of his own flesh, and he looked down in surprise to find himself drawn into large almond eyes of bluest topaz in which he feared he might drown. He wondered why he had never before noticed how beautiful this girl was? Her movements were delicate and graceful, her body lithe and well rounded, her mouth full and moist like a ripe plum. He let her eyes draw his head downward as they danced, until their lips touched, gently at first, and then hungrily.

It was time to depart. Marc was sitting on the beach in the same spot he had been when he'd met The Elders only a few days ago. The lights were gone from the boats, and the laughing crowds had gone home. Life on Hydra V had returned to normal and the *Golden Phoenix* was scheduled to leave for Carrandon tomorrow. This was their last night on the waterworld of Hydra.

Marc sighed. If only he hadn't been so foolish as to exhaust all his energies on thinking of Iris. If only he'd allowed himself to be attracted to the exquisite Tyla when he'd first arrived. Now there was no time for anything except goodbyes. He brushed the feeling of regret from his heart.

Someone touched him gently on the shoulder. It was Princess Iris. Although he hadn't heard her coming, he was not surprised at her arrival. After all, she had a powerful telepathic gift and she knew exactly what his feelings for her were. He knew she had come to say goodbye to him personally, out of earshot of the others.

"Don't be sad, Marc," she said softly, brushing his cheek with fingertips as gentle as a cloud. "You sensed we weren't meant to be together, but you did not heed that inner knowledge. And now you have transferred your affections to Lady Tyla. So you must call on your training and seek within yourself to regain your perspective. You are lonely, and everyone around you has paired off, which has only served to mitigate your loneliness. But you are a Jaira, and you can take command. Discipline yourself to wait for the love that will truly last."

She looked into his face, earnestly and saw only confusion. "Marc," she urged the young man, "you must remember your origins. Your people are too different from the Hydran race in basic ways. Lasting happiness is impossible for two races so opposed. You, for instance, are a man at home in the desert while the Hydran women must live on or in the water. You are a Starfleet Commander who's life is spent traveling the vast outer reaches of space while Lady Tyla is the strong right arm and dutiful daughter of a magistrate whose needs are the needs of his people." She sighed. "But although you must leave a piece of your heart on Hydra and bid Lady Tyla goodbye, I hope you will take courage from the fact that, against all odds, I miraculously found a compatible man to love from a distant galaxy. The fusion of his bloodline and mine will enhance and strengthen the royal Hydran legacy. And as member of a royal bloodline yourself, Marc, you have a duty to uphold the same ideals. But content yourself with this; I predict that one day soon, you will find your soulmate, too."

Marc lowered his head, his heart was heavy. It would be some time before he regained his objectivity and Iris' words would be accepted with a happy heart.

"I have so much to do in my new responsibility." Iris changed the subject diplomatically. "My program is to travel from island to island to meet all of my people and tell them about the changes and improvements our new government will institute very soon. Now that Sadra is only an unhappy memory, the Secret of the Elders will become public knowledge and our race will move forward rapidly in evolution as we make use of the gifts bequeathed to us by our wise Urfee predecessors."

"So, what you told Sadra about the Urfee legacy wasn't true?"

"Of course not! I was bluffing him, playing for time as you asked me to do. I would never have given our Secret away to the Tyrant. My family has always known it, and known that we dared not speak of it until our people came back into the Light. But I can tell you now. Do you remember the strange glowing structures that you saw when your aircraft was sucked into the sea? It sucked down the flotillas of wavehoppers, too."

Marc involuntarily recoiled from the memory of that experience. "I will never forget it as long as I live."

"Well, the Odman monarchy has known from the beginning what causes this phenomenon and we know the exact location of the undersea pyramids that create the electromagnetic vortex that sucked you in. But most importantly, we know how to control it. Just imagine what an evil ruler like Sadra could do with such knowledge? Anyone entering the orbit, let alone the atmosphere of this planet could have been controlled and made his slaves. Such absolute power had to be prevented at any cost." Her eyes darkened momentarily at the memory of her martyred family.

But her morbid mood was fleeting. "Marc!" she jumped up. "Come with me. I want to show you something."

A short walk took them to the smallest of the buildings around the temple pool. She approached what appeared to be an undecorated stone wall and made a strange sign with her hands while she murmured something incomprehensible. Then Marc stood, mouth agape, as the wall fell back and he saw a lighted, three-dimensional globe of Hydra floating in the dark interior. Princess Iris made another sign and the surface of the orb changed. The water receded and a plan of the ocean floor appeared instead. A network of huge pyramids covered the ocean floor and the symmetry with which they had been built indicated a master plan of incredible grandeur.

"Well, you've probably guessed that the Urfees were the master architects of this electromagnetic system. Now, under certain circumstances the pyramids create a whirlpool which moves either inward or outward. When the vortex turns inward, the ocean sucks down everything in the area, and when it spirals outward it creates the fierce tsunamis you experienced. Sometimes opposing energies are created that cause devastating electrical storms. But that's not all."

She hesitated, as if weighing her words. Marcd looked at her and saw lines of tension etched in her beautiful features.

"The power of the electromagnetic flow created by these pyramids can reach out into space and be used it to either transmit or receive messages from distant worlds. We dared not use it while Sadra was in power, for fear of being detected. But from now on I plan to have a regular communications link maintained between the neighboring worlds and beyond. Perhaps, when we decode all the wisdom recited to us by the Elders or Brubits, as our people know them, we will even be able to broadcast to Carrandon and other systems far out into space." Her eyes sparkled with pride and emotion.

"So it turned out to be a vital Secret that we were protecting, don't you agree?"

"I am stunned by its magnitude." said Marc truthfully. "But how do you hope to maintain control of such enormous power?"

"I can't explain at present," Iris' voice held a note of sadness.

"Not that I don't trust you." She read his mind. "But I promised my father not to reveal that part of the Secret just yet. One day all traces of the Dark Force will be erased from the minds of our people and that is when the Secret of control will also be shared."

"But I am not one of your people. I am a Jaira and your ally! How could satisfying my curiosity harm you?" Marc asked indignantly.

"Only a few weeks ago, Marc, you unleashed the Dark Force of against Sadra and, while that could be argued as a necessary act, my guess is that you are not ready for such knowledge just yet," she replied.

"Yes. I concede to your judgement. My father was right," he added, recalling the voice of warning. "We should never again let our minds enter the Dark Force. We must always use the Light for good." The way he said it, it sounded almost like a pledge.

\*\*\*

The surface of the watery planet shimmered with silvery lights and the sky above was brilliant with stars. Buck Salladian was swimming effortlessly, disturbing the glassy smoothness of the surface.

*"Perhaps I should return to Carrandon"*, he thought. He did his best thinking in the water. *"Perhaps Iris really prefers Marc, after all."* Jealousy nipped at

his heart and he thrashed out viciously at the water. He had seen them earlier, sitting on the beach, walking by the temple, talking avidly to each other, entering her private quarters.

\*\*\*

Buck felt miserable. *"Maybe she doesn't love me now that she has had a good look at me in her own environment"*, he thought. *"Only I don't know how I can live without her"*. His sorrow was so intense that he ached physically. The ocean stretched placidly in all directions and he flipped onto his back, floating as he looked at the stars.

Suddenly he caught a splash in the face and swallowed a mouthful of the briny water, blowing it out in a spurt, looking around to see what had disturbed his privacy.

"So! And what do you think you're doing out here all by yourself, Minister Salladian?" It was a mocking voice. He opened his arms. It was Iris! He closed his arms again. She was riding astride an Elder, standing on its back, her loose hair blowing around her head like a halo. She jumped into the water after giving the mammal a friendly slap of dismissal.

"All by myself, am I? Doesn't look like it to me!" Buck couldn't help joking back. "And what of Her Exalted Highness, frolicking out here on the back of a seal as if she didn't have a care in the world! Is that any way for a highness to behave?" He pulled her towards him and gave her a very wet kiss. She responded eagerly, and all his doubts dissolved without a trace.

"What's a seal? That was an Elder." Before he could answer, she changed the subject. "Buck, shall we visit the sea temple again?" she laughed up at him. "I'm in the mood for a little swim. How about you?"

"Well," he hesitated coyly. "I don't know if I should. Didn't you tell me something about a mating custom attached to that place?"

"Custom? Oh, yes! I did tell you about the bonding ritual. But I left out one teeny-tiny detail." She twinkled at him merrily and paused for effect.

"And what would that be, your royal mischief?"

"Well, I forgot to tell you that according to our custom we have been betrothed ever since you kissed me in the Temple!" She laughed merrily at his look of comic-horror. "You might just as well surrender, handsome. You must let you know, I never would have led you down to the Temple at all if I hadn't had my heart set on marrying you from the start!"

Buck was close to exploding with happiness. "You mean if we go there now, and spend the night, it will consumate our union and we will be wed?"

"Yes, my love," she looked at him shyly. "If it pleases you, tomorrow we can make the announcement and hold a small reception at court, and invite your friends to drop in to take a glass of nectar with us before they go."

"Why is the man always the last to know when the lady decides to marry him?" Buck made a mock sigh of exasperation.

"Then you'll come with me to the Sea Temple again tonight?" she crooned erotically, as she nuzzled his ear.

"With you, darling girl, I'll go tonight, and

tomorrow, and the next night, if that's what it takes to make you mine. Hey! Tell you what, I'll race you!"

Iris laughed like the sound of crystal bells and reached for his hand. Together they dove under the shimmering moonlit waves. Only a white flower from her hair remained behind to dance in the silver foam.

www.ingramcontent.com/pod-product-compliance
Lightning Source LLC
Chambersburg PA
CBHW050538260626
47157CB00002B/351